PART I

Faulkner's Narrative Poetics

University of Massachusetts Press   Amherst, 1978

Faulkner's Narrative Poetics
Style As Vision

Arthur F. Kinney

Grateful acknowledgment is made to the following for permission to reprint copy-
righted material:
The Estate of William Faulkner for material from *William Faulkner Collections*,
University of Virginia Library; and for material from *New Orleans Sketches* and
The Faulkner Miscellany, quoted with permission of Mrs. Paul D. Summers, Jr.
Journal of Modern Literature for material from "Faulkner and Flaubert," in the
Journal of Modern Literature 6, pp. 222–47, copyright © 1977.
Paintbrush for material from "Faulkner's Fourteenth Image," in *Paintbrush* 2, pp.
36–43.
Random House, Inc., for permission to quote from the copyrighted works of
William Faulkner and Joseph Blotner.
The Southern Review for material from "Faulkner and the Possibilities for Hero-
ism," which originally appeared in *The Southern Review*, October 1970, vol. 6,
no. 4, pp. 1110–25.
The Viking Press for material from James Joyce, *Dubliners*, copyright © 1958 by
The Viking Press; and for material from *Portrait of the Artist as a Young Man*,
copyright © 1956 by The Viking Press.

Library of Congress Cataloging in Publication Data
Kinney, Arthur F., 1933–
Faulkner's narrative poetics.
Based on lectures delivered at Oxford University during Hilary Term 1977.
Bibliography: p.
Includes index.
1. Faulkner, William, 1897–1962—Criticism and interpretation.   I.   Title.
PS3511.A86Z866   813'.5'2   77-90731
ISBN 0-87023-251-7

To the memory of
Richard P. Adams, Claude Simpson, Olga W. Vickery

"hearing, listening, and seeing too . . .
watching and hearing through and beyond.
. . . the clear undistanced voice"

Every style embodies an epistemological decision, an interpretation of how and what we perceive.   SUSAN SONTAG

Maybe nothing ever happens once and is finished. Maybe happen is never once but like ripples maybe on water after the pebble sinks, the ripples moving on, spreading.   WILLIAM FAULKNER

The most serious artists cling to their original vision with tenacity.
STEPHEN SPENDER

Style is more a question of vision than of technique. SAMUEL
BECKETT

That's a matter of style, and I am convinced that the story you tell
invents its own style, compels its own style. WILLIAM FAULKNER

A great author is of one substance and often of one theme, and
the relation between his various creations is bound to be reciprocal, even mutual; each is the other in a different form. R. P.
BLACKMUR

Contents

Preface

IN A PARADOX THAT William Faulkner himself would appreciate, his work has been best understood—but also misunderstood—among his European admirers. Gustaf Hellström of the Swedish Academy spoke for many of them in awarding Faulkner the Nobel Prize in 1950 when he remarked that

> side by side with Joyce and perhaps even more so—Faulkner is the great experimentalist among twentieth-century novelists. . . . [This] desire to experiment is shown in his mastery, unrivaled among modern British and American novelists, of the richness of the English language, a richness derived from its different linguistic elements and the periodic changes in style—from the spirit of the Elizabethans down to the scanty but expressive vocabulary of the Negroes of the Southern states.

Such comments may strike us now as commonplace, for anyone who has heard Faulkner reading his work—whether in person or on the recordings he made which now comprise an essential portion of his legacy—is astonished to learn that he does not even read syntactically, seems not to perceive his sentences as part of a customary grammar. Instead there is the persistent destruction of traditional speech rhythms so as to allow for new linguistic patterns, patterns based not on traditional phraseology but newly established through repetitive images and clusters of thought. Our trained habits of reading are rendered insufficient; his new grammatical alloys require that we attend to his very sentences in new ways. It follows that such experimentation with grammar and sentences extends to the arrangements of his novels; *everything* about his fictional strategies seems designed to demolish our worn anticipations. *As I Lay Dying* fractures the novel into fifty-nine discrete segments. *The Wild Palms* demands that we trace concordances between two narratives rather than the sequence of events in either one of them. *Requiem for a Nun*, despite its typographical arrangements as a play and Camus's attempted staging in Paris is, as Faulkner always said it was, a novel which in Faulkner's usual way traces the hesitant, confused, rationalizing consciousness of Temple Drake transforming into that of Temple Drake Stevens.

But Hellström only partially understood what Faulkner was attempting, for here is the passage omitted in the portion of his citation given above: "Scarcely two of his novels are similar technically. It seems as if by this continuous renewal he wanted to achieve the increased breadth which his limited world, both in geography and in subject matter, cannot give him." No matter where a study of Faulkner's narrative poetics may lead us—even when we concentrate on all his experimentations—we find that their deep structure is, as with any great artist, similar and even repetitive. The multiple perspectives on Addie's death which constitute *As I Lay Dying* are an extension of, but not fundamentally distinct from, the multiple perspectives in *The Sound and the Fury* concerning the loss of Caddy—and not simply the perspectives of Benjy, Quentin, Jason, and Dilsey, but those too which while more buried are equally important, those of Luster, Mr. Compson, Caroline, and Quentin IV. The Modern Library appropriately published the two novels together, making both serve as a prelude to the multiple narrations in *The Wild Palms* and the multiple narrators, implied and later direct, in the trilogy *Snopes*. As with any great writer, the poetics here, while growing progressively more complicated, remains unchanged in its essential characteristics.

Jean-Paul Sartre is perhaps most frequently quoted among Faulkner's European critics. But like Hellström, Sartre too is partly right, partly wrong (if always instructive). Here is the well-known passage I have in mind.

> The first thing that strikes one in reading *The Sound and the Fury* is its technical oddity. Why has Faulkner broken up the time of his story and scrambled the pieces? Why is the first window that opens out on this fictional world the consciousness of an idiot? The reader is tempted to look for guidemarks and to re-establish the chronology for himself:
>
> "Jason and Caroline Compson have had three sons and a daughter. The daughter, Caddy, has given herself to Dalton Ames and become pregnant by him. Forced to get hold of a husband quickly . . ."
>
> Here the reader stops, for he realizes he is telling another story. Faulkner did not first conceive this orderly plot so as to shuffle it afterward like a pack of cards; he could not tell it in any other way. In the classical novel, action involves a central com-

plication—for example, the murder of old Karamazov or the meeting of Edouard and Bernard in *The Coiners* [*The Counterfeiters*]. But we look in vain for such a complication in *The Sound and the Fury*. Is it the castration of Benjy or Caddy's wretched amorous adventure or Quentin's suicide or Jason's hatred of his niece? As soon as we begin to look at any episode, it opens up to reveal behind it other episodes, all the other episodes. Nothing happens; the story does not unfold; we discover it under each word, like an obscene and obstructing presence, more or less condensed, depending upon the particular case. It would be a mistake to regard these irregularities as gratuitous exercises in virtuosity.

The brilliant aperçu that each scene, each chapter, each confrontation in a novel by Faulkner correlates to all the other scenes, chapters, and confrontations, analogous to parts and a synecdoche for the whole, is surely basic to Faulkner's narrative poetics. But Faulkner does not dismiss those traditional structures we associate with the "classical novel" altogether in supplying this new arrangement; rather, he uses traditional linear arrangements of fiction as an understood subtext toward which the reader is always driving his impressions and judgments; the tensions in reading Faulkner come from what he provides for us and what we attempt to make of it, from formlessness *and* the desire for form—hence from *both* Sartre's first and second responses. Against the devices of realistic narration, of anticipated causation and sequence, Faulkner gives us only apparently unrelated details and unreconciled meanings—the excessive language of Rosa Coldfield, the gratuitous relationship of Horace and Narcissa Benbow, the biography of Popeye, the story of Rider in a novel on the McCaslins—so that, when we penetrate the complexities of style and presentation, when we see the analogies implied between structure and episode, we discover *for ourselves* the configuration that makes each emblematic scene a part of the artistic whole.

Moreover, these patterns which we wish to provide for each novel become, in reading Faulkner, unusually yet extraordinarily urgent. Thus the Dutch scholar Joachim Seyppel:

> Faulkner's formlessness serves the one purpose of finding "form": a seamless presentation of the deepest human conflicts. His novels therefore are actually without beginning or end; *Absalom, Absalom!*, one of the most personal, direct, and typi-

cal of Faulkner's works, begins with a leap into Miss Coldfield's room, into the office, and into speech: "Her voice would not cease, it would just vanish." It ends as abruptly with the exclamation: *"I dont. I dont! I dont hate it! I dont hate it!"* These novels seem eager to continue life itself and are continued later by life itself: fragments, rhetorical interruptions of life's flow, immense and unbroken rocks, jungles of words, swamps of sentences, spasms, tropical storms.

Much of the vitality in Faulkner's art stems from this indeterminacy of his characters' perceptions and from his own apparent denial of formal closure, even as we try to give the story a fuller shape.

But if Seyppel had not cited a particular work of Faulkner's, we should not know which one he had foremost in mind: talking about one of them, we comment on them all. Still his novels do not simply stop; each has its plotted climax. The "flash" and "glare" of recognition that Quentin and Shreve share near the closing of *Absalom, Absalom!* allows them to burst, spontaneously and jointly, into the final narration of Sutpen and Sutpen's Hundred that not merely makes a complete story but *makes profound sense*, that fuses perception (what we see) and conception (how we assimilate and interpret what we see; what we think) to allow judgment and even participation. To show this consistency within the Faulknerian canon, we can shift from an example in *Absalom, Absalom!* to *The Sound and the Fury:* we *feel* that the closing moment, with Benjy and Luster reversed in direction and heading the customary way to the Compson grave, is somehow *right*. Each thing in its ordered place at the end of the book relaxes the tension created by the chaos of mind and event that has taken so much attention and energy in the novel. But we want, in fine novels, to go beyond sensation and, when we do, we find conceptually that this scene, as Sartre would warn us, embraces each other scene, embraces them all. For one thing, the novel ends as it begins (hence supplying form if not closure): we begin with Benjy moving toward his make-believe grave and the bottle with jimson weed, accompanied by Luster; we end with his going, again with Luster, to the cemetery for all the dead Compson past—for the heritage he shares, remembers, honors. It is, in a sense, the broken family about to be reunited. For, after all, hasn't death always been seen in this novel as the uniting force, that which will secure each of the Compsons and anneal the family at the last? In their promiscuity and sickness, all of them have courted death—Mr. Compson through alcohol, Quentin with suicide, Jason with despair, his mother with hypochondria—and so Benjy's last act here is only a concrete representation of the perceptual awareness that has gone before. Luster, interested more in life than death, more in the circus than in the deadening routine of labor for the Compsons, resists this slow, steady march toward a dead past. *Of course* he takes the wagon the wrong way. But he is defeated, the past in this book indefatigable. Even the least of the Compsons, Jason, can stop him. And then, Luster and Jason alike are subjected to Benjy's wish, to go, and to go the traditional way, to the Compson grave. When we sense, finally, how the world of the book is subject at the end to the wishes of this thirty-three-year-old idiot and how Benjy's insistent correlation (only apparently disjointed) between life and death, between the promiscuity of Caddy and the death of Damuddy, is that precise union of ideas that stalks each Compson with the sense of his own mortality, only then do we realize what this final judgment of Jason and this surrender of Luster mean as concrete representation: *The Sound and the Fury*, from first to last, is Benjy's book. Benjy's fusion of life and death correlates to what seeing the first and last means to Dilsey and, finally, to us. And I think that is what Sartre sensed when he said (correctly) that each episode in Faulkner's novel stood for them all. What Sartre failed to acknowledge was that *we* make of each the synecdoche it most advisably is.

We are helped to such observations by the period in which we find ourselves—a period of indeterminacy in thought from Heisenberg's principle in physics to Godel's law of infinity in mathematics or, to move closer to people Faulkner read and acknowledged, the contiguity of existential writers like Dostoyevsky and psychologists like Freud. Faulkner's genius flourished at a time when there was new, exciting, and important work in the understanding of human perception and human consciousness and in the growing awareness that art originates in the human response to events rather than in the external world of discontinuous act. With his age, Faulkner recognized that the world was continually being reconstructed by the perceptions and conceptions of people interacting with it. It is this awareness that allows him to place something so mysterious and mischievous as the human consciousness within what is, after all, the art of a man who maintains an architectonic sense of his craft. If we remember that Faulkner could talk with equal earnestness about the pressures of duration on man's understanding—something he learned from Henri Bergson's *L' Evolution créatrice*—and also refer to his own fictive techniques as tools for the lumber in the attic of his imagination, we shall be very near to the heart of the matter. This matter is his trust in his own novels, a poetic under the pressure of human consciousness, to reveal what is most deeply true not only about his characters in Yoknapatawpha but, equally, about us in the world beyond.

A. F. K.
Oxford, England
Cortland, New York
Amherst, Massachusetts
November 1977

Note

Faulkner's Narrative Poetics is an expansion of a course of public lectures delivered at Oxford University during Hilary Term 1977.

Introduction

The initiative of prose normally has its center of gravity in the conscious mind.—NORTHROP FYRE

The very disintegration and inadequacy of the world is the precondition for the existence of art and its becoming conscious.—GYÖRGY LUKACS

Then they talked about what they would do with twenty-five dollars. They all talked at once, their voices insistent and contradictory and impatient, making of unreality a possibility, then a probability, then an incontrovertible fact, as people will when their desires become words.—FAULKNER

IRONICALLY, BEN WASSON, laboring in New York City to transform Faulkner's unacceptable *Flags in the Dust* into a publishable *Sartoris*, made of the first significant Faulkner novel a much diminished thing. Surely Wasson did not recognize the harm he was bringing to the first novel about Faulkner's land and people; most readers today do not sense the important loss, either. But it is not far to seek: both novels retain the central concern of Bayard Sartoris to continue living without his twin brother, but only *Flags in the Dust* provides us with all the necessary data to understand the final juxtaposed scenes detailed in that book—Young Bayard's visit to a seamy bar in Chicago (made puzzling because of Wasson's earlier cuts) and Narcissa's incessant piano playing at the Sartoris home (related to an earlier scene, reduced in *Sartoris*, concerned with Little Belle's public recital).

In either version this novel is not simply Faulkner's remaking of *Lord Jim*, although in its concern with the question of heroism under pressure and without forewarning, it is one of Faulkner's major tributes to Conrad; this novel is also a study of how man searches through external images of the self to find the measurement for his life. As events are filtered through Bayard's consciousness, we sense that John is the measure not only of life but of death for Young Bayard, and not simply because of the plane crash but because of the hate bounded with love, the competition intertwined with devotion, that characterized their life together both as children and as pilots. Young Bayard's enveloping awareness of John takes many forms—we see it in childhood games, in the choice of vocation, in the self-estimate of his worth as a child and as a Sartoris—and it is the chief motivation for many of his acts, for his shame over his survival after World War I, for his dark nightmares of brooding guilt, for his violent attempt to demolish John's remains with the embers of a black servant's fire, for his urgent need to marry his brother's girl even when he has no deep personal feeling for her.

We are private witnesses to Young Bayard's consciousness through the disjointed images that force him to act or think, conveyed by him or what appears to be an omniscient narrator in patterns which, however distant, still approximate his consciousness. In Bayard's obsession with such similar images as the stallion, the car, and finally the plane, we sense a progression of advancing time and speed which saves him from a vortex of past Sartoris legends only to destroy him, at the last, in a meager unsafe present. His displacement of John by his attention to such dissimilar characters as Horace, Old Bayard, and Harry Mitchell shows us Young Bayard's rooted need for companionship and approval that he lost when he emerged alive from the war. It is this sense of gaining significance only through dying, as all the famous Sartorises have done, that so urgently challenges Bayard's human will to live; it is instructive that he prefers working or racing outdoors to listening to Aunt Jenny or Narcissa within the Sartoris mansion and equally important to note that whenever he is in danger all his instincts are, unlike John's, those for self-preservation.

But self-preservation for what? Bayard's tragedy is compounded when he realizes that the Sartorises supply no model for living—Old Bayard is cemented to a dead time, a useless anachronism that all Young Bayard's love cannot give self-respect—and so the novel traces Bayard's quest for a new twin, a new pattern for behavior that through action will give some premium to his survival beyond combat. That Young Bayard's choices here are severely limited, are indeed seen by him as hopeless, is strong comment on the vitality of Aunt Jenny's legends, on Jefferson in 1918, on the values of the South that Jefferson is made to represent.

Still Young Bayard manages to contain his despair and so endure in the very search itself, even when circumstances test him at every turn. His homecoming is unheroic; Simon sees him " 'Jumpin' offen de bline side [of the railroad tracks] like a hobo. He never even had on no sojer-clothes. . . . Jes' a suit, lak a drummer er somethin'.' " His arrival is contrasted to the honor and decorum awarded the black servant Caspey (later encouraging Caspey to less decorous behavior). So Bayard seeks a new secret self in Horace—Horace who is, unlike Bayard, all form. The chief difficulty here is the essential bloodlessness and uselessness of form by itself; Horace's own strivings to shape his letters, his actions, his very life as a perfect poem underline the essential futility of the other "poem" in the novel, the legend that Aunt Jenny spins of Jeb Stuart and John Sartoris during the War between the States.

Horace is not the only person Young Bayard uses to displace and so rectify John and the death cult he stands for by way of youthful and reckless heroism. There is Rafe MacCallum; we sense the close association they have because Young Bayard first confesses to Rafe the more gruesome (and embarrassing) details of John's death. Rafe seems to understand; he drinks bootleg whiskey with Young Bayard in the back of the local Jefferson store and restaurant, accompanies Bayard to the wild stallion, and consoles Bayard through a night of debauchery. Yet Rafe, like Horace, offers *only* solace; he has no advice on how Young Bayard may countermand his heritage and so regain selfhood and self-respect. Since it is by now clear to Young Bayard that only a Sartoris can do that, he turns first to Aunt Jenny, then to his grandfather Old Bayard. With both he remains luckless. Aunt Jenny sees in Young Bayard's racing car only signs of John; she would deny Bayard his individuality. Although Old Bayard does sense his grandson's need for recklessness in association with his fundamental instinct for survival, he reverses their positions, using Young Bayard to rescue his own reputation as a disappointing and defeated Sartoris (the *other* Bayard). Ironically, he succeeds, for Young Bayard manages to provide his grandfather with the heroic death that seals his life with some minor tribute at the same time consigning Young Bayard to a perpetuation of that alien and death-oriented Sartoris tradition that he has tried to destroy from the time he flew his Camel to save his brother and almost lost his life in doing so. Shocked, angered, embittered, Bayard leaves his family to try to establish an alternative existence, first at the MacCallums' cabin where life among men who act as grown children only recalls John's childish behavior; then in Chicago where, seeing Harry Mitchell across the bar, Bayard is able to envision, in this last external image of himself, what a citizen of Yoknapatawpha can accomplish up North. Harry is drunk; he is wrestling with a prostitute who tries to steal his diamond stickpin; he is unable to pay his bar bill. Thus in a world turned by a mirroring consciousness into a sequence of misconstructions and dead ends,

Bayard relinquishes himself to the dangerous feat of testing a new plane, perhaps hoping to salvage in danger and death some scrap of purpose that will, at last, eradicate John's desire to turn danger and death in his Camel into some grand and absurd joke.

This brief synopsis of the novel's chief configuration is less clear in *Sartoris* than in *Flags in the Dust*—even the sense of dust with which the novel like life begins and ends is less obvious—because of Wasson's unfortunate omissions. *Flags in the Dust* (which Faulkner repeatedly wanted to publish during the last years of his life) makes more of Horace because, in seeking a purpose for life and in marrying out of a desperate but misdirected need to find sustenance, his situation almost precisely parallels Young Bayard's. And both of them, deliberately, are made analogous to Byron Snopes whose own anxious search for self-respect and love is, finally, not so much a parody as a broadening indictment of the frustrations in a Southern town caught in the heavy traditions of the past, of lives perpetually made to account backward for present diminution. The extra scenes Faulkner devoted to Byron in *Flags in the Dust* (his name reminding us of Horace as his flight anticipates Young Bayard's) were eliminated in *Sartoris* and so obscured the novel's central dilemmas. Wasson also cut the early scenes of Harry Mitchell, yet it is his ineptitude, forcing him North from Jefferson, that will adumbrate Bayard's journey at the end of the novel and may even have served him as his only envisioned escape. *Flags in the Dust*, like the other novels of Faulkner, is communicated through a presiding intelligence that becomes, in the course of understanding itself, an analogizing narrative consciousness.

Young Bayard is not always conscious of parallels and crosscurrents in this novel of his life, but we are as readers: our own attempt to drive disconnected episodes to a single frame of reference and meaning causes us to re-cognize and reconstitute the material that the novel brings before us. As Sartre found *The Sound and the Fury* whole in every scene, each scene echoing all the others, so we sense that Young Bayard's situation is deliberately reflected in Horace and Byron, in Old Bayard and Harry, in Aunt Jenny and Narcissa. This sense of the novel as a series of discrete scenes which through repetition, parallelism, and juxtaposition intimate a broader meaning for the whole is fundamental to Faulkner's narrative poetics. And we see this wherever we turn: Joe Christmas finds his own self-alienation and self-disparagement in Joanna Burden, Benjy and Quentin share the awful realization that the only beauty is the beauty of loss and death, Temple and Popeye sense their attraction to evil as a permanent cor-

ruption of the possibility of justice, and Ike McCaslin charts his life
as it is mirrored back to him in Sam, then in Boon, then in Roth; and
we, reading *Go Down, Moses*, find still greater significance in comparing Ike to Rider and to Gavin Stevens, to Cass and to Lucas in those
other segments, only assumed disjointed, of the novel in which Ike appears. The ripples of *narrative consciousness* thus spread out through
the various scenes of Faulkner's novels to embrace our sense of the
work *as a whole*, our *structural consciousness*, and, beyond that, to a
sense of the significance of the accumulation of incidents and images
as we put them together, what we may term our *constitutive consciousness*. The crime and punishment which Temple Stevens tries to
define in the dramatic segments of *Requiem for a Nun* Faulkner defines, in larger terms, in the prose prologues that parallel her sordid
story in the larger history of Jefferson, Yoknapatawpha, and even
Jackson, Mississippi, while the alienation and exile of Mohataha and
Cecelia Farmer are our most lucid clues for understanding and recognizing Nancy Mannigoe and Temple Stevens. In so aligning one or
more narrative consciousness with our own consciousness of the work
as a single unified aggregate, Faulkner's novels are persistently phenomenological in origin and shape.

As consequence, Faulkner's novels are never linear in development;
they *seem* impressionistic. They pursue, stumble, repeat, circle, stop
bewildered within the minds of characters who in turn judge, explore,
denounce, imagine. There is here a deliberate attempt to capture
the human processes of thought and growth which are never one-
dimensional, but which oscillate, expand, contract, retrogress, mobi-
lize, partially atrophy, proceed erratically. Quentin's anguished search
in *Absalom, Absalom!* and his morbid meditations in *The Sound and
the Fury* are obvious cases in point as are the multiple narrators of
The Town and *The Mansion;* but so is Joe Christmas in his inarticulate search for a fixed identity, Harry Wilbourne in his ruminations
on the designs and possibilities for love and grief, and Horace Benbow
in his romantic quest for justice.

Much of this was of course the direct legacy of the nineteenth-
century novel. Faulkner knew his Melville and his Dostoyevsky as
well as his Balzac and his Flaubert. Henry James, whom Faulkner
openly admired, insisted not only on the central intelligence as the
shaping force of the novel but on witnessing one troubled vision
through another; Conrad advanced this with his fascination for
multiple impressions and distorted chronologies; Joyce began to con-

centrate on the stillness at the moment of climactic discovery. Such techniques for fiction were widespread and well studied in the 1920s, during Faulkner's period of apprenticeship; and Ford Madox Ford's observations must even then have seemed a summing up when he wrote that "it became very early evident to us," to Ford and Conrad, "that what was the matter with the Novel, and the British novel in particular, was that it went straight forward, whereas in your gradual making acquaintanceship with your fellows you never do go straight forward." To form a strong character, to provide psychological realism, "you could not begin at his beginning and work his life chronologically to the end. You must first get him in with a strong impression, and then work backwards and forwards over his past." What was held *de rigueur* for Ford and Conrad became as well a kind of recipe for Faulkner.

"Lo, I have committed fornication / But that was in another country; and besides, / The wench is dead." This moral tag from Marlowe's *Jew of Malta* keeps recurring in the runner's mind in *A Fable*; it is a clue to our understanding of him and a choric reminder to the runner of his own self-discovery: even a runner cannot always run. Yet what is haunting the runner is equally applicable to the general who cannot forget his fornication or his days in the Tibetan lamasery. This persistence of the past likewise impinges on the present for the sentry and the corporal and, above all, for the Quartermaster General, although for them the fornication is figurative, metaphorical; and we make the application even when Faulkner's characters do not, cannot. Beyond the borders of *A Fable* and in retrospect, Marlowe's lines are central to Quentin's thought in *The Sound and the Fury* and to Joe Christmas's in *Light in August*. All of Faulkner's novels are thus cradled within one or more narrative consciousness, and the observations, openly admitted, merely felt, or strangely absent, "never do go straight forward" but analyze, sift, and integrate sensations, observations, and events, register and respond to what they consider significant. Faulkner shapes his work to reveal the visions of his characters; their visions thus become his style.

Faulkner takes us into such acts of perceiving, whether presented in first or third person, in soliloquy, interior monologue, or omniscient narration: not only do we share the thoughts of his characters but we also share the movement, quiescences, turbulence, tension, straining, bewilderment, and repetition that indicate their sensory and intellectual responses. There is never any real detachment; even descriptions and objects are important as perceptual indicators. We share not only insights and judgments but prejudices, blindnesses, and distortions. By displacing serial narrative construction with shifting perceptual planes, Faulkner provides us with actions as they press on the consciousness of major characters. Awareness may come after the fact, or independent of it; instead of extending forward or backward in a single sequence (as with Benjy Compson), a narrative consciousness may alternately move forward and backward in time (as with Ike McCaslin), may interject the present with memory or anticipation (as with Joe Christmas), or may slip repeatedly back to an event or to an image despite a struggle to forget or ignore it (as with Jewel Bundren). At the same time, the narrative is interlaced with suggestions of possible reasons for present observations or potential actions and for ways to deal with the past or present while the action continues to move forward, or backward, in time. Calendar time and conceptual time may be congruent or incongruent or both in turn. But always in Faulkner's works there is a persistent restlessness, a searching to know and a struggle toward self-control that resists any easy temptation to composure, the sort of restlessness exemplified by Young Bayard in *Flags in the Dust*. Indeterminacy in things (contingencies) and in consciousness (perceptions) characterizes Faulkner's view of Young Bayard and of the mind generally as it also characterizes his poetics, and always with a kind of urgency, until a final moment when everything converges, in the narrative consciousness of a character or in the all-embracing consciousness of the reader, and the deep structures of predispositions and unconscious impositions are disclosed.

Time, Faulkner once declared, does not exist except "in the momentary avatars of individual people"; he might have said the same for space. Neither is actual nor reportorial but imaginatively and individually constructed. For Ratliff, life is seasonal and cyclic and it repeats an annual pattern throughout northern Mississippi; the same is true for Anse Bundren. For both Ratliff and Anse, places too seem interchangeable. For Flem Snopes, on the other hand, life is a single progression in time and space from poverty to wealth, from country to town and to respectability. For Flem, place is as necessary an indicator of self-measurement as time.

Faulkner's novels seem so full of conscious and unconscious perceptions that there is, surprisingly, a minimum of fact. Instead there are many apparent facts which, when pressed, are mere illusion. Storytelling and rumor replace observation; judgment and memory displace witnessed knowledge. This is surely true of Joe Christmas's warped memory of his childhood, memory that becomes belief and thus directs and regulates his every thought and gesture. It is also true of Benjy, whose world is colored by loss (it is no accident that the novel opens with Benjy's search for something lost), and with Temple whose recollection for Horace of her rape by Popeye is totally concerned with the foreplay rather than with the act of fornication itself. Faulkner seems to invite us always to note discrepancies as if his sole emphasis often rested there, for he translates what sources his works have into semifictions and legends in much the way his characters do. Some time ago Ward Miner learned that, although Jefferson and Yoknapatawpha follow the grid of Oxford and Lafayette County with a high degree of accuracy, there are important differences in population, economy, and racial makeup. Elsewhere friends of Faulkner and critics of his work assure us that Old Reel-Foot is not simply and wholly Old Ben; William Clark Falkner is not Colonel John Sartoris; the criminal who suggested Popeye to Faulkner used something "more horrific" than a corncob (whatever that might be); and an unrelated lynching prompted Faulkner to describe the death of Lee Goodwin. The final focus is never on source as it is never on fact, but is rather on the perception of fact or the alternative ways of seeing facts. This is where truth finally lies for Faulkner, in fiction as in life, and it must be made sufficiently available within his novel so as to be embodied as perceptions not only in the characters but in us, his readers, as well.

So Faulkner would be pleased that Sally R. Page finds that "*Mosquitoes* is a successful novel at least in the sense that it creates within the reader the same frustration of expectation without resolution and the boredom of futile encounter that is its subject," for a reduplication outside the novel of perception that is within the novel (even when only dimly understood there) is a large measure of his aim. We join his characters in their need to explore and discover, connect and evaluate. We are to feel about *Light in August* as Irving Howe feels. "Chapter twelve of the novel, in which the affair between Christmas and Joanna Burden reaches its climax," he writes, "is surely one of the most powerful pieces of writing ever done by an American: a narrative which leaves one not so much with the sense of having witnessed an ordeal as having participated in it." The account is powerful because its very life stretches beyond the passage and page that provide it, and is renewed each time that it is shared: expanded knowing within the novel related to the expanded knowing in the reader.

Although Faulkner is primarily concerned with studying one or more narrative consciousnesses in various and discrete episodes, as he studies Young Bayard's in *Flags in the Dust* both in isolation and alongside the somewhat analogous consciousness of a Horace Benbow, a Harry Mitchell, or a Byron Snopes, still he does not openly integrate the units of his novels. The chapters of *Flags in the Dust* remain essentially disjunctive. Instead of providing connectives or transitions, Faulkner gives us central dramatic motifs and patterns of corresponding experiences which recur, correlating episodes and even taking on their own symbolic values. Elements scattered throughout a novel invite conflation or synchronization; while Faulkner is repetitive, he is never redundant.

Perhaps Faulkner learned some of this in Hollywood; surely it was corroborated there, for like most serious film makers who seem to recognize the necessity of engaging the spectator's imagination by making their shots somewhat inconsecutive so that the spectator must fill in the gaps for himself, Faulkner relies on our active collaboration when faced with discontinuities in time, space, and event. We know instinctively that what words most powerfully and naturally do is hang together, combine both ideationally and syntactically, and that certain clusters of words lead to anticipations of consciousness. To aid us in the process of reading his work, then, Faulkner makes all his narratives cognitive in aim and means while making them distinctive, from time to time, with perceptual synapses. So such baffling moments as Young Bayard's apparently arbitrary death, or the multiple ending of *Pylon*, or the temporal and modal dislocations at the center of chapter 5 of *Go Down, Moses* ("The Bear") followed by a flashback to an earlier day, require some explanation beyond the explicit data: while on the one hand Faulkner exercises a total claim on us, at the same time his novels remain limited and partial. This is because human truth for Faulkner can never lie in a single narrative consciousness; and we understand Young Bayard better when he is placed alongside Caspey and Horace, Aunt Jenny and Narcissa.

As consequence, Faulkner does not rely, finally, on any single narrative consciousness, but on the reader's own *constitutive consciousness*, his ability to select what terms he will accept, his means of combining them, and, just as importantly, what he will reject. This is a lesson Faulkner found not only in his James and Conrad but in Balzac and Flaubert. Just as the Sèvres dish and the box with the pearl-rimmed portraits, the garden bench and the map of the world constitute for us the consciousness and meaning of Eugènie Grandet, just as the dance and the auction, the woods and the cathedral, Tostes and Yonville-l'Abbaye constitute Emma Bovary for us, so we know Faulkner's corporal *only* by knowing the runner, the old general, Levine, and Marthe. We constitute the consciousness of Ike McCaslin not only by knowing the woods and the delta as he knows them, but by gauging his perceptions of Sam and Boon, of Cass and Roth, and of Lucas, Tennie's Jim, and Fonsiba. It is in just such combinations that we realize; it is by just such discrepancy and disjunction—by discrepancies in the recognitions of various characters and by disjunctions between episodes within a novel and between the novel and its title, as with *Absalom, Absalom!* and *The Wild Palms*—that Faulkner forces us from the field of his vision into the field of our own. Only thus, in art, can Thomas Sutpen be intimated as King David who weeps for his son Absalom or does not weep for him; only in art may Harry Wilbourne be reflected in the dry, wavering, sterile palm trees yet remain Harry Wilbourne.

The paradox in all this is that the more we consider Faulkner's apparently audacious experimentation in the novel, the more radically old-fashioned he becomes. His structures are at least as old as fable and myth, for they are arranged by scenes derived from thought, belief, and memory: as much inheres in the telling as in the tale. Thus Faulkner's units of narrative consciousness strike personal roots of some permanence; they are also reshaped with the momentary but imperative needs of his characters in their critical race toward self-knowledge; the whole world of experience and the narrow impulse of individual psychology alike impinge on a character's understanding as he relays it to us. Our constitutive consciousness of any given novel, then, will both reflect and judge, mirror and *re*-shape these events, recognize in the re-cognition of them.

Thus to extend the study of narrative consciousness in Faulkner leads to very different, but I think quite central, readings of most of his novels. We can understand, for example, why Faulkner was right to insist that *The Unvanquished, Go Down, Moses,* and *Requiem for a Nun* are novels. We can see why *Sanctuary* concludes, deliberately, with a flashback providing the biography of Popeye: only with such a biography does Faulkner address the last central questions of that book. We can see how Jason resembles Benjy and Quentin, is more like than unlike them. We can perceive, in our constituent reading, what allows Cash to survive while Darl cannot. We discover the wisdom of having the furniture dealer conclude *Light in August* and give new importance to the fact that even Thomas Sutpen, in relating his life story to Grandfather Compson, was doing just that and *only* that, " 'telling a story.' " We can even account, finally, for the failure of Ike's marriage and for the fact that Flem Snopes's motive for possessing Eula and the de Spain bank and mansion was not, after all, greed but simple self-respect: he is Ab Snopes's son to the end, just as Mink is Ab's nephew; and both end their lives in a final (and fulfilling) confrontation with the other as opposing selves.

In directing our responses in this way, Faulkner's style and vision fuse as a permanent possession of the imagination which is the basis of his narrative poetics. I think we can best appreciate such a poetics of consciousness by examining first its roots, then its techniques as Faulkner develops them, and, finally, his accomplishment in the major novels. Part I of the essay which follows, then, sums our understanding of human perception and conception by reviewing our current state of knowledge alongside *Light in August* as well as those novelists of consciousness whom Faulkner found most useful. Although what he took from his predecessors is for the most part general—and not especially startling to the students of Balzac and Melville, Joyce and Proust—this too gives us some indication of what to watch for. Part II of this essay, on Faulkner's method, examines those techniques most recurrent in his body of fiction, providing brief analyses of all his minor novels and detailed readings of his remaining major ones.

I Background for Faulkner's Narrative Poetics

Visions: Forms of Modern Consciousness

Thoughts need shape.—RUDOLF ARNHEIM

Form must be the form of the mind. Not a way of saying things, but of thinking them.—JEAN COCTEAU

Eventually man finds that his identity is not simply discovered but created.
—ENRICO GARZILLI

They were sitting again now, having decided that they had gone far enough for that night, and the niggers had made camp and cooked supper and they (he and Grandfather) drank some of the whiskey and ate and then sat before the fire drinking some more of the whiskey and he telling it all over and still it was not absolutely clear—the how and the why he was there and what he was—since he was not talking about himself. He was telling a story.—FAULKNER

SEEING (LIKE KNOWING) is a two-way process. Objects *out there* lead to our *inner* thoughts, lending them representation and significant form, while our thoughts simultaneously limit the ways and distort the things that we see. Our conscious perceiving and understanding, therefore, always superimpose our frames of reference on our observations, laminate act with precept, while experiences can swiftly or with imperceptible slowness change our preconceptions. We cannot escape interacting with our environment nor can we escape dynamic involvement with the books we read (although they are deliberately metaphorical): we are analogous to fictional characters, as Jorge Luis Borges has long since told us, but at a final remove. Faulkner not only understood this phenomenon, but he everywhere exploits it. Reading his fictions, we help make them.

The Ways We See: Elements of Perception

Faulkner's narrative poetics is first grounded, therefore, in human perception; he is in line with those modern thinkers who are as concerned with how we know as with what we know. As a random illustration of this from *Light in August*, here is our introduction to

Joe Christmas, neatly made analogous by Faulkner (like a box within a box) to Byron's introduction to Joe at Joe's first appearance in Jefferson.

> Byron Bunch knows this: It was one Friday morning three years ago. And the group of men at work in the planer shed looked up, and saw the stranger standing there, watching them. They did not know how long he had been there. He looked like a tramp, yet not like a tramp either. His shoes were dusty and his trousers were soiled too. But they were of decent serge, sharply creased, and his shirt was soiled but it was a white shirt, and he wore a tie and a stiffbrim straw hat that was quite new, cocked at an angle arrogant and baleful above his still face. He did not look like a professional hobo in his professional rags, but there was something definitely rootless about him, as though no town nor city was his, no street, no walls, no square of earth his home. And that he carried his knowledge with him always as though it were a banner, with a quality ruthless, lonely, and almost proud. "As if," as the men said later, "he was just down on his luck for a time, and that he didn't intend to stay down on it and didn't give a damn much how he rose up." He was young. And Byron watched him standing there looking at the men in sweatstained overalls, with a cigarette in one side of his mouth and his face darkly and contemptuously still, drawn down a little on one side because of the smoke. After a while he spat the cigarette without touching his hand to it and turned and went on to the mill office while the men in faded and worksoiled overalls looked at his back with a sort of baffled outrage. "We ought to run him through the planer," the foreman said. "Maybe that will take that look off his face."

In Byron's recollected struggle here to understand, what first strikes us as supplying and shaping the rhythm of the passage is his insistence on basing his *conception* in his *perception* and the perception of his associates (in whom his bewilderment here often takes refuge).

This comes as no surprise to us, of course, and doubtless we read the passage without pausing over it because long ago the Lockean notion that the mind is a *tabula rasa* until life plants succeeding images on it (turning us out, as Dickens remarks in *Hard Times*, like so many pianoforte legs) was discarded for the newer understanding of modern epistemology, prevalent since Kant, that reality is individually constructed by selecting and shaping ideas and images. So Byron here is not a receiver of images but a creator of awarenesses—he calls it *knowledge*, "Byron Bunch *knows* this"—because he chooses and shapes what he sees and so absorbs it into what he thinks. *Seeing* for Byron is thus indistinct from *thinking* for Byron. He practices what Rudolf Arnheim catches so well in his phrase, only apparently oxymoronic, "visual thinking." "My contention," comments Arnheim, "is that the cognitive operations called thinking are not the privilege of mental processes above and beyond perception, but the essential ingredients of perception itself. I am referring to such operations as exploration, selection, grasping of essentials, simplification, abstraction, analysis and synthesis, completion, correction, comparison, problem solving, as well as combining, separating, putting in context. These operations are not the prerogative of any one mental function; they are the manner in which the minds of both man and animal treat cognitive material at any level." Like us, Byron *mixes* levels of abstraction in order to perceive what is concretely before him: a strange man who, in the concrete, demands a concrete response. Byron sees (concretely) a stranger (the label is a simple name-calling abstraction); his consciousness then wavers between an attempt to define by analogy ("He looked like a tramp") and to limit himself to direct observation of facts ("His shoes were dusty and his trousers were soiled too"). This is an active consciousness, then, caught not only in the act of defining but in the act of absorbing; Byron wishes to analogize ("like a tramp") or classify ("the stranger") in order to give some meaning to the images he perceives ("His shoes were dusty"; "his trousers were soiled too") while not departing from those images. In fact he *hangs onto* images. Still focusing on the "stranger's" trousers, he records that "they were of decent serge, sharply creased," and goes on to note that "his shirt was soiled but it was a white shirt, and he wore a tie and a stiffbrim straw hat that was quite new." Now this is not simply a character description—or even scene painting—because it is all the direct object, for Faulkner and us, of the chief subject and verb of this paragraph, "Byron Bunch knows this." Byron is exercising his powers of visual thinking, as all of us do initially; "no ideas but in things," as William Carlos Williams puts it in *Paterson*. What is important here is not the unusualness of the image (as it is, say, with Vardaman's sudden attachment to the fish) but the socialized habit suggested by the choice of Byron's images; the network of concrete detail here speaks to the stranger's *social acceptability* and, beyond that, to his *social class*, as judged *and emphasized by Byron*, not by Faulkner. Image linkages, that is, have an internal relationship and consistency. Modern philosophers and psychologists never tire of telling us, as Ribot puts it, that "the logic of images is the prime mover of constructive imagination." Byron tries to define the stranger's *status* by his *appearance;* the focus is still on a *constructive perception* of the stranger which will result *in a relationship* that includes Byron, the observer. Having understood this, however, we see in Byron a rooted ambivalence. He both associates himself with the stranger and dissociates himself. *Stranger* and *hobo* are thoughts visually perceived which keep the man at some distance from Byron and so free Byron to react in a whole range of ways, from accepting him to rejecting (or even ignoring) the man. But the man's dress—the remnants of a suit and a professional appearance—speaks to Byron's weekend status in the church (which we shall learn about soon enough in his unfolding consciousness in *Light in August*) and so aligns Byron *with* the new man in a brotherhood which is *distinct from* the "regular" laborers at the sawmill who never assume a professional capacity. Thus the stranger attracts and intrigues Byron; his thoughts remain *wholly* concentrated on the stranger. He himself senses this and, uncomfortable in the relationship, Byron seeks to dissociate himself once more: "He did not look like a professional hobo in his professional rags, but there was something definitely rootless about him." Byron, as we meet him, is most confident of his being *settled*—that will be what Hightower points to in describing and evaluating Byron for us. Byron has a *place*. Whatever else he is, or wishes to become, he is *not a hobo;* hence he is not a *stranger.* So to dissociate himself ("there was something definitely rootless about him, as though no town nor city was his, no street, no walls, no square of earth his home"), Byron once more captures that freedom to accept, reject, or ignore the stranger. We perceive creatively not simply out of amusement or the need to respond but out of deeper desires and needs, betraying our values and wishes as much as our outer capacity to perform what a situation asks or demands of us. Behavior for Faulkner is always tied to inner choices, conscious or unconscious; these in turn help us to explore the person Faulkner is *really* characterizing.

"In order to interpret the functioning of the senses properly," Arnheim cautions us, "one needs to keep in mind that they did not come about as instruments of cognition for cognition's sake, but evolved as biological aids for survival." Biologically, the movement of our eyes, and the ability to have a field of vision within peripheral vision so as to amass and concentrate our responses, is an act which, once needed for physical self-preservation, has since become a matter of habit for preservation of our *selves*, that is, of our consciousness. So Byron too pushes what he doesn't want to see (the "stranger" as "ruthless") to one side, and beyond peripheral sight and thought; he pulls what he does want to see (the "stranger" as "lonely") *into* his (and our) field of vision.

In doing so, he is as wary of potential error as we are. We know that a straight stick looks bent if it is partially submerged in water; we know a distant object looks small not necessarily because it *is* small but because it is distant. Our eyes themselves deceive us *unless* we *think* about our perceptions so as to correct the potential margin of error. "He did not look like a professional hobo in his professional rags," Byron *knows*, but appearances can deceive, and he goes on, in the same unbroken thought, to add, "but there was something definitely rootless about him." Seeing the stick is in and out of water allows us to correct a possible misperception of the stick—even though the stick is a concrete object and right before our very eyes, in the center of our field of vision. The air of rootlessness which Byron perceives, secondarily to the concrete perception of the man's soiled trousers, is therefore a corrective to the easy identification of the stranger as a professional man. Moreover, modern physiology has taught us that the eye, constantly vibrating, moves even faster at moments of intense concentration, so as to supply unusually sharp images. It *literally* "sees more." This can be voluntary—as when we try to remember someone we are being introduced to—or involuntary—as when someone we are being introduced to "makes a strong impression" on us whether we wish it or not. Now because we are aware of these two alternatives, we cannot know, by the fifth sentence in the passage I have quoted, whether Byron's immediate and profound concentration on the stranger—resulting in a later obsessive memory of him—is voluntary or involuntary. I think because we are aware, at some deep level of *our* consciousness, that this is important—to understanding Byron, to understanding the novel—that we instinctively search in this passage for clues. We look, that is, to see if Byron is *consciously* stating sufficient reasons for his intense contration on the stranger. Since we have only just met Byron, this is difficult for us to judge, so we turn to the *terms in which* Byron evaluates the man who appears suddenly before him. In doing this, we may note—perhaps unconsciously ourselves, for we may concentrate, may "see more" in any good work of art than is made at once explicit—what Byron selects as important. He is not concerned about the abruptness of the stranger's appearance. He is not concerned about the stranger's manner (at least not at first). He *is* concerned about the stranger's appearance and he relates this appearance to his relationship with society—whether he is "professional" and a part of it, or a "hobo" and outcast from it. If we sense this as the primary dichotomy of terms Byron's perception imposes (in its thinking visually) on the stranger, we shall be prepared for the word "lonely" in the adjectives soon to be applied to the stranger by Byron. So far, so good. In scanning the parts of the whole in the field of vision—"like certain electronic devices, such as that used with television," says Susanne Langer, in talking about the way we see and perceive—Byron settles at once on the man's relationship to others. "Lonely" reaffirms that interest. "Ruthless" and "almost proud," however, seem to deny the portrait Byron is building, of a man down and out and in need of companionship, a man more openly unhappy and unfulfilled, although perhaps not less so than himself. "Ruthless" and "almost proud" divorces the two of them. But this too is in keeping with modern psychology, which argues that we define not only by likenesses but by binary oppositions—by seeing how *unlike* something we are. Dissimilarity preserves our uniqueness, our selving, and reaffirms *us*, rather than *them*. So another thing we learn from this passage—we sense, if we do not explicitly acknowledge—is that Byron is desirous of confirming himself.

Our concentrated field of vision seems realistic while it is decidedly unrealistic (in that it selects from, rather than leaves whole, a configured scene before it), but we accept this partial sight because our perception assumes (and goes on creating) what in fact it does not see. This is always happening to us; when we walk or drive past a barn, for example, we assume it has four sides, although we only see one or two of them; we assume further that the sides we cannot see resemble in color, material, and age the ones we do see; and if we know what goes on in a barn we may, in our "mind's eye," even complete the picture by imagining what is inside as furnishings, or what activity is occurring within. (This desire to control the field of vision by creating all of it is precisely why Darl opens *As I Lay Dying* seeing Jewel in the cottonhouse, although of course the walls separate them. Darl needs to understand Jewel, and to be with him. Without Jewel Darl's vision, his world, his life would be incomplete; he needs more than the cottonhouse.) What is true for us is true for Byron: he goes on to resolve his ambivalence about the stranger—so he can resolve tension and know how to respond—by choosing one alternative ("lonely" or "ruthless") and building creatively on it. " 'As if,' as the men said later, 'he was just down on his luck for a time.' " Yet such easy accommodation, rendering Byron superior to the man and the event, and so in more control in theory than in fact, causes Byron some further uneasiness, and he recalls an additional clause that restores the equivocation and reintroduces the tension: " 'and that he didn't intend to stay down on it and didn't give a damn how much he rose up.' " In selecting images for visual thinking and in designing coherent patterns or configurations for those perceptions, we reassert what we *mean* to see. The world makes sense because we *make it make sense;* understanding this, at least subliminally, we see Byron trying to make sense of the stranger. That he cannot easily do so betrays his own uneasiness that goes beyond the stranger, his uneasiness with himself. "Byron Bunch knows this," but what *does* he "know"? He knows that he does not know.

We perceive because of relevance, and also because of associations; it was Braque who once amusingly observed that a coffee spoon near a cup means one thing, when used to put on a shoe it means something else. So the stranger associated with Byron is one thing; when he is associated with the other men in the sawmill, he is another. He is no longer the potentially professional man who is wearing the stained dress of the professional; he is rather someone in old clothes who is chiefly characterized by his strength and self-reliance. "After a while he spat the cigarette without touching his hand to it and turned and went on to the mill office while the men in faded and worksoiled overalls looked at his back with a sort of baffled outrage." He " 'didn't give a damn much how he rose up,' " Byron has just recalled the men saying; " 'he didn't give a damn' " suggests the force of the men who see in the stranger a force potentially equal to their own; " 'how he rose up' " suggests their bafflement. They are not necessarily concerned that they do not understand the stranger; they admit freely that they do not "know," that is, understand, him. His physical habit with the cigarette—"he spat the cigarette without touching his hand to it"—is, as we shall see in the course of the novel, a kind of fierce physical gesture which aligns the stranger with the workmen more than with Byron, but even here Byron's visual thinking dwells on the similarity between the stranger and his fellow workers. It is the foreman, the spokesman for the group but not for Byron (we sense this because his language is so starkly disjunctive from Byron's language in his thoughts), who says, as forcibly as the stranger is now perceived by Byron, " 'We ought to run him through the planer. . . . Maybe that will take that look off his face.' " Both the foreman and the stranger are made similar here—are made doubles by Byron's analogizing consciousness in their "ruthless"ness and in their exercise, or threatened exercise, of "almost proud" power.

In so associating the stranger with the foreman, Byron's progressive perception (what Byron "knows") enables him not simply to sense a certain defeat in the stranger ("He did not look like a professional hobo in his professional rags, but there was something definitely rootless about him, as though no town nor city was his, no street, no walls, no square of earth his home"). It also allows Byron to establish, *within* his conscious perception, a kind of *pity for* the stranger. "He was young." He is "lonely." The "decent serge, sharply creased," is no longer stained or dirty in his thoughts. If this stranger frightens Byron ("his face darkly and contemptuously still"), he also arouses a kind of sympathy and fraternity within Byron. Thus "He was young" can come to suggest both the contemptuous strength of youth—the ruthlessness of youth—or the suffering of youth, a boy down on his luck. Forced to choose between the two—to commit himself to befriend the stranger and thus take a different stance from his fellow workmen or to ignore the stranger and thus not help one in need—is a quandary which Byron cannot, at the moment, resolve. (It is indicative of much we shall learn of him; he is a man who is both a hard worker at the sawmill and a hard worker, on Sundays, in the fields of the Lord.) So Byron temporarily resolves his puzzlement, and completes the design of his visual thinking, by omitting, from here on out, his own perceptions. Rather, the perceptions he gives to himself (and to us) are the perceptions *of the others—as if* they were his own.

Once we harbor certain thoughts, however, we precondition our future vision. Perception is not simply a matter of what we see, or even of what we remember of what we see, or even what we wish to remember of what we see, but of fulfilled anticipations of what we *expected* to see. Seeing is a matter of molding our sight day after day and year after year. So the artist Ben Shahn can remark in *The Shape of Content*—itself a revealing title—that new images are made up of inner vestiges of older images; we live, he says, in "that company of phantoms which we all own." Since this seems to say in a metaphoric way what we have all accepted as common knowledge, even as common sense, we can turn it around, as Faulkner does, and apply it to Byron. What he projects onto the stranger imagistically is a series of images he is most attuned to by his own previous experience—to dress, to "air," and to gesture. Those that set the stranger apart, give him "no street, no walls, no square of earth," make him sympathetic to Byron and therefore, we must assume, speak in some deep way to Byron's own past. We cannot tell from this single passage whether the stranger's current condition, *thus perceived by Byron*, reduplicates Byron's own past or present state of homelessness or whether it suggests the homeless persons Byron has known. (We shall learn it is the latter, for Byron likes best to serve others. He serves the church, he befriends Hightower, he aids Lena, he tries to save Joe. He is most frustrated, in the course of the novel now before us, when he can*not* help someone, as when Hightower refuses his help, or cannot get others to help where they should, as Lucas Burch should acknowledge his common-law wife and child.) What we do know, in this concern with homelessness, is that it is a central concern to Byron (as it is not to the other workmen). The stockpiling of images— "no *town* nor *city* was his, no *street*, no *walls*, no square of *earth* his *home*"—reveals a kind of obsessiveness with roots, with belonging, that is not displayed elsewhere here. In supplying this concern, through the images of his visual perception, Byron lets us know him— or, rather, Faulkner brings us into the field of his narrative consciousness while seeming to give us a detached, third-person narration. Moreover, Faulkner has so strategically arranged this necessary baggage of a scene for introducing the protagonist that he combines the "stranger" who is similar as well as dissimilar, through the perceptual discrepancy between what Byron sees and what the others see, to produce something new: the theme of home, of belonging. If we remember that Faulkner was writing for Hollywood at the time he was writing *Light in August* and was therefore well aware of Eisenstein's notion of a *tertium quid*—a new third thing that arises from an attempt to relate two juxtaposed but apparently discontinuous things, like scenes in film—we can understand what Faulkner hopes to achieve by bringing a stranger into Byron's consciousness through the confrontation of the stranger and the other workmen at the sawmill. And if we don't remember that Faulkner understood how movies work on our consciousness—and that they are not dissimilar from books in presenting images to our visual thinking—it does not matter. We see in movies as we see in life, for in both we construct meaning out of data that, left alone, are discontinuous, dissociated, and meaningless. Byron's perception, in solidifying a situation and imparting meaning and value to it, merely reduplicates our own effort in reading about it. Through establishing Byron's visual perception of events, Faulkner establishes our own.

Visual Thinking: Elements of Conception

"An image," Sartre tells us, "can only enter into consciousness if it is itself a synthesis, not an element"—a representative function, not an isolated observation. But images, as grasped by the *perception*, are finally absorbed into broader systems of conscious understanding; they enter into the *conception*. Conception deals primarily with abstract thoughts and principles as perception deals with the concrete and observable; conception is the locus of normative and subjective *ideas*; conception is the realm of *metaphor*. Conception works through stretches of time and space; it is the cognitive part of our mind which relates present to past experience, which makes analogies, which builds systems of thought, and which finally lends back to perception certain expectations, certain predispositions. Conception resolves what is contradictory or admits what is irreconcilable; it is the home of what is allowed to be paradoxical. In our discussion of perception above, certain extrapolations, showing the consequences of Byron's perceptions, dealt with Byron's conceptions. The *immediate* is perceptual; the *recollected* (and hence at least partly systematized) is conceptual.

Byron's first sight of Joe Christmas, the stranger, opens chapter 2 of *Light in August*. The passage quoted above continues as follows:

> They did not know who he was. None of them had ever seen him before. "Except that's a pretty risky look for a man to wear on his face in public," one said: "He might forget and use it somewhere where somebody wont like it." Then they dismissed him, from the talk, anyway. They went back to their work among the whirring and grating belts and shafts. But it was not ten minutes before the mill superintendent entered, with the stranger behind him.
>
> "Put this man on," the superintendent said to the foreman. "He says he can handle a scoop, anyhow. You can put him on the sawdust pile."
>
> The others had not stopped work, yet there was not a man in the shed who was not again watching the stranger in his

soiled city clothes, with his dark, insufferable face and his whole air of cold and quiet contempt. The foreman looked at him, briefly, his gaze as cold as the other's. "Is he going to do it in them clothes?"

"That's his business," the superintendent said. "I'm not hiring his clothes."

"Well, whatever he wears suits me if it suits you and him," the foreman said. "All right, mister," he said. "Go down yonder and get a scoop and help them fellows move that sawdust."

The newcomer turned without a word. The others watched him go down to the sawdust pile and vanish and reappear with a shovel and go to work. The foreman and the superintendent were talking at the door. They parted and the foreman returned. "His name is Christmas," he said.

"His name is what?" one said.

"Christmas."

"Is he a foreigner?"

"Did you ever hear of a white man named Christmas?" the foreman said.

"I never heard of nobody a-tall named it," the other said.

And that was the first time Byron remembered that he had ever thought how a man's name, which is supposed to be just the sound for who he is, can be somehow an augur of what he will do, if other men can only read the meaning in time. It seemed to him that none of them had looked especially at the stranger until they heard his name. But as soon as they heard it, it was as though there was something in the sound of it that was trying to tell them what to expect; that he carried with him his own inescapable warning, like a flower its scent or a rattlesnake its rattle. Only none of them had sense enough to recognise it. They just thought that he was a foreigner, and as they watched him for the rest of that Friday, working in that tie and the straw hat and the creased trousers, they said among themselves that that was the way men in his country worked; though there were others who said, "He'll change clothes tonight. He wont have on them Sunday clothes when he comes to work in the morning."

This long section also constitutes the direct object of the sentence which formulates the chapter—"Byron Bunch knows this"—and yet *knowing* has slipped quite subtly here from perception into conception. This is not because images are no longer present, for there is here an occasional image: "They went back to their work among the whirring and grating belts and shafts"; " 'He says he can handle a scoop, anyhow.' " Rather, it is because images have receded from the center of Byron's consciousness. They are now only the props which propel his recollections and so build on and secure his visual thinking by further abstraction.

At first, this progression seems doubtful, for the narration of the scene merely continues as we first read the passage. Yet something decisive has happened here: Byron has dropped out of the scene. What was first clearly a relationship being formulated between the stranger and himself—"He looked like a tramp" means "He looked like a tramp to Byron" since "Byron Bunch knows this"—has passed into a memory of *them*: "*They* did not know who he was." In thus comfortably distancing the stranger the better to recall and define him, Byron adds further space between them by dwelling for a short period on the total disappearance of the stranger within the superintendent's office. His absence is not cause for Byron's attempt to perceive, however, but a time for him to record the perceptions of others; *he* is abstracting his own relationship, or potential relationship, with the stranger in the voices and understanding of his surrogate fellow workers. " 'Is he a foreigner?' " " 'His name is what?' " Where before Byron had refused closure, had not completed his definition (perceptually) of the stranger because he felt both related to him and unrelated to him, now he is distanced by a different, wholly external, range of responses: from those of the laborers who proceed from distrusting the stranger to accepting him with hesitation to that of the superintendent whose support of the stranger is beyond question. Byron's own difficulties are submerged in the difficulties of the others— *they* must reconcile themselves to the stranger as coworker, to the stranger's strange name, and to bets on how he will dress the next day, bets which are clearly strategies preliminary to deciding whether to accept or reject the stranger.

Yet this displacement is only momentary in Byron's consciousness, for he is too honest, at least with himself, to deny his own interest in the stranger. So Byron transfers the mystery in the appearance and the employment of the stranger into a mystery which *seems* explained—the name which *he* makes an omen. "It was as though there was something in the sound of it that was trying to tell them what to expect; that he carried with him his own inescapable warning, like a flower its scent or a rattlesnake its rattle." The sense of *omen* is, at the conceptual level, Byron's way of managing to accommodate the stranger—and to prepare himself for *whatever* might happen, good or bad. What strikes us forcibly is that what Byron *thinks* supplies not prophecy but (once more) *equivocation*, for the omens he thinks of are neatly balanced—the flowers *and* the snake, beauty *and* death. He forestalls betrayal and disappointment by admitting the possibility of either *or of both*. And doing *this* arouses the last connection between himself and the stranger which had been the first part of his perception and now, conceptually, his *memory* of the stranger. By the close of this passage, with the half-joking wager on the stranger's garments the next day, Byron has managed to end what at first seemed to be a deep and unspoken relationship between the stranger and himself. If we, as readers, are to put together in *our* constitutive consciousness what has happened—that is, if we are to reconstitute the fragments of thought and image here to locate Byron's unspoken conception of the stranger—what emerges most clearly is that Byron has so arranged his "knowledge"—"Byron Bunch knows this"—that he has *released himself from* his early, compulsive attraction to the stranger. His conceptualization, then, has served a deep and important purpose: it has *divorced* him from the man named Christmas. And in this deliberate closure provided by the necessity to dissociate, we are led more deeply than ever into Byron's consciousness.

Faulkner's various ways of revealing narrative consciousness—what Gustaf Hellström of Sweden called experimentalization in the novel—are thus not always so easy to perceive on a first reading. We know that the process of conceptualization is acquired, and that adults do it more quickly and more satisfactorily than children. (We may recall here that Vardaman can accommodate the death of Addie Bundren only in haphazard ways, by associating her death with that of the fish he caught and by initial wild and random accusations of who or what might be to blame for Addie's death. His conscious conjectures are incomplete and often groundless, substituting coincidence or sequence for causation or purpose. Vardaman, however, does recognize the centrality of the conceptualization process; like most children he even formulates it egocentrically—not simply why did Addie Bundren die? but why did Addie Bundren leave *me*? The *process* here is identical with the one undergone by Byron Bunch in the passage we have been examining: who is Joe Christmas? and is this stranger like or unlike *me*?) But although Byron's process of conceptualization here is rapid and subtle, the passage before us is not, as it might at first appear, one of an omniscient narrator. It is clearly one of an evolving consciousness wrestling with what will become, for Joe, Joanna, and Hightower as well as Byron, the two key questions of *Light in August* generally: who is Joe Christmas? what does Joe Christmas's particular biography, as presented in this novel, mean for *me*? The lesson here is a necessary one in examining Faulkner's technique and in coming to understand his poetics, for Faulkner *never* provides us with an objective and omniscient narrator. *All* of the scenes in his novels, and all of the narrations of those scenes, are filtered through partial and prejudicial consciousness from which we, as readers still more remote from the action, must reconstitute or re-cognize so as to understand. *Not* to understand that Byron here remembers Joe in order to exorcise him is to *mis*understand the point of the whole passage and the reason for Faulkner's introducing Joe through Byron. *"Byron Bunch* knows this"—but we know more.

We understand Byron better than Byron understands himself because we are helped through Faulkner's precise and skillful choice and arrangement of fact and idea, image, perception, and conscious memory, all leading (as he will remark at the opening of chapter 6) to belief. "Memory believes before knowing remembers." *Knowing* here becomes farthest removed from what is actually held onto conceptually, from what directs thinking. "Knowing" simply "remembers," as Byron Bunch "knows" here only his selected and digested "memory" of that first appearance of the stranger Joe Christmas, and this "memory" in turn coalesces into "belief" that "that was the way it was." Memory *becomes* fact, as Byron's memory here of the first encounter with Joe is presented as unquestioned fact, reliable and authentic. The process we have seen in a small and specimen way at the beginning of chapter 2, in Byron's perception and conception, is a miniature of the whole long third of the novel which is its crucial center—Joe's biography. Byron's developing consciousness also anticipates Joanna's account of her life (for she tells a story about a Calvinistic grandfather, an abolitionist's burden, and the good intentions of an old maid practicing civil rights for others) in a way is, we sense, so far from the frustration and warped perception of the Joanna we see in action that we are able to judge clearly that, whatever the story of her life *really* is, what she tells herself (by telling Joe) about her reasons for serving blacks is an accommodating *fiction*. Her account of herself results from belief, not "knowing" in the sense of observation and objectified experience. And what is true for Byron, Joe, and

Joanna is also true of Hightower—his desire to accommodate both the glory of the Confederate army and the need to preach Christianity to the fallen postbellum South is to preach regional rather than biblical history and, by choosing his own grandfather as exemplar, to seek personal as well as historical heroism.

These symbolic structures of consciousness—by which Joe can be ruled by the Calvinist McEachern, Joanna can be eternal servant to an imaged black cross, and Hightower can change chicken coop to battlefield—can be reiterated as things "known" because consciousness works through an aggregate of similarly perceived images or ideas. The human mind "bundles" coordinate perceptions together to form concepts of some endurance. Most of the modern psychologists tell us this, from Piaget in *The Psychology of Intelligence* and *Structuralism* to Erikson with his work on the stages of growing up (and growing up well adjusted). Such "bundles" are reciprocal. They enforce what we want to believe, and we want to believe what they enforce. This would be psychology's way of putting Faulkner's own definition of epistemology, for *Light in August* and for all the other novels as well, that "Memory believes before knowing remembers." What distinguishes Faulkner from these psychologists, however, is that they see knowing as a progressive and contingent matter; we are always open to new experiences which will either reinforce or modify the beliefs we have come to live with and by. For Faulkner, epistemology can be endangering because it can be encircling, can be a trap rather than a pathway through life. "Memory believes before knowing remembers" is, after all, a *circular* statement; it brings us back to where we began and so encloses us, finally, in memory to which believing and knowing, at opposite sides of the moving circle of memory, are subordinate. *Light in August* traces, therefore, essentially circular movements—that or characters standing still. Joe's travels return him to where he began; Joanna and Hightower seem rooted and unable to move (in the sense that *move* signifies *change*). Only Lena and Byron seem to progress, even cutting a path spatially through Jefferson and beyond. Yet this is how Byron and Lena see *themselves*—as traveling forward to some acknowledgeable end. To make certain that *we* understand they too are trapped in their own circles of belief, their own bundles of reinforcing concepts which cause the most energetic of the novel to stand still, Faulkner introduces a furniture repairer and dealer who picks up Lena and Byron on their way out of Jefferson with Lena's and Lucas's new child. This new spokesman is not an afterthought; nor is he Faulkner's sudden (and total) reliance on a kind of cop-out in consciousness. Rather, he is given us as the only person *outside* Jefferson—as much as possible outside the novel itself—who, as our surrogate, tells us what he sees. What he sees— Byron *married* to a woman who strings him along, *father* of a child she will not give him half possession of—pointedly tells us that what we think is true, even at a factual level, is in the world of men and women, of human consciousness, always subject to *mis*construction. We *think we know;* perhaps we never do. "Byron Bunch knows this" is, paradoxically, a summary of the whole novel and none of it and, ironically, never true in the everyday parlance of *knowing.*

Fiction and the Reader

This "modern" understanding of human consciousness in Faulkner is a shaping factor of his narratives; it also assumes a certain collaborative and reinforcing relationship between author and reader, and between text and reader. Faulkner cannot hold the observations of how human consciousness functions that I have been describing and still manage to tell a story through omniscient narrators. Not that he is alone in this; from Balzac's elemental understanding of perceptual imagery through the experimentations with stream of consciousness in Conrad, Joyce, and Proust, this is common property of the modernist novel, as we shall soon see in some detail. But Faulkner *is* unique in his shifts within this understanding of consciousness, both in the subtle shift from image to concept that we have seen at the beginning of chapter 2 in *Light in August* and more radical segmentation of perceptions and conceptions, as in the various chapters of *The Sound and the Fury* and *As I Lay Dying.* Faulkner is able to do this because he is willing to assume certain expected reactions from his readers and because he trusts their good sense in attempting to fuse together what seem to be discrete parts of a novel. In *Light in August,* for example, he plays against our drive to make the text coherent and whole in some customary, traditional fashion by hinting sufficiently at the Christ story to allow *us* to analogize Joe Christmas and Jesus Christ (the characters *in the novel* never do; *we* do) and to see how that will help us to some degree (though finally, I think, not much). And he is willing to trust our ability, as careful and dedicated readers, to see the essential similarities among Joe and Joanna and Byron and Hightower. Having experienced their analogizing consciousness at work (just as Byron sees everyone as like or unlike him, Joe by analogy sees every woman as the dietitian or Mrs. Mc-Eachern and every man as Doc Hines or Mr. McEachern), we tend to analogize, too. Thus we are meant to go farther than analogizing the consciousness of Joe and Joanna, Byron and Hightower as those movements of mind which repeatedly return to the refuge of accommodating concepts or fictions. *We* come to understand that Lena is subject to this, too: her fiction is that one day she will find Lucas and he will settle down and be a good father to their child; her story, framing the other stories, is thus correlative to them. And so is the furniture dealer, for what does he do but *translate* his perception of Lena and Byron into the kind of traveling salesman's story that his wife would want to hear at bedtime? We all use our consciousness to serve our own needs, and so, our need being a unified novel, Faulkner relies on us to make the pieces fit.

When the pieces fit, the novel functions in a customary, unified way; it *makes sense.* At their most skeletal, the pieces form a pattern. I do not think we always see that pattern; I remarked in the Preface that the end of *The Sound and the Fury* makes sense, but when I have asked my colleagues and students to say precisely *how* it makes sense, seems sufficient closure for this particular novel, they are often at a loss to say. Strangely silent too, at first, are the critics who admire *Light in August*—regularly considered a "major" novel written during the period when Faulkner was at the "peak of his powers"—for no one seems especially concerned that a salesman, introduced in the last chapter, is the narrator who closes this many-voiced narration. Rather, there seems something sufficiently fitting about this closure that it has brought no aggrieved critical attention. What is equally important, it has brought no satisfactory critical exegesis. No one has explained why Faulkner, in his technical genius, shifts focus so radically at the very end of the book. I think this is because we do not feel the furniture dealer to be all that unusual here. *He belongs,* or *seems* to.

Modern students of epistemology have gotten at this phenomenon of consciousness, too, in what they variously call subliminal knowledge, or subception, or (for literary critics) the "subtext." *"We can know more than we can tell"* is the way Michael Polanyi puts it. We know things which we neither verbalize (because we do not have the words) nor perceive (because what we know is not openly called to the conscious state). To give a common but clear illustration of this phenomenon, we can appreciate what our consciousness holds at a level below the threshold of our awareness if we try to describe a friend of ours to someone who has never seen him. We find we can-

not describe him precisely enough to portray him to someone else,
yet we can easily accept or reject adjectives volunteered for such a
description by others. Or we can recognize a friend after not seeing
him for several years, even when he has grown a beard, gotten much
fatter, or changed his personality in some marked and visible way.
What is held in our consciousness below the threshold of awareness is
so strong that it can conduct us past minor changes wrought by a
shift in time, place, or condition; similarly, what narrative experiments Faulkner makes with the form of the novel as we have long
grown accustomed to expect it—whether in the disparate (and even
discordant) perceptions in *The Sound and the Fury* or the sudden appearance of the furniture dealer in *Light in August*—are forms we can
accommodate not so much by noting them as by relating them back
to and absorbing them within the fundamental form, the ur-form, of
the novel housed in our deepest consciousness. Our desire for order
that is there so handles the new, the potentially disordered, that so
long as there is some visible connection (and some commitment to
ordering the experience), we find ways of formulating the order. So
instinctive is this process that we *can* say, at the same time, "The
ending of that novel makes sense" and "I cannot explain the ending
of that novel in so many words."

The goal of our integrated consciousness, as readers, is consequently
an equilibrium of our consciousness of the novel and the text itself.
This does not necessarily mean final closure. If it did, a novel could
not be reread and of course we can continue to reread Faulkner's
novels with the increased delight that comes with acquaintanceship.
If it did, it would raise stasis and fixity to a much higher value
than Faulkner ever awarded them—privately in his unfolding novels,
publicly in his statements about them. No idea of Faulkner's is quoted
more often than the epigraph to *The Mansion* in which he argues that
motion is life, un-motion is death. He wishes, primarily, to catch the
flow of life by energizing our consciousness. This does not preclude
in his poetics, however, a moment of relative integration, a point
where things that *were* in flux are now *relatively* constant and therefore semipermanent features of whatever solutions may be available
in our understandings of the work, now and in the future. This idea
is not new with Faulkner; it was new with Joyce. He called the moment an "epiphany," and his young protagonist Stephen Hero first
defines it for Cranly: "By an epiphany he meant a sudden spiritual
manifestation, whether in the vulgarity of speech or of gesture or in a

memorable phase of the mind itself. He believed that it was for the man of letters to record these epiphanies with extreme care, seeing that they themselves are the most delicate and evanescent of moments." Thomistic thought becomes, for Stephen, a sublime aesthetic. "When the relation of the parts is exquisite, when the parts are adjusted to the special point, we recognise that it is *that* thing which it is. Its soul, its whatness, leaps to us from the vestment of its appearance. The soul of the commonest object, the structure of which is so adjusted, seems to us radiant. The object achieves its epiphany." The idea is refined in *A Portrait of the Artist as a Young Man.* " 'The esthetic image,' " Stephen tells Lynch, " 'is first luminously apprehended as selfbounded and selfcontained upon the immeasurable background of space or time which is not it. You apprehended it as *one* thing. You see it as one whole. You apprehend its wholeness. That is *integritas*.' " This sense of the world coming to temporary rest in a kind of completeness was Joyce's contribution to the novel as form; Faulkner's contribution is to move the sense of epiphany from the climax of the plot (Stephen discussing art; Stephen confronting Leopold Bloom) to the conclusion of the book, and to transfer the sense of wholeness from the protagonist to the reader. This is why, for so long a time, critical commentary has emphasized Faulkner's novels as a kind of collaborative art.

Conclusion

The elements of Faulkner's poetics of vision, then, are these: (1) it centers in the evolving human consciousness, which is always greater than the sum of its individually revealed perceptions; (2) it is distinctive from any presiding awareness in the novel, is, rather, a constitutive consciousness developed by the reader; (3) it makes the act of reading an active collusion; and (4) it gives to Faulkner's work investigative form. Although the form of the detective story is centuries old, Faulkner finds it appealing because it embodies as his works do the active search for understanding, the exploration of perception and knowledge, the quest for material for the integrated consciousness. "The writer is learning all the time he writes," Faulkner said in Charlottesville, "and he learns from his own people, once he has conceived them truthfully and has stuck to the verities of human conduct, human behavior, human aspirations, then he learns—yes, they teach him, they surprise him, they teach him things that he didn't know, they do things and suddenly he says to himself, Why yes, that is true, that is so." The mystery format so obvious in *Absalom, Absalom!* or *Knight's Gambit* or *Intruder in the Dust* is also present, if more recessive, in *The Sound and the Fury* and *Light in August*, where we are always trying to solve what made the Compsons come to their present sorry state, and whether Joe Christmas is black or white (and if it would matter).

This investigatory sense is guaranteed in part by Faulkner's insistence on employing multiple perspectives. We should give less importance to Joe's need to know if he is white or black, masculine or feminine, victimizer or victim, if we did not realize, in the course of reading *Light in August*, that all the central characters are by turn victimizers and victims, hurting others and hurting themselves. What is true for Joe slowly evolves, in our understanding of him, into what is true of the others, of Jefferson generally. The hints of doubling which Byron provides in the passage we have studied thus become a synecdoche for the whole novel, in much the way Sartre claimed any scene becomes in *The Sound and the Fury*. In that earlier novel, Benjy's loss of Caddy does not seem so important a matter to us, relatively sane as we are, until we learn that her loss is a contagious one, affecting generations of Compsons, through them generations of black servants (including those who only dimly understand, like Frony), and through *them* becomes a synecdoche for the loss historically felt by Jefferson and the South.

Art for Faulkner, then, is an activity, not an object. His works, like all good literature, are never meaningless, yet never finally susceptible to total verbalization—they remain mysterious, open, suspended in final significations. As these concentric circles of meaning take us ever outward from the core event of the book (Joe's search for self-identity by learning his race, the Compsons' search for a restored order by finding Caddy), we must wonder, at the outer circles, where we are leaving the novel behind and entering ourselves. This continuum which Faulkner would set up between art and life takes various forms. For me, it came in a visit to Oxford, Mississippi, where, after seeing how the town square resembles that of Jefferson, I found certain analogies close, perhaps, to the source material for the novels: there the Confederate soldier stands on his pedestal looking southward, surrounded by a drugstore like the one where Gavin Stevens buys sodas for Linda Snopes, the hardware store like the one where Jason Compson works, and the shiny bank near the site of the bank Flem took over from Manfred de Spain. Beyond these factual parallels, however, I noted that in the spring narcissus grow behind the courthouse and near the hardware store; they are near where Benjy held his mended narcissus before Jason. And I noted that the graveyard toward which Benjy is headed at the close of *The Sound and the Fury* is the one where the Faulkners are buried too: Faulkner's mother, with an inscription on her pillared monument resembling the one on the stone of Eula Varner Snopes; William and Estelle Faulkner lying north of—and quite apart from—the mound of cypress trees which, at the center of the older part of the cemetery, is the final resting place of General Lamar and other glorious Confederate dead of Oxford and Lafayette County. You can see these impressive graves, the graves of the *real* Sartorises, if you stand north of Faulkner's grave and look, again appropriately, south. But go around to the south of Faulkner's grave and look north and you see, on the town's horizon before you, the water tower where Flem Snopes hid brass as he started his steady progress to fortune in Jefferson. Faulkner the man lies *there*, between Snopes and Sartoris, much as those characters embody terminal points of the Southern consciousness as Faulkner unfolds it, perceptually and conceptually, in his canon. Perhaps seeing that grave there called to my consciousness something more fanciful than it would to most, yet it is Faulkner's narrative poetics that can begin such a train of thought. For it is just such a personal, integrated consciousness as this one—in a singular moment of time and on a singular plot of good Mississippi clay—that is what, finally, Faulkner's characters, and we with them, search after.

Styles: Novelists of Consciousness

Art is an intensification of reality.—ERNST CASSIRER

A novel is not, like a statue or a picture or a building or a short lyric poem, all there at once—it is an experience that unfolds in time, like a play or a musical composition.—ROBERT LIDDELL

One moment the road had been empty, the next moment the man stood there beside it . . . the same cloth cap, the same rhythmically chewing jaw materialised apparently out of nothing and almost abreast of the horse, with an air of the complete and purely accidental which [Jody] Varner was to remember and speculate about only later.—FAULKNER

FAULKNER WRITES IN THE tradition of the novelists of consciousness who reveal events by means of unfolding perspective; only the visual thinking and the thrusts of consciousness of Faulkner's characters make human reality and human truth possible for him. His novels do not progress evenly, but in fits and starts. Sometimes meaning is cloudy, at other times it is as clear and complete as in a Joycean epiphany, and at still other times it is contradictory or at best partial. The constant rearrangement of events conveyed by a progressive perspective is characteristic of Faulkner's novels throughout his career. We can say of them, as Leon Edel says of Virginia Woolf's, that "we are transposed into a relative rather than a fixed vision."

It follows that, while we are made gradually aware of Faulkner's people and their beliefs and attitudes through an accumulation of events and an accretion of their thoughts, our knowledge of them is always contingent and our reading about them is necessarily revisionary. In the trilogy *Snopes* we first think of Eula Varner as a lazy but erotic girl; we do not sense her full stature until some time later, when she marries Flem, pleads with Gavin, and finally commits suicide. Likewise we see Flem's exacting honesty at the cash register in Will Varner's store, but we do not see his relativistic morality until he reaches Jefferson, or his full potentiality until he succeeds Manfred de Spain in the presidency of the bank. The opinions of others—Ratliff, Chick, Linda, and Mink—are not always congruent, but they help us to formulate meaning in *Snopes* as the entire village of French-man's Bend helps us to assess Will Varner. But we never come to understand Ratliff, Gavin, or Linda completely; by the close of *The Mansion*, they, like Frenchman's Bend itself, remain "hill-cradled and remote, definite yet without boundaries." The chief problem in Faulkner, then, amidst such changing events, evolving attitudes and multiple perspectives, is to locate a reasonably coherent consciousness.

The Conditions of Narrative

In seeking a center for his fiction, Faulkner constantly looks inward, examines what Henry James has called the "atmosphere of the mind." Here places, events, and emotions impinge to form inter-pretations and judgments colored by memories, fears, hopes, and desires—conditions too subtle for absolute conveyance to outer be-havior and articulated thought. Subjected to the pressures of psychic needs, the consciousness attempts to guess the unseen from the seen, to trace the implications of things and the motives of others, to judge outcomes by perceived patterns and anticipations born of experience and habit: consciousness for Faulkner as for Bergson is a process of endless accretion, the endless functioning of the mind and the senses, "the continuation of an indefinite past in a living present."

Our search for meaning in Faulkner gains considerable support from the characters themselves, who are also frequently engaged in exercises of self-definition. Often they are confused because they can-not connect the larger meanings of history to the pressures of a mo-ment or because past irresolution is reawakened by informing present events, yet the interpenetration of thoughts and implications must often be realized in action. The objective reality and the subjective consciousness must not only be correlative; each also interacts with and affects the other, as in each of the four narrations of *Absalom, Absalom!* The minds of Rosa, Mr. Compson, Quentin, and Shreve, like the minds of others of Faulkner's characters, must allow for the extraordinary and the illogical as well as the anticipated and the habitual; they must be simultaneously open and closed. As a novelist, Faulkner hints at these complexities, which as directly perceived are, at least at the first, incomprehensible. He gains a greater realism of consciousness by subjecting even the description of events to it; as Ciancio has remarked, "Faulkner envelops rather than develops a story."

Place, time, gesture, and language are all strategic; as with Quentin and Shreve, so elsewhere Faulkner writes in the syntax and the grammar of the growing consciousness. Although the mind always wrestles with the perceptual world, its sounds and smells, such perceptions are joined by the consciousness to elusive memories, to evanescent thoughts, and to fantastic ideals. The outer landscape motivates and sometimes reflects the inner landscape, but geographical space and chronological time are relevant only if reduplicated by the consciousness. Alternatively, a character may perceive a consequence before its cause, or judge an incident with only a fraction of the necessary evidence. Faulkner is interested in whatever the consciousness draws on—the perceptual world, the preconscious reverie, the subconscious fear or desire—and we must come to understand characters by realizing their adequacy in their conscious formulation of whole structures and integrated, stable patterns that make sense. "One of the novelist's greatest problems," W. J. Harvey reminds us, "is thus to reconcile transparency and density."

This poetics and the techniques by which to accomplish it result from Faulkner's wide and intensive reading and study as well as from his conversations with such friends as Sherwood Anderson, whom he met and admired in January 1925 and who encouraged him to write about his own home region. Anderson and his early work are helpful indices to Faulkner's novels. At the age of forty-five, Anderson had walked out of his job at a small paint factory in Elyria, Ohio, leaving a life of security in order to devote his life to writing and "truth," encouraging a similar romanticism in Faulkner upon his departure from the postmaster's job at the University of Mississippi. In his fiction, Anderson uncovered the buried lives of small-town Midwesterners by showing in symbols, metaphors, images, and turns of phrase precisely what delineated their innermost selves. By recovering the residual past of a character's life in the presence of his thought, by building in apparently artless episodes, and by adding some authorial wisdom, Anderson was able to record the private psychology of the underprivileged and the repressed, the inarticulated and the misunderstood.

Winesburg, Ohio (1919) was one of Faulkner's favorite books, and its resemblance to his own subsequent fiction shows how closely Faulkner read and how well he learned. Winesburg is based on Clyde, Ohio, as Jefferson is based on Oxford, Mississippi. The novel is an assembly of personal portraits intimate and painful, both meaningless and meaningful, revealing lives "like the twisted little apples that grow in the orchards of Winesburg" which are grotesque in appearance yet sweet at the core of their consciousness. Some continually work at life, like Dr. Reefy, whose thoughts are always as present as his handful of paper balls, "little pyramids of truth [which] he erected and after erecting knocked . . . down again that he might have the truths to erect other pyramids"; others, like Elizabeth Willard and Alice Hindman, try to force adventure into their mundane lives while still others, like Enoch Robinson, turn inward to flights of imagination, peopling a room with spirits. Still others, like Wing Biddlebaum, are eternal victims of others' misunderstanding. Wing's self-portrait reveals his fond wish for friendship, but his hands, his means of showing his human compassion, are, unfortunately, seen by the town of Winesburg as gestures of homosexuality, and his outraged consciousness, scarred for life like that of Elizabeth, Alice, and Enoch, lapses into a psychic paralysis. Wing joins the other spiritual derelicts who are beyond salvation, lonely, frustrated, and eccentric; they expect no response or help from others and they get none, and Winesburg itself becomes a metaphor for their dissatisfied lives, its buildings and streets discrete arenas where the private occupations of men and women can only serve their private visions. Despite their compulsion for identification and recognition they remain, as Doctor Parcival puts it, all crucified like Christ by a careless ignorance.

Anderson's novel resembles *The Sound and the Fury* and *Absalom, Absalom!* because it, too, is a growing sequence of self-revelations. We come to understand the people of Winesburg by observing their attachments to inanimate objects, to secret fantasies, and to inaccessible dreams. Ebenezer Cowley identifies himself by his Prince Albert coat, Elizabeth Willard concentrates on the money hidden in her bedroom wall, Alice Hindman forms a blanket and pillow on her bed to resemble a man, and the Reverend Curtis Hartman breaks a church window with a stone so as to see Kate Swift undressing. In the chapter titled "The Untold Lie," Ray Pearson sees his double in a younger man whose sorrows he can anticipate but not prevent. Such a gallery of inner selvings, what George Willard calls the "ghosts, not of the dead, but of living people," shows the stark disparity between observation and inner consciousness. Such a disparity is also the core of Faulkner's fictions: like Anderson, he builds his novels around the moments of exposure and revelation which seize and preserve this private and secret selving. Quentin resembles many of Faulkner's characters when he considers himself in *Absalom, Absalom!* as "a barracks filled with stubborn back-looking ghosts still recovering."

Faulkner draws on other writers, too, on the strategies of the mind which he found recorded in Flaubert and Balzac, in Conrad and in Joyce: in the discontinuity of thought and place, in the simultaneity of perceptual experiences, in the scrambled data of visual thinking, and in the affinities of recollected spots of time. His work is an amalgam of these and other features we have found characteristic of human perception generally: distorted imagings, visual thoughts, self-projections, assimilation, abstraction, and configuration. In the chaos of experience and in the range of perspectives, under the continual formulations of the active consciousness, Faulkner shapes for us an integrated center in which resides his poetics of consciousness and to which his narrative form gives primary attention.

Faulkner's Predecessors

Historically, the novelty and effectiveness of Faulkner was amazing, Simone de Beauvoir recalls in *The Prime of Life*. "Not only did he show great skill in deploying and harmonizing multiple viewpoints, but he got inside each individual mind, setting forth its knowledge and ignorance, its moments of insincerity, its fantasies, the words it formed and the silences it kept. As a result the narrative was bathed in a chiaroscuro, which gave each event the greatest possible highlight and shadow." Such techniques as he used, however, were not, for the most part, his own invention. In providing us with a catalogue of Faulkner's library at the time of his death, Joseph Blotner notes "the absorbing interest which literary technique had always held for Faulkner and the enormous amount of reading he had done in studying it." Faulkner studied especially the novelists of consciousness whose interest in visual thinking and integrated conceptualizations matched his own. He learned much from their styles, and we can trace many of his strategies and techniques in the works of others: the autonomy of the novel in James, the use of images in Flaubert, the panoramic view of society in Balzac, the idea of the *doppelgänger* and the use of the family in Dostoyevsky and, most importantly, the development of consciousness in Melville, Conrad, Joyce, and Proust. Of his affinities with others, Faulkner himself was always aware; as early as 1932, in an introduction written for an unpublished edition of *The Sound and the Fury*, he wrote of *Light in August*, "I was deliberately choosing among possibilities and probabilities of behavior and weighing and measuring each choice by the scale of the Jameses and Conrads and Balzacs." Together they helped lead him to his understanding of style as vision.

For Henry James the novel is a "direct impression of life"; elsewhere in "The Art of Fiction" he calls the novel "a living thing, all one and continuous, like any other organism, and in proportion as it lives will it be found, I think, that in each of the parts there is something of each of the other parts." To supply "the air of reality" it builds by affinities of detail, what James called the "solidity of specification." Yet for James the focus of such autonomous works is always the same; he always writes of a person's relation of himself or of his vicarious reconstruction of other people's relation to the world: he places the observational center *inside* the novelistic field. This is true of *The Turn of the Screw*, a novel Faulkner enjoyed, where Douglas's ghost story is contained only in the worn manuscript of the governess's account, forever a mystery locked beyond any rational tests for authenticity, forever wholly in the realm of speculation. The tale is as reliable or as faulty as the governess's perception of events; as the center of intelligence for it, she supplies for James another necessary ingredient, "an immense sensibility, a kind of huge spider-web of the finest silken threads suspended in the chamber of consciousness, and catching every air-borne particle in its tissue." Despite the views of the governess herself, the actual facts are lost to us, as Sutpen's biography is lost to Quentin and Lucius McCaslin's is to Ike.

Assumption, anticipation, event, imagination, reflection, and memory blend in the Jamesian point of view; seeing tends to replace doing, to *become* the doing. The narrative consciousness is creative, shaping even the environment in which it discovers itself as Milly Theale (in *The Wings of the Dove*) transforms the park in the scene at the dinner party into a place of appropriate appearances and a metaphor for her own predicament—an identification more psychological than rhetorical. But the narrative consciousness also condenses: at its high pitch of awareness, it melds the self-interpretation which it constantly judges. The result is a closed self, one which never tests self-concept against a more general reality.

What Philip M. Weinstein finds true of *Roderick Hudson* is paradigmatic for all of James, this work "beginning as an exploration of untapped energies and ending as an imprisonment within stale roles." James's transparent prose is characterized not by its language but by its vision, its angle of seeing. Scenes are always filtered through the positional interpretation or the memory of a narrative perspective that enlarges its view by outside reporters—the celebrated *ficelles*, characters who give additional information to the central intelligence as Faulkner employs Gavin Stevens and V. K. Ratliff. Both the narrative consciousness and the *ficelle* allow James to present tales indirectly, surrounding dramatic fact with additional drama of the heightened perception, as the most significant part of Strether's life in *The Ambassadors* occurs in the reverberating theater of his mind. James writes in the preface to *The Awkward Age* what might be taken as a description for *Absalom, Absalom!*: "The central object was my situation, my subject in itself, to which the thing would owe its title, and the small rounds represented so many distinct lamps, as I liked to call them, the function of each of which would be to light with all due intensity one of its aspects. I had divided it, didn't they see? into aspects."

Faulkner did not own James's prefaces, although he may have read some of them, but Phil Stone did buy Faulkner Percy Lubbock's *The Craft of Fiction* in 1922. In summing James's theory of fiction there, Lubbock also writes what could be taken as one key to Faulkner's narrative method:

> The process of writing a novel seems to be one of continual forestalling and anticipating; far more important than the immediate page is the page to come, still in the distance, on behalf of which this one is secretly working. The writer makes a point and reserves it at the same time, creates an effect and holds it back, till in due course it is appropriated and used by the page for which it is intended. It must be a pleasure to the writer, it is certainly a great pleasure to the critic, when the stroke is cleanly brought off.

The stroke Lubbock speaks of is a confirmation of our hunch as readers, not a final conclusion; Conrad was later to note that James's novels "must always present *a certain lack of finality. . . . One is never set at rest by Mr. Henry James's novels. His books end as an episode in life ends. You remain with the sense of life still going on.*" Barbara Hardy agrees that with James "the conclusion is less that of a climax in action, like a death or a marriage, than a dissolution of local tension." The final relaxation without clarification is true for some of Faulkner's work as well—for *Flags in the Dust,* for *Go Down, Moses,* and for *A Fable.* The similarity in method between the two writers helps to explain Faulkner's professed admiration for James.

Gustave Flaubert once wrote to George Sand, "I try to think well in order to write well. But my aim is to write well—I have never said it was anything else." His care with words is the equivalent of James's care with point of view, and it is this concentration on *le mot juste* that most attracted Faulkner in his reference to Flaubert in a book review in January 1922 and in a passing reference to *Madame Bovary* in 1925. The inner coherence in Flaubert, simultaneous or successive, is the inner coherence of things as well as persons. Objects are blended by a sensualizing memory into meanings which dispel a bitter present or displace past disappointments and so always manage to stay the flux of a loosened consciousness. Consequently, Flaubert's chief efforts were spent eliminating any traces of an author from his work; for him the art of fiction was justified only when the consciousness of some character was made the plausible source of observation, allowing a novel to achieve its own fiction and its own reality which are in turn a replication of the reader's constitutive consciousness in the act of reading.

Faulkner spoke most often and admiringly of Flaubert's *La tentation de Saint-Antoine* as did Flaubert; "This is the work of my whole life; the first idea came to me in 1845 in Genoa, looking at a Breughel painting," Flaubert wrote to Mlle. Leroyer de Chantepie in 1872, "and since that day I have never stopped thinking of it and doing reading for it." Similar to *Requiem for a Nun*, *La tentation* is dramatic rather than narrative, so as to increase its impact; it too uses the special optics of theater—exaggerated ideas, broad gestures, strong phrasings—and in its three acts the series of temptations heralded by the Seven Deadly Sins which Saint Anthony faces tend to push the novel-as-play toward allegory as Nancy Mannigoe's act of murder and Gavin's moral counsel tend to push *Requiem for a Nun* toward allegory. And like the tortured Temple, Saint Anthony is too bewildered and too passive for *La tentation* to have much force. When Flaubert came to revise his 1849 version in 1874, he had Saint Anthony, a victim like Temple Stevens of *ennui*, discover that as he reviews his past, he finds his beliefs and knowledge—perhaps life itself—are only nightmarish illusion. During this process of self-realization, Saint Anthony learns that man cannot understand good and evil, although unlike God he is always subject to them; so much, in fact, is beyond man's understanding that dreams, desires, forgetfulness, rest, even death become for some time truly seductive: Faulkner may have returned to thoughts of *La tentation* during those long years he spent on *A Fable*.

Still, *Madame Bovary* probably showed Faulkner even more in narrative style: this novel remains for us, as for Faulkner, Flaubert's chief triumph in his art of narrative consciousness. Like a novel by James, this is a remarkably architectonic achievement. The novel is divided into three books, each polarizing Emma and Charles Bovary—book I lingers on Emma at the ball but Charles at their wedding; book II observes Emma at the opera contrasted to Charles at an operation, the dirty, bloody business of medicine that provides Emma with what luxuries she has; book III contrasts Emma at the grand cathedral hoping for another assignation and Charles, still relatively confined, mourning at her deathbed. Each book, like the entire novel, is built in contiguous blocks and each, for Emma, has its symbolic geography: Tostes, Yonville-l'Abbaye, Rouen. But very like filmic montage, the episodes are linked by our constitutive consciousness: in the affair with Rodolphe, for example, we note that Emma first sees him from a second-story window, vows her affection for him on the first floor, and consummates the affair in the woods. Networks of images also interweave discrete passages: we are meant to connect the black butterflies, the burning wedding bouquet, and the black spittle on Emma's lips as she dies; and all these are, in turn, linked to the torn bits of letters which Emma throws from the cab window in despondency, just before the end. Such linkages are likewise within a scene too, as in the famous *comices agricoles* where Rodolphe and Emma watch a cattle auction in the town square from her bedroom window. "*Everything should sound simultaneously*," Flaubert later commented on his own scene. "One should hear the bellowing of cattle, the whispering of the lovers, and the rhetoric of the officials all at the same time," and, of course, one should constantly compare them as well: the dumb, cowlike love of Emma, the bargaining for affection by Rodolphe to the bidder who best satisfies. Joseph Frank, who has especially admired this scene, writes further that it "illustrates, on a small scale, what we mean by the spatialization of form in a novel. For the duration of the scene, at least, the time-flow of the narrative is halted; attention is fixed on the interplay of relationships within the immobilized time-area. These relationships are juxtaposed independently of the progress of the narrative." Spatialization is a common factor of all Faulkner's novels, too, although it is perhaps most easily seen in the segments which compose *The Unvanquished* and *Go Down, Moses*.

Madame Bovary is a book about a woman who is too much influenced by books; Emma suffers from her authentic confusion of the imaginary and the real, wish and possibility. The fine dresses she longs for and the green silk cigar box that smells of masculinity to Emma are dangerous invitations to her sensibility, but men are likewise for her dreamlike objects. In book I she focuses on Charles as a source of security and respectability as well as escape from the farm of her father; in book II her desire grows for Léon and Rodolphe, representative of the sexual fulfillment and excitement she does not find with her husband; and book III relates her mounting frenzy, the consequence of her increased sense of emptiness, in the juxtaposition of her anxiety with Rodolphe, her confusion in Léon, and her sense of deadening routine personified by Charles. In turn each supplies her with one of the necessities for her emotional life: Charles (like Bidet, who mirrors him) provides devotion and stability, loyalty and service; Léon (mirrored in the adolescent mooncalf Justin) suggests to Emma the purity of Platonic love which suppresses the rawness of desire; and Rodolphe (whose double is the notary Guillaumin) represents practical and open sensuality, getting what he wants from life while avoiding any entangling alliances. Characters like objects image social classes to Emma, but her dependence on them becomes too strong, becomes total: when they are removed, her entire world collapses.

Flaubert's achievement, similar to Faulkner's, is to see that an antiheroic subject is sufficient for serious writing through the insinuation of the simple consciousness in images, events, positional perspective, and environment. Flaubert also recognized that the chief difficulty of the artist is the necessity to make language both precise and evocative, but in metamorphosing things into meanings, he transforms the least beautiful of experiences—one thinks analogously of Flem's dealings and Mink's murder of Houston—into high moments of distilled art. He does this, finally, without forsaking a static perspective and much of the mean truth which resides at the core of human experience.

It is likewise with Honoré de Balzac, whom Faulkner also openly admired and imitated: here, too, objects are transformed by an insinuating narrative consciousness. The "solidity of specification" radiates meaning in Balzac as it does in James, something James himself recognized when he praised Balzac for those "insistent particulars" in which he achieved the "love of each seized identity"; although he overloaded his printer's galleys with additions and corrections, Balzac needed such rich detail because it is, for him, not merely ornamental but intensely metaphoric. The long descriptions of the soldiers at the opening of

Les Chouans; Goriot's heart-shaped locket containing the hairs of his daughters and hung around his neck by the hair of his deceased wife; the garden of Mme. Vauquer's boarding house with its statue of Love from which a coat of varnish is "scaling off": such facts take on an iridescent quality, for Balzac is fundamentally a visual thinker whose fiction is akin to Impressionist painting and to Symbolist poetry. Objects are made images which introduce and even come to signify characters. Mme. de Langeais can refer to old Goriot as a well-squeezed orange, while M. Grandet is described in terms of speculations, investments, and loans, and Eugènie Grandet's cousin Charles is identified by his luxurious possessions: his scissors, his razor mounted with gold, and the box with the two portraits by Mme. de Mirbel "handsomely set in pearls"—it is the same technique we find in Faulkner when he refers to Sophonsiba by her roan tooth and to Flem by his machine-made bow tie.

Singly or in constellations, objects, circumstances, and scenes as acknowledged by Balzac take on symbolic meanings for the human consciousness (as the long march that opens *Les Chouans* resembles the march of the blacks in Faulkner's *The Unvanquished*). Even with his leisurely biographies of such major characters as Félix Grandet or his inventoried descriptions of such places as Mme. Vauquer's boardinghouse, we discover important emblems, hieroglyphs of the self. Thus the boardinghouse, which resembles Rosa Coldfield's office in its objects and its smells, builds in us a phenomenological awareness of the worn and the stale, the decaying and the tawdry, that might otherwise be inaccessible. Similarly, the rocky, unpredictable, and treacherous countryside around Fougères mirrors the impetuous Chouan Royalists while Galope-chopine's hut is characterized by the mugs of cider that convey the man's rudimentary and greedy nature. Nanon's kitchen is filled with signs of the pinched and the starved, and old Goriot's room, with its bare patches of plaster and its rag-covered bed, "reminded him of the saddest prison cell." Places are, for Balzac, psychological reflectors, allowing him to characterize his own work (in a review of Stendhal) as the synthesis of a literature of ideas and a literature of images.

But Balzac was also aware that such images are correlative, that they comment on each other tonally, leading to a wider panorama of French life as Faulkner's stories of Jefferson reflect all of Yoknapatawpha County and beyond. The bold uniforms of the Republicans in *Les Chouans* intimate power and wealth, while the goatskins of the

Royalists suggest need and ingenuity. Yet for Balzac both forces, both the Blues and the Chouans, are fanatic, implusive, and careless— beneath the apparent dissimilarities there is always harbored a replication of meaning. Thus Corentin and the marquis of Montauran, for all their differences, mirror each other in their affection for Marie, their need for duplicity, and their bondage to a cause, and like Marie herself they never come to understand or control their passions; Delphine and Anastasie, Goriot's daughters, are alike in their poor marriages, their foolish and selfish miscalculations, and their misuse of their father; even Eugénie Grandet is, finally, only a younger version of her mother. Balzac's crowded canvas is fashioned by such cross-references of character and event: in the detailed relationship between the ambitious Eugène and the criminal Vautrin, who tempts him to illegal fortune, there is even a private doubling, an early anticipation of the secret sharer of Conrad, in which people allow others to absorb their weaknesses and so try to evade responsibility for them. Vautrin's plan for an estate in America is similar to Sutpen's plan for founding a dynasty, and both share an ironic futility from the outset. In Balzac as in much of Faulkner, such detail is seen as it reflects human consciousness; nothing is ever wasted.

Yet in Balzac as in Faulkner, there is little separation between such images and the actual world they record; both believe in art as documentation. Balzac searched his own people, his own region, and his own recent past for his stories, holding them together by repetition of incident and the reappearance of characters. His fictional France, like Yoknapatawpha, sweeps widely in its coverage. For *Les Chouans* he went to Brittany to note the geography, customs, dress, and language as well as the buildings; his description of Le Vivetière is based on his intimate knowledge of Marigny Castle. When he came to write of prison life, he was not content to read the *Mémoires* of the convict Vidocq (who serves as the model for Vautrin in *Père Goriot*); he also met him and journeyed to several prisons as well. Félix Grandet, Eugènie's miserly father, has been identified as Jean Nivelleau, who made a fortune in the French Revolution before settling in a château just outside Saumur, as Félix does. Faulkner traversed French battlefields in research for *A Fable*; he also draws on his own family for the Sartorises and on his own experiences for *Pylon*, as Balzac drew on his miserly father and his own speculations and bad debts for characterization and incident. Such facts were never simply the inspiration for Balzac; rather, he made them (like Faulkner) significant substance of his life's work.

Moby-Dick, like *Les Chouans*, was one of Faulkner's favorite books as a child; he recommended it to his brother in 1915 and admitted his admiration publicly in 1931; ten years later he got out a copy and began reading it to his daughter Jill: little wonder, then, that in 1945 he named Herman Melville as one of the four greatest influences on his own work. Melville's shaping form and sentiment pervade Faulkner's canon, not only in particular echoes—where the White Whale seems a prototype of Old Ben, or where Ishmael gazing into the water or riding Queequeg's coffin prefigures Quentin watching the trout and Cash atop Addie's casket—but also in their more profoundly linked sensibilities, in their mutual understanding of life as an unfolding pilgrimage in which the goals of salvation and self-understanding are finally made indistinguishable. Consequently both Melville and Faulkner use the novel as a form of questing for self-definition, although in *Moby-Dick* the range of possible responses is unusually, even terrifyingly, great. Initially the voyage of the *Pequod* seems to propose two alternatives—either we can be ambitious and aggressive like Ahab, testifying to an antagonistic world and, striking through it like so many pasteboard masks, risk destroying ourselves; or we can be meditative and celebrant like Ishmael, watching, wondering, but removing ourselves from extreme acts for the sake of self-preservation. For Melville, Ahab's attitude is not distinct from Ishmael's but an inversion of it, and both responses confront us with an awesome and troubling infinity of meanings, within and without the stormy Atlantic of their beings. As Ishmael remarks of Queequeg, his close friend, he can only know "his outside." He is forever mysterious, like the whale: "Dissect him how I may, then, I but go skin deep; I know him not, and never will."

Kant's phenomenology lies just behind *Moby-Dick*, for Melville too witnesses to the world as a symbology, outer events full of hidden significations. Ishmael lives among omens and superstitions as well as the ritual of routine; all things, he reminds us, "are not without their meanings." The name of Peter Coffin; the painting at the Spouter Inn; the unfinished books and cathedrals of a more classical past; the present tasks of weaving mats, climbing monkey-ropes, and squeezing ambergris: to each and all of these, he tries to assign some reliable intention or purpose. His restless mind leads to his attempt to find himself in all that he studies.

But *Moby-Dick* is not confined to Ishmael's struggling consciousness; we are also supplied with Ahab's, Starbuck's, Queequeg's, Flask's, and Pip's: the novel consists of multiple perspectives, each

character searching for analogous people or incidents so as to understand himself better. In the fateful rush to encounter the whale, Queequeg sees his own doom in Pip, and Starbuck finds his secret sharer
in Ahab, while Melville's more pervasive perspective points repeatedly
to the central similarity between Ahab and Ishmael, both of them
essentially lonely men, frustrated by past loss and present limitation
and brooding over their self-induced sense of alienation while persistently clinging to that sense of wonder which may either save or
destroy them. Both are water-gazers who in staring out at the boundless ocean keep finding only themselves, like Narcissus. Nonnarrative
blocks, like the chapters on cetology, also provide resonances of narrative thinking by means of perceived analogy: Ishmael finds in his
unfinished catalogue of whales or his discussion of the grand armada,
his anatomy of the whale and his discussion of the color white, the
same sort of uncertainty he perceives in Ahab's behavior and in his
own faltering sense of purpose.

The long etymological listings for *whale* demand that *we* admit a
multiplicity of meanings too, while the final three entries in a mirroring list of uses compiled by a sub-sub-librarian—

> " 'Stern all!' exclaimed the mate, as upon turning his head, he
> saw the distended jaws of a large Sperm Whale close to the
> head of the boat, threatening it with instant destruction;—
> 'Stern all, for your lives!' " *Wharton the Whale Killer.*

> "So be cheery, my lads, let your hearts never fail,
> While the bold harpooneer is striking the whale!"
> *Nantucket Song.*

> "Oh, the rare old Whale, mid storm and gale
>   In his ocean home will be
> A giant in might, where might is right,
>   And King of the boundless sea." *Whale Song.*

—are, like Father Mapple's sermon and the reflections on the dou-
bloon, anticipations of the entire novel in miniature. "We know the
sea," Melville writes, his voice indistinct from Ishmael's, but we
know it "to be an everlasting terra incognita." Mystery for him, as for
the characters of *Absalom, Absalom!* and *A Fable*, is as necessary as
it is unbearable.

The meaning of the final imaging in *Moby-Dick*, of the *"unharming
sharks . . . with sheathed beaks,"* is forever locked away, inscrutable,
not simply because of an infinity of truths at the novel's end but also

because of a final skepticism about truth itself. Yet we know this from the beginning, when we try to wrest meaning from the painting in the Spouter Inn as practice for fathoming *Moby-Dick*. There, in the painting, "what most puzzled and confounded you was a long, limber, portentous, black mass of something hovering in the centre of the picture over three blue, dim, perpendicular lines floating in a nameless yeast. A boggy, soggy, squitchy picture truly, enough to drive a nervous man distracted. Yet was there a sort of indefinite, half-attained, unimaginable sublimity about it that fairly froze you to it, till you involuntarily took an oath with yourself to find out what the marvellous painting meant." So we too become transfixed before the driven mission of the *Pequod*, its potential significations rippling outward, vast in possibilities. For "Surely all this is not without meaning," we conclude, much as Ishmael began, "we ourselves see in all rivers and oceans. It is the image of the ungraspable phantom of life; and this is the key to it all"; still, as Mr. Compson tells Quentin, " 'It just does not explain.' " Not least significant for Melville is the fact that Ishmael finally circles back to where he began; Quentin Compson and Joe Christmas, Harry Wilbourne and Ike McCaslin, after their searches for self-signification, do also.

Fyodor Dostoyevsky's colleague on the *Vremya*, Apollon Grigoriev, once remarked of him, as he might have remarked of James or Melville, that the Russian novelist could never distinguish between life and thought; even today, Dostoyevsky remains one of the premier novelists of the human consciousness. The sole origin of consciousness, observes Dostoyevsky's Underground Man, is suffering. To be conscious is to be ill, yet the Underground Man will not rid himself of such torment. "Though I did lay it down at the beginning that consciousness is the greatest misfortune for man," he goes on, "yet I know man prizes it and would not give it up for any satisfaction." Such anguish is perpetual, stemming as it does from the eternal vacillation between noble impulses and ruthless skepticism, between high dreams and low achievements. Judgment and wisdom isolate Dostoyevsky's Russians with endless remorse; since their guilt is foremost in their minds, they become self-exiles, knowing that they are undeserving of another person's affection and unable to make any acceptable compact with society and with God. The passionate, like Dmitri Karamazov, are sullen and despondent; the intellectuals, like Dmitri's brother Ivan, remain bitter and ironic. Religion is no aid to them either since, as Ivan tells Alyosha, it does " 'nothing but talk of the eternal questions.' "

Trapped between the demands of body and mind and the legal and moral constraints of society and church, the luckless Dostoyevskian hero tries without success to cleanse his conscience and so give his consciousness rebirth. " 'Man is broad, too broad,' " Dmitri sums; " 'I'd have him narrower.' "

Like Balzac, Dostoyevsky introduces his characters with brief biographies, yet invariably (unlike Balzac) their behavior runs counter to what we know, and it falls on us as readers to reconcile this discrepancy, to broaden the initial sketch, and to supply a newly accommodating configuration of consciousness. Yet Dostoyevsky's whole canon insists on the impossibility of a coherent consciousness. Man is crushed by circumstances and driven by temperament to turn in on himself, the victim of inward and outward pressures which split his character in two. It is this pathological condition that produces Dostoyevsky's "double," which he told his brother (erroneously) in November 1877 was " 'the greatest and most important social type which I was the first to discover and proclaim.' " Occasionally doubling is imaginary, as when Smerdyakov thinks Ivan commands him to kill their father. But at other times, it is a willed hallucination: the skeptical Ivan tells of seeing a "devil" whose speech confirms his gravest doubts; " 'nothing but hosannah is not enough for life,' " the "devil" tells him, " 'the hosannah must be tried in the crucible of doubt.' " Man is often directed in Dostoyevsky, by what he identifies as his alter ego, and this in turn provides a dialectic with the self. Ivan's discussion with Alyosha about whether or not he is like God's damned is correlative to Shreve's and Quentin's analysis of Charles Bon and Henry Sutpen.

Faulkner autographed a special copy of *The Brothers Karamazov* inscribed by Wili Lengel in 1931 and another in 1932 at Rowan Oak; he owned three copies when he died. It was a book he praised in 1931, while two years later he recalled first reading it in 1923; in 1945 he was telling a class that Dostoyevsky, like Melville, was one of the four greatest influences on his work. Like so much of Faulkner's fiction, *The Brothers Karamazov* is the anatomy of a family, written like *Absalom, Absalom!* and *Intruder in the Dust* in the form of a mystery. But Ivan is aware of man's incapacity to tolerate mystery as well as miracle, and in destroying such faiths as depend on them, he exposes to Alyosha how Father Zossima's body, like any other man's, decomposes in its own stench: Alyosha's dread and sorrow at such decomposition parallels Darl's. The dead monk had once said that *Karamazov* was synonymous with *sensuality*, and the family is unable to handle the passions of the sons as well as the death of the father: the idiocy of Smerdyakov (like that of Benjy Compson and Ike Snopes) seems an outer signification of the inner condition of all his family. In the central chapter, yet another dialectic of consciousness titled "Pro and Contra," Ivan's language of philosophical rationalism is juxtaposed to Alyosha's language of poetry; the conflict cannot be resolved but, rather, tends toward solipsism or toward a blind faith. The will to evil which Ivan and Smerdyakov see in each other is only imperfectly answered by the suffering to which Dmitri and Alyosha submit themselves; the effects of vice here as elsewhere for Dostoyevsky are intimately conjunct with the effects of disbelief. " 'Who doesn't desire his father's death?' " asks Ivan. Dostoyevsky makes the question psychological, social, and metaphysical; but he gives us no answer.

Dostoyevsky's world is haunted by those yearning to be well again and those who are incurably sick. In his troubling amalgam of the psychological and metaphysical implications of sin and suffering, Dostoyevsky provides us only with a profound and urgent dilemma. "One can neither abstract an ethical imperative nor a systematic philosophy capable of doing justice to the dramatic tensions to be found in life as he grasped it," Eliseo Vivas tells us. The world of Dostoyevsky's fiction is a vast bleakness. " 'There is no place for [love] in the world today, . . . We have eliminated it. It took us a long time, but man is resourceful and limitless in inventing too, and so we have got rid of love at last just as we have got rid of Christ. . . . If Jesus returned today we would have to crucify him quick in our own defense, to justify and preserve the civilization we have worked and suffered and died shrieking and cursing in rage and impotence and terror for two thousand years to create and perfect in man's own image.' " This might be said by Dostoyevsky's Ivan or by the Underground Man, but it is not: the speaker is Harry Wilbourne, in *The Wild Palms*.

Joseph Conrad contributes to the fiction of human consciousness his own sense of the dislocated narrative, what he called the working backwards and forwards of the inquisitive mind, the relentless probing of the conscious understanding in long and complex containing sentences. "To snatch in a moment of courage, from the remorseless rush of time, a passing phase of life," Conrad remarks, "is only the beginning of the task." To "reveal the substance of its truth" we must dig deep into life, "disclose its inspiring secret." Conrad insists that acquisition of knowledge precede illumination of the consciousness; consequently, in the plots of his novels the climax often comes early— a method Faulkner likewise uses in *The Sound and the Fury, Requiem*

for a Nun, and A Fable. "Confronted by the same enigmatical spectacle" as the reader, Conrad writes, "the artist descends within himself,
and in that lonely region of stress and strife, if he be deserving and
fortunate, he finds the terms of his appeal." *The terms of his appeal*:
fiction for Conrad depends on *artist and reader* as secret sharers. Although Conrad called James his "très cher maître," he seems now more
closely aligned to Melville.

"Conrad does not get away from the event to concentrate wholly on
the psychological vibration, as does James," Leo Gurko notes. Instead,
Conrad uses the protagonist as the outward sign of the inward signification hinted by the narrator: their imaginative interplay is replicated
in that interplay between the storyteller and the reader which allows
us to see, but to see through a glass darkly. Truth in Conrad is urgent
but prismatic—in *The Nigger of the "Narcissus"* there are a half-dozen
interpretations of Jimmy Wait, all of them (on a ship of this name)
self-projections—for, as Conrad writes Richard Curle, human thought
is fluid, and our perspectives shift, our angles of vision grow alternately cloudy and bright, we see things partially, singly and in groupings, while the long-sought configurations of consciousness elude us.
Truth is both inaccessible and inescapable. The Kurtz of *Heart of
Darkness*, approaching and evading truth, is indicative of much of
Conrad; the baffled Marlow of *Lord Jim* has the same desire to know
but inability fully to understand.

For the parallel growth of both dramatic and narrative consciousness
in Conrad, *Heart of Darkness* is paradigmatic: at every point of Marlow's discovery, Kurtz's physical biography charts the growth of
Marlow's intellectual understanding and his increasing spiritual malaise. Past events and present moments, like the active subject and the
perceiving agent, are correlative; in Conrad's organic world, the
recollective tale opens in the "brooding" gloom at Gravesend, a proper
if civilized analogue for the blackness of the Dark Continent. The
scenes Marlow paints show his own preoccupations with death: the
black sky over the Thames, the "whited sepulchre" of Brussels, and
the fateful women knitting all coalesce finally in the bald skull and the
dying cry of Kurtz in the heart of the Belgian Congo. Marlow's narration shifts tonally—the early, humorous accounts of the pointless
shelling by the French gunboat, the parading pilgrims, and the meticu-
lously dressed Chief Accountant give way to the more drastic confusion
of Kurtz, whose talents and values have become twisted past comprehension and whose greatness of mind has collapsed because of the
fundamental incompetence of the human intellect. Marlow shares this

developing incapacity to cope in his new and uncertain tone, in his dislocations of time and place, his fragmentary episodes and disjunctive narrative, in his false distinctions and open contradictions in which he discloses his own inability to formulate any stabilizing structure of narrative consciousness. His report seems directed at himself when he says of Kurtz, " 'The wastes of his weary brain were haunted by shadowy images,' " but his frustrations and fears move outward too in anger. " 'You can't understand,' " he complains of his listeners. " 'How could you?—with solid pavement under your feet, surrounded by kind neighbours ready to cheer you or to fall on you, stepping delicately between the butcher and the policeman.' " In attacking the incompetence of the Intended and, here, of the men on the Thames, he turns both audiences into self-projections. In protecting both, he allows them to sustain his own last hope for the human powers of endurance. We see in Marlow (as we see in Benjy and Darl) that sanity is purchased by ignorance. Kurtz, like Sutpen and Ahab, " 'had kicked himself loose of the earth . . . he had kicked the very earth to pieces [yet] he was alone.' " In daring the entire world, such men destroy themselves.

At the time he died, Faulkner had a copy of *Lord Jim* in his bedroom at Rowan Oak. The novel is Marlow's attempt (and Conrad's) to move beyond the suicidal impulses of *Heart of Darkness;* when Marlow tells us in *Lord Jim* that " 'These were issues beyond the competency of a court of inquiry,' " he is speaking not only of Jim's resurrection, but of the possibility of reparation for us all. Jim dreams for self-esteem in a world where proof of that esteem is lacking or the challenges to it are too sudden and overpowering. Personal and public fates are intermeshed, yet incongruent. Jim's questions are conundrums: if you misjudge once, are you a permanent failure? can you arrange a second chance? in an irrational world, is even the concept of reparation valid? Such questions as these make Jim " 'one of us.' " But as in *Heart of Darkness*, the pattern of Jim's actions as mirrored in the patterns of Marlow's narration is one of attempted confrontations and continual avoidances. Those who feel deepest the compulsion to understand are those most fearful to learn: knowledge, as Ivan Karamazov knows, is both necessary and unbearable. The problem is not, as Marlow ventures early, only how to be, but as Jim recognizes in Patusan, *whether* to be. Analogous to Young Bayard and Joe Christmas, Jim finds the hazard of life total: with him the need to know runs the risk of oblivion, of final unknowing. Even the attempts at structure at the integrations of experience which will lend insight are as likely to be dreams and delusions. Stein's oracular advice to submit to the destructive element is at odds with his counsel to " 'follow the dream, and again to follow the dream,' " as his own equivocal life of chasing butterflies—an act of resignation and evasion—in either case betrays. But Jim's death is the correlative of Stein's advice and of his action, for Jim's murder is equivocally an act of heroic surrender and of suicidal despair. " 'We are only on sufferance here,' " Marlow confesses at the end of the adventure but at the outset of his narrative, giving us his premise all along, " 'and got to pick our way in cross lights, watching every precious minute and every irremediable step, trusting we shall manage yet to go out decently in the end—but not so sure of it after all—and with dashed little help to expect from those we touch elbows with right and left.' " His despair is less active but no less pervasive than Addie Bundren's in her integrated consciousness, characterized as it is by frustration, bafflement, and defeat.

Faulkner owned two sets of Conrad, and there are echoes of *Youth* and of *Heart of Darkness* in his work as early as the New Orleans sketches of 1925; *Heart of Darkness* resonates especially in the Haitian scenes of *Absalom, Absalom!* But it is finally in works like *The Nigger of the "Narcissus"* that we find the use of multiple narrative consciousness that is so central to such novels as *Soldiers' Pay* and *As I Lay Dying*, where the death of Jimmy Wait resembles the deaths of Donald Mahon and Addie Bundren as the center of a wide range of responses and the provocation for numerous acts of secret sharing.

For Conrad, the need to know and the impossibility of understanding result in a longer narrative of containing sentences, sentences filled with modifications, qualifications, digressions, and dislocations in their constant attempt to account for the frustrated and atrophied will. In this syntax as in his understanding of perception, Conrad writes a narrative that approaches the metaphoric rather than the explanatory. "A work of art is very seldom limited to one exclusive meaning and not necessarily tending to a definite conclusion," Conrad wrote Barrett H. Clark in May 1918. "And for this reason that the nearer it approaches art, the more it acquires a symbolic character." Conrad may have had in mind Kurtz's last words—" 'The horror! The horror!' "— but he could also be describing Shreve's necessary but unbearable demand of Quentin: *"Tell about the South. What's it like there. What do they do there. Why do they live there. Why do they live at all?"*

James Joyce transforms the dislocated narrative of Conrad into a fluid consciousness: as in Stephen Dedalus's unformed observations throughout the early parts of *A Portrait of the Artist as a Young Man* and on his early morning stroll in *Ulysses,* perceptions in Joyce continually reach outward toward universals. The consciousness thus becomes all-embracing, erasing any distinctions of time, place, or action, like the snow at the closing of "The Dead," "falling faintly through the universe and faintly falling, like the descent of their last end, upon all the living and the dead." Stream of consciousness in Joyce relies on an impressionism defined by Stephen's Thomistic aesthetic, on sorted and unsorted images characterized only by beauty, wholeness, and harmony (*integritas, consonantia, quidditas*). Such luminous acts of visual thinking are always contiguous but rarely causal or sequential; they are more customarily the result of accident and circumstance, of interruptive dream and involuntary memory, on the receptacle of a receiving but rarely selective mind: the early brief episodes of *A Portrait,* for example, abrupt, bewildering, foreshortened, remind us of the opening scenes of *The Sound and the Fury.* The consciousness in Joyce does not generally admit stable configurations; instead, it records sensations and impressions without anticipation or final judgment and without beginning and end, like Stephen's biography, Molly Bloom's soliloquy, and the whole of *Finnegans Wake.* Distinctions between what is important and what is unimportant in such an open consciousness may be reasoned or impulsive, idiosyncratic or nonexistent. For young Stephen, the wet bed at Blackrock and the word "smugging" at Clongowes are equally mysterious and equally significant, and Leopold Bloom is as easily rebuffed by Menton at Patty Dignam's burial as he is by thoughts of Molly in bed with Blazes Boylan. It is no surprise, then, that Dante's irrational defense of the church and Simon Dedalus's drunken comments to Stephen in *A Portrait* blend with the young boy's own wandering impressions of his childhood. By presenting the mind as an indiscriminate register, Joyce advocates the same freedom and lack of inhibition that Stephen defends so passionately to Cranly.

Yet it is precisely by means of such an extraordinary sense of formlessness that Joyce causes us to see his characters as creating selves: by recording and conveying impressions, the shaping power of the creative imagination and the shaping power of the personality are fused within our collaborative act of reading. In *Dubliners* we watch serially as men and women, young and old, perceive unassimilated confrontations with themselves. In *A Portrait* we watch Stephen progress as beneath his random but chronological recollections his syntax develops, his vocabulary expands, and his language matures. It is we, not

Stephen, who trace the growth of his mind and his concomitant growing disaffection for the priesthood, from his early intimidations when
caned by the prefect of studies through his serious deliberations on a
religious vocation to his final ability to scorn the "skull" of the
deathlike priest who teaches physics at the university. Such threads
multiply in *Ulysses*. Buck Mulligan replaces Cranly as a harsh teacher
to Stephen—much as Shreve serves Quentin—and Stephen's transformation from a self-proclaimed Hamlet to a self-proclaimed Christ finds
its correlation in Leopold's metamorphosis from cuckold to father.
The meeting of art and commerce in Stephen and Bloom and their
spiritual kinship is fragmentary and fleeting for them; but it is of
considerable thematic importance for us, for we attend to the way in
which they move toward and through their need for each other so as
to re-form themselves. Stream of consciousness in Joyce is not a matter
of cognition but of continual re-cognition.

Yet for Stephen (and for Joyce) the task of the artist is not one of
mirroring the random activity of visual thinking. "Beauty expressed
by the artist cannot awaken in us an emotion which is kinetic or a
sensation which is purely physical," Stephen warns Lynch. Rather, "It
wakens, or ought to awaken, or induces, or ought to induce, an esthetic
stasis, an ideal pity or an ideal terror, a stasis called forth, prolonged
and at last dissolved by what I call the rhythm of beauty," further
refined as "the first formal esthetic relation of part to part in any
esthetic whole or of an esthetic whole to its part or parts or of any part
to the esthetic whole of which it is a part." Impressions insinuate their
own potential rearrangements for a more stabilized meaning: we find
as collaborative artists that Stephen's relationship to the priesthood
goes through three distinct steps in *A Portrait*; that the central passage
in the book, the sermon on hell, is his reason for turning away after a
temporary conversion; and that the priesthood is strong in childhood
when it has no competing interests, an alternative when Stephen is
awakened sexually, and superfluous once Stephen replaces it with his
own religion of art. *The Unvanquished* is structured in the same fashion by Bayard's recollections of his own formation of consciousness in
three stages: in his ambush of Union soldiers, his vengeance on
Grumby, and his final confrontation, alone, with Redmond.

Joyce breaks the dynamic flow of human consciousness in his fiction
by the deliberate fragmentation of experience, "the first consistent use
of the technique of segmentation," as Stanzel has it. The opening
scenes of *Portrait* are disjointed because the child's-eye view of the
world is unable to discern relationships among sounds, sights, and

smells. But the novel itself is fractured into episodes without con-
necting links. Set off only by asterisks or chapter headings, independent blocks of visual thinking tend to freeze the consciousness at a
particular moment of time, to halt its flow. Joyce had learned this
technique in *Dubliners*, where each portrait served him as a separate
block of discrete awareness; we are given no history, no background.
The half-darkened araby, the ivy for Parnell, Eveline before the departing boat, the card game in "After the Race," Lenehan's date in
"Two Gallants," Maria's omission of a crucial verse in *I Dreamt That
I Dwelt* ("Clay"), and the lovers Mr. Duffy witnesses on Magazine
Hill ("A Painful Case"): all remain isolated photographs, each with
wholeness, harmony, and radiance, but truncated like the segments
composing *The Unvanquished* and *Go Down, Moses*. The analogy to
the snapshots of *Dubliners* in *A Portrait* is Stephen's own series of
independent roles, as student, son, and aesthetician, as Stephen Mar-
tyr, converted sinner, and Dedalus-artificer, while in *Ulysses* the
cross-cutting becomes even more extreme, the novel's paths moving
restlessly among Stephen, Leopold, and a larger Dublin. Here, in the
many layers of myth and historical narrative, the extreme ranges of
style and form, and the disjunctive scenes in the newsroom ("Aeolus")
and Night-town ("Circe"), in "The Sirens" and especially "The Wandering Rocks," the novel insists on its own fictive montage, it own
predilection for stasis. Such discontinuity results in a sense of intellectual indeterminacy. "The density of the presentational screen, the
confusing montage and its interplay of perspectives, the invitation to
the reader to look at identical incidents from many conflicting points
of view—all this makes it extremely difficult for the reader to find his
way," Wolfgang Iser writes. "The novel refuses to divulge any principle of how to bind together this interplay of perspectives." We are
faced with the primary impact of life itself, but a life which yearns to
be shaped into meaning. "The paradox of [*Ulysses*]," Harry Levin
sums, "is that it imposes a static ideal upon kinetic material."

Yet if the narrative impressionism cannot pattern observation and
experience, the constitutive consciousness of the reader can. By combining relative episodes, such as those involving Stephen and priests,
we are able to see beneath the surface of continual flow and so locate
meanings yet unuttered. "Real adventures," says the narrator of "An
Encounter," "do not happen to people who remain at home: they must
be sought abroad," and the observation is echoed in "A Little Cloud":
"There was no doubt about it: if you wanted to succeed you had to go
away. You could do nothing in Dublin." The snow that Gabriel sees in

the book's closing moments intimates in Dublin itself a kind of psychic paralysis which draws the book toward the configuration we must trace for ourselves. Likewise the relationship between Stephen and Leopold is visible beneath the confused events of their day; as Stephen provides Leopold with a substitute for Rudy (but one who can begin to teach him how to live with himself), so Leopold is more affectionate and helpful to Stephen than his father Simon; the contemporaneous walks of Stephen and Leopold, their meeting at the newspaper and later in Night-town and their drinking bout all disclose their essential affinity, their essential doubling. When we study *The Sound and the Fury*, we find that Benjy and Quentin share much, too, beneath their disjunctive narratives, and function in ways, revealing to us, as doubles.

It is by openly inviting just such responses from us as that of doubling that Joyce provides us with the same sort of epiphany he awards to his characters. This *quidditas* is a perceptual salvation, a religion of the consciousness. It appeals to us at a deep level, working actively below our intellection, addressing what Eric S. Rabkin calls the subliminal, with "privileged moment[s] of phenomenological perception without further cognitive assistance from the author: intuition beyond telling," as Grossvogel puts it. Both fragmentation of impressions and subliminal configuration or epiphany are thus necessary counterparts for Joyce's poetics—coordinate acts of body and mind which guarantee a heightened art grounded in both kinesis and stasis. It is in this peculiar joining that Faulkner comes closest, too, to Joyce —one writer Faulkner wished to see when he went to Europe in 1925 and the writer he called in 1947 the father of them all is the authority for those moments in Faulkner when Isaac faces Old Ben and when Chick goes to the grave with Aleck Sander and Miss Habersham, moments at which the arbitrary but burdensome flux of time stands still and, unspoken, makes sense at last.

In the seven volumes of *A la recherche du temps perdu*, Marcel Proust confines fiction to all the jumbled content within the recall of a single autobiographical consciousness: life and art, visual thinking and integrated consciousness are made conterminous. "From the start," Roger Shattuck tells us, "we are given the record of a sensitive consciousness eager to discover and enter the outside world of appearances, and apparently unable to do so in any satisfactory way. Marcel remains confined inside a pliable but impenetrable membrane of self-consciousness." Marcel's mental landscape supplies three analogous geographies—Paris at the turn of the century; Combray, a small provincial town in the Ile-de-France; Balbec, a Norman beach resort— and within the traceries of Combray, two distinct paths compete for attention, the bourgeois Swann's Way and the aristocratic Guermantes Way. For Proust the mind is a storehouse for the cross-cuttings of consciousness (a method Faulkner employs in *As I Lay Dying* and *The Town*); although the two routes through Combray are diametrically opposed and are begun from different doors of Marcel's house, they image for him endless configurations. Swann is Marcel's ideal father; and of the Guermantes, the duchess Oriane is his ideal lover. The families are joined by the marriage of Swann's daughter Gilberte and by his granddaughter Mlle. Saint-Loup. Although Oriane lives out the novel, Swann dies early, and the two come to represent for Marcel life and death, the duality of privation and resurrection, of destruction and preservation involved in every moment of voluntary and involuntary acts of consciousness. Taking Swann's Way or the Guermantes Way, Marcel invariably ends at the Church of St.-Hilaire, "a building which occupied, so to speak, four dimensions of space—the name of the fourth being Time—which had sailed the centuries," which "seemed to stretch across and hold down and conquer not merely a few yards of soil, but each successive epoch." As the church secures life through its ability to unite (much as Gilberte's marriage and daughter), so, too, will Marcel's novel. And like the church, Proust calls the volumes of *La recherche* "travaux d'architecte," architecturally structured, like *A Portrait of the Artist* and *Ulysses*. Fifty pages of the Combray section are held together by the question of whether or not Mme. Goupil arrived at mass on time, for instance; the axis of Swann's life is the question of who was with Odette when, one afternoon, she did not answer her bell. Proust means for us to accept such images in his shifting consciousness—to stay time by formulating circuits and linkages—but he also provides us with analogues which Marcel does not see, such as Swann-Odette: Marcel-Albertine, so that we, like Marcel, are required to combine and recombine. What Wallace Fowlie calls a "veritable obsession" with Proust, the preoccupation with the irrevocability of time, is wrested into control within the domain of art: *La recherche* is Proust's twenty-year attempt to stop the flux of life while capitalizing on it. The larger dimensions of his concern are seen in the later volumes; as social decadence increases, so Proust's treatment of homosexuality, from *Sodome et Gomorrhe* on, becomes more prominent, a rapid outgrowth of the earlier insinuations concerning Marcel and Albertine. All is terrifyingly open and hence diminished; the loss and decline evident in the Zeppelin raid over Paris and Jupien's brothel for male prostitutes in *Le temps retrouvé* are analogous to Popeye's presence in Yoknapatawpha and Memphis and to Faulkner's world of Snopesism. Proust wrote *Le temps retrouvé* immediately after *Du côté de chez Swann* as a book of complementariety and completion. The other five books are the long middle, so long we experience an *oubli*, a forgetting, and *moments bienheureux*, realized resonances: our consciousness comes to replicate Marcel's. Proust's France is panoramic, like Balzac's, but it is transferred into the theater of the mind and placed under constant scrutiny, as Yoknapatawpha is under perpetual and revisionary analysis by Young Bayard, Quentin, and Ike. Faulkner owned a complete set of Proust's *Remembrance*, and in 1952 he recalled to Löic Bouvard that when he read it he remarked, "This is it!"

Like Proust's novel, *The Unvanquished* and *The Reivers* are twice-told tales, both experienced and recollected. But Proust's presentation is actually threefold, because it also includes the novelist's involvement in the recovery of his own past. Like Faulkner, Proust works in associative blocks which are often imagistically based. *Du côté de chez Swann* opens with the following cross-cutting episodes:

1. *Recent past:* Marcel has retired early but in a fit of insomnia he begins to relive his past

2. *Childhood at Combray:* Swann visits, and Marcel's mother is delayed in kissing him good-night

3. *Period within 1:* dipping the *madeleine* in tea calls up a discrete childhood experience

4. *Second return to Combray (2):* the entire Combray childhood is surveyed; this is an "envelope passage" for 2

5. *Distant past (pre-1):* Marcel attempts to understand Swann (episode 2) by remembering a love experience Swann had before Marcel was born

Proust (like Joyce) splinters time to study its fragments; the narrative forms pools of consciousness, so that Marcel's consciousness is not as free as Stephen's: the restless mind in Proust concentrates on relationships and outlines of meaning built on anticipations, retrospections, and correlations. The presentation of consciousness in Proust thus more nearly resembles Melville's and Conrad's. Still it is more positive; where Melville and Conrad search for a cause, Marcel seeks a reincarnation; he lives in a world where everything such as the *madeleine* is immanent, always a part of himself and always at the service of his recollection. There is no such thing as *was*. With Proust as with Balzac and Flaubert, every object tends to metaphor. "The rhetorical equivalent of the Proustian real is the chain-figure of the metaphor," Beckett writes. "It is a tiring style, but it does not tire the mind. The clarity of the phrase is cumulative and explosive. One's fatigue is a fatigue of the heart, a blood fatigue. One is exhausted and angry after an hour, submerged, dominated by the crest and break of metaphor after metaphor: but never stupefied. The complaint that it is an involved style, full of periphrasis, obscure and impossible to follow, has no foundation whatsoever." It is, rather, a moving and poetic style about a search that is not only successful but substantial and significant as well. *La recherche* "indicates a quest, a mission to recover something holy," Wallace Fowlie tells us, resembling the directed consciousness of Benjy and of Quentin, who, awakened by the smell of roses and honeysuckle, search restlessly for Caddy.

From Bergson (with whom he studied at the Sorbonne) Proust learned that time is a matter of duration and that the memory of past time, when activated, displaces and becomes present time: the force and effect of chronology are dissolved. "No image can replace the intuition of duration, but many diverse images, borrowed from very different orders of things, may, by the convergence of their action, direct consciousness to the precise point where there is a certain intuition to be seized," Bergson says in his *Introduction to Metaphysics*. "Consciousness must at least consent to make the effort." Like Quentin's and Shreve's presentation of Sutpen and Faulkner's own presentation of *A Fable*, Proust's organization of *La recherche* is fundamentally by *rapport*, by creative analogies, in which one term is made consciously to correlate with another. Because memorial reconstruction relies on relationships, recollections for Marcel relate the individual consciousness to a social milieu—the double appeal always apparent and accessible in Faulkner. In Proust voluntary memory gives kinetic life to expectations and sought recollections, but there is also the involuntary memory triggered by the *madeleine*, the steeples of Martinville, even the unbuttoning of shoes. The three trees of Balbec lead, for example, through the trees of Hudimesnil (in *A l'ombre des jeunes filles en fleur*) beyond memory and dream to hallucination: the trees seem to be dead friends reaching out for—or at—Marcel, but as the ghosts of John Sartoris and Sam Fathers reach out to Young Bayard and to Ike and the ghosts of Henry Sutpen and Charles Bon are twinned in Quentin and Shreve. The axis of sensation in the Proustian consciousness so abstracts its material that finally it is the unexpected, the anachronistic, that blends into new signification in the act of intellection. It is the diminishment of experience that results in a new compound and so a re-enlargement of experience. Beckett describes the process of the Proustian consciousness this way:

> The total past sensation, not its echo nor its copy, but the sensation itself, annihilating every spatial and temporal restriction, comes in a rush to engulf the subject in all the beauty of its infallible proportion. Thus the sound produced by a spoon struck against a plate is subconsciously identified by the narrator with the sound of a hammer struck by a mechanic against the wheel of a train drawn up before a wood, a sound that his will had rejected as extraneous to its immediate activity. But a subconscious and disinterested act of perception has reduced the object—the wood—to its immaterial and spiritually digestible equivalent, and the record of this pure act of cognition has not merely been associated with this sound of a hammer struck against a wheel, but centralised about it. The mood, as usual, has no importance. The point of departure of the Proustian exposition is not the crystalline agglomeration but its kernel—the crystallised.

When "we hear endlessly, all around us," Marcel remarks, "that unvarying sound . . . is not an echo from without, but the resonance of a vibration from within." The scent of hawthorn or of dog roses, the sound of footsteps on a gravel path, a bubble formed at the side of a waterplant become the new possessions, first seen, then divorced from their environments; like Flaubert's, Proust's novel is stuffed with images to connect. *La recherche* does not alternate between dramatic and summary scenes but between the singular and the iterative images; the ideal and the real marry; imagination merges with apprehension, symbol becomes substance. Anxiety is supplied to Marcel's narrative only because this merging is never complete: Marcel is always aware of his intervening consciousness between the act and his perception. "When I saw any external object, my consciousness that I was seeing it would remain between me and it, enclosing it in a slender, incorporeal outline which prevented me from ever coming directly in contact with the material form; for it would volatilise itself in some way before I could touch it, just as an incandescent body which is moved towards something wet never actually touches moisture, since it is always preceded, itself, by a zone of evaporation." Survival then becomes the exercise of habit and this "is survival on a low level of being," as Roger Shattuck puts it.

Still Marcel's aim—to have his impulses formulate his own pattern of consciousness, his own autonomy—suggests that in attempting to possess the world he, like Sutpen, means ultimately to possess the self. Marcel moves from scattered impressions to constructions of consciousness. His endless examination for analogies, for comparisons of the way he appears to other people and at different times, for associations with different objects and locales, all come down to the continual reformulation of himself. "Man is the being who cannot get out of himself, who knows others only in himself, and, if he denies it, lies," the Narrator of *La recherche* remarks. Even the increasingly open interest in homosexuality, Bersani reminds us, "is the next-to-last step in a turning away from the world of others and toward a world in which there are only mirrors." It is difficult for us to know, finally, if the Proustian consciousness emphasizes the beauty of flowers along the Guermantes Way or the pleasure in re-creating that beauty—if Marcel shows us Paris, Combray, and Balbec, or if they only show us Marcel. The widest of experiences in the Proustian consciousness finally resolves in sameness, not diversity; like consciousness in Conrad and in Faulkner (with Quentin, Isaac, and Gavin), a consciousness is continually rebeholding itself. Proust means to convey a vision but also to convey the experience of envisioning: a prophecy self-perpetuating and self-fulfilling. For the "excluded" Proust, asthmatic, half-Jewish, homosexual—"yesterday's gardenia" writing in his isolated chamber of cork—"knowledge can never cease to remain impression," as Poulet has it. With Proust, we have arrived at the point where consciousness has become wholly ontological.

Conclusion

Fiction by the novelists of consciousness provides us with helpful confluences to Faulkner's own stylistic experimentation. Other ideas and methods he assembled from other sources: the use of archetypal stories and the measure of the accidental against the eternal from the Old Testament, the use of parables and the positive significance of suffering from the New Testament, imagistic clusters and the sense of the permanence of art against the ravages of time from Shakespeare and Keats. In his interview with Jean Stein vanden Heuvel, he admits his fondness for Mrs. Gamp in Dickens's *Martin Chuzzlewit*, and this may suggest a model for his exaggerated comedy, his burlesque, even his grotesque characters; and from other long, loose novels of the nineteenth century he borrowed a structural sense of antithesis and parallelism, anticipation and echo, correlative digressions and emblematic scenes. Recurrent references to the deaths of John Sartoris and Old Ben are not unlike the structural importance of the railroad station as a scene of death in *Anna Karenina*, a novel Faulkner especially liked, and in both *Flags in the Dust* and *Go Down, Moses* he uses such *leitmotifs* as Tolstoy does to achieve the dramatic impact afforded the consciousness by premonition as well as by enactment.

In his later years, Faulkner was fond of saying that he read Cervantes every year, and he commissioned a sculptor in South America to carve a bust of Don Quixote out of Brazilian mahogany for his study. Faulkner's many affinities with this one novel are instructive to us, showing us how deeply and how well he read his predecessors. Cervantes' mingling of the comic and the tragic in the man who can see giants in a land no longer imaginative enough to sustain any magic, a man who can metamorphose his comic role as the Knight of the Woeful Countenance into the sort of behavior fitting for the original Man of Sorrows, is an extraordinary testimonial to the power of the human personality and the endurance of the human will—and to those "old verities and truths of the heart" that Faulkner kept praising so lavishly. Cervantes (like Faulkner) was fundamentally concerned with the potential congruence between the world's possibilities and man's expectations, with self-definition as it is formulated by man's premises and by the authenticity of experience itself: not only Quentin and Darl but Bayard, the tall convict, and Gavin Stevens learn, like the don, that the inner vision becomes more difficult to prove the more intrusive the world becomes, with its self-contradiction, capriciousness, irrationality, and impermanence. Yet Don Quixote clings to his belief in the golden age even when Sancho Panza reminds him of the iron age in which he is luckless enough to find himself—as Faulkner's present-day characters recall the antebellum South, the old hounds running the Big Woods, and the possibilities for a Sutpen's Hundred.

The inherent fragmentation of personality between the don and Sancho which makes them secret sharers hints from the outset Cervantes' dependence on multiple perspective: the views of different characters on a single event (such as the battle with the Knight of Mirrors), the view of different events by the same character (such as Sancho's increasing commitment to the pastoral), and even accidental and staged "truths" (such as the flight on Clavileño). In these various responses, as well as in the analogies provided by the interpolated stories, the necessity and treachery of fiction itself become the basic issues. "Don Quixote *saw*"; "things *seemed*"; "he *thought*" that: moments of arrested and examined action show the limitation and relativity of human perspective generally, and the whole is nearly undone when Cervantes explains evasively that his tale is from a faulty manuscript written by one Cide Hamete Benengeli, a notoriously unreliable narrator. Cervantes' interpenetration of life and art, truth and history, is of a piece with Quentin's and Shreve's in *Absalom, Absalom!*: both are fragmentary, partially (or potentially) inauthentic and unreliable. Faulkner's characters who protest in their tales too much—Horace, Darl, Hightower, the reporter, Harry Wilbourne, V. K. Ratliff—sense that, too.

"Faulkner dramatizes on every page the futility of imposing any kind of order or pattern upon human life," Duncan Aswell writes, "while at the same time revealing with the utmost compassion, and making us feel with the greatest poignancy, that the yearning to make logical sense out of events is a compulsive, inescapable need, one of the defining characteristics of the human soul." Although he is speaking particularly of *Absalom, Absalom!*, his observation applies to all of the Yoknapatawpha fiction. In its struggle for structural ordering, the narrative consciousness in Faulkner, as in other novelists of consciousness before him, attempts to secure a contingent integration of mind and experience. This immense act of impulse and of will is finally confirmed or denied in our conscious act of reading.

II Faulkner and the Modernist Tradition

Style as Vision: Method

The difference between content, or experience, and achieved content, or art, is technique.—MARK SCHORER

A poet's function—do not be startled by this remark—is not to experience the poetic state: that is a private affair. His function is to create it in others.—PAUL VALERY

I was deliberately choosing among possibilities and probabilities of behavior and weighing and measuring each choice by the scale of the Jameses and Conrads and Balzacs.—FAULKNER

WILLIAM FAULKNER OPENLY associated himself with those modernist writers he repeatedly studied for purpose and strategy; what at first may appear as artistic eccentricity or deliberate obscurity in structure and expression has deep roots in those novelists of consciousness who preceded him. Faulkner's art allies itself to European fiction as much as to Southern regionalism, and it is no surprise that the French, heirs to Balzac, Flaubert, and Proust, have been quickest to recognize this. "If there is one fault which Mr. Faulkner does not have, it is surely incoherence," M. Coindreau tells us. "His writing techniques are no more arbitrary than his psychology." Both his technique and his psychology account for the experience of fiction on us too, by which reading as well as writing becomes a dynamic, literary act.

Structural Consciousness

Faulkner is aware, for example, of our deep need to integrate experience and knowledge and to build, as Arnheim claims many artists do, toward a configuration of the whole; his first appeal to us as readers is to our *structural consciousness*. *Absalom, Absalom!*, therefore, can be read as an attempt to answer those questions that Shreve poses to Quentin at dead center: what is the South and what is it like to live there? In their joint attempt to reply, Quentin and Shreve build a *pattern* to identify Thomas Sutpen, a pattern that will account for the facts (Quentin's visit to Sutpen's Hundred, the letter from his father), their opinions, and the reports. In finally viewing Sutpen as a man whose sense of self-respect was badly assaulted by his rejection in Tidewater Virginia, they are able to integrate the founding of Sutpen's Hundred with Rosa's hatred and Wash's murder; in establishing Sutpen's need to keep up appearances they account also for the actions of Henry, Judith, and Clytie. At last it all explains—for both the Southerner and the Canadian. Quentin and Shreve demonstrate Faulkner's interest in such patterns. "One must first grasp the whole," Szanto writes in another context, "whereafter [any] particular segment will illuminate itself."

Faulkner underwent just such a process of locating the necessary patterns in writing *The Hamlet*. His account in a private letter to Malcolm Cowley shows how for him the integration of parts or episodes into the proper configuration also supplies a kind of organicism.

> THE HAMLET was incepted as a novel. When I began it, it produced Spotted Horses, went no further. About two years later suddenly I had THE HOUND, then JAMSHYD'S COURTYARD, mainly because SPOTTED HORSES had created a character I fell in love with: the itinerant sewing-machine agent named Suratt. Later a man of that name turned up at home, so I changed my man to Ratliff for the reason that my whole town spent much of its time trying to decide just what living man I was writing about, the one literary criticism of the town being "How in the hell did he remember all that, and when did that happen anyway?"
>
> Meanwhile my book had created Snopes and his clan, who produced stories in their saga which are to fall in a later volume: MULE IN THE YARD, BRASS, etc. This over about ten years, until one day I decided I had better start on the first volume or I'd never get any of it down. So I wrote an induction toward the spotted horse story, which included BARN BURNING and WASH, which I discovered had no place in that book at all. Spotted horses became a longer story, picked up the HOUND (rewritten and much longer and with the character's name changed from Cotton to Snopes) and went on with JAMSHYD'S COURTYARD.

Faulkner's own groping toward the final story occurred in part during the years he wrote *Absalom, Absalom!*, and the result, like the final story of Quentin and Shreve, circles back to its beginning. From the opening passages of *The Hamlet*, in which we learn that the only thing Frenchman's Bend remembers about Grant's march through the county is the gold Grenier buried to keep from him, until the final pages when Ratliff and his companions are tricked by Flem into digging for that gold, we are given a study of the various forms of human greed. *The Hamlet* is an anatomy of possessiveness. Frenchman's Bend is obsessed with who owns what, with who gains and who loses what. All the Snopeses represent a threat because they are better at getting things, yet the truth is that they are simply quicker and colder about it than Will Varner (who cajoles his customers into serfdom while keeping out the competition) or Ratliff himself (who persuades women to buy sewing machines they cannot afford); Will and Ratliff are poor parodies. Henry Armstid's compulsion to buy one of the spotted horses is a consequence of this dream to own, but he is no greater a victim than Mrs. Ab Snopes, who wishes to buy a cream separator and to trade their only cow for it! In earlier and more expansive times at the hamlet, Ab and Pat Stamper bartered in good humor for the ownership of a horse because to them the means were always more enjoyable and important than the ends. But in the cramped present, the very nature of these people after Flem arrives is perverted: even love becomes a matter of possessiveness. Who will possess Eula and whether Ike possesses the cow in sodomy become questions of overriding importance. As the novel moves inexorably from tall tale to exploitation that is real, from a relaxed store veranda to a compulsive auction, and from Labove's dream of law school and of Eula to the peep show which capitalizes on Ike's sense of beauty, Frenchman's Bend reveals more and more its own capacity for self-victimization.

Once we find the theme that is Faulkner's structural principle, his novels are instantly more comprehensible. In *Soldiers' Pay*, for example, he portrays a wide range of sexual longings which only the Reverend Mahon is able to subordinate to a religious faith. In *Mosquitoes* we are provided with a fugal study of loneliness on Mrs. Maurier's yacht before the scene finally shifts into Gordon's studio where the needs of life are only inadequately met by art. Even so apparently simple a novel as *The Reivers* is a structured if final glossing on Faulkner's aphorism in *Light in August* that "Memory believes before knowing remembers." The entire novel is one sentence, most of it the direct object to the opening words, "Grandfather said:." Although the bulk of Grandfather's recollection is an account of

Lucius, Boon, and Ned following a Yellow-Brick Road through Tennessee to a childlike vision of Memphis and an impossible condition of freedom and Non-Virtue, this vision is sternly bounded by death, by the real death of a grandfather at the beginning and by the death of Grandfather's childhood at the end. This cyclic view of life is captured not only in the circular journey to Memphis and back but in the core image of the adventure, the racetrack. Lucius loses his innocence when he trusts Boon with the family car, Otis with his friendship, and Ned with an ability to train horses. The trick with sardines and the childhood perspective to which Grandfather returns to tell this story reveal beneath the plot a Lucius now grown old and near death himself attempting through humor and memory to confront his own limitations. This structural awareness of *The Reivers* shows us that, for all his good humor and in spite of the tall tale with which he entertains his grandson, Grandfather Lucius now charts his life as progressive loss, the tale as his stay against mortality. Backward-looking is what revitalizes him; the full title of the novel is *The Reivers: A Reminiscence*. The significance here as elsewhere in Faulkner lies in the configuration that embraces every part.

"Our own minds and our sensory equipment organize our world; it is we who establish these *a priori* connections which we later discover and sometimes describe, mistakenly, as natural laws," William H. Gass writes in *Fiction and the Figures of Life*. "We are inveterate model makers." From such form alone we gain a sense of integration and, hence, of significance. We *need* to be bound in. This understanding is especially prevalent in *The Sound and the Fury*. The Compsons maintain life by reasserting respectability and routine while the idiot Benjy, unable to rely on conceptualized order, is bound in by the fence along the golf course and the front walk, and by Luster, who accompanies him as he plays about the yard. Only Quentin, Caddy, and Quentin IV are unable to accept such restraints. But their escape is only temporary; Quentin's suicide is a tragic synecdoche of their denial of boundaries.

Faulkner is fond of revealing a basis for structural patterns in the first and last scenes of his novels. Yet even here he often sets up a dialectic with the middle of the book which we must resolve, as in *The Reivers* and *The Sound and the Fury*. Consequently, *Flags in the Dust* opens with Old Bayard and Old Man Falls preserving by conversation, as Jenny and Narcissa do at the end, a South which Young

Bayard is unable to accept: the novel is at first a testament to, then finally an indictment of, the romance of the antebellum South fostered by willed ignorance, the suspension of disbelief. *Light in August* begins with Lena Grove, whose self-containment is antithetical to Joe's inability to be at peace with himself. This dialectic confronts us almost at once: Lena's placid journey halts at Jefferson, where her first sight is smoke from Joanna Burden's house, the scene of Joanna's and Joe's greatest act of desperation. Although Lena's peace of mind is restored to us at the center of the last chapter, she presents by then in her calmness a grim comment on the peace of mind which Joe sought and won at the cost of life and identity. *Intruder in the Dust* has a similar structure; it commences with Chick Mallison's fall into the creek and Lucas's rescue of him; here the upsetting of social and racial roles strikes an imbalance that is reiterated when Lucas is accused of murder and the white boy Chick feels obliged to save the black man who rescued him. Within this confusing set of circumstances, both Chick and Lucas become secret sharers, learning that in pursuing a lower form of justice in connection with the Gowrie murder they both must compromise the higher form of justice which maintains human dignity only by abolishing the distinctions of race and class permanently. The use of the secret sharer occurs again with the reporter and Hagood in *Pylon* and with Minnie Cooper and McLendon in "Dry September," these last two linked sardonically by the glow of the silver screen and the glare of headlights on the blank wall.

The use of multiple perspective enhances but complicates this basic structural principle because several characters pursue correlative paths in the middles of these novels. *As I Lay Dying* is essentially a dialectic on action and language, but the polar responses indicated by Jewel and Darl (the one who rarely speaks and the one who rarely acts) are parallel in their growth and in their last extreme acts despite the modifications of the dialectic afforded by Anse, Cash, Dewey Dell, and Vardaman. Gavin's chivalric attempts to save Linda from Flem in *The Town* are made analogous to the larger and more generous desires of Chick and Ratliff to save Jefferson itself. In the first version of *Sanctuary* Faulkner expanded Horace's secret desires for incest, his own inner corruption with Narcissa and Little Belle a replication of Temple's with Popeye and Red; in the novel as it was published, Horace's untried beliefs are the perverse inversion of Temple's and Popeye's unthinking actions.

Perhaps the most difficult novel of all structurally, however, is *A*

Fable; Faulkner worked longest on this self-confrontation with the individual's yearning for freedom opposed to his need for restraint, testing the basis of his own poetics. In *A Fable*, the massive but fluid responses are to the dialectic on power between the corporal (whose name also designates the sacramental cloth placed on the Eucharist during the Holy Mass) and the Old General (whose name insinuates the voices and beliefs of the multitude). Fundamentally, the corporal's actions argue that power resides in individual freedom, commitment, and will while the Old General places it in established, traditional, and institutional authority. Their unresolved debate echoes at every level and in every incident in the novel: in the simplest personal and social needs of the horse-thief episode; in the financial arrangements the sentry proposes; in the institutionalized actions of the law, the military, and the organized church; and in the metaphysical speculations which necessarily center on the possibility and potentiality of the Passion, the archetypal confrontation between the authority of the Father and the freedom of the Son. The Old General's offers—temptations, really, that suggest in their number the three temptations of Christ in the wilderness—are promises of liberty, compassion, and fame in a traditional society; he tries to end the dialectic by forcing one side of it. He is supported in this effect by the Quartermaster General (who supplies the military), by General Gragnon, the division commander (who insists on a military orthodoxy), the whole of the allied forces, and ironically, even Levine, who would welcome just such an occasion to honor the military by significant service. But the other force in the dialectic ranged behind the silent corporal is equally prominent—the runner, the corporal's sisters Marthe and Marya, his whole squad to a man, and, ironically, even the groom who would do anything to save the liberty of his horse.

This irresolute paradox is also embodied by the strongest advocates on either side. The Old General acts the part of both Satan and God, as if man could not have one without the other; despite his damning temptations, he was once a hermit at a Tibetan lamasery, prefigured by the man sacrificed with the camel and himself prefiguring the corporal's retreat from the front lines; he knows that the conspiracy of peaceful resignation from war is the gravest challenge to the institutionalization of force. On the other side, the sentry embodied a love of freedom as the groom, but now he embodies a love of power by selling life insurance—his love of risk has led to power over men. The slow corrosion of Levine's Sidcott is only a physical manifestation of the corruption of the Old General's argument, the transformation of the groom into the sentry, and the diminishing effect of the rebellious squad's heroic gamble. The resolution of this debate between the Old General and the corporal, between father and son, past and present, society and freedom, is essential to know but beyond the capacity of man to comprehend, the mystery within the Mystery, passion within the Passion, reminiscent of Dostoyevsky.

Both the need and the bafflement form the extraordinary balance of forces in the novel's closing scene. We never know if the corporal is the man buried as the Unknown Soldier, but this very mystery is enclosed in the paradox of the act of burial itself. It is fitting that the corporal is made an emblem for sacrifice and a memorial to the cost of peace, but it is also bitterly ironic that this man who refused to kill is honored as a soldier who fought to the death for France. Only two men who could appreciate this paradox are present, and they do not know it is the corporal's burial to which they have come. The runner has returned proclaiming the liberty of man, but his body is so maimed that he is unable to effect his own freedom; his Conradian secret sharer, the Quartermaster General, is also at the ceremony, but without troops to supply now and so relatively harmless. But the crowd is not. This same milling mob—mankind generally—which had opened the novel by turning out to scorn a traitor now unknowingly honor him as a hero; they take their scorn out instead on the runner by attacking him. They have learned nothing from the war and their actions mock the memorial they came to admire. Only the Quartermaster General cares for the sick and dying runner.

> The man in the gutter opened his eyes and began to laugh, or tried to, choking at first, trying to turn his head as though to clear his mouth and throat of what he choked on, when another man thrust through the crowd and approached him—an old man, a gaunt giant of a man with a vast worn sick face with hungry and passionate eyes above a white military mustache, in a dingy black overcoat in the lapel of which were three tiny faded ribbons, who came and knelt beside him and slipped one arm under his head and shoulders and raised him and turned his head a little until he could spit out the blood and shattered teeth and speak. Or laugh rather, which is what he did first, lying in the cradle of the old man's arm, laughing up at the ring of faces enclosing him, then speaking himself in French:

"That's right," he said: "Tremble. I'm not going to die. Never."

"I am not laughing," the old man bending over him said. "What you see are tears."

The military man and the persevering rebel, the "old man" who "cradles" the laughing, bloody remnant of the war and ignores his own "three tiny faded ribbons"—a new *Pieta*. This delicately balanced magnification of the book's central paradox—Balzacian in placement and effect—remains surrounded by the larger crowd of humanity who in Faulkner's fable are quite willing to transfer their faith in the military to their part in this civil and religious ceremony, the rite of a new scapegoat—acting once more with a willed blindness to their own loss and shame, and by instinct to their own hungers and needs.

Although the final scene of *A Fable* blends all the forces and ideas of the novel in a way that appeals to our structural consciousness, this structure of the work, beneath the more blatant allegory of the Passion Week, is not immediately clear. One major reason for this is that Faulkner, like Joyce, builds his novels in discrete episodes that we must pull together for ourselves. Writing a novel, Faulkner once remarked, is "a good deal like dressing a showcase window. It takes a certain amount of judgment and taste to arrange the different pieces in the most effective place in juxtaposition to one another." His presentation is by scenes rather than by sequence, creating the dialectic of our response. We know because of his comment to Cowley that this is the way he constructed *The Hamlet*.

"At least since Homer, readers of extended narratives have expected categorically that such works will be divided, that they will contain within their beginnings and ends a series of subordinate beginnings and endings," Philip Stevick reminds us. This expectation evokes in the reader something not unlike the abstract formal pleasure one finds in a Grecian vase, one of Faulkner's more persistent allusions. The episodes of novels seem most discrete when they are given separate titles as in *The Unvanquished* and *Go Down, Moses*, but in the twenty novels he has left, Faulkner has incorporated thirty-three previously published stories and an unknown number of unpublished ones (such as "Elmer," near the close of *Mosquitoes*), the residue of which is still sometimes slightly traceable. The episode in which McEachern punishes Joe Christmas is complete in itself, but the placement of this punishment in *Light in August* urges us to look backward to the dietitian and the janitor at the orphanage and forward to Joanna Burden and Percy Grimm in Jefferson. The result of such placement of episodes is not linear but a pattern that tends to be geometrical rather than chronological.

Although this technique is familiar to readers of *The Sound and the Fury* and *As I Lay Dying,* it is not so often noted in *The Wild Palms* and *Requiem for a Nun*—works which Faulkner also called novels. Yet it is fundamental to both. In many respects *The Wild Palms* is Faulkner's most interesting experiment in constructing a novel. Both Harry Wilbourne and the tall convict have outwardly similar experiences at about the same time and at roughly the same age: they are uprooted and taken out into a larger world by others, begin to drift and become disenchanted, and without regret return to the same place, the penitentiary at Parchman, willingly accepting their own sense of guilt and hence a life of perpetual imprisonment. But Harry's adventures are also the inverse of the convict's; the roughly parallel segments comment on each other.

Harry's story is a domestic tragedy of willed self-defeat. In wishing to escape the intellectual and scientific life of medical school, Harry is an easy prey to Charlotte Rittenmeyer, whose irresponsibility encourages his own, but like her he subsequently remains too calculating in all that he does. His lovemaking is a series of forced gestures; after his tins of food are exhausted in Wisconsin, he tries to practice medicine at a mining camp in Utah; the childbirth he assists is an abortion. Even the stories he writes in Chicago are not art but commercial perversions of the truth, analogous to Charlotte's window displays and twisted creatures of papier-mâché. Yet Harry fails to learn from his frustrating and deadening experiences. He rents a beach cabin on the Gulf coast for the last days of his failed romance from the sort of doctor he could have been, but he fails to see the grim, instructive irony in his landlord's unhappy life; in jail, he is content to watch fondly a young couple on "one of the emergency ships built in 1918 and never finished," as if they were ideal secret selves to Charlotte and himself. In his last act—choosing a live martyrdom for romantic love instead of accepting cyanide from Charlotte's husband—he acts out of the same self-pity that attracted him to Charlotte initially.

While the convict's story has a similar outward shape, inwardly it is the comedy of a man unwillingly reborn. The unnamed convict was originally betrayed by a cheap adventure story, but he moves away from a life shaped by pulp fiction as Harry moves toward one. The convict is unskilled, possessed with human rather than technical or professional knowledge, instinctive rather than trained. Loosed upon the flood waters of the Mississippi, he befriends an unidentified woman and works with a Cajun whose language he cannot understand, he assists in a natural childbirth, and he earns a living temporarily by hunting alligators. When he is able to return to prison at last, he has had the adventure that makes him a hero to others that he had hoped to win by robbing a train, and at a cheap price—at the cost of a freedom which for reasons quite unlike Harry's he cannot handle and does not wish. Both narratives thus end ironically. Yet together they constitute (by "counterpoint," according to Faulkner) a single novel which argues the desirability and danger of total liberty and the necessity and treachery of romance.

The correlations in *Requiem for a Nun* are more obscure, but here too the prose and dramatic segments are analogous, this time in tracing the efforts of men to assert themselves against the eroding forces of time and history. The novel opens with the story of Thomas Jefferson Pettigrew, a lonely man who yearns for immortality and achieves it by lending to the new town his middle name. In doing this, he must agree first to bribery, thus corrupting the town at its beginning as well as the names of Thomas Jefferson and himself. In the final prose segment Cecelia Farmer gains immortality of a kind by scratching her name on the windowpane of the jail out of boredom just before seeing a Southern soldier who later will come to take her to Alabama. Both Pettigrew and Cecelia are deluded, however, for we learn that people who visit the town of Jefferson or look at the windowpane no longer know of either of them. Despite the scratches that we may imagine indicate Cecelia's sharp cry for selfhood ("*Listen, stranger; this was myself; this was I!*"), she and Pettigrew as individuals are lost to a modern world where the attention is on railroads, buses, radio stations, and the local Basketball Tournament and where religion and politics are only acute diversions. Yet even this consequence can be laid at Pettigrew's feet, for he agreed that the town draw up account books, causing an interest in capital investment to replace the simple Chickasaw interest in bartering and trading; from his own psychological bondage, Pettigrew helped to enslave the town to a capitalistic economy (a further irony to his and the town's name). It is symptomatic, then, that Jefferson built a jail before it built a courthouse, and that its last act before incorporation was to buy off the last inhabitant of regal splendor, the Indian Queen Mohataha. Like Pettigrew and Cecelia, she too is now forgotten, while Jefferson continues to live on in its various states of physical, social, economic, and moral bondage.

But Pettigrew's legacy is not altogether harmful. In insisting on reparation for the stolen lock, he introduces into Jefferson the idea of accountability: the jail was followed by a courthouse. It is to this trust in accountability rather than to the desire for immortality or the fear of oblivion that Nancy Mannigoe turns when she risks her own life in order to restore Temple's sense of responsibility. Nancy's appeal is not to the lower court of Yoknapatawpha nor to the governor at the statehouse in Jackson, for she is well aware that people's laws and institutions only imprison them; rather, she appeals to a sense of decency and love in Temple that will take her beyond the judge and the governor and allow her to see (as she does in the second dramatic segment) that she stands before the judgment of God and not of men. Unlike Pettigrew, Temple cannot bribe the state for Nancy's freedom; unlike Cecelia, she cannot run away from her husband and remaining child with a new man. The future of Temple is not clear at the end of *Requiem*, but we do know from the segments of prose and drama in which the novel is written that she is finally aware of her own bondage to her family, and that she begins to understand freedom as a matter of the soul, a liberty within. In demonstrating to Temple that a "nigger dope-fiend whore" can perform acts of mercy befitting a nun, Nancy shows Temple Drake the way to become Temple Stevens. Faulkner's irony, however, is that this response is one of two possibilities for Temple; the other is that Nancy, like Mohataha, may be removed from society so that other people, the white ruling class of Yoknapatawpha, can go on doing as they wish. In a novel structurally similar to Flaubert's *La tentation de Saint-Antoine*, the conclusion resembles that of Joyce's *Dubliners*. We must attend, at the end, to the narrative's broad but ironic analogy to the novel's title. A requiem mass can only *pray* that the departed soul may find peace. It does not guarantee salvation for the living, either.

"The true business of the literary artist," Robert Louis Stevenson wrote in 1885, "is to plait or weave his meaning, involving it around itself; so that each sentence, by successive phrases, shall first come into a kind of knot, and then, after a moment of suspended meaning, solve and clear itself. In every properly constructed sentence there should be observed this knot or hitch; so that (however delicately) we are led to foresee, to expect, and then to welcome the successive phrases." This is true not only of Faulkner's sentences but of his novels—of their related opening and closing episodes and of certain interior segments, such as McEachern's beating of Joe Christmas in *Light in August*. In addition, Faulkner often provides us with smaller emblem passages within a particular segment which (similar to Flaubert) alike illuminate the segment in which they appear and the whole structure and meaning of a work by gathering together constituent perspectives and themes. The opening paragraph of *Pylon* is a case in point.

> For a full minute Jiggs stood before the window in a light spatter of last night's confetti lying against the windowbase like spent dirty foam, lightpoised on the balls of his greasestained tennis shoes, looking at the boots. Slantshimmered by the intervening plate they sat upon their wooden pedestal in unblemished and inviolate implication of horse and spur, of the posed countrylife photographs in the magazine advertisements, beside the easelwise cardboard placard with which the town had bloomed overnight as it had with the purple-and-blue tissue bunting and the trodden confetti and broken serpentine . . . the same lettering, the same photographs of the trim vicious fragile aeroplanes and the pilots leaning upon them in gargantuan irrelation as if the aeroplanes were a species of esoteric and fatal animals not trained or tamed but just for the instant inert, above the neat brief legend of name and accomplishment or perhaps just hope.

Jiggs's world here is unreal, phantasmagoric. On display inside the shop window yet clearly beyond his reach are a jumble of objects including expensive boots alongside a slick testimonial to the air show in town; both are as artificial and as glossy as photographs of aristocratic life in the coffee-table magazines. There is a sheen here but no humanity; animal life is seen reduced to the mechanical, the inert, and the fragile. The view, like the compound words in which it is expressed, is so strange that we have difficulty recognizing it. Jiggs, standing in dirty cloth shoes amidst the refuse of Mardi Gras, at first seems a mockery of the wealth which so fascinates him, yet the purple and gold tissue is also a festive sign for royalty, a correlative and corporate representation of unachieved wealth. Jiggs sees the boots as a completion of his secret selving, but we can see that his world is already a tawdry replication of the display, and we are able to anticipate that the life of the stunt fliers whom he serves will be no more human or alive, no less slick and contrived, and finally no less vulnerable than the exhibit with which he is first paired.

A similar emblem passage occurs in *The Sound and the Fury* near the close of the fourth chapter when Jason has at last grabbed one of the circus hands in his attempt to locate Quentin IV. "Jason glared wildly about, holding the other. Outside it was now bright and sunny, swift and bright and empty, and he thought of the people soon to be going quietly home to Sunday dinner, decorously festive, and of himself trying to hold the fatal, furious little old man whom he dared not release long enough to turn his back and run." The little old man is a sad substitute for the circus worker Jason wished to punish, another signification of the diminished state of the Compsons, and his own desire to run reveals to us that Jason is not only unable to contend with the world in which he finds himself but that he finds himself in a world which he distrusts and despises. His obligation to play the part of the enraged uncle, like his roles as head of the family and obedient son, mocks him even when he tries his best to fulfill it. He acts with reluctance and irritation, knowing that other people in other worlds have festive occasions and enjoy the sunshine and peace of a normal and sustaining family life. All that Jason wants is described in this passage, as well as all that he is and all that he cannot have. His shock of self-recognition, the sound and fury that hasten to hide the void of his "empty" world, resemble the activities of Benjy and Quentin and underline the quiet desperation of the present-day Compsons. It is a tense but pathetic moment of Joycean epiphany, not unlike that moment in *Absalom, Absalom!* when, in the tomblike atmosphere of Rosa's office, Quentin sees "the dim face looking at him with an expression speculative, urgent and intent," inviting him to a life which he wants very much to avoid for himself even as he feels irrevocably borne into it.

The Unvanquished is exemplary of all Faulkner's appeals, at various levels of sentence, scene, and juxtaposed episodes, to our structural consciousness. Essentially, the novel is not about blacks against whites, or even the South against the North, but the enslaved, both white and black, against those at liberty. The titled segments of the novel, while independent in themselves, build by correlations to the work's final dialectic of meaning, Bayard's alternative commitments to the old or new law, the Old South of romance or the New South of realistic compromise. In the last segment, "An Odor of Verbena," Bayard is able to see the range of analogues provided for him in the opening chapter, "Ambuscade," even as Ringo, who would be Bayard's secret self, suggests on the way to Jefferson an easy solution for the two of them: they can plot another ambush.

Bayard's recollection of the past and his re-experience of his childhood show how he, like Colonel John Sartoris and Granny, began in a state of innocence fundamentally incongruent with a world at war. His father means to protect their home and culture from Northern incursion just as Granny means to protect the family property from Yankee raids, but they, like young Bayard and Ringo, see the war as a game, too. The simulated Battle of Vicksburg in which Ringo willingly joins (but on the losing side) is an emblem passage; the game is easily destroyed by Loosh because, like the trunks of family silver and the twisted railroad tracks, the battle is an attempt to preserve old and challenged myths unchanged. Bayard's own romantic name, drawn from medieval chivalric romance, warns us that his culture reveres a kind of gallantry that blinds its people to the inhumanity of enslavement and serfdom. Colonel John's prearranged escape from the barn and Granny's attempt to hide the boys under her skirts are also the blind sentimentality of pulp fiction. Although such tricks do not fool the Yankee for long, such delusion is widespread among the Southerners of Faulkner's Yoknapatawpha: it begins with Loosh's notion that by destroying the childhood battle of Bayard and Ringo he can establish his own freedom from slavery and the past; it reaches its apogee in the mass of newly freed blacks who in seeking Jordan march to their own doom.

Looking back on Granny from the older Bayard's perspective at the close of the novel, we can see that her plan to cheat the Yankees of booty is her attempt to trade Bayard's games of war for Ringo's games of black survival customary to the enslaved; her own actions mock her. She seeks mules (eunuchs, significantly), her actions prefiguring those of the carpetbagger. Her death is, consequently, fit punishment for such greed, for her hypocrisy about prayer had grown into something deadlier and more serious. When he discovers her, Bayard compares her to a toy, acknowledging the childishness of her escapades. "She had looked little alive, but now she looked like she had collapsed, like she had been made out of a lot of little thin dry light sticks notched together and braced with cord, and now the cord had broken and all the little sticks had collapsed in a quiet heap on the floor, and somebody had spread a clean and faded calico dress over them." His repetition of words conveys his grief just as his revisionary perspective of her stature, smaller now as his father's has become, discloses a critical stage in his maturity. Bayard's subsequent murder of Grumby, although prompted by Ringo's romanticism, is accomplished after Grumby has shot twice at him and, missing, has jumped him before Ringo forces the man to flee.

When Ringo depicts the Sartoris house, he sees it as it once was, although it is actually burned and gutted; the illusion is carried forward when Colonel John rebuilds the house on its old foundations. By sheer will John and Drusilla, without the help of Bayard, restore their antebellum life—even at the expense of stuffing ballot boxes, killing carpetbaggers, and cheating Redmond. They recapture form but forfeit substance; bravado and claims to gentility have little room for honesty and realism in such postwar years, their actions too quickly forgetful of such meanness and danger that caused Bayard to pull the trigger on Grumby. The Colonel's death is therefore as fitting as Granny's, which it resembles, while the reactions—save for Bayard's—are the same: Professor Wilkins expects Bayard to do a son's duty; Ringo sees the opportunity for new strategies of war; Drusilla, in her theatrical request with the dueling pistols, is an analogue to John and Granny—but for Bayard she is the double of Grumby, urging on a murder he wills himself—this time—*not* to commit. In a novel which portrays a South dedicated to romantic absolutism—John's sense of honor; Granny's sense of property; Drusilla's sense of vengeance—Bayard's relativism is always misunderstood. But in his final confrontation with Redmond he chooses his own correlative, his own Conradian secret self; he denies his previous actions with Grumby and he rejects the foolish heroism of his father and the scorn of Loosh in the opening segment of the novel for the example of the Yankee colonel: in sparing Redmond, he responds at last to his Northern counterpart who with his humanity and humor had spared him. As a Southerner, Bayard thus displays not only hard-won tolerance of belief but an especially difficult form of heroism.

We move in *The Unvanquished* from our sense of its structure to the narrative consciousness of Bayard; with him we sort through the past events in order to determine his response in the final segment. But in employing our own constitutive consciousness (as Joyce would ask of us, given his discrete episodes), we come to judge Bayard as well: and what are we to make of him at the last? His final act of refusing to fire at Redmond is heroic enough to earn from Drusilla the verbena she leaves him, but this is an insufficient, even irrelevant token for him. He cries—whether from relief or for the death of the old code we are uncertain—and then seeking additional solace from Aunt Jenny he takes the position by her feet he had so often assumed with Granny: he retreats to the posture of childhood.

> "Kneel down." So I knelt beside the chair. "So you had a perfectly splendid Saturday afternoon, didn't you? Tell me about it." Then she put her hands on my shoulders. I watched them come up as though she were trying to stop them; I felt them on my shoulders as if they had a separate life of their own and were trying to do something which for my sake she was trying to restrain, prevent. Then she gave up or she was not strong enough because they came up and took my face between them, hard, and suddenly the tears sprang and streamed down her face like Drusilla's laughing had. "Oh, damn you Sartorises!" she said. "Damn you! Damn you!"

Her tears are analogous to Bayard's; unlike the men in the streets of Jefferson, she does understand what he has done and why. In damning the Sartorises, Jenny also damns herself, for she is one of them, like the others inescapably grieved by the death of the old and the emergence of the new consciousness. Life without honor is cursed, but as the terms of honor have been transformed so have the terms of life. Aunt Jenny damns Bayard for facing Redmond and causing her to fear for his life, but also for vanquishing the old sense of honor for the new, and vanquishing all the Sartorises in the process. The novel's title is ironic, for only Redmond is unvanquished—and only because he has abruptly left town. As in Melville, the final range of tones in *The Unvanquished*, like its final range of meanings, is held poised, in a delicate balance, similar to the close of *A Fable* and similar to *Requiem for a Nun*.

Narrative Consciousness

"If experience consists of impressions," writes Henry James, "it may be said that impressions *are* experience": we are helped to the meanings of Faulkner's novels by the pressures of their *narrative consciousness* on events. It is a necessary limitation, for few of us are tolerant enough to observe fictional events in full neutrality; one task of fiction, Simon O. Lesser reminds us, is "the scaling of time to a dimension our minds can compass." Our conscious act of reading is controlled in large measure by what R. S. Crane calls "determinate desires," initial formulations of the narrative consciousness, the primary function of which is to shape events for us. In Faulkner our visual thinking relies on the orientation, authority, bias, and involvement of the screening perspective, on the logic of the narrative subjectivity. Jason's frantic chase after the man from the circus in chapter 4 of *The Sound and the Fury* could, in any other context than that in which we have it, become low comedy. But we have shared a day with Jason in chapter 3; we know how he is mocked and scorned and ignored by others, and we are accustomed to the elaborate behavior and sentiment which he employs in order to move with a little freedom and self-respect in his sharply constricted world. In *The Wild Palms*, the young couple in the emergency warship would seem gratuitous if Harry Wilbourne had not implied, through his presiding intelligence, that he has not known any happily married couples. If Bayard did not tell us the events of *The Unvanquished* retrospectively, *after* he had faced Redmond, we should not be as aware as he may be of the alternatives, posed first in the novel by the Yankee colonel, on the day of his final duel. With Faulkner (as with Melville or Conrad) this open but dislocated narrative consciousness requires us to enter the fictional field, yet it is this same narrative consciousness that provides us with our point of entry. We know Faulkner's characters, says Mary Cooper Robb, "inside-out, not outside-in."

But we must also be aware that the screening perspective will necessarily be somewhat distorted because it comes directly from the simulated human source. We have seen that Granny's vision is astigmatic in *The Unvanquished*, for instance, because the older Bayard recalls it that way; seen frontally between Bayard and Ringo and caught in the havoc of the War between the States, she would appear to us quite differently. McEachern sees Joe's tendency to sin because he *wants* to see it: sinning is for McEachern a natural condition of the human personality and a verification of God. The matter of race is more complicated yet. Faulkner's narrative consciousness, participant in the regional consciousness of Yoknapatawpha, is open enough in Quentin's and Chick's observations on blacks in *The Sound and the Fury* and in *Intruder in the Dust,* but it is less visible (yet more significant) in other instances: Caspey's return from the war provides Young Bayard with a secret self that determines many of his early actions in *Flags in the Dust;* Dilsey's natural affinity for motherhood shames Caroline Compson while her insinuating authority often undermines Jason; and Nancy Mannigoe's trust in her ability to teach Temple to "believe" is modified, as we have seen, because she neglects to take race into account. Yet here as elsewhere, Faulkner removes himself from the narrative perspective; his "Craft and raw material are in such lucid balance," says Wright Morris in reference to *The Sound and the Fury*, "that it seems the craftsman himself is missing. We are *within* the picture; it seems no outside force had a hand in it." Faulkner's ideal as a functioning artist is simply to provide and juxtapose the necessary episodes; ideas renewed in patchwork, while the role of the artist remains, as Stephen Dedalus notes, "within or behind or beyond or above his handiwork, invisible, refined out of existence, indifferent, paring his fingernails."

Faulkner also shares with his predecessors in the fiction of consciousness an unfolding perspective: it is fundamental to his narrative poetics that the material which prompts visual thinking is relatively static while the narrative consciousness in its act of recording and integrating is in constant movement. "What I see and hear in the soar and thud of [Faulkner's] details," Alfred Kazin remarks, "is an effort to convey—not merely *to* the consciousness of a single mind but *along* the whole circuit of time and thought through which we move— that which *is* our life in all its presentness." In *The Unvanquished*, visual thinking grows before us as Bayard matures, much as the language and perceptual awareness deepen in *A Portrait of the Artist as a Young Man*. Chick's early bewilderment at his rescue and subsequent treatment by the black man Lucas after falling into the creek in *Intruder in the Dust* is pointedly differentiated from his later, more mature determination to dig up the Gowrie grave to ascertain Lucas's innocence of a white man's murder. The single, puzzled response to Lucas on the earlier occasion is likewise changed into a capacity for those multiple meanings he is able to bring to this later act, for the dust into which he intrudes is not just the dust of the ground and the dead, but the dust of history, of superstition, of prejudice, and of myth —all the dust that blurs and obscures our insight. This progressive perspective in Faulkner is accretive—by impressions—rather than causal by observation or chronological in time, additive in a way that allows us, by recurrence and selective emphasis, to anticipate, to understand, and finally to interpret and judge.

Our response is shared by Faulkner's characters themselves; they like to tell stories. Grandfather Priest sees his childhood as a kind of fable; Shreve requests a story from Quentin as Quentin received an account from his father; and Ike, when confronted by the commissary ledgers, attempts to decode them as a narrative. Some of Faulkner's narrators, like Old Bayard, Aunt Jenny, and Temple Stevens, are compulsive storytellers, and some novels, like *Sanctuary*, retell the same story: we have alternative versions of Temple's provocation and rape from Ruby, Lee, Horace, Temple, and Eustace Graham, Temple's lawyer. At times it is difficult, as it is with Ratliff in *Snopes*, to know when the storyteller is reporting events and when he is fabricating them. *Light in August* is one of Faulkner's most popular works in direct proportion to the relatively easy availability of its narrative consciousness; *A Fable* and *Absalom, Absalom!* have been, historically, the least accessible because the narrative consciousnesses there are multiple and unusually guarded.

But the progressive perspective in Faulkner, as we have seen in *A Fable* and *The Unvanquished*, is probationary: it stops at provisional truths. Habitually searching, it refuses to accept conclusive opinions but seeks to integrate contingent images and structures in the consciousness. Isaac's vision of the magnificent buck in "The Old People" chapter of *Go Down, Moses* is evanescent, fleeting; his incantatory experiences with Old Ben are transcendent; his recollections of the former hunts in the chapter "Delta Autumn" are deliberately nostalgic and incomplete: he refuses at each stage in his life as a hunter to assess with any finality the experience of the hunt or the significance of his quarry. Before Ratliff is tricked by Flem at the Grenier place and especially after his fool's hunt for gold, he is unwilling to predict the next movement of any Snopes; the tribe of young Snopeses that arrives from Texas at the close of *The Town* is essentially a metaphor for the inherent boundlessness of truth. Despite the progressively detailed conjectures of Quentin and Shreve and the hypotheses of Rosa and Mr. Compson, the final assessment of Thomas Sutpen lies beyond the boundaries of *Absalom, Absalom!*

The hesitation to limit the range of perceptual experience is both encouraged and discouraged by ritual, legend, and myth. Harry Wilbourne and the tall convict use the ready-made formulas of pulp fiction to define their lives and to trace their own relative success, but they are unwilling, finally, to recognize their own practice. Neither Aunt Jenny nor Narcissa Benbow is willing to subscribe to the Sartoris legend absolutely, but it is a useful index for them in appraising the actions of their ancestors and in assimilating the death of young John. Hightower is able to accept his grandfather's raid on the hen house by transforming it into an act of great bravery during a wartime mission, but in moments of illumination he knows that he has been able to live with his past only by lying about it, by avoiding it. It is this unfolding narrative vision, along with a passion to explain contingencies, that gives narrative consciousness in Faulkner its dynamic quality. "Our eyes [are] hypnotically fixed on the skein of plot as it unravels itself," as Simon Lesser puts it elsewhere, "on the moving tip of the story line." This progressive unfolding, which runs counter to Faulkner's arrangements of discrete episodes, provides his novels with their own inner energies and a dialectic of forces we, as readers, must resolve.

The narrative consciousness in Faulkner focuses first on images. "Things, it is true, are not complete without minds," Bosanquet reminds us, "but minds, again, are not complete without things." The primacy Faulkner awards to visual thinking suggests the intensity of experience as well as its shape. Visual thinking is essential to his narrative poetics, as the revisions in his holographs and typescripts repeatedly indicate. In the holograph of *As I Lay Dying*, for example, Darl describes seeing Jewel's horse as "a gaudy instance among the pines"; in the book, this has become "a gaudy instant among the blue shadows." In the holograph, Dewey Dell says, "I sit naked on the seat above the mules"; the book reads, "the unhurrying mules." Such revisions attempt not only to capture the angle of vision but to employ the special language of the particular narrative consciousness. In the holograph, Faulkner has pasted in this additional passage for Darl:

> For an instant it resists, as though volitional, as though within it her pole-thin body clings furiously, even though dead, to a sort of modesty, as she would have tried to conceal a soiled garment that she could not prevent her body soiling. Then it breaks free, rising as though the emancipation of her body had added lightness buoyancy to the boards or as though, seeing that the garment is about to be torn from her, she rushes suddenly after it in a passionate reversal of concealment. The reason lost in the compulsion of the need. Jewel's face goes completely green and I can hear teeth in his breath.

Moreover, the visual possibilities of Addie's coffin are heightened in the revisions in numerous places. In the holograph, Faulkner adds to Tull's monologue this description of the flood:

> It was nigh up to the levee on both sides, the earth hid except for the tongue of it we was on going out to the bridge and then down into the water, and except for knowing how the road and the bridge used to look, a fellow couldn't tell where

was the river and where the land. It was just a tangle of yellow and the levee not less wider than a knife-back kind of, with us setting in the wagon and on the horse and the mule.

Elsewhere Whitfield's language is also intensified. What reads "I won" in the holograph is published as "I emerged victorious"; "His holy love" becomes "His holy peace and love"; "for by those dangers and difficulties" becomes "for by those dangers and difficulties which I should have to surmount"; "I deceived" becomes " 'I betrayed' "; "let the tale come from my lips and not hers" becomes " 'let not the tale of mine and her transgression come from her lips instead of mine.' " Holograph 96 has Cash thinking, "So he stopped there like he knowed, before that little house" but the book changes the passage to "So he stopped there like he knowed, before that little new house, where the music was. We waited there, hearing it. I believe I could have dickered Suratt down to five dollars on that one of his. It's a comfortable thing, music is." Dewey Dell's language is made less similar to Darl's throughout, and a number of Christian overtones are added to monologues by Darl and Vardaman. In each instance, the change is toward perceptual consciousness, within the confines of the narrative angle of vision.

"An 'image,' " Gombrich writes, "is not an imitation of an object's external form, but an imitation of certain privileged or relevant aspects." For Faulkner, images are synedoches for the narrative consciousness which they help to define. There are the soap bubbles which characterize the beauty and vulnerability of antebellum life for Bayard as he looks backward on the first chapter of *The Unvanquished*, and—later, after his baptism in war—the mutilated hand of Grumby. The roadsign for New Hope which is registered in the consciousness of Dewey Dell not only comments on her own interest in the trip to Jefferson but reminds us of the real motivations for other members of the Bundren family who are making the arduous journey. The tube of toothpaste which Joe Christmas squeezes when he innocently eavesdrops on the dietitian's sexual encounter has later ramifications in scenes with Bobbie Allen and Joanna Burden and (for us, if not Joe) is finally correlated with his castration by a butcher knife at the hands of Percy Grimm. The smell of Lucas Beauchamp's house for Chick, the black man's food, and Chick's inability to recognize Molly in a picture because she is not wearing her headrag all remind us, at the outset of *Intruder in the Dust,* of the depth of Chick's racial consciousness. In *The Mansion,* Linda's gift to Gavin of a cigarette lighter engraved with both their initials—*GLS*—suggests the warmth of her feeling for him and her desire to be remembered by him after she leaves Jefferson. " 'It's by pictures, pictures . . . that one must get at you,' " says one of Dostoyevsky's characters.

Often Faulkner uses perceptual imagery to suggest the associations within the unconscious rather than in the conscious recognitions. We define the Sartorises initially in part by their house; we measure Sutpen's fate by the damage done to Sutpen's Hundred during the war, and mourn its final destruction by Clytie; we are able to judge Fonsiba ironically (although Isaac cannot at first) by her mean dwelling: "just a log cabin built by hand and no clever hand either, a meagre pile of clumsily-cut firewood sufficient for about one day." Temple's appearance in *Sanctuary*—first seen in a dancing dress, then in a Chinese smock, finally identified only by her cosmetics—helps us to trace her decline and her corruption. Byron Bunch aids us in identifying Hightower by personifying his canvas deck chair, "mended and faded and sagged so long to the shape of Hightower's body that even when empty it seems to hold still in ghostly embrace the owner's obese shapelessness; approaching, Byron thinks how the mute chair evocative of disuse and supineness and shabby remoteness from the world, is somehow the symbol and the being too of the man himself." When such possessions become consciously important and jealously guarded, the narrative consciousness works from another direction. There are Flem's restaurant, water tower, bank, and mansion, and Granny Millard's expanding horse pen, Boss Priest's car and the MacCullums' dogs, the coins Lucas saves to pay Gavin and Linda's foreign Jaguar. Most revealing of all are the images of other people rather than the realities themselves to which narrative consciousnesses cling: images of Caddy, Thomas Sutpen, and Lucius Quintus Carothers McCaslin— those characters in Faulkner whom we never seem to meet in the novels, except in the memories of others.

In such instances as these last, visual thinking in the Faulknerian narrative consciousness becomes metaphoric. The narcissus which Benjy carries not only suggests his essential self-centeredness, even when he thinks of Caddy, but, like the cornflower and jimson weed with which he is also associated, it is a superstitious sign of death. In *Sanctuary*, Popeye carries a pistol (a "sex-surrogate," Swiggart calls it), Horace carries a book, while our introduction to Ruby—"A woman stood at the stove. She wore a faded calico dress. About her naked ankles a worn pair of man's brogans, unlaced, flapped when she moved"—tells us of the drudgery of her labor, her poverty, and her dependence on others as well as her capacity to be satisfied with very little. (Later she will finger the chocolates Horace brings her in Jefferson, but she will not eat them.) The elaborately "flowered china" clock in Temple's room in Memphis is stopped at 10:30: the hour of college chapel and, at evening, of college dances. The oleanders which divide Harry's and Charlotte's beach cabin from the doctor's and which reappear at the hospital and the jail are poisonous evergreen bushes. The spotted horses from Texas—strange, uncontrollable, fantastic, yet always fascinating—become metaphors for the Snopeses themselves, just as Flem is mirrored at the last in a mansion which he reconstructs on the outside but which is rotting away within. Chains of such metaphors can become choric, as with the buzzards in As I Lay Dying, the bird call which is simultaneously a sign of life and a warning of death in A Fable, and Mink's various relationships to the land throughout Snopes. Such poetic images, Northrop Frye reminds us in his Anatomy of Criticism, "do not state or point to anything, but, by pointing to each other, they suggest or evoke the mood which informs." Donald Mahon's blindness is an ironic commentary on all the characters in Soldiers' Pay, just as the mosquitoes of Faulkner's second novel are the basic metaphor for the vicious, pointless, and disgusting behavior of Mrs. Maurier's guests aboard her yacht on Lake Ponchartrain.

The developing narrative consciousness in Faulkner proceeds by correlations of whole chains of such images as these. Uncle Buck and Uncle Buddy open Go Down, Moses with their deliberate analogy between their ritualistic hunts for the fox and for Tomey's Turl, insinuating a moral equivalency that becomes a central belief of the McCaslins throughout the remainder of the novel. In Knight's Gambit, Gavin Stevens moves from a relatively simple problem of deduction in which he comes to realize that crime is a matter of understanding human nature and that solving crime is less important than preventing it; the final chapter, "Knight's Gambit," conflates both the psychological and the moral lessons in the chess metaphor which Gavin and Chick use to describe their protection of Captain Gualdres and Melisandre Harriss before forcing the Captain's departure in order to save her. Our awareness of such correlations, often implicit in the novels and stories, helps us to understand the action. When in Flags in the Dust, for instance, we hear Virginius MacCallum question the need to buy a Christmas turkey since there is already so much food on hand—using almost precisely the words Old Bayard uses about Thanksgiving dinner just before Young Bayard accidentally kills him—we can see the efficient cause for Young Bayard's abrupt departure. Emily Grierson refuses to admit Colonel Sartoris's death in "A Rose for Emily," not because she wishes to avoid paying taxes but because in her mind his death is correlative to that of her father and of Homer Barron: and the death of the old order and of herself as well.

Such analogous perceptions lead to habitual behavior. Apparently Quentin has a strong memory of brushing Caddy when she falls into the branch, for he brushes Natalie's back and pauses to brush his teeth just before drowning himself, as if preparing to meet Caddy again. Quentin views his entire last day in creative analogies, the one between Caddy and the little Italian girl only the most explicit of them. Mink discloses his years of single-minded concentration on Flem's death and his opinion of his cousin when he plans the murder by ambush and with an archaic weapon: the act as performed is a counterpart to his killing of Jack Houston. The ability to analogize does not merely supply models of action, however. It can also lead to original and ingenious actions. Flem learns how to relate two things so that he may deal with them both at once: he arranges to rid himself of the Old Frenchman place as well as Henry Armstid and Ratliff with the same land-salting plan, and in exposing Montgomery Ward Snopes's parlor of pornography, he rids himself of a troublesome cousin, finds a way to keep Mink under observation at Parchman, and begins to form his public reputation as a leading citizen of Jefferson. In other instances, creative analogies are meant as implicit replies or reprimands, as when Mrs. Hines in showing warmth to Joe and to Lena's baby at their births tries to counteract and so compensate for the brutal treatment by her husband. The depth of human need for analogies in the formation of consciousness is made most forceful, though, when there is only incomplete correlation, as Joe Christmas and Temple Drake, Thomas Sutpen and Ike McCaslin learn to their own final ruin.

A particularly common method of creative analogy in Faulkner's narrative consciousness is doubling, in which characters reify themselves or portions of themselves in other characters, similar to the double in Dostoyevsky, or the secret sharer in Conrad. Otto Rank tells us that the double may project the character's narcissism or his wish fulfillment; or as a haunting presence from the past he may serve as an embodiment of guilt, shame, or envy, acting as a kind of conscience control. Ovid's Narcissus is an instance of doubling in its simplest forms: "Am I the lover / Or beloved?" he asks. This is the conception behind the numerous mirror images in The Marble Faun, Faulkner's early book of poetry—but it is also Quentin's silent question when he confronts Caddy and when, thinking of her still, he sees his own mirrored self in Dalton Ames or Julio or Gerald Bland. The relationship between Horace and Popeye in *Sanctuary* is first established when Horace sees Popeye's straw hat instead of his own face reflected in the natural spring at the old Frenchman place. It is Temple who keeps looking in a mirror in this novel, however, illustrating Rank's theory that the mirror often images both the libidinous desire and a death wish (as it does elsewhere with Benjy and Quentin). "Maeterlinck says: *If Socrates leave his house today he will find the sage seated on his doorsteps. If Judas go forth tonight it is to Judas his steps will tend,*" Stephen Dedalus recalls in *Ulysses*. "Every life is many days, day after day. We walk through ourselves, meeting robbers, ghosts, giants, old men, young men, wives, widows, brothers-in-love. But always meeting ourselves."

This sense of the other self often directs the narrative consciousness in Faulkner, as it does in Dostoyevsky, Melville, Conrad, and Proust. Jason and Caroline Compson facing each other across the dining table recognize their own deep similarities; so do Joe Christmas and Bobbie Allen across the counter of the restaurant, confessing their own guilt and their own sexual longings while believing, somehow, in their trapped innocence. Marthe sees in the corporal her own capacity to love and her own victimization by others who misunderstand her; Boon Hogganbeck finds a suitable companion for his journey into Non-Virtue in the eleven-year-old Lucius Priest. Temple Drake, "with her high delicate head and her bold painted mouth and soft chin, her eyes blankly right and left looking, cool, predatory, and discreet," sees an open resemblance in Popeye, to whom she is drawn as a kind of secret sharer. Emmy's conscious doubling of Donald Mahon as a boy and Januarius Jones as a man, permitting her to surrender to Jones at last, is one of the chief revelations of Emmy's character (as well as Mahon's) in *Soldiers' Pay*. Ike sees himself as the secret sharer of Sam Fathers, childlike and pure, but in repeating Sam's " 'Grandfather!' " to a snake rather than to the magnificent buck, and omitting the word "Oleh!," Ike betrays his own inner sense of fatality and unintentionally mocks Sam's earlier transcendent vision.

This secret selving as a form of wish fulfillment explains Quentin's strong attraction to Caddy; it also explains Harry Wilbourne's uncommon fascination for the young couple on the World War I hulk. Thomas Sutpen functions as a wish fulfillment for a number of characters in *Absalom, Absalom!* Henry sees him as patriarch, Charles as the means to self-respect, Wash as a sign of his own chance for advancement, Mr. Coldfield as a wise if immoral business investment, and Rosa (like Ellen) as the means for a marriage which advances the cherished values of the antebellum Southern culture. But here as elsewhere in Faulkner, intense doubling can lead to anxiety. The double can become a "love-hate object," Robert Rogers informs us, "the object of conflicting emotions so powerful that the unstable perceiver cannot tolerate the resultant anxiety. The perceiver attempts to dispel this anxiety by the magical gesture of separating the seemingly untidy whole into tidy compartments. Actuality is denied, a good-bad father becoming in the sublogic of the primary process the good, loved father and the bad, hated father." This psychological interpretation clarifies Rosa's demonic hatred alongside her intense admiration of Sutpen. Quentin's and Benjy's profoundly felt ambivalence toward Caddy shows how their own identities are essentially grounded in their view of her: she is both the faithful companion—the beloved—and the greatest possible loss—the chief threat. But they cannot rid themselves of thinking of her as their other self.

Furthermore, the sense of the secret self can become so powerful to the inner vision that the narrative consciousness is obsessed with annihilating it. Rank tells us that shadows and reflections in water and mirrors are ways in which the consciousness tries to destroy what it most cherishes and fears. Faulkner, who had heard some Freudian ideas by the mid-1920s, seems to have this in mind in charting Quentin's last day among shadows, the Charles River, and his projections of himself on the men and boys he meets and remembers. Even the secret sharer with whom the narrative consciousness may profess friendship on the surface can represent a bitter antagonist beneath conscious statement, as Rat Rittenmeyer hates Harry Wilbourne and as Darl fears and hates Jewel. The same relationship may exist between Thomas Sutpen and Charles Bon, if the reconstruction of them by Quentin and Shreve has merit; it is surely true of Mink Snopes and Jack Houston. Mink is drawn to destroy Houston not simply because of the extra pound fee for a month's feeding and pasturage of his cow, but because Houston so resembles Mink's hated self in his pride, his irascibility, his toughness—and in his subjection to a woman who, however admirable she may have been, consumes him in marriage. This secret selving in Faulkner is often decisive in the behavior of the narrative consciousness and often reinforces its actions: in hanging on to each other inside their rotting house, the Compsons cling to the several symbolic presences (in love and hate) which provide companionship in the irrevocable erosion of whatever claims to merit and stature they and their family once possessed.

Hume believed that the mind perceives no more than a composite of sense impressions; its only creative act, he said, is to juxtapose them. "Creation of this kind we practise every day," Percy Lubbock adds in *The Craft of Fiction*. "We are continually piecing together our fragmentary evidence about the people around us and moulding their images in thought. It is the way in which we make our world; partially, imperfectly, very much at haphazard, but still perpetually, everybody deals with his experience like an artist." Bayard Sartoris fashions his crucial responses because of his juxtaposition of Yankee courtesy and Confederate deceit. Anse Bundren's remarriage on the day of Addie's burial is prompted by his lifelong commitment to the forces of growth over the forces of decay. Much of the dramatic impact of the Jefferson scenes in *Sanctuary* is the juxtaposition, in Horace's mind, of the carelessness of Popeye and Temple on the one hand and Narcissa's lack of concern on the other; the dry rot of inhumanity which he comes to see as characteristic of his hometown ironically enervates him at the crucial moment in Lee Goodwin's trial. Rider is likewise enervated in *Go Down, Moses* when he discovers that whites and blacks treat him the same after Mannie's death as before: the world has not trembled nor graves yawned at the incomprehensible death of so central a force in his life. In comparing the commercial force of the plantation to that of the woods by juxtaposing the images of the ledger books and the railroad, Isaac McCaslin rejects two tainted landscapes only to learn, in later years, that he has left himself no suitable geography in which to continue living.

This juxtaposition of mental geographies is peculiarly strong in the narrative consciousness in Faulkner. The American backwoods freedom afforded the British groom in *A Fable* is sharply curtailed in wartime France, where he changes his position to that of a sentry; and his black companion, once the lay preacher and stablehand the Reverend Tobe Sutterfield, is likewise corrupted by the war, changing his name to "Monsieur Tooleyman" of the Association Les Amis Myriades et Anonymes à la France de Tout le Monde of Paris, his second, grander, but more institutionalized self. In *Intruder in the Dust*, Chick Mallison finds that his growth—his baptism, maturity, and awareness of last things—comes in the country; Jefferson images only stratification, and a kind of numbness and sterility, a stasis. Chick is drawn to the Gowrie grave not only to save Lucas Beauchamp, although that is his first conscious motive, but, finally, to save himself. "If William Faulkner is occasionally obscure, he is not willfully so," Coindreau remarks. "His complexities, whether of content or of form, are never gratuitous": the narrative consciousness in Faulkner, by its combinations and correlations of images, exposes in much of Faulkner's fiction the fundamental significations of his novels.

Faulkner's characters are first defined, then grow, by developing intricate conscious and unconscious relations between their inner and outer worlds. This takes most of their time, attention, and psychic energy, yet often the rewards are frustrating or sharply restrictive; often they reduce their spheres of choice and action, ending up confused, alone, and shut off from the main currents of life. They are unable or unwilling to reconcile their deepest needs in their restricted worlds. *Pylon*, while it lacks the inner density and resonance of many of Faulkner's novels and while it does not have the consistency of a singular presiding intelligence, is nevertheless illustrative of several of his methods of narrative consciousness.

The central perspective in *Pylon* is that of the reporter; he is the one who is able to draw the similarities between the opening celebration for Feinman Airport and the Mardi Gras of New Valois. The new airport, built on land reclaimed from Lake Rambaud, is named in honor of the chairman of the Sewage Board who is more interested in the profit motive than in human safety; its buildings and runways are modernistic and ugly, twisted by the needs of the planes and equipment and by the donor's desire to engrave his initial into the design wherever possible, both consequences of the dehumanization which characterizes the contemporary world in the reporter's consciousness. Yet the gold and purple pennons at the airport have their correlative in the gold and purple tinsel which transforms the noisy, mechanical, stinking city into a festival that mocks both pagan and Christian beliefs with its excessiveness and its excrement: the crepe streamers in New Valois read *inri* ("Jesus of Nazareth, King of the Jews"), an ironic allusion to Feinman himself. Fundamentally, it is the mechanical life that is common to both, Feinman Airport filled with its stunt planes which turn around metal pylons and New Valois directed by newspapers and clocks. The telephones and cars which connect both locations tie them together more securely. The reporter's dilemma is that from such a world corrupted by technology he is constantly urged by his editor Hagood to write stories of moving human interest.

Like most narrative consciousnesses in Faulkner, the reporter is
mirrored in the objects he perceives. He is not alien to this city, much
as he might wish to be. He depends on its gadgets, contributes to its
newspaper, lives on a street labeled "The Drowned," and drinks
absinthe, which is made from wormwood. But we know that he has
some pretensions to art from his apartment in the Vieux Carré (although we can also see that his taste is limited).

> It was a gaunt cavern roofed like a barn, with scuffed and worn
> and even rotted floorboards and scrofulous walls and cut into
> two uneven halves, bedroom and studio, by an old theatre cur-
> tain and cluttered with slovenly mended and useless tables
> draped with imitation batik bearing precarious lamps made of
> liquorbottles, and other objects of oxidised metal made for what
> original purpose no man knew, and hung with more batik and
> machine-made Indian blankets and indecipherable basrelief
> plaques vaguely religio-Italian primitive.

The reporter's insufficient appreciation of art is revealed more pointedly by Jiggs, his surrogate consciousness in the opening pages, whose
unrealistic desire is for riding boots which are lavishly displayed
rather than beautiful in themselves and which represent wealth rather
than utility, for he has no horse; he buys them without even trying
them on for size. Although the reporter and Jiggs are from different
worlds, they have striking similarities. Both are derelicts of humanity
whose labor causes machines to run, yet, while contributing to this
mechanical society, they profess close relationships to humanity, living
on borrowed money and dependent on others.

Because the reporter sees in the fliers the loneliness and tawdriness
that he wishes to escape, he does not like or admire them at first; he
sees them as robotlike; " 'they aint human like us.' " He makes the
plane, rather than the attractive Laverne or the young boy Jackie, the
center of their perverted, modern and mechanical life; he is quick to
image them as objects rather than as human beings, as Hagood might
have predicted he would. But the reporter is an example of the unfolding perspective in Faulkner. From the moment he begins to study
the fliers, the reporter finds his observations challenged. He feels
sexual attraction for the woman and to his surprise learns that she is
genuinely concerned about the safety of Jack Holmes during his free
fall; she is obviously in love with Roger Shumann; and she oversees
her boy (even though she does not know which of her lovers is his

father) by teaching him how to handle taunts from others. Moreover, the ability of the fliers to create a form of art within their machine-ridden environment, along with their insistence on a kind of independence, generosity, and freedom which sets them apart from modern society, attracts the reporter's admiration as well as his bewilderment, and he invites them to spend the night with him. Although his motives are mixed, for he hopes to make love with Laverne, the reporter shows us by his change of attitude, behavior, and language that the fliers are awakening their emotions in him. He sees them, though unconsciously at first, as secret selves.

The reporter has a reputation for gathering facts, but he is not skilled at understanding human psychology. He does not understand the dynamics of the group of fliers, and, ignorant of the fact that Holmes is threatened by Shumann's leadership, he is surprised when Jack turns him out of his own apartment. The next day, he avoids Jack and seeks out Roger as his secret self. The two men are instinctively friends, bonded by their seriousness, their professionalism, their concern for Laverne and the baby soon to be born, and their anxiety to win big money to provide for them. From the start it is a bad match; both the reporter and Roger are romantic and well intentioned, even courageous, but they lack sufficient mechanical knowledge and realistic self-appraisal. In their misguided attempt to show their concern for others, both become *un*professional; they arrange, at some illegality, for Roger to fly Ord's unsafe plane in the big race. As the reporter takes the fliers on a taxi ride nowhere, as he betrays them in getting their mechanic drunk, he is now a direct participant causing Roger's death. This scarecrow, this cadaverous corpse of a man has helped to create his own double in the corpse of the best flier of the group and the man he sees as his only friend. Ironically, neither makes the correlation to Roger's prototype, Lieut. Frank Burnham, described only the day before in the reporter's own newspaper as being burned alive, the air meet's first fatality.

But if Roger Shumann dies in an effort to provide for Laverne, Jack, Jackie, and the baby, he also inadvertently provides for the reporter. Awakened to a love of mankind which he finds impossible to bear, the reporter leaves three accounts of the death of his other self. The first is his initial attempt at poetry; the second, a turgid journalistic report; the third, his first openly confessional and autobiographical writing. The reporter has learned at last to give Hagood the humanity and warmth his employer has wanted, for it is Hagood, not Shumann, who we discover has—through cajolery, concern, and patience—been the reporter's real secret sharer all along. Because Hagood remains the living double who represents to the reporter his own guilt and short-comings, for Hagood is a generous man who has succeeded profession-ally in the world of New Valois, there is some doubt that the reporter will be able to return to this father figure whom he both hates and loves. But there is no doubt that he has moved beyond the contrived and the mocking which his world, until now, has stood for. *Pylon* concludes with its own balance of forces; the reporter with his newly found love for others has returned to the world of absinthe, but he has left behind a letter in an attempt to save himself, as he was not, in the end, able to save Shumann and the rest. The birth and growth of the human consciousness of a reporter forced to anonymity by his gadget-ridden culture is the theme—and the triumph and the tragedy—of *Pylon*.

Constitutive Consciousness

Faulkner's meanings come not simply in the narrative con-sciousness of one or more characters (such as Jiggs and the reporter, the Bundren family, or Quentin and Shreve) but in our *constitutive consciousness* as readers, the integrated sum of our awareness of the structure of the work and the perceptions of all the characters whose thoughts are explicitly or implicitly provided for us: the epistemologi-cal emphasis in Faulkner's narrative poetics is finally on the reader. Traditional omniscient narration is blended with stream of conscious-ness and multiple perspectives to allow for a wider range of visual thinking, correlation, and juxtaposition. The increased possibilities are what give to Faulkner's work its distinctive quality of seeming to be both inside and outside the characters, inside and outside events simultaneously. "Faulkner has the best of both worlds," François Pitavy observes;

> by amplifying all the vague, fleeting, latent, or forgotten thoughts of a character without being restrained by the latter's limited intelligence or consciousness, he gives the reader the impression that he participates in that character's life. He re-tains the emotional force of a subjective account while giving it the fullness and fluency of an objective one. Since a voice thus

modulated seems at once external and internal to the character, both emanating from him and enveloping him, a three-dimensional effect not unlike that of stereophonic sound is produced.

The key to this effect, produced in the constitutive consciousness, is the use of multiple perspective.

"It is customary to think that objective reality is dissolved by such relativity of terms as we get through the shifting of perspectives (the perception of one character in terms of many diverse characters)," Kenneth Burke tells us. "But on the contrary, it is by the approach through a variety of perspectives that we establish a character's reality." A helpful paradigm for the use and effect of multiple perspectives is supplied by Ortega.

A great man is dying. His wife is by his bedside. A doctor takes the dying man's pulse. In the background two more persons are discovered: a reporter who is present for professional reasons, and a painter whom mere chance has brought here. Wife, doctor, reporter, and painter witness one and the same event. Nonetheless, this identical event—a man's death—impresses each of them in a different way. So different indeed that the several aspects have hardly anything in common. What this scene means to the wife who is all grief has so little to do with what it means to the painter who looks on impassively that it seems doubtful whether the two can be said to be present at the same event.

It thus becomes clear that one and the same reality may split up into many diverse realities when it is beheld from different points of view. And we cannot help asking ourselves: Which of all these realities must then be regarded as the real and authentic one? The answer, no matter how we decide, cannot but be arbitrary. Any preference can be founded on caprice only. All these realities are equivalent, each being authentic for its corresponding point of view. All we can do is to classify the points of view and to determine which among them seems, in a practical way, most normal or most spontaneous. Thus we arrive at a conception of reality that is by no means absolute, but at least practical and normative. . . .

[Comparing the relationship of each to the event] enables us to speak in a clear and precise way of a scale of emotional distances between ourselves and reality. In this scale, the degree of closeness is equivalent to the degree of feeling participation; the degree of remoteness, on the other hand, marks the degree to which we have freed ourselves from the real event, thus objectifying it and turning it into a theme of pure observation. At one end of the scale the world—persons, things, situations— is given to us in the aspect of "lived" reality; at the other end we see everything in the aspect of "observed" reality.

This sense of real and conflicting claims to perceptual authority and received consciousness which Ortega describes is a sense of reality which was likewise shared by the Cubists. They too felt that a single, fixed point of view in painting distorted reality because it limited the painterly vision to a flat, two-dimensional plane. By breaking up the surface of the canvas into multiple planes and perspectives, they felt that they were adding a necessary third dimension. The Cubist use of planes instead of lines is similar to the panels of multiple narration in *As I Lay Dying*, where the use of lines would result in a single narrative development from a single angle of vision. This resemblance between Faulkner's method and that of the Cubists helps to explain his early interest in Cézanne and later Cubist painters through the work of Eric Faure, Clive Bell and others, and may help explain, too, why he lived only one short block from the Luxembourg Gallery when he stayed in Paris for a time in 1925.

Multiple perspective in literature is as old as the two stories of creation conflated in Genesis and for Faulkner as recent as the experimentation with it in such writers as Melville, Conrad, and Joyce. The technique serves as a prism which (1) invites the reader's involvement, active association with the characters, and judgment of them and events, while (2) it breaks the epiphany into radiating angles of vision, single colors, so that events and meanings can be better understood. Such a use of multiple perspective, and multiple narrative consciousnesses, conveys to us the loss of the Compsons, the significance of Addie Bundren's death, and the rebellion of the corporal. In *The Sound and the Fury*, the loss of Caddy, central to the perspectives of Benjy and Quentin, is used to establish her relationships with all the remaining Compsons in the last two chapters. In *As I Lay Dying*, the death of Addie, which threatens to remove the stability of the Bundren family, awakens in her husband and all her children—to varying degrees —their own recognitions of bitter isolation and their need for each other, and explains why the title of the novel is a dependent clause. In *A Fable* the corporal sees his relationship to the Old General as that of son to father, of servant to master—and of brother to brother in the greater community of mankind.

In Faulkner such "plurisignificant" and "multidimensional" narrative perspectives are a series of filters, whereas analogues are a series of mirrors. These multiple perspectives are used throughout the canon in various and subtle ways. In *Soldiers' Pay*, they lend to Margaret Powers a split consciousness, for she moves between her public and her private selves in her thinking. When she recalls privately the death of her husband while Mrs. Burney publicly mourns the death of the man who killed him, and when she confesses her past to Joe Gilligan in their hotel room in Cincinnati, she reveals a power of sympathy and a sense of guilt which are not exposed elsewhere. The private frustrations of Mrs. Maurier's guests in *Mosquitoes*—the lesbianism of Mrs. Wiseman, the impotence (and fetishism) of Mr. Talliaferro, the perverseness of Major Ayers, and the timidity of Miss Jameson—not only provide a range of visual thinking about life and love but correspond analogously to the artists whose more abstract ramblings in other portions of the novel suggest the bonds that tie together so seemingly disparate a group of people. In their separate driftings, Harry Wilbourne and the tall convict share a parallel sense of powerlessness and disintegration because they both lose direction and points of reference. In *Knight's Gambit*, it is the multiple perspectives of minor rather than major characters on Gavin Stevens—of Monk, Lonnie Grinnup, Jackson Fentry, and Joel Flint—that supply us with a greater reality about human nature by fragmenting it. But perhaps the most pervasive use of multiple perspective in Faulkner comes in his juxtaposition of past and present. It is the basis for the chief tensions in *Flags in the Dust*, *The Sound and the Fury*, *Absalom, Absalom!*, *Light in August*, and *The Unvanquished*—while in *Go Down, Moses* it so fractures the forces of human history and personal understanding through generations of mistrust and ignorance that neither the will of Ike McCaslin nor that of Gavin Stevens can find any means of reconciling them.

Faulkner's longest work, the trilogy *Snopes*, both within each volume that comprises it (*The Hamlet*, *The Town*, and *The Mansion*) and among them, carries multiple perspective into its greatest range. The outer tale of the trilogy as conceived by the omniscient and narrative consciousnesses is a study in acquisitiveness; the story of the Snopeses is the story of what each of them gets, whether he earns it fairly (as Eck does) or unfairly (like I. O.). From the beginning of Flem's rise,

symbolized by his winning Varner's business and house in Frenchman's Bend, until the end when he takes over the analogous De Spain
bank and mansion in Jefferson, we watch variations of greed at work.
It is by a mirroring accumulation of objects made images—the black-
smith shop, the restaurant, the power plant's brass, the mansion—that
the people of Frenchman's Bend and Jefferson measure Flem's success.
But their narrative perspectives are distinct from our constitutive consciousness, for they omit Flem's own implied sense of himself; and
what motivates him is respectability, not greed. Ever since his father
Ab was shot in the heel by Colonel Sartoris, Flem has wished (rather
like a latter-day Thomas Sutpen) to achieve the status of the man who
humiliated his father. His first attempt is to displace the aristocrat of
the hamlet where the Snopeses live, but this is insufficient—it is essentially not correlative. He sets his sights on Jefferson, the home of the
Sartorises. Although clever in the ways of business and determined to
get ahead, Flem suffers from one weakness, his sexual impotence. This
sense of impotence may be caused by his secret selving with Ab or
his single-mindedness to get ahead—it is never made clear—but,
robbed of human emotions (again like Sutpen, in Quentin's version
of him), he turns even this situation to his advantage. He in effect
cuckolds Hoake McCarron and (by humorous analogy) Will Varner to
win and marry Eula. His future acts are analogous: by threatening to
expose cuckoldry, he manages to steal brass from the power plant; by
cuckolding himself—a sure sign for our constitutive consciousness—
he succeeds Manfred De Spain in the presidency of the bank. Since
Colonel Sartoris is himself the president of the town's other bank and
the resident in the town's other mansion, Flem has achieved his ends.
The correlation his consciousness sought to establish has been effected,
although for us De Spain's breeding—his father sold the wilderness to
the railroad; he went to West Point—makes the comparison ironic.
But Flem is unaware of this. In *The Mansion*, therefore, we see a man
who is lackluster, inert, without purpose or desire. Flem, in using
others to achieve his end (including members of his own family), has
as his final reward not so much self-justification or even peace of mind
as loneliness of spirit. When Mink comes for him, seeking his *own*
vengeance, Flem is ready to die; his last act at the expense of his relatives is to cheat Mink and Linda of the right to cause his unwilling
death. Thus they, too, find their end achieved, their lives empty. After
Flem's death, Mink runs back to the earth he once knew and the deaf
Linda races away in her new Jaguar: both commit gestures of suicide

correlative to Flem's. Within its broadly conceived comic contours an inversion of *Absalom, Absalom!*, *Snopes* leads not to moral and psychological but to poetic justice.

Flem's movement through the landscape of Yoknapatawpha also provides us with a parallel perspective of the other inhabitants of the county. The interior story for our constitutive consciousness is in our juxtaposition of their visions of Flem, whom they use as a projection of their own inner selves: Flem proves to be the mirror of selfishness (not the yearning for self-respect) of the county generally. To distance themselves from their own possessiveness, however, the people in *The Hamlet* move from acts to words, from involvement in their own greed (such as Labove's desire to possess Eula) to their narratives (Labove's self-portraiture as a knight and as a distressed lover). Even the simplest of them, like Tull and Bookwright, turn to stories about the Snopeses; Frenchman's Bend strains toward explicit myth making. In *The Town* this tendency toward abstraction becomes more intellectual; it also becomes more obvious and more mannered. While Chick supplies the developing perspective customary in Faulkner, he is ranged on one side by Ratliff's instinctive hunches and second guesses and on the other by Gavin's contingent theories and scrupulous reexaminations (tempered by his concern for Linda). Caught in the middle, Chick sees Ratliff and Gavin use him to test, confirm, supplement, and compete with each other as secret sharers in their saga of Snopes-watching. Their narcissistic acts are largely displaced in *The Mansion*, however, when Linda and Mink join forces to act rather than to think. Before they meet, Linda fights in the Spanish Civil War, studies communism, and works at upgrading black schools, and Mink joins in a communal project of building a church: their acts of socialism indict Flem's more individualistic and selfish ends. These activities allow Linda and Mink to interpret their murder of Flem as an act of moral justice, but their deed is also vengeance made acceptable by rationalization, correlative to Flem's.

Faulkner's final irony, then, is that all the efforts of Flem, Linda, and Mink are to no avail: no one gives them self-respect in Jefferson, because it is not seen that that is what they want—and because self-respect must come, finally, from within. Even in those citizens of Yoknapatawpha County who mean most to be compassionate, thoughts displace feelings and narratives displace deeds. In their relative ignorance of one another, they too share a portion of Flem's loneliness: in *Snopes*, Faulkner demands that our constitutive consciousness penetrate the multiple perspectives of self-serving narrative consciousnesses at which time the fact of their shared loneliness is made startlingly clear.

We can guard against overreliance on the narrative consciousness in Faulkner by training our constitutive consciousness to attend to all the available perspectives and, beyond them, to acknowledge and integrate the greatest range of images, metaphors, analogues, and juxtapositions congruent with them and with the shape and structure of the work. In the matter of images—Josh's pipe or Mrs. Maurier's grapefruit in *Mosquitoes*, for instance—our constitutive consciousness must identify all the useful meanings not recognized explicitly in the narrative itself. Some are relatively obvious: when Horace Benbow describes his life with Belle as an endless series of Friday-afternoon errands after shrimp, he is ironically telling us more of himself than he is aware; when Harry and Charlotte hear the sound of the wind in the dry palms mocking the wind Harry's knife lets into her uterus, we are made aware of the *un*natural act of the abortion. The water tower in Jefferson with its hidden brass is as much a monument to Flem as is Eula's grave marker—and as much a symbol of the town as the statues of Colonel Sartoris in the cemetery and the Confederate soldier in the town square. When the prison camp in *A Fable* is described by the omniscient consciousness as having barbed wire that resembles Christmas tinsel, the approaching death of the corporal makes the reference sardonic—but it is a paradoxical reference, since the corporal's effect on the runner, the Quartermaster General, and even the sentry suggests that the spirit of Christ is also being reborn.

We have already seen Byron identify a deck chair with Hightower, but often we understand characters by acknowledging such associative images ourselves, as in the reporter's room in the Vieux Carré. Hightower's house is described to us as remote, unkempt, unobtrusive, something ignored by the town, a kind of mausoleum for the living. Lena is much like the wagon where we first find her—passive and peaceful, yet tired and dusty, always moving apparently without thought. The imprisoned Mink at Parchman represents a caged animal. Constitutive images often gather multiple meanings, as the planes do in *Pylon*. The bridge that is washed out in *As I Lay Dying* is also such an image, since the novel itself is about destroying and rebuilding bridges between people; still other constitutive images are water in *The Sound and the Fury*, the churches in *Intruder in the Dust*, and the car in *The Reivers*.

Occasionally, Faulkner's novels have extensive networks of images which are necessarily beyond the visual thinking of any character. In *Go Down, Moses*, the bed over which Lucas challenges Zack reminds him of home, of marriage, and of his absent wife Molly; Rider has the same associations of marriage and home in mind when he finds himself in jail with only a cot; ironically, Ike's cot in the "Delta Autumn" chapter seems to suit him, even when the mulatto makes an oblique reference to it in her discussion of love. *Absalom, Absalom!* has an elaborate network of banking and commercial imagery which suggests that human relationships are measurable and human dreams quantitative, but it also raises the problem of accountability; the image pattern in *The Hamlet* moves from fertility to sterility by the closing episodes. There is, finally, the overarching image or metaphor, such as Mahon's blindness in *Soldiers' Pay*, the insects in *Mosquitoes*, and the multiple meanings assigned to *confession* throughout the prose and drama of *Requiem for a Nun*.

In Faulkner's novels geography too is not so much an environment in which characters find themselves as a force with which they interact; an outgrowth of images in Faulkner's narrative poetics is the use of geography as metaphor. Significantly, all the characters in *Mosquitoes* are drawn to a yacht—"a nice thing, with her white, matronly hull and mahogany-and-brass superstructure"—that is called the *Nausikaa*. The three separate geographies in *Sanctuary* help us to locate the values of certain characters and to trace Temple's fate; we watch her move from the open and natural environment at the Old Frenchman place to the corrupt and openly criminal underworld of Memphis and then to Jefferson, which is, because of its hypocrisy, the most corrupt and dangerous place of all. Joe Christmas's biography in three distinct locales—the scenes of childhood, the town of white Jefferson, and Freedman's Town—allows our constitutive consciousness to isolate the common factors and so more clearly define his problems of self-identity. *Go Down, Moses* generally admits of a diptych, the plantation (including the commissary) and the woods (the land of the hunt), with a coda in Jefferson suggesting that the hunt of men as animals first portrayed in chapter 1 ("Was") has not ceased in the present time of chapter 7 ("Go Down, Moses"). Within this broader set of comparative values, Ike McCaslin suffers a serial diminishment: he moves in the trilogy of chapters in which he is the chief character ("The Old People"; "The Bear"; "Delta Autumn") from the big, boundless woods to the bounded plantation, to a rented room in Jefferson to the cramped front seat of a truck and his cot in a shared tent. We can expect that nearly any place in Faulkner will sooner or later take on metaphoric values that instruct our constitutive consciousness; for Yoknapatawpha County, even the North, Chick Mallison tells us, is not "a geographical place but an emotional idea, a condition of which he had fed from his mother's milk to be ever and constant on the alert not at all to fear and not actually anymore to hate but just—a little wearily sometimes and sometimes even with tongue in cheek—to defy."

Whereas analogous persons or events better enable a developing consciousness to reach self-definition in Faulkner, the reader's constitutive consciousness uses analogues which surpass the character's limited understanding of himself. In *Flags in the Dust*, the fact that the names of Isom and Simon are nearly anagrams of each other reinforces the confusion of Bayards and Johns in alternating generations, and the generations, we find, tend to meld together: the important thing is to be a Sartoris. Each of the three Compson brothers— Benjy, Quentin, and Jason—wants to impose on his sister Caddy, for his own selfish purpose, a different yet confining pattern of behavior, making of her a mother, a virgin, and a housekeeper. In *Sanctuary* Miss Reba's pride in her house and her social position is correlative to Narcissa's, just as the conversation of Miss Reba and her friends in the Memphis brothel is openly analogous to the conversation of the Baptist ladies in Jefferson. Harry should have some premonitions about Charlotte's concern for him when he observes the ease with which she leaves Rat and the children, but our constitutive consciousness is further warned when her comment to Harry concerning her family foreshadows what we know, from chapter 1, will also be the conclusion of their affair: " 'It's not finished. It will have to be cut,' " she tells Harry. " ' "If thine eye offend thee, pluck it out, lad, and be whole." That's it. Whole. Wholly lost—something. I've got to cut it.' " But such analogues also provide information on a developing consciousness. On his way to kill Flem, Mink is not given the money he expects from Mrs. Holcomb: he is confronted with a situation analogous to his being cheated, thirty-eight years earlier, by Houston, but he will not now rob Goodyhay for it as he had robbed Jack Houston; his single-mindedness on revenging himself on his cousin cleanses him and allows, though with severe limitations, a kind of moral advance. But analogues enable Faulkner to communicate directly to us over as well as through his characters in order to establish or emphasize his meanings. We are to recognize, for instance, that Sydney Herbert Head's repulsive language and behavior in chapter 2 of *The Sound and the Fury* is correlative to Jason's in chapters 3 and 4. The cigarettes which Popeye is always smoking are a direct link to his arsonist grandmother, but they link him, too, to Temple (whose body is always "on fire") and to Lee Goodwin's savage assassination by a lynch mob; the analogous imagings of fire thus tie together the sources of violence in *Sanctuary*. Such analogues also underline central themes; Judith Sutpen hands Charles Bon's letter over to Mr. Compson for the same reason Rosa calls on Quentin—to " 'have the marble [of time] scratched.' " Uncle Buck and Uncle Buddy redefine the debt they owe to their black relatives in *Go Down, Moses*—what matters is *their* truth, not *the* truth—but Aunt Mollie reverses this resorting to cash payments when she demands her version of a proper human burial for Butch from Gavin Stevens and the other white citizens of Jefferson. An analogue alone provides a grimmer conclusion for *The Hamlet* than it might otherwise have. Riding by the frantic Henry Armstid on his final departure for Jefferson, Flem leaves, with wife and baby, as the serene conqueror at last of all Frenchman's Bend. Across the fence, Mrs. Armstid is making her way with lunch for her husband. The two families thus juxtaposed suggest a hollowness in each, a certain loss beyond recall, a death-in-life. We have seen how analogues provide extensive parallel and counterpoint in *The Wild Palms*. The same technique is repeated in *A Fable*. The mob which comes to scorn those who would save it in the opening and closing scenes of that novel are offset by the two groups of thirteen men—the corporal and his squad who temporarily halt the war at the outset of their Passion Week and Sergeant Landry and his twelve men, who seek a body for the Tomb of the Unknown Soldier, who would again elevate the dignity of man in the closing episodes. In both instances, however, the mob has nearly the last word. Although it gives bread to Marthe in the opening scene, it maims the runner at the end.

Our constitutive consciousness also replicates the narrative consciousness in locating and understanding through doubles with this distinction: our doubling tends to be objective, while the doubling accomplished by the narrative consciousness usually reveals self-pride, self-delusion, or ignorance. We can see that Old Bayard and Young Bayard are twinned, that they rightly share the same name in *Flags in the Dust*. Young Bayard's homecoming, furthermore, is commented on by the homecomings of Caspey and Horace, who serve briefly as other doubles for Young Bayard in our reading of the novel. In *Sanctuary*, Horace is implicitly mocked by the people on the train as he goes to Ole Miss in search of Temple; Ruby is explicitly mocked by the church-women and citizenry of Jefferson. We are to see both of them as out-casts and as just and loving people unable to save Lee Goodwin or what they believe in. In the sequel, *Requiem for a Nun*, Cecelia Farmer is as imprisoned by her frustrations as Nancy Mannigoe is by her knowl-edge. One of Joe Christmas's doubles in *Light in August* is Gail High-tower. Both men search the past for their identity, and both men feel more at home there than in the present; both are to blame for the deaths of the women for whom they feel most responsible; and their secret selving blends in their joint process of realization and acceptance of death within hours of one another, deaths that they seem to will for themselves—one in brutal and violent murder, the other in a vision of the present which, at last, the trampling hoofs of the past beat to the ground with the force of finality. In *The Hamlet*, Ratliff's celibacy links him to Flem long before he falls victim to the land salting of the Old Frenchman place, while Eula—relatively passionless, yet arousing a passion to possess in others—shares these characteristics with Flem, causing their marriage to be in some ways predictable and fitting. Eula's subsequent suicide in *The Town* prefigures Flem's resignation to death in *The Mansion*, for both of them experience the demoral-izing, depersonalizing effects of their particular forms of pride and rapacity. And David Levine commits suicide when he loses his protec-tive sense of war's glory in *A Fable* while the priest falls on a sentry's bayonet after advising the corporal not to insist on peace; the larger institutions which they serve, the military and the church, neverthe-less (analogously) survive untouched.

"The twentieth century has addressed itself to arts of juxtaposition as opposed to earlier arts of *transition*," Roger Shattuck writes. As we have seen, the juxtaposed episodes in Faulkner's novels work dis-continuously but provide us with a sustained way of seeing. Plots are juxtaposed in *The Wild Palms* and *Snopes*, generations are juxtaposed in *Flags in the Dust* and *The Unvanquished*, members of the same family are juxtaposed in *The Sound and the Fury* and *As I Lay Dying*, past and present are juxtaposed in *Absalom, Absalom!* and *Requiem for a Nun*, races are juxtaposed in *Go Down, Moses* and *Intruder in the Dust*, and actions and words are juxtaposed in *Pylon* and *A Fable*:

the panels of experience in which Faulkner structures his novels suggest that for him this is the fundamental way in which his style and visions are made inseparable.

The broadest juxtapositions are between the titles of novels and the works themselves; we have already seen how *As I Lay Dying*, as a title, reflects a dialectic fundamental to that novel and how the title *Requiem for a Nun* is both paradoxical and ironic. The titles for *Mosquitoes, Sanctuary*, and *Pylon* elevate obvious images of visual thinking to the demands of metaphor on our constitutive consciousness. *Soldiers' Pay* refers not only to Donald Mahon's maimed body but to Joe Gilligan's maimed spirit, both victims of World War I. Much has been written about the appropriateness of the Shakespearean soliloquy from which the title for *The Sound and the Fury* is drawn, but we will also find the context instructive: Macbeth grieves because a messenger has just told him that his queen is dead. The Old Testament story of David and Absalom is part of a larger attempt to trace a lineage for Christ, to locate the dynasty that will produce a Messiah; the title of *Absalom, Absalom!* is what our constitutive consciousness must finally correlate with Shreve's sardonic summation that in a few thousand years the Jim Bonds will rule the Western Hemisphere.

But juxtaposition is also important within each of Faulkner's twenty novels. Horace's innocence in *Sanctuary* alongside Narcissa's demand for respectability gives the novel a sense of paralysis. *The Hamlet* proposes through juxtaposition the similarity of the courtroom scenes and the scenes of bartering, as if law were a matter of horse trading and bartering were always a matter of sticking to the rules. In the story "Red Leaves," Faulkner supplies an early and condensed version of a juxtaposition seen throughout his work. A black slave who has run thirty miles at the age of forty to avoid a ritual death is confronted at last by a "burgherlike" Indian. They sum the two cultures of Faulkner's fictional South, the slaves and the rulers, in a harsh indictment of the latter: "They were both on a footlog across a slough —the Negro gaunt, lean, hard, tireless and desperate; the Indian thick, soft-looking, the apparent embodiment of the ultimate and the supreme reluctance and inertia." Over a century later, Rider shows us in *Go Down, Moses* that the situation has not changed in Yoknapatawpha; his own frustrations undercut the meager attempts of the white McCaslins to buy off the good will of the blacks and anticipate Gavin's naive gesture of charity. Nor have matters improved in *Requiem for a Nun:* by juxtaposing Nancy in the Jefferson jail and

Temple before the governor in Jackson, Mississippi, both pleading for clemency for a black who would lay down her life for a white, Faulkner suggests that Yoknapatawpha County remains unwilling—perhaps incapable—of confronting and so judging itself. In such a world, understanding by means of the constitutive consciousness is both necessary and inevitable.

"Memory believes before knowing remembers": *Light in August* is explicitly concerned with the problems of narrative and constitutive consciousness. The emphasis on perception is realized throughout the novel in the relatively high frequency of the verbs of visual thinking (*look; see; watch*); at one point, *look* and *watch* appear fourteen times in two pages. The interrelationship of these three means of understanding—observation or knowledge, belief, and memory—connects the three fairly disparate stories of Joanna Burden and Joe Christmas, Gail Hightower, and Lena Grove and Byron Bunch, but because of the multiple perspectives in which the novel is presented, our constitutive consciousness must finally locate the important analogues and juxtapositions and so make of the work an integrated fictive structure.

Joe Christmas supplies the central narrative consciousness in the long middle section of the book, where in third person his life is recounted from his perspective. Joe envisions his problem as one of race, sin, and sexual relations in a region where all three are necessary means of identification. The man in the orphanage has told him he did not know who he was, and the problem troubles him. Joe's foster parents seem to differ on the matter; Mr. McEachern punishes him cruelly as if he were guilty of some religious or sexual sin of thought or deed, or as if (for Joe) he were black as the man in the orphanage claimed; Mrs. McEachern treats him sympathetically, as if he had committed no sin at all (as if he were white). Their radically differing behaviors recall to him the attitudes of the dietitian and matron in the orphanage (as well as the janitor and Alice), and he grows up tense and confused. When he leaves home, he dedicates himself to finding further knowledge which will coincide with his racial and religious beliefs and his childhood memories and thus substantiate a clearer self-definition. But his consciousness of his life is so highly selective and so patterned by analogous people and situations that it seems to rely more on memory's ordering and the anticipation of beliefs than on the discontinuous facts of experience: his life reinforces his confusion because he insists on seeing it as a series of repetitious and self-fulfilling observations and events.

When he arrives in Jefferson, Joe meets Joanna Burden, and he senses in her another person, like himself, who is troubled by self-identity. Outward similarities reinforce their instinctive relationship; they are conscious secret sharers, as their names indicate to us. Both are obsessed with the problem of the black race, both have a deep sense of sin and suffering, and both are sexually masochistic. Beneath this conscious sharing, however, Joanna appeals to Joe's analogizing unconsciousness because she coalesces for him, for the first time, disparate, fracturing events and people of his past—she represents *both* Mrs. McEachern and Bobbie Allen. He responds so habitually to this awareness that he fails to recognize that he has caused Joanna's crisis by awakening sexual responses that she cannot correlate with her Calvinist upbringing. At first, this does not matter. They share a belief in life as a form of continual punishment and they seek the grace of self-respect by insisting on their own guilty actions; the relationship takes the form of an encapsulated but obsessive catechism. They are both the persecutors and the persecuted; their social and sexual roles become interchangeable. Yet the dynamics of their partnership require them to be both mirror images for each other *and* each other's opposing self. They are not only doubling but complementing secret selves—they use each other to satisfy basic longings, she for a black man to serve and he for a strong moral authority. The conflict between this conscious doubling and unconscious manipulation is too unstable to last. Moreover, Joe needs to know his racial and sexual identity, and the fluidity of his relationship with Joanna prevents such certain knowledge. Paradoxically, when she makes him a black man for her own sexual and religious gratification, she reinforces his memory and belief but robs him of the possibility of gaining new knowledge of himself. By requiring that Joanna remain his moral judge, he in turn robs her of the freedom of her newly acquired sexual release. Unable to make their secret other selves coincide with their conscious needs and demands, they bury their efforts in increased (and increasingly anxious) sexual activity.

Unlike Joe and Joanna, Gail Hightower does not wish to know himself; his biography is not revealed to us until well after that of Percy Grimm. Instead, Hightower loses himself by resurrecting his grandfather in memory and belief as an active new self, thereby dismissing any need to find an alternative, modern identity. Hightower's act restores the perspective to history and to past heroism which he believes is most just. It also provides him a way to suppress his hatred of his father and the fact of his own failed marriage. He joins his own private needs with his public vocation by preaching his faith in Confederate heroism, but his memory and belief are so clearly disjunctive to the needs of his wife and of his parish as they know them that he drives both from him. When his wife commits suicide and his church dismisses him, he retires to a small house at the edge of town to recover the past in a series of willed visions and imaginings. But he, too, is troubled, because his isolation also leads to a renewed self-examination brought on first by Byron, who keeps him informed of current changing events, and finally by Joe's self-confrontation (and Percy's) at Joe's death. Hightower's discomfort is aggravated by his knowledge that for him the final consequence of his memory and belief was *self*-alienation from God; even as a preacher, he senses he was "a figure antic as a showman, a little wild: a charlatan preaching worse than heresy." His life is further interrupted when he is asked to deliver babies—first a black baby and, later, Lena's.

This is the point at which our constitutive consciousness can make Joanna, Joe, Hightower, and Lena correlative. It is the pressure of present knowledge which finally breaks the hold of past memory and belief on each of them. In the instances of Joanna and Joe, Joanna's menopause ends her sexual activity; she is confronted by the fact of her sinful relationship with Joe and unable to take any further joy in it. Because she still feels herself his partner, she suggests a joint act of suicide as just punishment for them both, but her plan supplies Joe's consciousness with all that he has come to fear as well as need—moral authority, a strong woman, and fervent prayer. He responds to her as he responded to Mr. McEachern and as he wished to respond to Bobbie Allen's allies: he attacks her, with a razor, after her gun misfires, one last ironic analogy to the sexual encounters which had held them together. But he does not kill himself; instead, he takes flight once more in search of his identity.

Joe's earlier inquiry had taken him in a wide arc to Chicago and back; this time his circular journey is confined to Yoknapatawpha County and to nearby Mottstown. But the outer map of his travels resembles his inner consciousness; although the events at the black home, the church, and along the roadside encapsulate all the motifs of his earlier biography, his route remains formless and apparently aimless, his movements confused, blurred, and unassimilated. Yet his struggling consciousness does manage to reify the past once more. In entering a black church he shouts the dangers of sin, replicating Doc Hines; in seeking black food, he receives a meal similar to those Mrs. McEachern provided; and in surrendering at last in Mottstown, he acknowledges the necessity for a second Mr. McEachern to punish him as he deserves. All actions have also called forth responses to Joe that remind him of Joanna Burden: he is caught in the swirls of his own circling consciousness. Joe's last willful act calls up an image of Joanna too: he wills forth another secret self in Percy Grimm. Grimm was born too late to serve in World War I; like Joe, he needs to find a means of self-definition. His racial memory and his belief in heroism as a matter of law and order overcome his knowledge—that Joe is guilty on hearsay evidence only and does not necessarily appear to be black—and he moves to punish Joe as Joanna would have done and as Joe now desires. Joanna had figuratively emasculated Joe; Percy Grimm does so physically. But in the course of his being maimed, Joe becomes the black cross shadowing the land that Nathaniel Burden had predicted would fall over the South. Joe's final actions of the present thus serve primarily to confirm and secure the beliefs and memories from Yoknapatawpha's past.

Hightower's reveries are also interrupted by a forced knowledge of the present problems facing Lena and Joe. Both appeal to Hightower's beliefs in the impoverishment of man's condition and in the beauties offered by acts of heroism. Unaccustomed to public and present action, he nevertheless deliver's Lena's child and attempts to save Joe's life by supplying him with an alibi for the time of Joanna's death. Although Hightower succeeds with Lena, he is ineffectual in Joe's behalf and he retreats again from the present. He refuses to inquire after the truth; like the town of Jefferson, he is content with the account of Grimm and the imaginative rationalizations of Gavin Stevens, both analogously blending a few facts comfortably with the racial and regional prejudices—the beliefs and memories—of Yoknapatawpha. By accepting these stories, Hightower is able to return to his reverie, melding the people of the present back into the heroic past of his Confederate grandfather's raid. Hightower's situation is potentially analogous to the situations of Joe and Joanna, but he asks and risks less; he does not, until his final vision, challenge the beliefs of the town and the town does not bother him. In counterpoint to these three, Lena and Byron always manage to work contentedly within the strictures of the community. The values of Jefferson, in fact, are what they hold and emulate, Lena in locating the father of her baby and Byron in trying to provide responsible care for Lena and the child. Lena is never self-conscious; Byron has never wished to be disagreeable or learned to be especially curious. By ignoring or subordinating whatever is incongruent with the predispositions of their culture—such as

Hightower's defrocking and Lucas's betrayal of Lena and Joe—they are able to leave peaceably. For them memory, belief, and knowledge are correlative.

Light in August concludes with the report of the furniture dealer. Like Percy Grimm, he enters the novel late; but also like Percy he is not new, only a reification of what has gone before, and hence, for us, part of an integrated work. Like Byron, Hightower, Gavin, Joe, and Joanna, the furniture dealer is a compulsive storyteller. Ironically enough, he tells his story to his wife in bed, and he speaks of Byron and Lena, not Joe and Joanna. Even so, he informs our constitutive consciousness by embellishing what he knows just as Percy Grimm and Gavin Stevens do. The furniture dealer construes things according to his beliefs about men and women and about love generally. He does not know that Lena and Byron will have more children, but he believes that they will. His story is a self-fulfilling prophecy, a self-projection rather than simply an observed account. It is also erroneous, since Byron is not (as the furniture dealer assumes) the father of Lena's baby. This too makes Byron's story analogous to Grimm's and Gavin's stories—and to Joe Christmas's perceived biography as well. Moreover, all four stories, like Joanna's narrative of the black shadow and Hightower's visionary wheel, remain circular; all image their ends in their beginnings. Movement in Light in August, no matter how energetic or intense, seems to our constitutive consciousness to become a standing-still. Yet it could hardly have been otherwise: the very proposition that "Memory believes before knowing remembers" is circular. In attesting to the power of belief and memory, Light in August places the residual power of narrative consciousness in cultural attitudes— in the patterns of religion, sex, and race in Yoknapatawpha—which absorb the present but are not transformed by it. Certain insistent questions in the novel are never finally answered: does Joe have black blood? did he kill McEachern? did he kill Joanna, or did Lucas Burch? why did Joe escape when he agreed with the sheriff to plead guilty, and why did he choose to run to Hightower's house? These are the questions that call for factual answers; they are thus beyond the province of this novel. What Light in August finally tells us—all that Light in August finally tells us—is what is known to belief and memory, what is known to the regional consciousness on which it always, ultimately, rests. This is why the multiple perspectives it contains, implicitly and explicitly, correlate with each other and blend into the omniscient perspective so well: as Cleanth Brooks has remarked, Light in August is a profoundly Yoknapatawphan tale, and this most detached observation—which sums the characters and events as analogously regional by moving outward past Percy Grimm and the furniture dealer—can only arise in our constitutive consciousness.

Conclusion

" 'I don't claim that words have life in themselves,' " Dawson Fairchild, the character based on Sherwood Anderson, remarks in *Mosquitoes*. " 'But words brought into a happy conjunction produce something that lives, just as soil and climate and an acorn in proper conjunction will produce a tree.' " Words themselves can be clumsy, opaque, recalcitrant; they are often poorly or wrongly used; they resist the hallucinatory vividness of life which we wish them to have. They are "defaced," as Conrad puts it, "by ages of careless usage," their capacity seriously impaired. They are, at best, an imperfect medium. This, or something very nearly like it, seems to be a basis for Faulkner's narrative poetics, for instead of relying on words alone, he relies on the configuration of language, his narrative consciousness formulating life in the ways our integrating and structuring minds, our constitutive consciousnesses, wish to perceive life, to create and re-create it. Faulkner conveys his people through perceptual screens, full of mistakes, prejudices, self-projections and dreams. They present us with developing ideas and possible alternatives, as perceivers caught in the act of visual thinking. "The woman had never seen him but once," we are told in *Light in August*, for example, "but perhaps she remembered him, or perhaps his appearance now was enough."

In supplying material to our constitutive consciousness, Faulkner's narrative consciousness does not, in the end, *tell* so much as *intimate*. The choice of material, the angle from which it is seen, its inherent correlations and obvious juxtapositions with other observations it images—these are the ways Faulkner uses visual thinking to help him transcend the limitations of language. Even Byron Bunch has some inkling of such a possibility. *"It was like me, and her, and all the other folks that I had to get mixed up in it,"* he says in *Light in August*, *"were just a lot of words that never even stood for anything, were not even us, while all the time what was us was going on and going on without even missing the lack of words."* This is why Warren Beck can claim that in Faulkner's style "with its epithets, its alternative speculations, its multifariously detailed imagery, and its juxtaposition of the sharply factual and the fantastic, there is nevertheless the opposite of any pretense to complete comprehension and definitiveness, but rather the hint, by extensions that fade out like searchlights into space, as to the only partially penetratable mysteries of being and conduct." The sudden awareness of self, the epiphanies in Faulkner, as in Dostoyevsky, Joyce, and Proust, are to be our epiphanies as much as anyone's; we shall, in the end, manage our own estates. Yet even here Faulkner may also be indebted to the French novelists he admired as much as the English, for it is Stendhal who tells us that "Un roman est comme un archet; la caisse du violon qui rend les sons, c'est l'âme du lecteur": the novel is the bow, but the reader is the violin.

Style as Vision: Accomplishment

Forms in art arise from the impact of idea upon material, or the impinging of mind upon material. They stem out of the human wish to formulate ideas, to recreate them into entities, so that meanings will not depart fitfully as they do from the mind, so that thinking and belief and attitudes may endure as actual things.—BEN SHAHN

What I want to do in writing novels is very much what you want to do when you play the piano, I expect. We want to find out what's behind things, don't we?—Look at the lights down there scattered about anyhow. Things I feel come to me like lights.... I want to combine them.... Have you ever seen fireworks that make figures?... I want to make figures.
—VIRGINIA WOOLF

There are two worlds of art: the realm of *design* and the realm of *experience*, universes whose reciprocal action is as inexplicable as it is certain.
—RAYMOND BAYER

The aim of every artist is to arrest motion, which is life, by artificial means and it fixed so that 100 years later when a stranger looks at it, it moves again since it is life.—FAULKNER

"THERE IS A RIDGE," Gavin Stevens tells us in *The Town:*

you drive on beyond Seminary Hill and in time you come upon it: a mild unhurried farm road presently mounting to cross the ridge and on to join the main highway leading from Jefferson to the world. And now, looking back and down, you see all Yoknapatawpha in the dying last of day beneath you.... First is Jefferson, the center, radiating weakly its puny glow into space; beyond it, enclosing it, spreads the County, tied by the diverging roads to that center as is the rim to the hub by its spokes, yourself detached as God Himself for this moment above the cradle of your nativity and of the men and women who made you, the record and chronicle of your native land proffered for your perusal in ring by concentric ring like the ripples on living water above the dreamless slumber of your past; you to preside unanguished and immune above this miniature of man's passions and hopes and disasters.

Gavin's perspective of Yoknapatawpha from the ridge is vital if he is to make sense of Flem Snopes and the rest of Jefferson; below in the city, Gavin is too prone to the unthinking traditions that caused him to attack Manfred de Spain at the Christmas Cotillion and too vulnerable to the instincts that urge him to protect Linda from Eula's adultery, while at a greater remove, such as his two-year residence in Heidelberg, he is too remote from those forces—"all here, supine beneath you, stratified and superposed, osseous and durable with the frail dust and the phantoms"—to re-cognize life and so come to terms with himself. This mediate point, on the ridge, is where light gathers, "pooling for an unmoving moment yet," where the "earth itself is luminous."

Such distancing is essential too for us, a necessary act of our constitutive consciousness. The density of Faulkner's own vision—like the rich texture of his style—is the consequence of nearly four decades' labor, in which he wrote twenty novels and nearly a hundred short stories concentrating on his "little postage stamp of native soil" below the ridge. Sixteen of his twenty novels are placed there and many of his characters—some 1,309 of them in the novels alone—are based on people he knew or heard about in Oxford, Mississippi, while some of the events, such as the idiot Benjy waiting behind an iron fence for schoolgirls to return home or the burning of Jefferson as Cecelia Farmer watches from the jailhouse window, are founded on his own observations or on historical occurrences. Faulkner transplants his grandfather's monument in Ripley to Jefferson as Colonel Sartoris's gravemarker, while his grandmother's stone is transformed into a memorial for Eula Varner Snopes. Such details accumulate, compact and resonant; the "plurisignificance" of Byron's description of Joe Christmas' arrival at the sawmill which we studied at the outset is replicated again and again: in the meetings of Harry and Charlotte, the Old General and the corporal, and Lucas and Chick; in the descriptions of Miss Rosa's office, the reporter's room in the Vieux Carré, and the McCaslin commissary; in the thoughts (of events both imagined and real) of Bayard, Temple, and Mink. We need such details for only in our recombinations of such data can we, through our constitutive consciousness, arrive at the designed meanings of Faulkner's novels. We too must climb as Gavin does, moving away from the close view we have taken until now so that, at the last, we discover the wider significations each novel intends. In tracing Faulkner's style back to his vision, we must always accommodate those words and observations that, through corresponding images and scenes, through juxtapositions, doublings, and analogues, lead to the larger meanings we find in each work. Yet we must also realize that such readings are still limited, like the narrative consciousnesses of which they are composed, to the partial, the provisional. Gavin himself knows that also: he concludes his meditation from the ridge by noting that life is "inconclusive and inconcludable, in order to be life." We shall see that vision too embraced and affirmed in Faulkner's major novels as we have already witnessed in our more distanced views of *Snopes* and of *Light in August*.

"Flags in the Dust"

Flags in the Dust, Faulkner's least known major work, is concerned (as Joyce is) with studying the effect of the dead upon the living; it opens and closes in a family atmosphere heavy with death. The peculiar moribund state of the Sartorises is emphasized early in the initial description of their house.

> The white simplicity of it dreamed unbroken amid its ancient sunshot trees. Wistaria mounting one end of the veranda had bloomed and fallen, and a faint drift of shattered petals lay palely about the dark roots of it and about the roots of a rose trained onto the same frame. The rose was slowly but steadily killing the other vine.

Whatever tender beauty lingers here is overshadowed by an inevitable process of decay and death, and the exterior of the Sartoris house has its correlations within: to the walls of Young Bayard's room which hold memories of Caroline Sartoris "like a withered flower in a casket"; to the attic trunk where Old Bayard digs forth a derringer which resembles "a cold and deadly insect between two flowers" alongside the family Bible of recorded births and deaths, "a fitting place for dead Sartorises to gather"; and to the main parlor, once a scene of lively parties but now characterized by a "macabre fustiness . . . in which the shrouded furniture loomed with a sort of ghostly benignance." Such a house is a fitting environment for Aunt Jenny and Old Bayard, twinned relics from the past War between the States, ghosts in the present, who perpetuate the somnolence of the opening pages of the novel where the palpable presence of Colonel John Sartoris's ghost has a kind of vitality that Old Man Falls and Old Bayard do not, "cemented" as they are "by deafness to a dead time and drawn thin by the slow attenuation of days."

Like the first spectral meeting between these two men, the Sartoris family activity seems limited to willing the past alive so as to join it. The same black family is retained as household servants: Simon comes each day for Old Bayard, uniformed and in the family carriage, and Elnora has grown up to cook for them, preparing toddy late each afternoon before the evening meal. After they eat, Aunt Jenny reads "accounts of arson and murder and violent dissolution and adultery" in the newspaper or retells the family legend, and "as she grew older the tale itself grew richer and richer, taking on a mellow splendor like wine." Although the ancestral story is one of the superb recklessness and foolishness of youth, time has stilled its action into a hushed reverie and made it striking only in the primary colors of a romantic rhetoric.

> Against the dark and bloody obscurity of the northern Virginia campaigns, Jeb Stuart at thirty and Bayard Sartoris at twenty-three stood briefly like two flaming stars garlanded with Fame's burgeoning laurel and the myrtle and roses of Death, incalculable and sudden as meteors in General Pope's troubled military sky, thrusting upon him like an unwilling garment that notoriety which his skill as a soldier could never have won him. And still in a spirit of pure fun: neither Jeb Stuart nor Bayard Sartoris, as their actions clearly showed, had any political convictions involved at all.

Bayard's gallantry with the enemy and his impulsive ride for anchovies are directly analogous to Colonel John's surprise jump into the enemy camp; yet in both, the beauty of the past is joined inextricably with death, the reaffirmation of the linkage extended by memory and speech into an infinity of present and future tellings. Before this stilled and glorified past the present recedes, humbled at the rooted permanence of the Sartorises' ancestral tribute.

In sharp disjunction to this settled accommodation to history, Young Bayard's ride on an unbroken stallion erupts with a fierce, cruel, and even threatening force.

> The stallion moved beneath him like a tremendous mad music, uncontrolled, splendidly uncontrollable. The rope served only to curb its direction, not its speed, and among shouts from the

pavement on either side he swung the animal into another street that broke suddenly upon his vision. This was a quieter street; soon they would be in the country and the stallion could exhaust its rage without the added hazards of motors and pedestrians. Voices faded behind him into the thunder of shod hooves: "Runaway! Runaway!" but this street was deserted save for a small automobile going in the same direction, and further along beneath the slumbrous tunnel of the trees, bright small spots of color scuttled out of the street and clotted on one side. Children. Hope they stay there, he said to himself. His eyes were streaming a little; beneath him the surging lift and fall; in his nostrils a pungent sharpness of rage and energy and heat like smoke from the animal's body, and he swept past the motor car, remarking for a flashing second a woman's face and a mouth partly open and two eyes round with a serene astonishment. But the face flashed away without registering on his mind and he saw the children, small taut shapes of fear in bright colors, and on the other side of the street a negro man playing a hose onto the sidewalk, and beside him a second negro with a pitchfork.

Someone screamed from a neighboring veranda, and the group of children broke, shrieking; a small figure in a white shirt and diminutive pale blue pants darted from the curb into the street, and Bayard leaned forward and dragged at the rope, swerving the beast toward the opposite sidewalk, where the two negroes stood. The small figure came on, flashed safely behind, then rushing green beneath the stallion's feet; a tree trunk like a wheel spoke in reverse, and the animal struck clashing fire from wet concrete, slipped, lunged, then crashed down; and for Bayard, a red shock, then blackness.

To our constitutive consciousness this wild ride appears to be Young Bayard's attempt to achieve at home the glamorous and heroic death that belongs to a Sartoris by fabricating a danger analogous to that experienced in war: he is daring and reckless, a one-man show in the streets and lanes of Jefferson. But here as elsewhere Young Bayard refutes such easy anticipations; as conveyed by his narrative consciousness, this event is neither what the crowd believes nor the story Aunt Jenny would wish to tell. Bayard is drawn to the horse not as an object to test himself but as a companion who desires freedom from the restraints of Jefferson. Bayard rides the horse because he wants to take it out into the country where it can achieve a renewed liberty, where it can exhaust its inner frustrations. Bayard chooses to be neither a spectacle for the town's enjoyment nor a danger to it; at real danger to himself, he swerves to avoid children who suddenly appear in his path. Like his other compulsive attempts to relieve himself in his new car, when he seems most to endanger himself or others, he swerves back *into* life feeling both "savage and ashamed." For Young Bayard, the heroism of the Sartorises is not so much a matter of glory as a basis for guilt; he is the only Sartoris who had actually seen a Sartoris die, and it was ugly. Repeatedly, his actions seem to realize the awareness of Old Man Falls which opens the novel: " 'When a feller has to start killin' folks, he 'most always has to keep on killin' 'em. And when he does, he's already dead hisself.' "

The chief irony of the novel is that, in attempting to void the Sartoris legend, Young Bayard seems to others to perpetuate it. The stallion ride, for instance, is to Young Bayard's analogizing consciousness a corrective to Sartoris history, but the other Sartorises do not understand. Moreover, it is for Bayard the direct consequence of Rafe MacCallum's remembering John—not Bayard—on a previous fox hunt, and Bayard's response—his discussion of the "meteoric violence" of war and his first public description of his twin brother's death. Although Young Bayard confesses only to Rafe, a childhood friend, and despite his attempt to screen himself from the harsher realities of John's death by drinking bootleg liquor, he cannot shake his brother's behavior as it has been conditioned by the forces inherent in the Sartoris perspective.

> He drank his whisky and set the glass down on the table, still clutching it. "Damn ham-handed Hun," he said. "He never could learn to fly properly. I kept trying to keep him from going up there on that goddam popgun," and he cursed his dead brother savagely. Then he raised his glass again, but halted it half way to his mouth. "Where in hell did my drink go?"
>
> MacCallum reached the bottle and emptied it into Bayard's glass, and he drank and banged the thick tumbler on the table and rose and lurched back against the wall. His chair crashed backward, and he braced himself, staring at the other. "I kept on trying to keep him from going up there, on that Camel. But he gave me a burst. Right across my nose."

Bayard is haunted by the needlessness of his brother's death and by his own inability to prevent it: what grieves him even more is the stark memory that—something he has also told Old Bayard and Aunt Jenny —his own brother shot at him, glorying in his danger and extending it to Bayard. The brutality of war has been enlarged by the Sartorises into the brutalization of their own spirit. Only Narcissa dimly understands this. " 'You do things to hurt yourself just to worry people. You dont get any fun out of doing them,' " she tells him, and he agrees. In denying himself the proper Sartoris behavior and sufficient respect for the proper Sartoris grandeur, Bayard translates his own instincts and his own searching inquiry into a will for truth that arises, consciously and deliberately, from a fierce will to live.

Young Bayard supplies the presiding intelligence in *Flags in the Dust*. As in *Sanctuary*, which revolves around five multiple views of Temple's rape, in *Flags in the Dust* we are supplied with Young Bayard's four accounts of the needless, ugly death of his twin brother. It is the core motif. At his homecoming, Young Bayard tells his grandfather and Aunt Jenny the bare outlines of John's crack-up rather than saying anything about his own war experiences; with Rafe in the Jefferson store and restaurant, he publicly admits John's final burst of gunfire at the nose of his plane as if the dying twin hoped for their double heroic deaths. When he divulges to Narcissa still further detail, we learn that John thumbed his nose at Young Bayard, fulfilling the Sartoris legend while Young Bayard does not, and that John's plummeting plane almost struck Bayard's as he sought to save his brother from his death-fall. Our constitutive consciousness senses in each of these not only the increasing intensity of Young Bayard's morbid pain and fear but the growing implications of his self-understanding. We are not surprised, then, when he finally confesses to himself at the MacCallums' that he caused John's death because he did not save him. This final self-realization will, in a matter of days, expel him from Yocana County and exile him forever, a victim of guilt and self-condemnation.

But these are the last stages of his progressive consciousness. For much of the novel, Young Bayard pushes off these darker speculations: the novel moves from dust to dust, from John's reckless death to Young Bayard's own, but all the central panels dealing with Young Bayard deal with his unsuccessful accommodations to *living*. The daredevil stunts of childhood behind him, he internalizes the war, controlling his consciousness with a cold, leashed violence. "Surrounded by coiling images and shapes of stubborn despair," his is the "ceaseless striving for . . . not vindication so much as comprehension, a hand, no matter whose, to touch him out of his black chaos. He would spurn it, of course, but it would restore his cold sufficiency again." His task is that of formulating a separate peace, with his family and with himself.

At first, the awful discrepancy between the demands of his family and his meager accomplishments during the war unnerves Bayard. Arriving in Jefferson, he wanders the back lots and visits his brother's grave, disturbed and distracted. When he does emerge from the bushes of his home after dark, he rushes to give his grandfather and Aunt Jenny a description of John's death, ridding himself of the memories of John's virtual suicide. But he cannot erase the haunting consequences of the Sartoris legacy for the reckless grandeur nor, the first night back in their old bedroom, dismiss the keen sense of his twin brother's loss. So he tries to sublimate it to new interests. He purchases a car, choosing it for his joy in its appearance ("long and low and gray") and equipment ("the four-cylinder engine had sixteen valves and eight spark-plugs"). Although he endangers his passengers in his brooding and despairing attempts to forget John and the tradition he embodies, that is neither his purpose nor his expectation. " 'I didn't mean—,' " he tells Narcissa at one point, after racing when he sees a stone bridge, " 'I didn't mean—,' he essayed again." Submerging his past confrontation with death even further, he turns to the more mundane life of farming. "For a time the earth held him in a smoldering hiatus that might have been called contentment. He was up at sunrise, planting things in the ground and watching them grow and tending them." But his insistent memory prevails even so: "he still waked at times in the peaceful darkness of his familiar bed and without previous warning, tense and sweating with old terror." His second car accident, when he is saved by two well-meaning but bewildered blacks, brings on a delirium that becomes emblematic of his state. "At times it seemed to him that they were travelling backward, that they would crawl terrifically past the same tree or telephone post time after time; and it seemed to him that the three of them and the rattling wagon and the two beasts were caught in a ceaseless and senseless treadmill, a motion without progress, forever and to no escape." In an enormous effort of will, he attempts to exorcise John's presence by annihilating the physical remnants of their past; unlike Old Bayard, whose earlier visit to the attic was to caress the Sartoris treasures and even add to them, Young Bayard's journey is tense and driven, and his inventory desperate and frenzied.

There was not much . . . : a garment; a small leather-bound book; a shotgun shell to which was attached by a piece of wire a withered bear's paw. It was John's first bear, and the shell with which he had killed it in the river bottom near MacCallum's when he was twelve years old. The book was a New Testament; on the flyleaf in faded brown: "To my son, John, on his seventh birthday, March 16, 1900, from his Mother." He had one exactly like it; that was the year grandfather had arranged for the morning local freight to stop and pick them up and carry them to town to start to school. The garment was a canvas hunting coat, stained and splotched with what had once been blood and scuffed and torn with briers and smelling yet faintly of saltpeter. . . .

Then he rose and gathered up the book and the trophy and the coat and crossed to his chest of drawers and took from the top of it a photograph. It was a picture of John's Princeton eating club group, and he gathered this also under his arm and descended the stairs and passed out the back door.

Young Bayard burns these tokens with a fresh armful of pine logs placed atop Elnora's coals left from washing the family clothes, indiscriminately destroying the hunting coat alongside the Bible, the bear's paw alongside the photograph from Princeton, just as his brother John had, indiscriminately, destroyed himself. By destroying the remnants of John's life, he may also rid himself—and the Sartorises—of any living legacy concerning a shocking and hideous death that time and Aunt Jenny might mellow, like wine.

But the general pain of life is a sign of the cost of humanity, we learn in *Flags in the Dust;* "not [to be] assaulted by temptations nor flagellated by dreams nor assuaged by visions" is to be a mule. So it is the acuteness of Young Bayard's special anguish on which we focus: the pain of his frustration radiates throughout the novel, his own psychological state a synecdoche of the larger world about him. Aunt Jenny's sardonic humor, Old Bayard's attraction to fast rides in his grandson's car, even Narcissa's fascination with the letters of Byron Snopes all demonstrate the vulnerability and corruptibility just beneath the social and verbal patina of Jefferson. But Young Bayard suffers most, for his honesty and integrity cause him to realize in himself the psychology of the twin; he must seek a replacement for John in one who, like him, honors *life*.

At first there is Horace, whose condition resembles Bayard's in our constitutive consciousness. Both return from the war with no taste for it; both are without purpose, without true vocation. Both are relatively shy and inarticulate: Horace's random gestures toward Belle Mitchell resemble Bayard's toward Narcissa. But Horace does not own a car and cannot drive one; he does not share Bayard's mechanical ability and his love of the outdoors; he is not drawn, as Bayard is, to the physicality of life. Instead, he is interested in blowing vases of glass, in quoting the poetry of Keats, and in making and collecting art. His life is artificially constructed, is itself something of a poem; in his letters to Belle from overseas and in his later letters to Narcissa— letters she does not pretend to understand—he refashions his experiences, as Aunt Jenny does hers, in the satisfying rhetoric of fiction. Like Aunt Jenny too, Horace denies the present reality by substituting a legendary existence as a fundamental, last stay against mortality. It is instructive that of all the characters in the novel, Bayard sees himself mirrored less in Horace and in Aunt Jenny than in any of the rest.

So it is to Narcissa that Young Bayard turns: he not only correlates her loneliness and frustration with his but comes to lean on her "serene and steady waves, surrounding him unawares." Her detachment from life is for him a comforting mirror of "the bleak and lonely heights of his frozen despair." Far more seriously, however, acknowledging her plan to marry John, he is determined to blot out his brother's influence by replacing him. But this gesture of his own marriage to her, like the purchase of the car and the ride on the stallion, is shortsighted and naive, even *dis*honest; Bayard is incapable of providing Narcissa with the respectability of custom on which she most depends. Her response is a natural extension of her own superficiality. Physically, she is frigid; psychologically, she is bewildered. She does not satify Bayard. In his strong desire to make their marriage work, Bayard takes his wife on a possum hunt—he brings her outdoors, into his world, a world in which she (like him) must confront the prospect of death and overcome it with her own deep instinct for survival. Her reaction to the possum they kill is telling. "Narcissa saw the creature in the pool of the flashlight, lying on its side in a grinning curve, its eyes closed and its pink, baby-like hands doubled against its breast": the creature reifies her husband in his illness and their baby which she is carrying in her womb. With sudden clarity her world too is revealed to be, if unconsciously, one of beauty edged by the intimations of death. She is, moreover, both attracted and repelled as Bayard is by this emblematic view of her own condition.

> She watched the motionless thing with a little loathing—such a contradiction, its vulpine, skull-like grin and those tiny, human-looking hands, and the long, rat-like tail of it. Isom dropped from the tree, and Caspey turned the two straining clamorous dogs he held over to him and picked up the axe, and while Narcissa watched in shrinking curiosity, he laid the axe across the thing's neck and put his foot on either end of the axe, and grasped the animal's tail. . . . She turned and fled, her hand to her mouth.

It is an extraordinary scene, for Bayard—were he to recognize it—has found the potential double he has been seeking. But he does not see her own flight adumbrating his; all he witnesses is Narcissa's inability to adjust to the cruel realities in life. Her fear and grief replicate Young Bayard's own at the death of John. It is a searing moment for them both.

Bayard's moral condemnation of war is reinforced by the other wartime experiences that are recounted in the novel. There are four, and all are correlative: Old Man Falls's opening story about Colonel John's escape from home and his later story about the Colonel's unexpected confrontation with a Yankee cavalry company at the creek, Aunt Jenny's memories of Jeb Stuart capturing a major in Pope's command, and Caspey recounting his massacre of German soldiers he caught swimming all raise battle to the level of romance and so sentimentalize it. They rob war of its danger and pain. By making it adventuresome or humorous, by shaping it into fictions, they make it not only palpable and palatable but attractive. These are the uses of war to which Young Bayard would put a stop.

Bayard's frustration is reflected (in other terms) in other characters. Horace is stifled by all sorts of conventions such as those practiced at Little Belle's recital. "The clothes they make them wear, the stupid mature things they make them do. And he found himself wondering if to be cultured did not mean to be purged of all taste." Horace's difficulty, however, is that life for him must remain *simply* a matter of taste. When someone more physically vital like Belle or her sister Joan appears, he is unable to locate proper modes of response. The man who went to war by serving the YMCA and whose most active joy is found in his father's lawbooks and glassblowing is an easy victim to such foreign forces. "Somewhere, everywhere, behind and before and about them pervading, the dark warm cave of Belle's rich discontent and the tiger-reek of it." In marrying Belle, he is exiled to a cramped rented house with an empty garage, and his life is measured in his weekly task as the Carrier of Shrimp—"H. Benbow, M.A., Ll.D., C.S."

Horace is thus transformed into a double for Harry Mitchell, Belle's first husband, who, without the intelligence and breeding of Horace, also could not satisfy his wife. The repeating rifle he shows Horace, his invitations to Horace to join him for tennis, and his constant retreat to the upper floor of his house to drink privately all underscore Harry's painful loneliness and shame. His ugliness—"His heavy prognathous jaw narrowed delicately down, then nipped abruptly off into pugnacious bewilderment"—only recalls for us that this man, despite his masculinity and generosity, is a social misfit in the artificial respectability of Jefferson. All his awkwardness is disclosed on the social occasion of his daughter's recital.

> "Daddy's gal," Harry, in his tight, silver-gray gabardine suit and his bright tie with the diamond stud, chortled, putting his short thick hands on her; then together they examined the latest addition to the array of gifts with utter if dissimilar sincerity—little Belle with quiet and shining diffidence, her father stridently, tactlessly overloud. Harry was smoking his cigarettes steadily, scattering ash; he had receptacles of them open on every available flat surface throughout the lighted rooms. "How's the boy?" he added, shaking Horace's hand.

Harry's crudity is as incongruent to the scene as Young Bayard's coldness often is in the Sartoris household, yet both Harry and Young Bayard are well intentioned, shaken only by their own feelings of inadequacy and guilt.

Still Harry possesses more self-control than Byron Snopes. The ugliest, poorest, and meanest man in the Jefferson of *Flags in the Dust*, Byron differs from the other men only in degree. He too is troubled and anxious, because his own self-doubts prevent his ever realizing the dreams he can fashion and the physical urgings he daily feels. He is humiliated to turn to the boy Virgil Beard to write love letters for him, yet he finds even these are ignored. Almost pathologically shy, but with a will that he must have Narcissa, Byron turns to voyeurism, and later, breaking into the Benbow house, to fetishism. He searches Narcissa's bureau and fondles her undergarments. "He groped his way across to the bed and lay face down upon it, his head buried in the pillows, writhing and making smothered, animal-like moanings. But he must get out, and he rose and groped across the room again." Unable to relate to his coworkers or the men on the street corner at night, unable to establish himself in Jefferson with any personal satisfaction, Byron finally robs the Sartoris bank and leaves town for the hill girl who represents to him his one remaining chance for love and peace. Even there, he is unable to control himself and is firmly rejected. He tries to elope with Minnie Sue, but, although her father wakes her and she comes willingly to see Byron, she will not go away with him.

> "You aint ready fer our marryin' yet, are you?"
>
> But he made no answer. He was trembling more than ever, pawing at her. They struggled, and at last he succeeded in dragging her to the ground and he sprawled beside her, pawing at her clothing; whereupon she struggled in earnest, and soon she held him helpless while he sprawled with his face against her throat, babbling a name not hers. When he was still she turned and thrust him away, and rose to her feet.
>
> "You come back tomorrer, when you git over this," she said, and she ran silently toward the house, and was gone.

Byron's final scene of self-degradation is one of the most painful presented to our constitutive consciousness.

Alongside the agony of Young Bayard, Horace, Harry, and Byron, we find several women—Aunt Jenny, Narcissa, Belle, and Little Belle —who have, inversely, found ways to accommodate themselves to Jefferson society. Belle, Little Belle, and Narcissa all share piano playing as an impressive social and soothing personal ritual; Narcissa often substitutes her piano music for conversation, especially when Aunt Jenny asks her most impertinent questions. Narcissa is also a compulsive reader, although she reads only novels. Among her piano, her charity work (her surrogate life with a refugee family during World War I is analogous to Horace's service with the YMCA in Europe), and her habitual books, Narcissa formulates alternative patterns of escapism. They are more varied but no less escapist than Aunt Jenny's recurrent retreats to the past of Jeb Stuart, and Belle's insistent planning for a future where wealth will award her with pleasure and satisfaction: " 'Have you plenty of money?' " she whispers to Horace; it is her only question of him. With such a society of open and hidden frustration, for men and women alike, we must sympathize with Young Bayard's harsh judgments, and his passionate desire to find self-respect in another kind of life more worth living.

From the moment of the possum hunt onward, Bayard's search for an alternative way of life which can embrace a substitute for John becomes increasingly agitated, and the results increasingly ironic. He returns to the car and renews his partnership with the other Bayard, who was also no wartime hero. But each time he attempts to be reckless, he instinctively pulls himself back to safety: it is his will to live that is dominant. Unfortunately, Young Bayard loses again; and the accident that follows almost at once is fatal to Old Bayard, although Young Bayard reaches out to save him from going through the windshield. Such a death for the grandfather is a bitter parody. It mocks the Sartoris legend, for Old Bayard dies of natural causes, of a heart attack; yet, unintentionally, it forces a distorted heroism upon him, for he dies in a foolish accident. This horrible ambiguity is not lost on Young Bayard, for he sees how his desire to escape John's fate has only caused its recurrence: he thumbed his nose at danger and has killed one of the Sartorises (as his brother almost killed him). Dedicating his life to transforming the Sartoris legend, Young Bayard has inadvertently preserved and renewed it. These larger implications of what he has done cause him to run.

For us, this flight reveals the last unexposed portions of Young Bayard's consciousness. He turns to the MacCallums, for Rafe knows already much of the truth about John's death, and at first their house appears more inviting to Young Bayard than his own did when he first returned to Jefferson.

> At last a pale and windless plume of smoke stood above the trees, against the sky, and in the rambling, mudchinked wall a window glowed with ruddy invitation across the twilight. Dogs had already set up a resonant, bell-like uproar; above it Bayard could distinguish the clear tenor of puppies and a voice shouting at them, and as he pulled Perry to a halt in the yard, the fox was vanishing diffidently but without haste beneath the back porch. A lean figure faced him in the dusk, with an axe in one hand and an armful of wood.

The MacCallum home is unpretentious and undisguised; it has no correlation to the air of false respectability that had so stifled him in Jefferson.

The walls were of chinked logs; upon them hung two colored outdated calendars and a patent medicine lithograph. The floor was bare, of hand-trimmed boards scuffed with heavy boots and polished by the pads of generations of dogs; two men could lie side by side in the fireplace. In it now four-foot logs blazed against the clay fireback, swirling in wild plumes into the chimney's dark maw.

Bayard is warmly received, treated as a guest, and provided with food and drink. This other homecoming is for him a welcome relief even while, for us, it is uneasily (if surprisingly) correlative. For the Mac-Callums, like the Sartorises, are extraordinarily childlike; their stories of camping and hunting life look backward to an earlier, less realistic time; imaged in their precious clock on the mantel which no longer runs, the past seems permanently reinstituted for them too. What is true of their surroundings is also true of the MacCallums. Just as Aunt Jenny regiments behavior by repeating her tales as archetypal, so Virginius MacCallum at the age of seventy-seven requires excessive dependence of his children, and all of them, six boys ranging in age from twenty to fifty-two, have remained bachelors in his service. Henry, in fact, has assumed the tasks of keeping house; he is "domestic, womanish . . . with his squat, slightly tubby figure and his mild brown eyes and his capable, unhurried hands"; Lee, "his womanish hands moving restlessly on his knees," seems forever depressed; and Jackson sits by his bastard pups, "in a sort of hovering concern, like a hen." We also see them compensate for an emptiness in their fond dreams for the youngest; "they would sit in silence, looking at Buddy's lean, jack-knifed length with the same identical thought, a thought which each believed peculiar to himself and which none ever divulged —that someday Buddy would marry and perpetuate the name." Rather than an alternative mode of living for Bayard, the MacCallums represent a sterile doubling—literally sterile since there are no women, no children, and no plans of marriage, the only births coming from the bastardization of a fox and a dog with offspring which are, to Bayard, "something monstrous and contradictory and obscene."

In this choking and unnatural atmosphere of malaise, Bayard's thoughts once again become morbid as his mind turns back to John's death. Moreover, the conversations and activities of the outer world now only confirm his inner turbulence by repetitive associations of Young Bayard with John. Mandy wonders if Bayard brought her a trinket as John would have; he no sooner lies down for the night with

Buddy than Buddy recalls John and extends his sympathy; with genuine delight, Jackson recalls the day John floated down the river on a log with a fox. The old times, the good times now resurrected and reborn, are of John—something we recall is true, too, in Jefferson, where Aunt Sally Wyatt recalls that John rather than Bayard " 'tipped his hat to a lady on the street.' " It is not simply that the citizens of Jefferson like these inhabitants of the Yocana woods admire John more; it is that they admire John for his recklessness, for the youth and foolishness and flair which, forced on him by his name, brought about his death. In this shock of recognition—that he cannot escape John, or, more precisely, the fictional John of others—Bayard leaves once again, before the news of his grandfather's death reaches the MacCallums, but this time he does not merely depart Yocana County. Instead, he leaves the Confederacy itself, because he sees the origin of the Sartoris code, four generations back, in a willful rhetoric to transform their defeat in the War Between the States into an occasion of courage and triumph. The dishonesty of the Sartorises in confronting the *anguish* of death is seen by Young Bayard, perhaps too simply, as the dishonesty of the entire South.

Bayard's inability to locate a homeland which can accept him on his own free and life-giving terms is marked by his aimless and anonymous wandering to Tampico, Mexico City, San Francisco, and Chicago. At the end of this travelling, he finds, at last, a new living twin. We recognize what he has found because of his pronounced fixation. "For a while Bayard had half listened [to his companions], staring at the [shabby] man with his bleak chill eyes, but now he was watching something across the room, letting the man talk on, unminded." Bayard has come to a Chicago bar with a man whose eyes mirror his own, but he is distracted by still something else. His change of mood frightens the prostitute who has come with him, but she cannot break his distraction or get him to drink. Finally, pressed by her inquiries, he speaks.

> "Brother-in-law over there," he said, speaking slowly and carefully. "Dont speak to family. Mad at us." They turned and looked.
> "Where?" the aviator asked. Then he beckoned a waiter. "Here, Jack."
> "Man with diamond headlight," Bayard said. "Brave man. Cant speak to him, though. Might hit me. Friend with him, anyway."

Bayard has discovered someone else who, like him, was forced to leave Yocana County and come North; they are, moreover, distantly related through their marriages and in Bayard's cloudy mind potentially friends since both are set apart from Jefferson. The conversation at Bayard's table, meant to involve him, is blocked from his thoughts; when sometime later he speaks aloud, it is from his unbroken stream of consciousness that he remarks. " 'Not brother-in-law,' he said. 'Husband-in-law. No. Wife's brother's husband-in-law. Wife used to be wife's brother's girl. Married, now. Fat woman. He's lucky.' " For Bayard Sartoris in Chicago, Harry Mitchell has succeeded—although we saw Harry on the tennis courts of his Jefferson home assertively and cruelly masculine, and at his daughter's recital with the same flashy stickpin awkward to Little Belle, boring to his wife, and repulsive and stupid to Horace. But these reflections belong to our constitutive consciousness; Bayard never witnessed them. And to Bayard, Harry now offers the possibility of a renewed friendship. When his companions prepare to leave, Bayard compulsively turns from them and toward Harry.

> In a small alcove Harry Mitchell sat. On his table too were bottles and glasses, and he now sat slumped in his chair, his eyes closed and his bald head in the glow of an electric candle was dewed with rosy perspiration. Beside him sat a woman who turned and looked full at Bayard with an expression of harried desperation; above them stood a waiter with a head like that of a priest, and as Bayard passed he saw that the diamond was missing from Harry's tie and he heard their bitter suppressed voices as their hands struggled over something on the table between them, behind the discreet shelter of their backs, and as he and his companion reached the door the woman's voice rose with a burst of filthy rage into a shrill hysterical scream cut sharply off, as if someone had clapped a hand over her mouth.

It is a moment of epiphany for Bayard: he has seen his double and he now knows what it is to be from Jefferson and out of it. Harry is drunk, a tart is after the diamond stickpin (it is all she sees in him, apparently), and Harry needs the jewel to pay the bill. Now we see the whole pattern: Bayard's sense of twinship has caused him to search himself so deeply that the hypocrisy he finds in himself, his family, and his county allows him no suitable arena for living by his own code; the only place he found total honesty and warmth was among the blacks at Christmas where race and class even then separated them because he was " 'Banker Sartoris's folks.' " Bayard's analysis replicates our own. Although he had refused before, he now accepts an assignment to test a dangerous plane, for it is one way he can still be useful, can still preserve the lives of others if not his own—perhaps the only way. Still, such an extreme recoiling from Harry Mitchell suggests to us, as it must suggest to Bayard, that with Mitchell he has looked into himself and at himself for the last time.

Young Bayard's death is therefore only apparently reckless; the burden of his unfolding consciousness in *Flags in the Dust* is to show how agonizing and unavoidable his death became. Although it has none of the dash and color of Colonel Sartoris's plunge for the Yankees' anchovies, the analogous death of Young Bayard at the close of the novel, if disappointing in form, has gained in substance. Narcissa and Aunt Jenny see Bayard's death as a poor attempt to fulfill the Sartoris legend, of course, but Young Bayard never sees it that way himself: he does not accept a proffered garter as he takes off in flight, because he does not mean to be a hero and the flight is for him not in the least glamourous. Instead, he is grim and determined; if he has lost hope, he retains both purpose and integrity, and once again, when the plane begins to go down, he struggles to save his own life. The fragmentation of the test plane, like the fragmentation of Bayard's hopes, mocks his integrity, for his death most closely resembles that of his twin brother John (who never tried to save himself).

In the end Young Bayard is unable to eradicate the Sartoris legend nor can he shape his life in any alternative way which is as perfect or artful as one of Horace's bloodless letters. It is this unnatural beauty of art that outlives him. We see it in Narcissa's uninterrupted piano playing and in Aunt Jenny's return to the tale of the Carolina Bayard, yet it is not clear whether these activities succeed in erasing Young Bayard from their minds. Narcissa's son by him has his name changed to Benbow and Aunt Jenny, who has chiseled on John Sartoris's gravestone

> Soldier, Statesman, Citizen of the World
> *For man's enlightenment he lived*
> *By man's ingratitude he died*
> *Pause here, son of sorrow; remember death.*

and has carved as a memorial for Young Bayard's twin brother

> Killed in action, July 19, 1918.
> *"I bare him on eagles' wings*
> *and brought him unto Me,"*

places on Young Bayard's tomb only his name and the date of his birth and death. He has broken the chain of the Sartoris tradition—but to what little effect and at what cost! It is Young Bayard who gives Horace's choric observation—" 'Perhaps this is the reason for wars,' he said.'The meaning of peace.' "—any lasting significance in this novel, but the act is lost on the past, the living, and those to come. The name Bayard chose for his son is changed; the inscription on his tomb by those who continue on insinuates his failure. Most damning of all, the generosity of his death is severely diminished by the reiterative art which formulates beauty only in the presence of death, the words and music of Aunt Jenny and Narcissa outliving all the hopes and deeds, alone now filling the room or shrouded furniture where "the window curtains hung motionless" and "beyond the window evening was a windless lilac dream."

"The Sound and the Fury"

The Sound and the Fury is Benjy's book: *his* consciousness begins and closes the novel, and it is to his memorialization of death at the small graveyard alongside the golf course and at the family plot in the Jefferson cemetery that we first and last attend. From the very beginning, Benjy transforms the significance of loss—the lost Caddy which our constitutive consciousness will make analogous to Luster's lost quarter, the lost golf ball, and Benjy's emasculation—into something greater, something which transcends clock time and allows Benjy to fuse both a memorable past and a painful present, joy and grief, love and death. Such equations tend to cancel out permanent anguish and provide for Benjy a compromise with existence. He locates the same solutions that the other Compsons do, more or less successfully, but with greater concentration. His perceptions consequently provide us with the basic epistemological question in the novel: is the idiocy of this tale told by an idiot in the tale itself or in the telling of the tale? Benjy's narrative consciousness supplies discrete episodes linked in ways both seen and unseen which in turn demand our own constitutive consciousness to connect them. Benjy's world is grounded in a trust based on familiarity. His direct responses are to stimuli he has long since learned—the sound "Caddy," his sister's slipper, the smell of trees, the sight and warmth of fire, even a new wheel on the old family carriage—and he has built from them a neat and safe world of patterned structures. He has, at these moments of configuration, an integrated consciousness. Only when there are no known things for him to assimilate—only when order is deliberately interrupted or dismissed —does he know anxiety and terror; his only fear is a fear of removal, never a fear of encounter. Benjy's stability, then, is from within; his world is organized by the centrifugal forces of his own self and the power of his stubborn and continual will. Conversely, he is helpless when the support of tradition is withdrawn, when his trust is betrayed. Thus his personal tragedy—with widening implications through the remainder of the novel—is an enlarging sense of loss, for he makes correlations among the deaths of Damuddy, of Jason III his father, and of Quentin III his brother; the departure of Caddy his sister; and the loss of his masculinity. Through this progressive demise of the Compsons, he can share the emotions of others, even strangers, from the outset of the novel: his identity, like theirs, is stripped from him bit by bit. His perceptions have become so acute by training that when Benjy bellows in the first scene, it is not only to the sound of a call for "Caddy" but also to the voice of someone who like himself has found something missing and whose entire being is concentrated on its recovery.

Not merely Caddy but Caddy and Benjy are at the center of Benjy's perceptual life; his memories revolve not around her, but around his relations with her and her absence from him; and much of his effort goes into willing her presence, her return, or in finding simulations of it in others: in the behavior of Quentin IV, in the maternalism of Dilsey, and in the companionship of T. P. and Luster. When he is attracted to mirrors (as he always is, for they increase his perceptual range), he does not see himself but Caddy or metonymies of her in a slipper, firelight, or the cushion she would hand him from his mother's chair; for Benjy, even the mirrors become Caddy's surrogate. Moreover, at the heart of his recollections of his sister is one day in particular which he recalls in eighteen distinct episodes (including most of the longest), the day he played with her and with Versh and Quentin in the branch and Caddy got her drawers muddy; significantly, it is also the day of Damuddy's funeral. It is in fact this juxtaposition that filters his perspective on life. " 'I dont care whether they see or not,' " Caddy says of her dirty drawers to Quentin, " 'I'm going to tell, myself,' " but she does not tell because the house itself is shut off to the children —their father meets them on the back steps, hustles them into the kitchen, locks Benjy into a high chair, and leaves Dilsey in charge. Dilsey will explain neither the crowd in the front parlor nor the great hush and their mother's tears. " 'You'll know in the Lawd's own time,' " is all that Dilsey will say. So Caddy never explains the fight at the branch, and this secret, which is also Benjy's secret, correlates with the secret in the front room—how, Benjy is not quite certain. To this he adds one final secret which also seems to him correlative, because it too brings a crowd to the front room of their house, it too is not explained, and it too sees Caddy in trouble (or so he feels and so Quentin intimates). It is Caddy's wedding: "Caddy put her arms around me, and her shining veil, and I couldn't smell trees anymore and I began to cry." These three troublesome visions of Caddy—Quentin angry with her and hitting her when she is in dirty clothes, his father keeping her from the front room, the family ridding themselves of her to a man he does not know—coalesce at the core of his consciousness and shape his visual thinking.

The force of Benjy's narrative consciousness comes in the narrow sharpness of his focus and in his ability to see certain discrete moments as reduplicative. The opening series is indicative of the whole first chapter. We first see Benjy and Luster walking along the fence that separates Compson land from the golf course; they turn and head for the branch, and for Benjy this change in direction triggers a memory of Caddy, when she was cold like Benjy, but when she befriended him, when their cold was privately shared and no one came between them; this in turn reminds him of Caddy and the out-of-doors, and he recalls that she smells like trees; he next thinks of his own connection with nature in the jimson weed which he puts on graves. He apparently does not wish to recall Caddy's naturalness and his own in connection with death, however, a sign of permanent loss, so he rejects this memory and returns instead to the thoughts of the cold day when he and Caddy were alone. Unfortunately, this memory is interrupted when Luster leads him by the carriage house and he sees the carriage that took them all to his father's burial. No matter how hard he tries to concentrate on the present, on objects, on nature itself, Benjy's thoughts return constantly to Caddy and this in turn leads him to impressions of privation and of death. The branch scene juxtaposed to Damuddy's death and to Caddy's wedding, his repeated attempts to find an associative parallel with Caddy's several losses, consumes most of his attention

and response, his sight and hearing; only at night, when his analogizing memory turns persistently to a fusion of Caddy and Quentin
IV, is he able, however tentatively, to forget about death.

It is by their boyfriends' dismissal of him that he first links Caddy
with Quentin IV.

> "Send him away." Charlies said.
> "I will." Caddy said. "Let me go."
> "Will you send him away." Charlie said.
> "Yes." Caddy said. "Let me go." Charlie went away. "Hush."
> Caddy said. "He's gone." I hushed. I could hear her and feel
> her chest going.
> "I'll have to take him to the house." she said. She took my
> hand. "I'm coming." she whispered.
> "Wait." Charlie said. "Call the nigger."
> "No." Caddy said. "I'll come back. Come on, Benjy." . . .
> *You old crazy loon, Quentin said. I'm going to tell Dilsey*
> *about the way you let him follow everywhere I go. I'm going to*
> *make her whip you good.*

The assimilation of Caddy and Quentin IV in their effect of removing
him from watching them—his visual thinking here seems not to distinguish their markedly differing tones—allows him to recognize
Quentin's escape down the pear tree as the completion of the analogy,
for one of his last memories of the day at the branch is Dilsey pulling
Caddy down from that same tree, where she climbed to see what was
going on in the Compson parlor. Thus Benjy's day ends as it began: it
is totally enclosed, and he is back, comfortably at last, to the day he
knows best, the day he knows as much of as can now be known. It
contains its mysteries for him still, but it also has his secrets. It is his
day, he *possesses* it, and his perceptions are confirmed by present patterns of behavior, so he can sleep.

Benjy recalls and visualizes not in single concrete images but in
associative clusters of images. His fluid consciousness seems to fasten
on two primary groupings, those that represent Caddy or accompany
her—rain, trees, slipper, fire—and those that are associated with privation, loss, and death. His jimson weed, for example, *Datura stramo-
nium*, native to Mississippi, is ill scented and is said to have been fatal
to children; the squinch owl like the blue jay is a superstitious sign of
death as are the jars of poison that decorate his homemade grave; even
the narcissus he holds at the end of the novel is associated with Neme-

sis because its scent was so sweet it was supposed to have made the Furies mad and frenzied. The farther reaches of allusion are beyond the boundaries of Benjy's consciousness but are meant to signal our own: they reinforce Benjy's fundamental analogy which makes the branch scene, Damuddy's death, and Caddy's wedding not merely correlative *but identical*. With Benjy sin, death, and promiscuity are interchangeable, are made one—and it is this felt impression that will govern not only his perception of life but Quentin's, Jason's, and Dilsey's as well. It is because he fastens in memory on these common themes which join episodes of his past into a seamless coherence that his mind moves so freely from one time and place to another, for it also insists on the linkages of sex, promiscuity, and death. It is instructive that on the holograph, Faulkner has *Twilight* as the working title of this novel.

Not only the absence of Caddy but the enforced synonymity of copulation and death is fundamental, too, to Quentin's outlook: " 'Is it a wedding or a wake?' " Shreve asks him as he dresses in his suit for a death that will marry him to Caddy for eternity, marry them in the clean flames of hell. It is a conjunction Caddy had also made for him; bewildered by her promiscuity and fearful of the sexual act itself, he asks Caddy if she enjoys it. She does not; *"When they touched me I died."* It is important that our constitutive consciousness recognize that at the deepest levels of their experience Benjy and Quentin, in their separately voiced threnodies, are true doubles, brothers in the Dostoyevskian sense.

Like Benjy, Quentin absorbs into his morbid celebrations fundamental concrete images of the past which they share—the pasture, the swing under the cedars, Caddy's treelike smell, her wedding veil—and like Benjy when he looks in the mirror he too sees Caddy, although for him it is, significantly, an image of her wedding day and she is running *away* from him:

> *In the mirror she was running before I knew what it was. That quick, her train caught up over her arm she ran out of the mirror like a cloud, her veil swirling in long glints her heels brittle and fast clutching her dress onto her shoulder with the other hand, running out of the mirror the smells roses roses the voice that breathed o'er Eden. Then she was across the porch I couldn't hear her heels then in the moonlight like a cloud, the floating shadow of the veil running across the grass, into the bellowing.*

We can recognize the similarity of vocabulary here as well as the similarity of statement—Caddy resembles flight, privation, loss; the distance between them, from Quentin's view, widens irrevocably, as in a dream. Where Benjy buries one memory in another, blurring the roughest and most anguishing edges in the final mystery of the day at the branch, Quentin tries to cover grief over with abstractions. He claims his father rather than Benjy as his conscious model: his opening remarks (like Benjy's) serve as an index to the operation of his thoughts.

> When the shadow of the sash appeared on the curtains it was between seven and eight o'clock and then I was in time again, hearing the watch. It was Grandfather's and when Father gave it to me he said, Quentin, I give you the mausoleum of all hope and desire; it's rather excrutiating-ly apt that you will use it to gain the reducto absurdum of all human experience which can fit your individual needs no better than it fitted his or his father's. I give it to you not that you may remember time, but that you might forget it now and then for a moment and not spend all your breath trying to conquer it. Because no battle is ever won he said. They are not even fought. The field only reveals to man his own folly and despair, and victory is an illusion of philosophers and fools. . . .
>
> If it had been cloudy I could have looked at the window, thinking what he said about idle habits. Thinking it would be nice for them down at New London if the weather held up like this. Why shouldn't it? The month of brides, the voice that breathed *She ran right out of the mirror, out of the banked scent. Roses. Roses. Mr and Mrs Jason Richmond Compson announce the marriage of.* Roses. Not virgins like dogwood, milkweed. I said I have committed incest, Father I said. Roses. Cunning and serene. If you attend Harvard one year, but dont see the boat-race, there should be a refund. Let Jason have it. Give Jason a year at Harvard.

As with Benjy, the clustering here and the linkages that remain unspoken are extraordinary and revealing. The conceptual—time, marriage, virginity, incest—are aligned so as to make them all susceptible to foolishness and despair, but also to make their conquering power equally foolish. Quentin is struggling here toward a life philosophy, not a death philosophy; the sunlight and Jason's renewal of the Compson legacy at Harvard frame for him those troublesome thoughts of sin, promiscuity, and death that will not stay down. In addition, beneath these conscious attempts, Quentin must know that as his father dismisses the story of incest so he dismisses the power Quentin assigns to virginity and to time. What then of the loss of Caddy? Can this be truly tragic? Is it possible—the thought occurs to Quentin several times in chapter 2—that, as Caddy once remarks, Mr. Compson will die within the year, his philosophy possibily disappearing with him? Does this make him the final proof or the final victim of his own views of triumph and of time? Quentin's consciousness is governed by abstractions, but, like Benjy's, it is primarily reflexive, his morbid intellection really the equivalent of the idiot's memorial reconstruction as both spend their day searching for Caddy and reconstituting her in their own dimensions. Quentin shares with Benjy a deep trust in the world and an extreme self-centeredness which produce in him his father's despair and his brother's sense of progressive loss: Benjy's stream of consciousness from Damuddy's funeral through Caddy's wedding to the imminent loss of Quentin IV is mirrored by Quentin in the movement from Caddy's wedding through an attempted substitute in the little Italian girl to Little Sister Death as the last and final reality. Correlative to Benjy's, Quentin's day is also circular; it moves from the mutilation of the watch (of time) and self-mutilation (the stopping of human time, of human life *in* time); although he is attracted to water as Benjy is to fire, both end their days by submitting themselves to the element that most attracts them only to assure themselves of its destructive properties.

But there is also a significant difference between the two brothers. Benjy *wills* Caddy back; Quentin tries to *win* her back. From the moment he awakens, he makes his day a response, by replication, of the day he fought Dalton Ames, for this time he means to earn possession of his sister, to *deserve* Caddy. His elaborate plans for suicide reflect his elaborate stance the day he told Dalton Ames to get out of town—it is just as unreal, just as sentimental—and he images the day through the same visual prisms of birds, water, shadow, and broken sunlight. When he takes the train from Cambridge to find a suitable place to hide the flatirons until later that day, he chooses a bridge reminiscent of the site where he fought Dalton and lost. As he looks in the water, the morbidity of his plan fuses sex and death as they swell up in his consciousness.

Where the shadow of the bridge fell I could see down for a long way, but not as far as the bottom. When you leave a leaf in

> water a long time after awhile the tissue will be gone and the
> delicate fibers waving slow as the motion of sleep. They dont
> touch one another, no matter how knotted up they once were,
> no matter how close they lay once to the bones. And maybe
> when He says Rise the eyes will come floating up too, out of the
> deep quiet and the sleep, to look on glory. And after awhile the
> flat irons would come floating up. I hid them under the end of
> the bridge and went back and leaned on the rail.

Again he feels the imminence of an earned death, for he did not save
his sister. Yet now as then his plans for self-immolation are purifying
and restorative; the water gives him once more that vision of the
"clean flame the two of us more than dead." Even when a trout appears, commanding and killing mayflies, he subjects it to his willed
reenactment, for, after darting about, it "hung, delicate and motionless
among the wavering shadows." Three young boys come along, resembling the Compson boys, and talk idly of winning a prize by
catching the fish. "They all talked at once, their voices insistent and
contradictory and impatient, making of unreality a possibility, then a
probability, then an incontrovertible fact, as people will when their
desires become words." Even the unfamiliar children have been absorbed into his mind to reflect himself: their pattern is a paradigm for
his own mental processes and they talk, too, of violation as death.

Like Benjy, Quentin wants to possess Caddy; he is jealous of her
sexual attractiveness, her men, and her promiscuity. His real enemies,
then, are as basic as human nature and as wide as the world, but in his
own mind they are all embodied in Dalton Ames, whom—despite his
attractiveness to Caddy—Quentin knows to be slippery, thoughtless,
crude, and selfish, a meddler. He finds it easy, then, to see Dalton
Ames in Gerald Bland.

> Bland came out, with the sculls. He wore flannels, a grey jacket
> and a stiff straw hat. Either he or his mother had read some-
> where that Oxford students pulled in flannels and stiff hats, so
> early one March they bought Gerald a one pair shell and in his
> flannels and stiff hat he went on the river. The folks at the boat-
> houses threatened to call a policeman, but he went anyway. His
> mother came down in a hired auto, in a fur suit like an arctic
> explorer's, and saw him off in a twenty-five mile wind and a
> steady drove of ice floes like dirty sheep. Ever since then I have
> believed that God is not only a gentleman and a sport; He is a
> Kentuckian too.

By means of Quentin's sardonic humor, we learn that Gerald rows on top of the water; he never goes below the surface, never achieves depth. Perhaps what galls Quentin additionally is that Mrs. Bland in her " 'eight yards of apricot silk,' " protects and supports her son in a way that Caroline Compson never supported Quentin. But the chief thing that Quentin envies is "Gerald's horses and Gerald's niggers and Gerald's women"—his attractiveness and his sexual exploits.

Quentin no sooner sees Gerald than he juxtaposes him, in his mind, to Dalton—

> Dalton Ames. Dalton Ames. Dalton Shirts. I thought all the time they were khaki, army issue khaki, until I saw they were of heavy Chinese silk or finest flannel because they made his face so brown his eyes so blue. Dalton Ames. It just missed gentility. Theatrical fixture. Just papier-mache, then touch. Oh. Asbestos. Not quite bronze.

—and then both blend, in his mind, into Sydney Herbert Head, "Hearty, celluloid like a drummer. Face full of teeth white but not smiling." Herbert, like Gerald, went to Harvard; like Dalton, he is "*A liar and a scoundrel Caddy was dropped from his club for cheating at cards got sent to Coventry caught cheating at midterm exams and expelled.*" Later in the day, Gerald and Mrs. Bland save Quentin from arrest by a marshal, much as Dalton tried to save Quentin by giving him an excuse to avoid their duel, but Quentin is provoked by a remark Gerald makes and they fight. Since we do not hear the remark— since no one hears it—it was likely never made: Quentin has projected his memorial anticipation onto present reality stimulated by Bland's boasts of exploiting women successfully, like Dalton Ames. But like Benjy, Quentin makes present reality serve him as an analogue—once again he is bloodied, and Shreve, whom Spoade was "Calling . . . my husband," reifies Caddy in helping him to clean up. In fact, the only period of the day when Quentin's mind is not analogously fixed on Dalton Ames in one surrogate or another is the time he spends with the little Italian girl. She is dark like Natalie, a girl he used to arouse Caddy's envy, but even here he is served by his myopic intellection, for Julio's attack on him for stealing his sister is a more humiliating fight than the one with Bland or Ames or the argument with Head. Throughout his final day in what he insists is an antagonistic world, Quentin can amuse himself best by stepping on shadows, by cheating time, by gazing into water: by the known acts of simulated suicide.

Conceptually, he projects his own death to join a dead Caddy. *"When they touched me I died."*

Much of Quentin's effort is spent reaffirming scenes of his past in which Caddy is absent, not, as with Benjy, scenes where she is an active participant. The reason emerges in the course of his monologue: although Caddy always shows affection for Benjy, she finally found Quentin too unrealistic. She becomes as cruel to him as Ames, Bland, or even (verbally) Spoade. "You're meddling in my business again didn't you get enough of that last summer"; *"I dont give a goddam what you do."* His consciousness screens this actual Caddy out with discomfort. What he remembers best are the scenes he sentimental-izes: the dirty drawers, the elaborate suicide pact, his arrangements to meet Dalton Ames. Other memories, such as the knife at Caddie's throat and Dalton's gun, are phallic images that both attract and repel him, so his thoughts then move to mirror images: the reflections of loneliness ("murmuring bones"; "roof of wind"; "lonely and inviolate sand"); the sense of inevitability ("Spoade was in the middle of them like a terrapin in a street full of scuttering dead leaves, his collar about his ears, moving at his customary unhurried walk"); the movement toward death that will reunite them. In self-fulfilling images of an abstracted sentimentalism, Quentin reemerges as Caddy's hero and as his own best champion.

Quentin's chapter also charts a spreading sense of loss and decay paralleled by the underplot of his father's morbid vision and death; his stilted college rhetoric can only meld into his father's grandiose philosophizing, can only return him to thoughts of decay and mean-inglessness. Like his mother, Quentin can handle—indeed, cannot escape—the concrete images of his past: Caddy's men, her pregnancy, her veil. But he cannot accommodate his father's abstractions of these because they are meant to criticize and correct his self-indulgence.

> and he every man is the arbiter of his own virtues whether or not you consider it courageous is of more importance than the act itself than any act otherwise you could not be in earnest and i you dont believe i am serious and he i think you are too serious to give me any cause for alarm you wouldn't have felt driven to the expedient of telling me you have committed incest other-wise and i i wasnt lying i wasnt lying and he you wanted to sublimate a piece of natural human folly into a horror and then exorcise it with truth and i it was to isolate her out of the loud world so that it would have to flee us of necessity and then

the sound of it would be as though it had never been and he
did you try to make her do it and i i was afraid to i was afraid
she might and then it wouldnt have done any good but if i
could tell you we did it would have been so and then the others
wouldnt be so and then the world would roar away and he and
now this other you are not lying now either but you are still
blind to what is in yourself

It is in this final montage that we come to know Quentin best. In this
reconstructed conversation with his father (whether actual or contrived, we cannot be sure) it is his father who drives Quentin to commit suicide, for it is his father who trusts most that he cannot do it—
who challenges him, in the end, *as Dalton and Herbert and Bland had.*
The abstraction that Quentin supplies and clings to—incest—is significantly an abstraction of restoration: he means to reunite the family.
That his father will have none of it suggests that his own basic value—
that of the family and of Caddy herself—is now jeopardized. In a
nearly incoherent rush of words Quentin admits, for the first and last
time, that she was pregnant when she was married; he finally surrenders temporarily to his father's insistent (but morbid) superiority.
But he restores himself, too, in the last lines of his chapter; in brushing
his teeth in preparation to meet Caddy, he reinstates his dream of a
cohesive family, and in his imagery and his linked concerns he also
wills Benjy's world back into his own.

Neither Benjy nor Quentin lives in the world of actuality; to them,
the real world is composed of memories and voices wholly subjective
and internal. The external world is composed only of stimuli which
awaken and confirm the foregone conclusions of their recollected
pasts. This activity of perception and conception proclaims the idiocy
in one, leads to suicide in the other: both are analogous and both are
radically correlative to Caddy's flight, to Jason III's alcoholism, and to
Caroline's hypochondria, all versions of willed self-destruction. It is a
bleak picture—bleaker even than similar portraits in Balzac and Flaubert—and we are tempted to ask if there is no alternative. Could the
Compsons survive by escaping from the claustrophobic atmosphere of
the family and these self-indulgent revisitings of their past? It is at
precisely this point that we are supplied with the narrative consciousness of Jason.

The middle son, Jason IV, moves in the wider world of Jefferson. He
works at the hardware store, he does a certain amount of bank busi-

ness, and he visits the Western Union regularly; on the day we see him, he gets two letters and receives and sends a number of telegrams. He has a woman in Memphis. By his varied activities, he manages to keep the Compsons going by keeping one foot in the mercantile world of Jefferson, one foot in the antebellum Compson household. But Jason's narrative consciousness tells us that he finds Jefferson and his home both sources of humiliation, analogous trials where he is put upon by those who refuse to accord him the proper respect. For him, values are easily transferred from one environment to the other because the two are correlative. Neither exercises his imagination or his true talents because both demand only that he contribute to situations established prior to his time. His profoundest interpretation of the Compson dilemma is his ability to see that, like the Bascombs, like business generally, appearances are more important than realities where they happen to differ, and that, if one is skillful and persistent enough, in time appearance can bring reality up to its own standards, substance up to form. Jason finds an articulate, even insistent supporter in his mother, much as Benjy and Quentin found support in Caddy and Jason III. Caroline Compson's own myth, that Jason is a Bascomb not a Compson (although to our constitutive consciousness the names seem similar), underscores Jason's sense of his business acumen and reinforces his sense of superiority to Earl, to Job (whom he correlates with Dilsey), and to the men who hang around the Western Union office; it also reinforces the necessary lies about Caddy's support of Quentin IV, the thousand dollars he invested in a car instead of the hardware business, and his own diligence and shrewdness.

From all this we might conclude that Jason is free of much of the Compson morbidity, their thoughts displaced by his action. We should have thought so if we had been introduced to him first. Now, however, we see ways in which he resembles Benjy and Quentin. He is as self-centered and self-indulgent as they are, caught up by his memory of the past and haunted by a sense of persistent personal loss. Jason, too, has trusted to the Compson name and been betrayed in that trust. Now his central fantasy is that he is victimized by everyone. It makes a strangely acute analogue to Quentin's own fantasy of virginity and incest, for both accommodations to fact—Quentin's of the past, Jason's of the present—build on real truths. Quentin is virgin and he and Caddy did contemplate, however briefly and with whatever aimlessness, an act of incest. Jason is victimized—by Quentin IV, by the man with the red tie, and by himself. His excited movements, his constant action, his spiteful tyranny at home, his real nastiness, pettiness, and meanness are all deliberate attempts to hide his sense of humiliation and failure from his family and from himself. But his perpetual frenzy and his series of incompleted actions show us that beneath his anxiety and his acts of deliberate cruelty are self-hatred and despair, for he is more Quentin's brother than he knows.

Yet Jason is not so confused that he does not dimly recognize this himself. Where Quentin III is hounded by thoughts of Dalton Ames, Jason IV cannot help but compare himself to his older brother. References to Quentin's year at Harvard are choric. "Selling land to send him to Harvard and paying taxes to support a state University all the time that I never saw except twice at a baseball game"; "I says no I never had university advantages because at Harvard they teach you how to go for a swim at night without knowing how to swim and at Sewanee they dont even teach you what water is." This sardonic humor is grounded in hatred and runs as deep as envy, for it too is essentially as self-accusatory as Quentin's recollections of Dalton Ames have been. Jason sees his own double in Quentin: they both stand on ideals, and both are aware of their own defeats long before defeat arrives. Jason is as much concerned as Quentin with managing time (both make constant references to clocks), with worrying about personal honor and family position, and with leaning, for final judgment, on public opinion: to be governed by inner and outer senses of respectability. Jason also shares with Quentin and with Benjy an analogizing consciousness. He continually measures the present state of the Compson household against its past and sees the present as a poor parody. He sees Quentin IV as another Caddy, she who first betrayed him when her marriage broke up and Sydney Head withdrew his promise of a position in the bank for Jason. Caddy once said to Quentin, "Im bad anyway you cant help it"; significantly, Quentin IV modifies this when she tells Jason, " 'If I'm bad, it's because I had to be. You made me.' " Quentin IV's provocative behavior in dress and manner, her continual acts of promiscuity, her secret dates and her flaunting of boyfriends while walking down the alley behind Earl's hardware store are all analogous to Caddy for Jason, and all promise to him a repetition of loss, this time the real loss of financial support.

Like his father and like Quentin, Jason tries to abstract his position. Jason's own terms are financial: investments, projected income, hoarded savings, and Wall Street speculations. The philosophy he builds on such a shaky foundation—that one must deal shrewdly to stay alive, that victory belongs to the greedy and to the clever—is at once a debasement of his father's sense of decadence and a vulgar parody of Quentin's musings on morality. Yet it also parallels them, for at the center of his corruption is Jason's yearning to re-create the past. Jason bolsters himself, as his brothers do, by living in a world of self-projections. Benjy replaces his uncomfortable present with correlative moments in the past; Quentin lives the fantasy of incest and of challenging Dalton Ames successfully; Jason lives with his fantasies of his cleverness at business dealings—in his quips on the market, his high-handedness with Earl and Job, his affair with Lorraine, and his treatment of his niece. But such fantasies display meanness rather than shrewdness, disproportionate meanness rather than common sense. Lorraine's letter mocks him even more than he realizes. Dilsey's efficiency is seen by him (significantly) as a constant affront. In chasing Quentin IV through Jefferson and out the back roads onto Ab Russell's lot, Jason reifies his own frenzy, his own needless secrecy and confusion, and his summary of the chase—"Like I say it's not that I object to so much; maybe she cant help that, it's because she hasn't even got enough consideration for her own family to have any discretion"—is for us a pathetic *self*-condemnation.

This like all else Jason proclaims—and he talks largely in declarative sentences—has the hollow ring of self-defeatism. He too builds his own defenses. He reorders the world by his ideal form of logic and his imposed sense of business, of clever acquisition and the shrewd deployment of resources. His thoughts constantly turn on logical connectives, on *because, when, where,* and *if.* He maintains authority by withholding some of the facts, such as the forged checks he gives Caroline to burn and the amount of the money order Caddy sends her daughter. Where he cannot maintain this kind of absolute control, where he is at the mercy of others, he turns uncertainty itself into virtue by presuming to understand it: " 'Cotton is a speculator's crop. They fill the farmer full of hot air and get him to raise a big crop for them to whipsaw on the market, to trim the suckers with.' " He does not converse with others but talks *at* them, in incomplete sentences and in clichés. In apposition to his mother's platitudes and his Uncle Maury's written circumlocutions, he manages to retain authority by using his cruel and embittered wit; his images are not from nature, as Benjy's and Quentin's are, but from man-made objects: Quentin IV's face looks "like she had polished it with a gun rag"; her nose, puffed from crying, "looked like a porcelain insulator." All these defenses are obviously strained, for Jason is also essentially suicidal: in seeking confirmation of his own self-deprecation from the outside world, he willfully insults others; he provides for his family in a way he knows may collapse at any moment; he even risks his uncertain position at the store. " 'I dont know why you are trying to make me fire you,' " Earl tells him.

Fearfully competitive to survive, Jason also becomes, in his decline, merely contentious. He quarrels over trivialities. His notion of life as a contest replaces Benjy's notion of life as family love and Quentin's view of life as chivalric adventure. Jason is very much of the present century, yet he argues from nothing to nothing; his narrative consciousness itself, like his arguments and actions, is largely a sham, and his conclusion, that one gesture is as good as another, forces Lorraine, Quentin IV, Caroline Compson, Dilsey, and Caddy into an unfortunate and misleading equivalency. Jason's final torrent of words functions for us precisely as Benjy's last perceptions of the early fall of 1898, the day of the scene at the branch, and Quentin's kaleidoscopic jumble of facts, ideas, and delusions just before his suicide.

> When I finished my cigar and went up, the light was still on. I could see the empty keyhole, but I couldn't hear a sound. She studied quiet. Maybe she learned that in school. I told Mother goodnight and went on to my room and got the box out and counted it again. I could hear the Great American Gelding snoring away like a planing mill. I read somewhere they'd fix men that way to give them women's voices. But maybe he didn't know what they'd done to him. I dont reckon he even knew what he had been trying to do, or why Mr Burgess knocked him out with the fence picket. And if they'd just sent him on to Jackson while he was under the ether, he'd never have known the difference. But that would have been too simple for a Compson to think of. Not half complex enough. Having to wait to do it at all until he broke out and tried to run a little girl down on the street with her own father looking at him. Well, like I say they never started soon enough with their cutting, and they quit too quick. I know at least two more that needed something like that, and one of them not over a mile away, either. But then I dont reckon even that would do any good. Like I say once a bitch always a bitch. And just let me have twenty-four hours without any damn New York jew to advise me what it's going to do. I dont want to make a killing; save that to suck in the smart gamblers with. I just want an even chance to get my money back. And once I've done that they can bring all Beale

Street and all bedlam in here and two of them can sleep in my
bed and another one can have my place at the table too.

It is all there with Jason as with Benjy and Quentin—the inescapable
past, the deep sorrow over the family's loss of pride and honor, the
self-justifications and rationalizations strongly argued, the lack of self-
confidence, and—most of all—the overwhelming self-pity. His day,
like theirs, has been circular, and his consciousness ends too where it
began: "Once a bitch always a bitch, what I say." Although Jason has
been considerably more active, he has accomplished less and told us
less about the Compsons and himself: he is distinctively Benjy's and
Quentin's brother, but he is also the least of them.

No matter how thoroughly and painfully the events of Jason's
crowded but empty day mirror his consciousness, his inner self, we
cannot tell at the close of his chapter whether his debasement is the
result of his character or whether his character is the result of the
Compsons' own decline. Chapter 4 is meant to answer this essential
question of our constitutive consciousness in its more fluid and multiple
perspective on the present-day Compson household.

We have seen contradictory images of Dilsey; while Quentin's view
of her as a devoted and loving surrogate mother confirms Benjy's
attitude, Jason sees her as meddling, old, and inefficient, now more of
a burden than a contribution to the Compsons. At last we meet her
directly; and the passage surprises.

The day dawned bleak and chill, a moving wall of grey light out
of the northeast which, instead of dissolving into moisture,
seemed to disintegrate into minute and venomous particles, like
dust that, when Dilsey opened the door of the cabin and
emerged, needled laterally into her flesh, precipitating not so
much a moisture as a substance partaking of the quality of thin,
not quite congealed oil. She wore a stiff black straw hat perched
upon her turban, and a maroon velvet cape with a border of
mangy and anonymous fur above a dress of purple silk, and
she stood in the door for awhile with her myriad and sunken
face lifted to the weather, and one gaunt hand flac-soled as the
belly of a fish, then she moved the cape aside and examined the
bosom of her gown.

The gown fell gauntly from her shoulders, across her fallen
breasts, then tightened upon her paunch and fell again, balloon-
ing a little above the nether garments which she would remove

layer by layer as the spring accomplished and the warm days, in colour regal and moribund. She had been a big woman once but now her skeleton rose, draped loosely in unpadded skin that tightened again upon a paunch almost dropsical, as though muscle and tissue had been courage or fortitude which the days or the years had consumed until only the indomitable skeleton was left rising like a ruin or a landmark above the somnolent and impervious guts, and above that the collapsed face that gave the impression of the bones themselves being outside the flesh, lifted into the driving day with an expression at once fatalistic and of a child's astonished disappointment, until she turned and entered the house again and closed the door.

What we are given is not so much a person as an emblem passage of the Compsons, *The Sound and the Fury* in miniature. "Regal and moribund": her weakened attempts to don the splendid garments of the past and the regal purple associated with Christ on Easter Sunday upon her own body, no longer large and splendid enough to hold them, is correlative to the condition of the family itself; hers is a collection of worn ornaments from a tired and long ago time. She has been "consumed" by the past, "the days" such as we have been given in the first three chapters "or the years" which have witnessed her decline. She is as "fatalistic" in her expression as Benjy, Quentin, or Jason, and like them she has apparently fought against the inevitable; she too has "a child's astonished disappointment." Her one gesture in response to the "bleak and chill" world is to examine "the bosom of her gown," to look inward. But she resembles her environment in what she sees; there we find an indomitable "skeleton." Her movement, correlative to those we have seen, is circular; she steps out of her house only to return into it once again.

Beyond all this her resemblance is a resemblance to death; she has declined almost beyond recognition. In her barren landscape there are no alternatives: no postures for continuing save by willful endurance. What we have, then, is a description of doom. We are further startled to find her double, physically, in Benjy: "His skin was dead looking and hairless; dropsical too, he moved with a shambling gait." Dilsey like Benjy retains the strength of her own fortitude. " 'En who gwine eat yo messin?' " she says to Caroline, scoffing at her offer to make breakfast (for it is not, we may be sure, a genuine offer), yet she continues to do her chores "with a sort of painful and terrific slowness." Dilsey's faith, like that of Benjy and Quentin, is self-generated, trusting, and futile, working through its own persistent sense of charity against her husband Roskus's choric comment, repeated by her children, that " 'Taint no luck on this place.' "

The cause for Dilsey's exhaustion is not far to seek. Like Benjy, Quentin, and Jason, she has persisted in her loyalty to the Compsons and to the Compson past. She is the retainer, the perennial house servant whose source of authority, compassion, and self-possession come from Christianity now ignored by Caroline, Jason, and Quentin IV, and from an antebellum tradition that has long since passed its usefulness. She too would perpetuate the myth of former Compson grandeur. As we move outward, however, we see that Dilsey is indirectly described by her surroundings. She is an older version of Luster: while he feeds Benjy with assurance and compassion, his "other hand lay on the back of the chair and upon that dead surface it moved tentatively, delicately, as if he were picking an inaudible tune out of the dead void." The cause for demise—the combination of sin, promiscuity, and death—is figured upstairs, where Quentin IV's room has "that dead and stereotyped transcience of rooms in assignation houses." The entire house, seen full and from the outside, not only reinforces our new view of Dilsey's limitations but undercuts Jason's pathetic attempts at preserving the past by sheer effort of will: it is now only a "square, paintless house with its rotting portico." If there is any large resemblance to the Compson household in chapter 4, it is (tellingly) in the description of Nigger Hollow, where "What growth there was consisted of rank weeds and the trees were mulberries and locusts and sycamores—trees that partook also of the foul desiccation which surrounded the houses." Although we may first hope for order, what we are presented with is the shabby and decadent, the consequence of a long erosion of past life into something like the prescience—even the presence—of death. Caroline Compson's reaction to the departure of Quentin IV—" 'Find the note,' she said. 'Quentin left a note when he did it' "—is neither the confusion of senility nor a poor joke, but a summing up of the mood, the inner awareness and weariness of them all.

Against the weight of this signification of attrition, Faulkner juxtaposes the sound and the fury of the Easter service at Nigger Hollow. The church itself, like the landscape before it, seems unreal.

> The road rose again, to a scene like a painted backdrop. Notched into a cut of red clay crowned with oaks the road appeared to stop short off, like a cut ribbon. Beside it a weathered church

> lifted its crazy steeple like a painted church, and the whole
> scene was as flat and without perspective as a painted cardboard
> set upon the ultimate edge of the flat earth, against the windy
> sunlight of space and April and a midmorning filled with bells.

The emphasis is on the simulation of authenticity which reflects other
simulations: Dilsey's of the past, Jason's of success, Quentin's of
Dalton Ames, and Benjy's of Caddy. The inside of the church mirrors
the outside; it is another attempt to create a cause for celebration.

> The church had been decorated, with sparse flowers from
> kitchen gardens and hedgerows, and with streamers of coloured
> crepe paper. Above the pulpit hung a battered Christmas bell,
> the accordion sort that collapses. The pulpit was empty, though
> the choir was already in place, fanning themselves although it
> was not warm.

The Christmas bell at Easter—perhaps a deliberate linkage by those
faithful who serve the church—strikes also at the theatricality of the
event, and this is personified in the Reverend Shegog himself, a traveling show " 'fum Saint Looey.' " " 'Dat big preacher' " does not match
local expectations either.

> The visitor was undersized, in a shabby alpaca coat. He had a
> wizened black face like a small, aged monkey. And all the while
> that the choir sang again and while the six children rose and
> sang in thin, frightened, tuneless whispers, they watched the
> insignificant looking man sitting dwarfed and countrified by
> the minister's imposing bulk, with something like consternation.
> They were still looking at him with consternation and un-
> belief when the minister rose and introduced him in rich,
> rolling tones whose very unction served to increase the visitor's
> insignificance.
> "En dey brung dat all de way fum Saint Looey," Frony
> whispered.

Yet what follows is the spectacle they had hoped for, the act they came
to see. "He tramped steadily back and forth beneath the twisted paper
and the Christmas bell, hunched, his hands clasped behind him. He
was like a worn small rock whelmed by the successive waves of his
voice." He moves the audience to compassion, to communal anguish,
"so that when he came to rest against the reading desk, his monkey
face lifted and his whole attitude that of a serene, tortured crucifix that

transcended its shabbiness and insignificance and made it of no moment, a long moaning expulsion of breath rose from them, and a woman's single soprano: 'Yes, Jesus!' " The brief description of Reverend Shegog deliberately recalls the description of Dilsey which opens the chapter, and this scene isolated and given us anywhere else might be, in its pitiful meagerness transformed to joy, a moving testament to faith, a transportation into tongues. But it cannot be so here, in chapter 4 of *The Sound and the Fury*, where it is charged with the burden of all that has gone before it and all that is hinted to come; here it is almost unbearably tragic. The congregation at Nigger Hollow reflects the Compson family, working at their own hope, living on their own faith, communally and spiritually willing to themselves the belief in a glorious past and the promise of a glorious future. They, too, see life as a trial which anticipates a resurrection after death. Although Quentin III sees spilled blood as useless when cleaning up after his fight with Gerald Bland while the Nigger Hollow congregation sees the blood of the Lamb, the blood of possibility, both views are self-fulfilling prophecies. Just as the Compsons re-form life to their own expectations, so the worshipers at Nigger Hollow see what they came to see, find what they planned to find. So the power of Shegog's Word —in a novel so concerned with the power of words—does not, finally, convert anyone previously unconverted. Everyone and everything return to what they were before. Frony leaves church still worried about their appearance, their respectability, as Caroline Compson might worry (" 'Whyn't you quit dat, mammy? . . . Wid all dese people lookin. We be passin white folks soon.' "); Dilsey has confirmed what she knew with her sacred sense of time and history (" 'He seed de power en de glory' . . . 'I've seed de first en de last' "); and Benjy, who has "sat, rapt in his sweet blue gaze" throughout the service, is still actively engaged in his separate and interior world.

Juxtaposed to this climatic scene is Jason's bloody fight with the old circus hand, sound and fury without *any* religious signification. It is no accident and no sly parody, but the secular parallel to what goes on in Nigger Hollow. Jason enters Mottstown with the reputation worthy of a Shegog, "his file of soldiers with the manacled sheriff in the rear, dragging Omnipotence down from His throne, if necessary." His fight is the good fight, too, for he defends (if only ironically, interested as he is in appearances) the pride and honor and decency—the moral up-rightness—of his family line. But the tinsel trappings of the church have no parallel in a circus tent; he finds only unloaded boxcars as earlier he had found Quentin IV's room empty. The joy at the church service is countered and seriously modified in his total frustration, his overwhelming despair. He has from the outset of his day been witness to the most serious progressive loss of all, for no one has understood or befriended him—not his mother or Dilsey, whose income is gone; not the sheriff, who exposes at last his own legal and economic corruption; and not the old man at the circus, who, with his butcher knife, would disclose Jason's essential ineffectiveness. The smell of gasoline which overcomes him is analogous to the smell of trees for Benjy and the smell of honeysuckle for Quentin, but this time there is no love or salvation in the most mundane (and mechanically produced) sensation. " 'What were you trying to do?' " asks a man who intervenes in his behalf, a stranger. " 'Commit suicide?' "

Dilsey herself, returned to the Compson household, is refreshed, but as for Jason there is no permanent relief for her among the Compsons. Christ may have risen, but he has not harrowed Jefferson on his way. In her routine round of resumed duties—the meal; Caroline's Bible and hot-water bottle; the supervision of Luster, who is twanging on the saw; and Benjy, who is moaning—she lives her own diminished present, her kitchen as limited an environment as Quentin's private hell and Quentin IV's upper room. In this mundane and repetitive existence, her activities are caught up in the same clop-clop rhythm as Queenie's, soon to be harnessed and taken to the graveyard. Both echo the inherent lines of the title: "Tomorrow and tomorrow and tomorrow" creeping in its petty, repetitive, unrelieved pace. This becomes the final irony for the Reverend Shegog's sermon, and for the insistent but futile dreams, sacred and secular, that barely sustain the still-living Compsons.

The confusion of names in *The Sound and the Fury*—the Quentins, Jasons, Maurys—suggests the essential unity of the family's vision: its agreement on purpose, its strident devotion to a reliance on appearances, and its compulsive and obsessive need to look inward and backward, its steady myopia. Benjy's castration like his idiocy seem outer images for them all: on Holy Saturday they have only the idiot's birthday to celebrate, and a circus is in town; on Easter Sunday Quentin IV has escaped her tomb, but the novel implies that she will only follow Caddy's path into an inevitable promiscuity and despair of her own (as well as her world's) making. Dilsey's spiritual and spirited opposition to the selfish, secular Jason remains futile. There is no resurrection here, no reconciliation; there is only resignation.

Each chapter of the novel circles around and back into itself; each ends in its beginning, like the narrative consciousness in *Light in August,* or the brooding tale of Conrad's Marlow on a barge at Gravesend. Despite the unique perspective and mental geography of each of the Compsons, we are given an essential unity in the emptiness of their present lives, in the lost vitality of their visions, and in the hopelessness of their dreams. Even the novel ends, as it began, with Benjy, for everyone comes, at last, to meet him on his own terms. They are the terms that correlate Damuddy, his father, Quentin, and Caddy, the terms of loss and of death. In a short time we find him "squatting before a small mound of earth. At either end of it an empty bottle of blue glass that once contained poison was fixed in the ground. In one was a withered stalk of jimson weed." This is a memorial celebration to all that he holds dear—to his family now gone, to his childhood, to the past generally. His Sunday ride to the larger graveyard, the family and community memorial to the past, is also just such a tribute. His insistence on the primacy of the past—of *their* past—is maintained even when Luster disrupts Benjy's careful construction of eternal time by driving old Queenie clockwise around the town square. Powerfully, fatefully we learn with Benjy that the establishment of peace and eternity by limited and mundane routine—Dilsey's means of survival too—is harrowingly, tragically vulnerable. Jason races out to confirm Benjy's patterning of events, to preserve appearances and secure the preservation of the Compsons. So they pass backward now, physically as well as mentally and spiritually, back over the ground they have just covered. Above them and behind, the Confederate soldier looks out, facing south, facing in the direction of the Compson home. Nothing has changed—"Ben's fist and his eyes were empty and blue and serene again as cornice and façade flowed smoothly once more from left to right; post and tree, window and doorway, and signboard, each in its ordered place"—except for one thing. Benjy is holding a flower, significantly a narcissus and significantly one that is broken. It has been straightened and mended, however, with twigs and a bit of string, by the black servant. Benjy does not see that. But we do.

The circle around the courthouse is a reduced replica of the circularity of the largest hopes and fantasies of *The Sound and the Fury.* It is fitting that, a quarter century later in the 1945 Appendix to this novel, the larger chronology of the Compsons begins with the heroism of Andrew Jackson ("who set the wellbeing of the nation above the White House and the health of his new political party above either and above them all set not his wife's honor but the principle that honor must be defended whether it was or not because defended it was whether or not"), and the line ends with Benjy's dishonorable incarceration in the state asylum at Jackson, Mississippi. From Jackson to Jackson; from insistence on abstract honor and glory to concrete idiocy; from dust unto dust. *The Sound and the Fury* is life itself; it draws its final terms beyond what the Compsons find at either end. In that sense, our constitutive consciousness alone draws its most comprehensive circle; and we are invited, in this last analysis, to include ourselves.

"As I Lay Dying"

As I Lay Dying, like *The Sound and the Fury*, is essentially a family novel; it too portrays the dissatisfaction of a willful mother whose family repeatedly fails to live up to her expectations. Addie Bundren is a stronger and more complicated character than Caroline Compson, but as *The Sound and the Fury* measured the Compson decline through Benjy's idiocy—as Benjy began and ended the novel—so *As I Lay Dying* measures Addie's failure in the progressive sickness of Darl's narrative consciousness.

As the presiding intelligence within *As I Lay Dying*, Darl's perspective is divided from the outset. He introduces the novel with this monologue.

> Jewel and I come up from the field, following the path in single file. Although I am fifteen feet ahead of him, anyone watching us from the cottonhouse can see Jewel's frayed and broken straw hat a full head above my own.
>
> The path runs straight as a plumb-line, worn smooth by feet and baked brick-hard by July, between the green rows of laid-by cotton, to the cottonhouse in the center of the field, where it turns and circles the cottonhouse at four soft right angles and goes on across the field again, worn so by feet in fading precision.
>
> The cottonhouse is of rough logs, from between which the chinking has long fallen. Square, with a broken roof set at a single pitch, it leans in empty and shimmering dilapidation in the sunlight, a single broad window in two opposite walls giving onto the approaches of the path. When we reach it I turn and follow the path which circles the house. Jewel, fifteen feet

behind me, looking straight ahead, steps in a single stride through the window. Still staring straight ahead, his pale eyes like wood set into his wooden face, he crosses the floor in four strides with the rigid gravity of a cigar store Indian dressed in patched overalls and endued with life from the hips down, and steps in a single stride through the opposite window and into the path again just as I come around the corner. In single file and five feet apart and Jewel now in front, we go on up the path toward the foot of the bluff.

There is an absolute clarity of vision, Jewel's rigidity and sexuality measured against Darl's circuitous and more fluid movements, but what is disturbing to us is what he sees. "Fifteen feet ahead of [Jewel]," he can see what Jewel looks like; he knows how many paces behind him Jewel is; outside the cottonhouse, with Jewel inside, he can still see him, know that he takes only one step, know how he appears. Darl's visual thinking is split between recording what he *sees* and projecting what he *thinks*, the realized and the imagined; further confused yet, he sees not only from two perspectives but from *three*, for he also thinks about the way *both* of them would look to someone at the cottonhouse as they approach it. What begins here as a juxtaposition of what is experienced and what is thought, what performed and what imagined, will grow progressively throughout the novel, the gap between the two becoming irrevocably wider. Multiple perspective in *As I Lay Dying* is not merely the presentation but the subject; despite the fragmentation of the novel—itself the larger analogue to Darl's fractured mind—nineteen of the fifty-nine sections, the bulk of them, are given over to tracing his progressively divided vision. Darl persistently stands between us and events, observing, relating, imagining, projecting, shaping, yet it is through his troubled and distorted vision that our constitutive consciousness must make its way for much of the time.

Like Bayard and John Sartoris, and like Benjy and Quentin Compson—or like offspring in Dostoyevsky, Joyce, and Proust—Darl is the child of his parents. He shares the lazy physical indolence of Anse since his activity is nearly all mental, yet his agitation and deep-seated anxieties are akin to his mother's. His thoughts, like those of all the others save MacGowan, dwell on his mother and on her death, for Addie Bundren is the imagistic center of the novel; his own forming philosophy, like hers, is death oriented, correlative to her corpse and its progressively stronger smell. Addie tells us that what she thinks also has no relationship to what she says and does.

> I would think how words go straight up in a thin line, quick and harmless, and how terribly doing goes along the earth, clinging to it, so that after a while the two lines are too far apart for the same person to straddle from one to the other.

That is Addie; here is Darl:

> How do our lives ravel out into the no-wind, no-sound, the weary gestures wearily recapitulant: echoes of old compulsions with no-hand on no-strings: in sunset we fall into furious attitudes, dead gestures of dolls.

As the novel unfolds we see Darl's relationship with his mother become obsessive and debilitating; he is not only estranged from his family (like Addie) through an impulse to metaphysics, but her bodily presence, try as he does to shake it from him, persists in forcing him to answer questions of existence which are beyond his capacity to resolve. His clairvoyant description of Addie's death demonstrates his intense mental involvement with her despite their deliberate physical separation, and his clairvoyant description of Cash and Vernon Tull completing the coffin for Addie in the dark, the wind, and the rain while Anse only watches reveals to us that his involvement is only heightened, not released, by her death. We are not surprised, then, when Cora Tull tells us that he came silently to see Addie one last time before going on an errand to earn three dollars; her superficial chattiness moves upward in the thin, harmless line of religious clichés while Darl's own troubled, tragic wisdom clings terribly to the earth.

As I Lay Dying is Darl's autobiography of consciousness; we learn from him that his ability to abstract himself from life itself began as a child. He recalls drinking from a cedar bucket as a youngster and later, during adolescence, masturbating in strangely remote terms.

> I used to lie on the pallet in the hall, waiting until I could hear them all asleep, so I could get up and go back to the bucket. It would be black, the shelf black, the still surface of the water a round orifice in nothingness, where before I stirred it awake with the dipper I could see maybe a star or two in the bucket, and maybe in the dipper a star or two before I drank. After that I was bigger, older. Then I would wait until they all went to sleep so I could lie with my shirt-tail up, hearing them asleep, feeling myself without touching myself, feeling the cool silence

blowing upon my parts and wondering if Cash was yonder in the darkness doing it too.

Darl first finds his other self in Jewel, whose ability at physical activity he much admires. We know the depth of his attachment to Jewel from the first and third segments; in the latter, his interior vision is so intent that he sees Jewel an impossible distance away, down in the pasture past the young pines.

> Down there fooling with that horse. He will go on through the barn, into the pasture. The horse will not be in sight: he is up there among the pine seedlings, in the cool. Jewel whistles, once and shrill. The horse snorts, then Jewel sees him, glinting for a gaudy instant among the blue shadows. Jewel whistles again; the horse comes dropping down the slope, stiff-legged, his ears cocking and flicking, his mis-matched eyes rolling, and fetches up twenty feet away, broadside on, watching Jewel over his shoulder in an attitude kittenish and alert.

If there is envy, it is the envy that Jewel need not worry his way to a primitivistic metaphysics. The description we get, however, bursts with admiration and the picture, while sexual, is also vibrantly poetic.

> When Jewel can almost touch him, the horse stands on his hind legs and slashes down at Jewel. Then Jewel is enclosed by a glittering maze of hooves as by an illusion of wings; among them, beneath the up-reared chest, he moves with the flashing limberness of a snake. For an instant before the jerk comes onto his arms he sees his whole body earth-free, horizontal, whipping snake-limber, until he finds the horse's nostrils and touches earth again. Then they are rigid, motionless, terrific, the horse back-thrust on stiffened, quivering legs, with lowered head; Jewel with dug heels, shutting off the horse's wind with one hand, with the other patting the horse's neck in short strokes myriad and caressing, cursing the horse with obscene ferocity.
>
> They stand in rigid terrific hiatus, the horse trembling and groaning. Then Jewel is on the horse's back. He flows upward in a stooping swirl like the lash of a whip, his body is midair shaped to the horse. For another moment the horse stands spraddled, with lowered head, before it bursts into motion. They descend the hill in a series of spine-jolting jumps, Jewel high, leech-like on the withers, to the fence where the horse bunches to a scuttering halt again.

Vernon Tull will later corroborate this view of Jewel astride his horse as a thing of power and beauty, and so will Cash.

But Addie's death undoes all this. We know because Darl's very first speculation on the meaning and value of existence is prompted by his vision of her death. It comes in a strange bed and a strange place, while he and Jewel are absent from the protection of the Bundren household.

> In a strange room you must empty yourself for sleep. And before you are emptied for sleep, what are you. And when you are emptied for sleep, you are not. And when you are filled with sleep, you never were. I dont know what I am. I dont know if I am or not. Jewel knows he is, because he does not know that he does not know whether he is or not.

Since Darl has such an intense affinity with Addie (as no one else in the family does), her death suddenly presages his own. Sleep may be analogous to death—or it may be the signification, given his ability at abstraction, of his own nonbeing. This bothers him immensely, not least of all because it discloses that his real identity remains with his mother, not with Jewel.

> Since sleep is is-not and rain and wind are *was*, it is not. Yet the wagon *is*, because when the wagon is *was*, Addie Bundren will not be. And Jewel *is*, so Addie Bundren must be. And then I must be, or I could not empty myself for sleep in a strange room. And so if I am not emptied yet, I am *is*.

His tangled logic folds in on itself, goes nowhere. Yet Addie's presence is inescapable once he returns home, her corpse so tangible a reminder in sight and smell that his own existence is threatened and his mortality certain. By sheer will, the boy who others tell us does nothing much but think throws himself into family activity. He intervenes between Jewel and Tull to calm them both when Anse insists on crossing the swollen creek. He helps to fetch Cash's tools from the creek bottom and later carries them into Armstid's house. At Grummet's Hardware in Mottstown, upon Cash's insistence, he goes after more cement. In Jefferson, he prevents a fight between Jewel and the man with the knife. In his own consciousness he clings desperately to the appearances of others, to events, to actions; he appropriates the language of others rather than of himself. Now his divided mind is increasingly torn not between what he images at some distance and what he sees about him, but between his attempts to rid himself of Addie altogether and his own tendency toward morbid and impossible speculations. For Darl wants to comprehend the world not by aping Addie's nihilism and not by re-forming it after some pattern of his own, but by *realizing* it in its own image. His fight is not for his own reality but for everyone else's, even as Addie's body drags him back to her own morbidity and decease.

" 'Well, it is a kind of sterility—Words,' " Dawson Fairchild remarks in *Mosquitoes*. " 'You begin to substitute words for things and deeds, like the withered cuckold husband that took the Decameron to bed with him every night, and pretty soon the thing or the deed becomes just a kind of shadow of a certain sound you make by shaping your mouth a certain way.' " Darl's progressive reliance on his mother—his license to a life of the mind—transforms his exercises in split vision, in looking on Jewel as a secret model or his relatively harmless abstraction of physical experience, into something more deeply serious. His clairvoyance threatens a permanent splintering of mind, as his brother Vardaman recalls for us.

> "Jewel's mother is a horse," Darl said.
> "Then mine can be a fish, cant it, Darl?" I said.
> Jewel is my brother.
> "Then mine will have to be a horse, too," I said.
> "Why?" Darl said. "If pa is your pa, why does your ma have to be a horse just because Jewel's is?"
> "Why does it?" I said. "Why does it, Darl?"
> Darl is my brother.
> "Then what is your ma, Darl?" I said.
> "I haven't got ere one," Darl said. "Because if I had one, it is *was*. And if it is was, it cant be *is*. Can it?"
> "No," I said.
> "Then I am not," Darl said. "Am I?"
> "No," I said.
> I am. Darl is my brother.
> "But you *are*, Darl," I said.
> "I know it," Darl said. "That's why I am not *is*. *Are* is too many for one woman to foal."

With Vardaman as a sounding board, Darl maintains a fragile equilibrium. But this is not true when he meditates alone. "If you could just ravel out into time. That would be nice. It would be nice if you could just ravel out into time." Then he becomes suicidal.

It is our constitutive consciousness that determines the persistent grounds for this instinct to self-annihilation. Besides Addie's dominance, Darl experiences, as we do, all the other reactions to Addie's death. He is in fact the only one in whose consciousness all the other fragments of the novel inhere and the acknowledgments of the others undo him. Darl can see (as Anse, Cash, Dewey Dell, and Vardaman cannot) the increasing embarrassment of taking Addie's stinking body to Jefferson for burial. The elements—the flood especially—seem against them. The neighbors are not appreciative or respectful but puzzled and mocking. The coffin itself has holes drilled in it by Vardaman and patched by Cash's plugs; it is drawn by an old team of mules and later an unmatched team, and it transports in time a man whose leg is mended with cement. Such agonizing ludicrousness points out to Darl the absurdity of their entire journey; for him, the Bundren odyssey is not richly humorous (as it is, at times, for us) but painfully grotesque. This would of course be sufficient reason to compel Darl to set Armstid's barn afire when Addie's coffin is placed there to keep the odor under control, but his unnatural clairvoyance has also admitted Darl to the motives of his family for their mission and, Jewel aside, he sees all the other Bundrens as blindly selfish. Anse seeks false teeth, although he rarely speaks; Dewey Dell seeks an abortion, yet her one natural ability is for conception and childbearing; Vardaman looks for an electric train that has long since disappeared from the Christmas display in the shop window; and Cash seeks a phonograph, although he owns no records and has little means by which to purchase them.

As Addie's body decomposes, so for Darl does the significance of the journey. Their fates become parallel. The funeral journey becomes funereal for Darl; its cost is too high. The family loses its only team and damages its only wagon. Jewel is required to sacrifice his horse—that which he loves most and which has afforded the means for his reconciliation with the loss of the mother he is now burying—and Cash may lose his leg, perhaps sacrificing his life as a carpenter and certainly restricting his life as a craftsman and his stature as a man. It is no wonder, then, that even if he could dismiss Addie as a double, Darl finally cracks under the impossibility of reconciling these absurd events (and the absurdity of death itself, which they mirror) and his own hope for order and meaning in the world. His attempts to end their pain—by letting Addie's coffin slip into the creek, by setting fire to Armstid's barn—are both frustrated. Moreover, he is betrayed by

Jewel, the one he loves most. We understand the precipitating effect of this final horror as he looks upon his earlier secret self. " 'I thought you would have told me,' " he says to Cash in shock and disbelief. " 'I never thought you wouldn't have.' " Thus the ludicrousness he saw at the outset of that awful journey which so annoyed Anse— "Darl begun to laugh. Setting back there on the plank seat with Cash, with his dead ma laying in her coffin at his feet, laughing. How many times I told him it's doing such things as that that makes folks talk about him. I don't know"—intimates his final indictment by his own family and his incarceration, just as his initial ability to see *himself* from the cottonhouse prefigures his final full projection into a completed second self. "Darl has gone to Jackson," Darl himself tells us.

> They put him on the train, laughing, down the long car laughing, the heads turning like the heads of owls when he passed. "What are you laughing at?" I said.
> "Yes yes yes yes yes."
> Two men put him on the train. They wore mis-matched coats, bulging behind over their right hip pockets. Their necks were shaved to a hairline, as though the recent and simultaneous barbers had had a chalk-line like Cash's. "Is it the pistols you're laughing at?" I said. "Why do you laugh?" I said. "Is it because you hate the sound of laughing?"

Not absurdity, finally, but the horrors of life overtake Darl and fix him in bewildered uncontrol.

The analogue to Darl's predicament—and his double to our constitutive consciousness—is Addie; if Darl's is the most prominent voice, Addie is the novel's most prominent presence. Like Darl, Addie has also, all her life, felt unloved by people and so alienated from life itself. "Words are no good," she tells us; "words dont ever fit even what they are trying to say at. When he [Cash] was born I knew that motherhood was invented by someone who had to have a word for it because the ones that had the children didn't care whether there was a word for it or not"; "love" is only a word and language "just a shape to fill a lack."

As Darl inherits his sense of death from his mother, Addie has inherited hers from her father. She recalls as her earliest memory how his words led her to inflict pain on schoolchildren when she was a teacher in an attempt to feel and live life, to become another person too, in order to escape a sense of not-being.

I could just remember how my father used to say that the reason for living was to get ready to stay dead a long time. And
when I would have to look at them day after day, each with
his and her secret and selfish thought, and blood strange to
each other blood and strange to mine, and think that this
seemed to be the only way I could get ready to stay dead, I
would hate my father for having ever planted me. I would
look forward to the times when they faulted, so I could whip
them. When the switch fell I could feel it upon my flesh; when
it welted and ridged it was my blood that ran, and I would
think with each blow of the switch: Now you are aware of me!
Now I am something in your secret and selfish life, who have
marked your blood with my own for ever and ever.

Surely a large part of Addie's difficulty is her sexual frustration.

In the afternoon when school was out and the last one had left
with his little dirty snuffling nose, instead of going home I
would go down the hill to the spring where I could be quiet and
hate them. It would be quiet there then, with the water bub-
bling up and away and the sun slanting quiet in the trees and
the quiet smelling of damp and rotting leaves and new earth;
especially in the early spring, for it was worst then.

Her marriage to Anse results from her frustration sexually and physically, but she has not anticipated his relative indolence. She takes no
joy in the birth of Cash or in Darl; Anse has promised her a kind of
love and sensation which she does not experience. Instead, she counts
up her children, giving Anse two for her act of commission and her
act of omission, sacrificing life to thought, the concrete childbirth to
the abstract idea of love. Her joy with Whitfield, on the other hand,
is compulsive and exuberant. It gives her the sense of sin which her
father had also intimated.

I believed that I had found it. I believed that the reason was the
duty to the alive, to the terrible blood, the red bitter flood
boiling through the land. I would think of sin as I would think
of the clothes we both wore in the world's face, of the circum-
spection necessary because he was he and I was I: the sin the
more utter and terrible since he was the instrument ordained by
God who created the sin, to sanctify that sin He had created.
While I waited for him in the woods, waiting for him before
he saw me, I would think of him as dressed in sin. I would think

of him as thinking of me as dressed also in sin, he the more beautiful since the garment which he had exchanged for sin was sanctified. I would think of the sin as garments which we would remove in order to shape and coerce the terrible blood to the forlorn echo of the dead word high in the air. Then I would lay with Anse again—I did not lie to him: I just refused, just as I refused my breast to Cash and Darl after their time was up—hearing the dark land talking the voiceless speech.

But Whitfield is her undoing as Jewel is Darl's. For it is Whitfield who, ironically enough, can separate words from acts and can so twist words that he can cleanse his conscience. He is the one who can derive from words alone a power sufficient to excuse his own guilt, to explain his own acts, and even to convince others of his innocence. He does so, betraying her again and for the last time, as he goes to give her a final blessing on her deathbed.

I have sinned, O Lord. Thou knowest the extent of my remorse and the will of my spirit. But He is merciful; He will accept the will for the deed, Who knew that when I framed the words of my confession it was to Anse I spoke them, even though he was not there. It was He in His infinite wisdom that restrained the tale from her dying lips as she lay surrounded by those who loved and trusted her; mine the travail by water which I sustained by strength of His hand. Praise to Thee in Thy bounteous and omnipotent love; O praise.

Addie dies before he can arrive, but he takes no offense, for she has kept their adultery secret. In confirming his faith (he says) she merely gives to his words a potency she spent her life denying. We can sense the force of this confrontation to our constitutive consciousness because it falls near the center of the novel; the twinned chapters of Addie and Whitfield are the fulcrum of the novel's movement. In addition, Addie's thoughts are preceded by Cora's, and that too is no accident. Cora's language repeats and balances Whitfield's, and both serve as illustrations of Addie's philosophy about the treachery of words, about the radical divorce between saying and acting. Addie courted Anse to be disappointed; she courted Whitfield and listened to Cora only to be confirmed in that disappointment.

More truly akin to Darl than she realizes, Addie is herself a nascent psychotic, unable to marry her anticipations of life to its realities. She reminds us of Dostoyevsky's tormented Ivan—or of R. D. Laing's recent description of a schizophrenic:

> One schizophrenic woman who was in the habit of stubbing out her cigarettes on the back of her hand, pressing her thumbs hard against her eyeballs, slowly tearing out her hair, etc., explained that she did such things in order to experience something "real." It is most important to understand that this woman was not courting masochistic gratification; nor was she anaesthetic. Her sensations were not less intense than normal. She could feel everything except being alive and real. Minkowski reports that one of his patients set fire to her clothing for similar reasons. The cold schizoid person may "go for kicks," court extreme thrills, push himself into extreme risks in order to "scare some life into himself," as one patient puts it.

This is an adequate summary of Addie's recollection of life (and precisely the reverse of Cora's and Whitfield's). But her willed death is not a final attempt to feel *something*; it is, rather, a resignation to the emptiness of life. Darl wishes to find purpose and order while contemplating non-being; Addie actively wills to die.

Life fails Addie because Addie fails life. She does not experience the tumult of love save with Whitfield, and she gives it to no one else, save Cash, and save Jewel, in the dark, when a horse has become her surrogate and it is too late for her to do anything but mourn her loss. By refusing to give to life, Addie loses any sense of it. Cora tells us that in her last days "Her face is wasted away so that the bones draw just under the skin in white lines. Her eyes are like two candles when you watch them gutter down into the sockets of iron candle-sticks." And, perhaps tellingly, "But the eternal and the everlasting salvation and grace is not upon her." Even this inane woman of words has a bit more of the truth than Addie does, for all we may scoff at her. Addie's sense of life-as-death, especially in her marriage, is fittingly imaged by her family: she is buried in her wedding dress—she marries death at last—even though she is turned the wrong way around to allow the dress to fit the coffin.

Addie's perspective consequently corroborates Darl's and helps our constitutive consciousness to fathom and pity his own turmoil. But Addie herself receives corroboration in the novel, and it comes, as it properly should, from the general practitioner who with some difficulty is hauled up the hill by a rope to visit her in her sickness. The two do not need to meet; they understand well enough the cause of her illness and the imminence of her death as they look at each other at the end. Afterward, Doc Peabody explains.

> I can remember how when I was young I believed death to be a phenomenon of the body; now I know it to be merely a function of the mind—and that of the minds of the ones who suffer the bereavement. The nihilists say it is the end; the fundamentalists, the beginning; when in reality it is no more than a single tenant or family moving out of a tenement or a town.

Doc Peabody confirms Addie and Darl and the dialectic of *As I Lay Dying*, the relationship between word and deed, thought and existence. But in his final homey image, he also provides us with a solution. In his union of abstraction and concretion, fact and metaphor as exact and interchangeable, he points to an answer to Addie's sense of death in his own ideas and expressions of life.

There are twelve other narrative consciousnesses in *As I Lay Dying* to juxtapose alongside Darl, Addie, and Doc Peabody; but all of them, in thought and deed, develop or reveal epistemologies which radiate from the core linkage of Addie and Darl. What separates them is their shared physical involvement in life; neither threatened nor especially aware of the metaphysical, they are full of vitality and, generally, unaware of mental or physical illness. They are seemingly immune to death. Their narrative consciousnesses are essentially visual; they provide the novel with a zest and a pictorialism that make it seem primitive next to *Flags in the Dust* and *The Sound and the Fury* and provide this work with its dimension of comedy. Their direct apprehension of life also frees the book, finally, from the self-pitying, self-sustaining view of life of Addie and Darl and so frees it from the sense of inevitability we feel in *Flags in the Dust* and the sense of claustrophobia that pervades *The Sound and the Fury*. By enlarging the physical journey to the psychological journey of death and renewal of life, they expand the horizons of the novel to achieve what Darl only imperfectly realizes and so embrace a wider, if not necessarily truer, reality.

This primitive pictorialism is seen nearly everywhere. It is seen, for instance, in the visual thinking of Vardaman, whose chief contribution in interpreting Addie's death is to analogize his mother with a fish. Since both died simultaneously, his childish logic tries to establish some relationship, even that of causation. Although it reveals his conscious love and involvement with his family, the fish itself is insufficient as a symbol or explanation and, after his first angry round of random accusations, after freeing Peabody's team, and after his initial stumbling grammar, his mind adjusts (as Darl's does not) to the new reality and his thoughts refocus on the electric train he has wanted since Christmas. This visual thinking is seen too in Jewel. His interest in the physical and his initial directionless grief are analogous to Vardaman's; his profanity is also as inept as his younger brother's scattershot observations. The horse is a replacement for Addie, from Jewel's perspective, as the fish has been for Vardaman. For both, Addie's death forces on them, finally, the end of such needs: Vardaman forgets the fish, and Jewel, with less effort than we might have supposed, is able to surrender the horse, perhaps because he got it when his mother ignored him, perhaps because his getting it initiated her decline. It is after the fish and horse are gone that these two can directly face the problem of Addie's burial—and after his loss of the horse that Jewel can concentrate on pulling Addie's body from the blazing barn.

Next to these children, Anse seem surprisingly unaffected by the loss of his wife. Instead, his mind seems to be on his teeth and, we see by the end of the novel, on remarriage. Yet he is able to win his way to this reconciliation with events only after struggling in his own elemental way with a philosophy of life. For Anse is humpbacked; his feet are splayed and twisted from his youth, when he was forced to work in the wet in homemade shoes. Marriage to Addie has not been pleasant for him either, and he may know that Jewel is not his child. We must have some sympathy, then, for his endurance and for his lack of rancor. His philosophy comes from the land; he formulated it early, perhaps before he married Addie, and he has stuck to it.

> I told Addie it want any luck living on a road when it come by here, . . . because the Lord put roads for travelling: why He laid them down flat on the earth. When He aims for something to be always a-moving, He makes it longways, like a road or a horse or a wagon, but when He aims for something to stay put, He makes it up-and-down ways, like a tree or a man.

Anse's name may be an anagram for *sane*, illustrating as he does the essential rightness of the forces of life. He and his children, like his crops, live; Addie, who is dead, moves horizontally in her funeral procession: Anse finds his own visual accommodations for the fact of death that integrate it into a universe of living things. As a farmer, he is dedicated to his land and to his crops and harvest; by analogizing Addie to all nature, his whole action in the course of the novel—his marriage, his pledge for burial, and his remarriage—are of a piece. The "duck-shaped woman" is not an affront to Addie's memory but a reaffirmation of the simple and single value to which his life has always been directed, the natural, organic cycle of life and death.

Dewey Dell is, throughout, a true child of Anse: she too is dedicated to feeling and life and alien to thought and to death. Her response to Lafe when he approaches her in the cotton field is to react instinctively, to enjoy the foreplay and copulation indiscriminately. She pays no attention to his words but only to her own physical yearnings and to her own bodily responses to his actions. In fact, Dewey Dell is so complete in her responses that she does not need words, even resents and fears their intrusion. She avoids the word *abortion*, for example, although she does not fear the actions it may engender, and she submits to Moseley and MacGowan without distinguishing clearly between them. Like Tull and Cash as well as Anse, she dedicates herself to life by abjuring thought and by refusing to dwell on the dominance of language.

Of all Addie's children, however, Cash is the best adjusted, because he is the only child born in wedlock whom Addie truly loved. He returns her love in full measure in the way he can best—by crafting for her a perfect coffin. Cash's carpentry began when he worked on a church—an analogy made repeatedly in the novel—and he is dedicated to the beauty, the duty, and the religiosity of his work. "Cash bevels the edge of it with the tedious and minute care of a jeweler," Darl tells us, and Tull adds,

> Cash is filling up the holes [Vardaman] bore in the top of it. He is trimming out plugs for them, one at a time, the wood wet and hard to work. He could cut up a tin can and hide the holes and nobody wouldn't know the difference. Wouldn't mind, anyway. I have seen him spend a hour trimming out a wedge like it was glass he was working, when he could have reached around and picked up a dozen sticks and drove them into the joint and made it do.

When his toolbox is smeared with mud on the trip, Cash washes it clean with wet willow branches.

In the design and production of Addie's coffin, Cash unites the abstract and the concrete, idea and execution. His words do the same. His rules of carpentry are both literal and figurative, metaphoric.

I made it on the bevel.
1. There is more surface for the nails to grip.
2. There is twice the gripping-surface to each seam.
3. The water will have to seep into it on a slant. Water moves easiest up and down or straight across.
4. In a house people are upright two thirds of the time. So the seams and joints are made up-and-down. Because the stress is up-and-down.
5. In a bed where people lie down all the time, the joints and seams are made sideways, because the stress is sideways.
6. Except.
7. A body is not square like a crosstie.
8. Animal magnetism.
9. The animal magnetism of a dead body makes the stress come slanting, so the seams and joints of a coffin are made on the bevel.
10. You can see by an old grave that the earth sinks down on the bevel.
11. While in a natural hole it sinks by the center, the stress being up-and-down.
12. So I made it on the bevel.
13. It makes a neater job.

So at the start. Near the close of the novel, the same metaphors are applied to Darl's arson and permanent hospitalization.

But it's a shame, in a way. Folks seem to get away from the olden right teaching that says to drive the nails down and trim the edges well always like it was for your own use and comfort you were making it. It's like some folks has the smooth, pretty boards to build a courthouse with and others dont have no more than rough lumber fitten to build a chicken coop. But it's better to build a tight chicken coop than a shoddy courthouse, and when they both build shoddy or build well, neither because it's one or tother is going to make a man feel the better nor the worse.

The perfect construction of the coffin makes it relatively watertight, as it turns out; Jewel can rescue it from the flood. In addition, the search for Cash's lost tools is the first fully unifying force in the family; as he supplies the coffin which brings them together in their ritual celebration of death, so his leg brings them together for the repair and renewal of life. Cash is ever concerned with *is*, unlike Darl and Addie who are concerned with *ought*.

Cash alone in the Bundren family locates by instinct and thought a response to Addie's distress over the fundamental division between doing and speaking. In using all his words as facts and as metaphors for action, in seeing the abstract conception behind and within the concrete act, Cash wins his way to life rather than death. His position, then, is the active counterpart to Doc Peabody's verbal solution: it is fitting that they meet each other in Jefferson at the end. Both function in a way that directs the body toward physical action; the two co-ordinately *produce*, even if the product is a coffin, even if the doing is at the approach of death. It is therefore not only physically necessary but metaphorically fitting that Cash builds the final home for Addie, that his thoughtful action contains her so that the Bundren family can move on. It is also just that he gets his Gramophone, for that is an instrument that in its concrete use realizes the abstractions of music. It is a self-sufficient image for Cash, providing its own life out of inertia and supplying its own abstract rewards, again (as with Cash's carpentry) creating art.

Not all versions of the narrative presented to us in *As I Lay Dying* are true as they are not all congruent: Cora, Dewey Dell, and Darl give various accounts of Addie's death, for example. But they are all psychologically true, true to the narrative consciousness that relays them to us at the time. Together they provide us with a multidimensional view of the journey, the factual/metaphorical structure of the book itself. The novel is slow to start, segments even overlap, but it accelerates as it progresses; portions of time and space are then even omitted. As the gaps become greater, Darl's narrative consciousness becomes more frequent and his passages longer so that his mixture of reportage and speculation, record and delusion becomes our main entry to the Bundrens. Yet the other consciousnesses, as the novel unfolds, come more and more sharply to modify his, to correct his by providing alternative possibilities: he openly becomes one side of a dialectic that opposes him to the larger community. Indeed, in one long antiphonal section between Darl and Vardaman, when there are no other corrective postures, the novel buckles out into nightmarish fantasy: the buzzards appear and multiply, the barn is burned. After this, the others gain force, and by the end we are given Cash, not Darl: as the novel charts the end of life in the slow and laborious journey to the graveyard and in Darl's own mental breakdown, so in the process it also reabsorbs life in the presence of the remaining Bundrens and returns us to it; in the larger perspective of our constitutive consciousness, the segments in *As I Lay Dying,* as in *Dubliners,* congeal, and as they do so, they test and affirm Anse's natural vision of the resurgent forces of nature.

At first, we watch the journey in *As I Lay Dying* chart certain issues—Dewey Dell loses her innocence; Vardaman loses Darl; Cash, the use of his leg; Jewel, his horse—yet, in a movement antiphonal to Addie and Darl, these are subordinated to a sense of life. And all of life is put before us: the natural and the civilized, the rural and the urban, the designed and the accidental, the mundane and the elegiac, instinct and craft, devotion and envy, the fire, flood, warm air, and cold earth. It is, like the image of the bloody egg which introduces the novel, a study in the paradoxical union of grief and joy, pain and pleasure: the balance which is Cash's insistent base principle. The image, should we miss it, reappears in Darl's understanding of a looped string and in the buzzards of death transformed into the circle of art, metaphors which catch the attention of Vardaman, Anse, Darl, and Cash. When we think about something too long it begins to lose itself, Darl tells us. The achievement of *As I Lay Dying* is that, with thoughts dwelling on death and burial, reality is achieved, not lost. The novel denies Addie (and Darl, her double) and so insures its validity—and its vitality. A last recognition by our constitutive consciousness is that *As I Lay Dying* is nearly all in an ongoing *present* tense.

"Sanctuary"

Sanctuary juxtaposes the worlds of Memphis, Tennessee, and Jefferson, Mississippi, as they are embodied by Popeye and Horace Benbow. Their confrontation is radically imaged only once, in the opening of the novel which is set at a third location, the natural spring on the Old Frenchman place, where Horace pauses to drink.

> From beyond the screen of bushes which surrounded the spring, Popeye watched the man drinking. A faint path led from the road to the spring. Popeye watched the man—a tall, thin man, hatless, in worn gray flannel trousers and carrying a tweed coat over his arm—emerge from the path and kneel to drink from the spring. . . .

In the spring the drinking man leaned his face to the broken and myriad reflection of his own drinking. When he rose up he saw among them the shattered reflection of Popeye's straw hat, though he had heard no sound.

He saw, facing him across the spring, a man of under size, his hands in his coat pockets, a cigarette slanted from his chin. His suit was black, with a tight, high-waisted coat. His trousers were rolled once and caked with mud above mud-caked shoes. His face had a queer, bloodless color, as though seen by electric light; against the sunny silence, in his slanted straw hat and his slightly akimbo arms, he had that vicious depthless quality of stamped tin. . . .

From his hip pocket Popeye took a soiled handkerchief and spread it upon his heels. Then he squatted, facing the man across the spring. That was about four oclock on an afternoon in May. They squatted so, facing one another across the spring, for two hours. Now and then the bird sang back in the swamp, as though it were worked by a clock; twice more invisible automobiles passed along the highroad and died away. Again the bird sang.

"And of course you dont know the name of it," the man across the spring said. "I dont suppose you'd know a bird at all, without it was singing in a cage in a hotel lounge, or cost four dollars on a plate." Popeye said nothing. He squatted in his tight black suit, his right-hand coat pocket sagging compactly against his flank, twisting and pinching cigarettes in his little, doll-like hands, spitting into the spring. His skin had a dead, dark pallor. His nose was faintly aquiline, and he had no chin at all. His face just went away, like the face of a wax doll set too near a hot fire and forgotten. Across his vest ran a platinum chain like a spider web.

By all counts, this is an astonishing and bewildering scene. No two men could seem at first more unlike: the "bloodless" Popeye, looking like "stamped tin," his cigarette slanting from a chinless face, carrying a gun; the "tall, thin" Horace Benbow with his tweed coat and gray flannel trousers, carrying a book. Horace's clothes are professional, neat and comfortable; Popeye's are slick and tight, and look artificial even in the sunlight. Horace has stopped for a drink of natural water and to listen to the birds. Popeye pays no attention to the birds, may not know what kind they are, and spits into the water; his element is fire, he is a chain smoker. Although Horace attempts a formal yet polite conversation, Popeye remains sullen and laconic. While Horace is deliberate and formal, Popeye remains sneaky, mysterious, unpredictable. There would seem to be nothing to draw them together or to hold them there, yet we are told they remain, staring at each other across the reflecting water, for *two hours*. We cannot say why, for Horace is en route to Jefferson and Popeye, everywhere else an impatient man, could force Horace on with the actual threat of his revolver. Even though our perspective shifts, midway, from Horace's side of the spring to Popeye's, we are given no answers; all we know is that in some profound way these two men attract each other. From the outset, *Sanctuary* asks us in what ways Popeye and Horace are doubles and in what way their confrontation serves as an introductory emblem passage to the novel.

Horace Benbow's developing narrative consciousness is the most thoughtful, yet he is also unusually naive for a man in his forties. " 'What sort of men have you lived with all your life?' " Lee Goodwin will ask him. " 'In a nursery?' " Horace is not only ill adjusted to the Old Frenchman place, but we learn that he has arrived there from a troubled marriage and is on his way to the family house, where he will find himself relatively unwelcome: like Popeye, he is childless and unloved; like Popeye, he is relatively homeless. His sister Narcissa, with whom he was once so close, now sees him as a meddler who threatens her comfortable respectability. She wants nothing to do with him.

> "Dont you see, this is my home, where I must spend the rest of my life. Where I was born. I dont care where else you go nor what you do. I dont care how many women you have nor who they are. But I cannot have my brother mixed up with a woman people are talking about. I dont expect you to have consideration for me; I ask you to have consideration for our father and mother."

Narcissa's attitude toward him is dictatorial and condescending, analogous to that of his wife Belle. Horace is painfully aware of this; he is vulnerable and always on the edge of self-pity. His one anecdote of his marriage—which he tells in identical versions to Ruby at the Old Frenchman place and to Narcissa and Aunt Jenny in Jefferson— embodies his own sense of his unimportance and his impotence.

"Why did you leave your wife?" she said.

"Because she ate shrimp," he said. "I couldn't—You see, it was Friday, and I thought how at noon I'd go to the station and get the box of shrimp off the train and walk home with it, counting a hundred steps and changing hands with it, and it—"

"Did you do that every day?" the woman said.

"No. Just Friday. But I have done it for ten years, since we were married. And I still dont like to smell shrimp. But I wouldn't mind the carrying it home so much. I could stand that. It's because the package drips. All the way home it drips and drips, until after a while I follow myself to the station and stand aside and watch Horace Benbow take that box off the train and start home with it, changing hands every hundred steps, and I following him, thinking Here lies Horace Benbow in a fading series of small stinking spots on a Mississippi sidewalk."

Earlier, Horace has told us that in leaving Belle and her daughter, " 'I had no money with me. That was part of it too, you see; I couldn't cash a check. I couldn't get off the truck and go back to town and get some money.' " This essential self-deprecation runs so deep that he is willing to assume the same posture with Senator Clarence Snopes, although he has no respect for the senator. Defensively, Horace aligns man to progress, women—and also himself—to mirrors.

Horace fancies himself an intellectual, and he still quotes snatches of poetry, if less frequently than he did in *Flags in the Dust*. Although he does display some ingenuity in questioning Ruby Lamar and in tracking down Temple Drake, his thinking is pathetically shallow. When he assures Lee Goodwin that they will win his case because Lee is innocent, because " 'You've got the law, justice, civilization,' " Lee only scoffs at him. The moment is echoed once more with Ruby just before the last day of the trial. He tells her not to worry. " 'God is foolish at times, but at least He's a gentleman. Dont you know that?' " to which Ruby replies, " 'I always thought of Him as a man.' " This would seem rather dense on Horace's part, since the other gentleman he has identified, Gowan Stevens, is for him the basic cause of Goodwin's difficulty—it was Gowan who first took Temple to the Old Frenchman place and then abandoned her. Yet it is not especially surprising, for Horace's chief insight through much of the novel— "Perhaps it is upon the instant that we realise, admit, that there is a logical pattern to evil, that we die"—is hardly profound, either; rather, it resembles the reaction of an adolescent who has just discovered the presence of evil and understands for the first time that not all evil is unplanned.

Ruby's remark is interesting and revealing in another way. Horace is innocent in the ways of women. Both Ruby and her baby bother him; twice he tells her she carries the child too much, misunderstanding that love and devotion are her fundamental characteristics, as her own biography with Lee should have shown him amply enough. He is ill at ease in Miss Reba's establishment; he prejudges Temple and has difficulty asking her questions or listening to her story and completely misjudges what she may do when she appears at the trial; and he is so distraught by her capacity for evil that he blends her with a picture of his stepdaughter upon returning to Jefferson, judging from this composite that evil is the property of women.

> The photograph sat on the dresser. He took it up, holding it in his hands. Enclosed by the narrow imprint of the missing frame Little Belle's face dreamed with that quality of sweet chiaroscuro. Communicated to the cardboard by some quality of the light or perhaps by some infinitesimal movement of his hands, his own breathing, the face appeared to breathe in his palms in a shallow bath of highlight, beneath the slow, smokelike tongues of invisible honeysuckle. Almost palpable enough to be seen, the scent filled the room and the small face seemed to swoon in a voluptuous languor, blurring still more, fading, leaving upon his eye a soft and fading aftermath of invitation and voluptuous promise and secret affirmation like a scent itself.

Horace sees something more here than Little Belle's potentiality to be Temple Drake or that, like Temple, she is corruptible. What he sees— in this scene which shows us how he has transferred his incestuous fantasies from his sister to his stepdaughter—is his essential fear and ignorance of women. Because incest can only be fantasized but never realized in the respectable society he knows, Horace has until now been relatively safe in his daydreaming romanticism. But Ruby Goodwin has shown him that for many women sexual love is natural, not bound by social restrictions, and Temple has shown him that even the young enjoy their sexuality. In their implied doubles within Horace's consciousness—in Belle and in Little Belle—they have suggested to him the fundamental nature of women as well as his own naiveté. They have confirmed his story of the shrimp in Jefferson and in Memphis as well as in Kinston. Like characters in James and Conrad, Horace does not tell his story again: Faulkner now makes silence our clue. From this point forward, Horace Benbow is as much on trial in Jefferson as Lee Goodwin, and, acknowledging this, Horace grows more secretive (with his sister and with Ruby), more defensive (in his actions), and more rigid (in his blind, dumb faith in justice): he grows toward Popeye's posture in the opening passage. In working with a mounting anxiety for Lee Goodwin's exoneration, we see Horace primarily attempting to exonerate his own ability as a lawyer and as a man.

So much is, by the end, within the range of Horace's narrative consciousness, although he resists most of his potential re-cognition. But *Sanctuary* also relies heavily on juxtaposition, and it is our constitutive consciousness, recalling the premise that Popeye may be a secret sharer, that allows us to understand Horace even more deeply. Both Horace and Popeye are spectators rather than participants in much of life; as impotent men, they rely either on the power of force or on the power of social and legal codes to cloak their weakness, to show the pretense of strength. Both fear nature, especially the natural instincts of women. Both fight resignation and self-defeatism through sheer will, although both are given to moments of self-pity. Popeye's spying on Temple at Miss Reba's, like Horace's continual contact with Narcissa, discloses that both of them lack confidence in what they set out with such public assurance to do. Popeye, by violence, and Horace, with his personal interest in Ruby and in his fantasies and daydreams, try to break through their fundamental isolation. Although one is a force in the Memphis underworld and the other an established personage in Jefferson society, neither feels any stable communal role. Both men are ridden by fear, self-doubt, and self-recrimination.

Further, in keeping silent about the rum-running he sees at the Old Frenchman place, Horace becomes a petty criminal himself, an accessory after the fact, and paying off Clarence Snopes for information leading to Temple, while it parallels Narcissa's tip to Eustace Graham, displays Horace's own willing corruptibility. Popeye and Horace become two sides of the same coin of inherent human evil—those who aggressively perform evil acts and those who compromise with evil or, with the best of intentions, are unable to prevent or contain it. Aunt Jenny warns Horace that he is sliding into evil himself just after he takes Lee Goodwin's case and shelters Ruby.

"But, Horace, aint that what the lawyers call collusion? connivance?" Horace looked at her. "It seems to me you've already had a little more to do with these folks than the lawyer in the case should have. You were out there where it happened yourself not long ago. Folks might begin to think you know more than you've told."

"That's so," Horace said. "Mrs Blackstone. And sometimes I have wondered why I haven't got rich at the law. Maybe I will, when I get old enough to attend the same law school you did."

"If I were you," Miss Jenny said, "I'd drive back to town now and take her to the hotel and get her settled. It's not late." ...

"I cannot stand idly by and see injustice—"

"You wont ever catch up with injustice, Horace," Miss Jenny said.

In showing us the fundamental likeness of Horace and Popeye—their true doubling—*Sanctuary* is a study in the resources of human evil.

The major narrative blocks we are asked to juxtapose in *Sanctuary* are geographically defined. Together with the Old Frenchman place, Memphis and Jefferson form a significant triptych; they are equally weighted. The Old Frenchman place is the setting for nearly all the first third of the novel; Memphis and Jefferson are the settings for the second third, linked by Horace's trip to Miss Reba's at the close; and they also provide the environment for the final third, linked at the close by Temple's journey to Jefferson. It is no accident, either, that these three environments are carefully defined and distinguished in cosmic terms in a novel which anatomizes the nature of evil and examines the possibilities for justice.

The Old Frenchman place is the most natural and earthy of the three geographies. It is the home of two "naturals"—an idiot and a feeble old blind and deaf man—as well as the home of a common-law (or natural) marriage and a child born out of wedlock. The house itself has been taken over by the weather, and the people in it eat and drink from its crops, sleep on corn-shuck mattresses, and drink water from a natural spring on the land. It is described twice.

The house was a gutted ruin rising gaunt and stark out of a grove of unpruned cedar trees. It was a landmark, known as the Old Frenchman place, built before the Civil War; a plantation house set in the middle of a tract of land; of cotton fields and gardens and lawns long since gone back to jungle, which the people of the neighborhood had been pulling down piecemeal for firewood for fifty years or digging with secret and sporadic optimism for the gold which the builder was reputed to have buried somewhere about the place when Grant came through the county on his Vicksburg campaign.

The gaunt ruin of the house rose against the sky, above the massed and matted cedars, lightless, desolate, and profound. The road was an eroded scar too deep to be a road and too straight to be a ditch, gutted by winter freshets and choked with fern and rotted leaves and branches.

The description of the earth here concentrates on disorder and decay; it is a nature which is ransacked for its wood and buried (unnatural) gold deposits; the house itself is a kind of skeleton. Although we are first introduced to this land by hearing a bird and seeing a natural spring, it is the spring in which Popeye spits and the bird's notes are regular, "as though it were worked by a clock." It is an essentially forbidding landscape and one that does terrify Temple and disorient Gowan and Horace. Our last scene there is of Tommy's murder and Temple's rape.

Next to this portrait of Earth is a portrait of Memphis imaging Hell. It is the underworld we see, a world of prostitution, violence, and crime, and its description as the Inferno is nearly classical in its dimensions.

They reached Memphis in midafternoon. At the foot of the bluff below Main Street Popeye turned into a narrow street of smoke-grimed frame houses with tiers of wooden galleries, set a little back in grassless plots, with now and then a forlorn and hardy tree of some shabby species—gaunt, lopbranched magnolias, a stunted elm or a locust in grayish, cadaverous bloom—interspersed by rear ends of garages; a scrap-heap in a vacant lot.

The outer landscape is mirrored in Temple's room.

The light hung from the center of the ceiling, beneath a fluted shade of rose-colored paper browned where the bulb bulged it. The floor was covered by a figured maroon-tinted carpet tacked down in strips; the olive-tinted walls bore two framed lithographs. From the two windows curtains of machine lace hung, dust-colored, like strips of lightly congealed dust set on end. The whole room had an air of musty stodginess, decorum; in the wavy mirror of a cheap varnished dresser, as in a stagnant pool, there seemed to linger spent ghosts of voluptuous gestures and dead lusts.

This is a society beyond conventional law; it is unnatural, mechanical, and grotesque, death-ridden. It is also, startlingly, accusatory yet empty of meaning. "Temple began to hear a clock. It sat on the mantel above a grate filled with fluted green paper. The clock was of flowered china, supported by four china nymphs. It had only one hand, scrolled and gilded, halfway between ten and eleven, lending to the otherwise blank face a quality of unequivocal assertion, as though it had nothing whatever to do with time." Although our chief setting is a whorehouse, we see no active sexuality, only frustration; the environment exploits, commercializes, and degrades human passion. Within the tawdry room that Miss Reba provides there is a kind of frozen quality, a routine essentially hollow that is almost Dantean. What activity there is we find both sinful and repetitive, compulsive rather than free—in the whorehouse, the Grotto (the speakeasy), and even the streets. It is the place where Popeye reveals himself.

> His hand clapped over her mouth, and gripping his wrist, the saliva drooling between his fingers, her body thrashing furiously from thigh to thigh, she saw him crouching beside the bed, his face wrung above his absent chin, his bluish lips protruding as though he were blowing upon hot soup, making a high whinnying sound like a horse. Beyond the wall Miss Reba filled the hall, the house, with a harsh choking uproar of obscene cursing.

In Memphis, Popeye's hellish animality, his grotesque monstrosity, seems peculiarly fitting.

In contrast to both jungle and underworld, the Old Frenchman place and Memphis, Jefferson images society—home, business, church, courtroom. As a guardian of the best of civilized values, it is as heavenly an environment as the novel can supply. Even the convicted black murderer sees it as a place which will lead him to possible salvation—

> He would lean in the window in the evening and sing. After supper a few Negroes gathered along the fence below—natty, shoddy suits and sweat-stained overalls shoulder to shoulder— and in chorus with the murderer, they sang spirituals while the white people slowed and stopped in the leafed darkness that was almost summer, to listen to those who were sure to die and him who was already dead singing about heaven and being tired

—within the shadow of a heaven tree itself. Yet the peacefulness of this scene—its sad beauty—is ironic, for the murderer has been condemned to hell by his white society, not to heaven. The useless spiritual is reflected in the crowded streets of market day where Horace sees only the hypocrisy of fancy dress; even the country folk, he tells us, are "unmistakable by the unease of their garments as well as by their method of walking, believing that town dwellers would take them for town dwellers too, not even fooling one another." Such false respectability is ironically correlative to Narcissa's anger—" 'now to deliberately mix yourself up with a woman you said yourself was a street-walker, a murderer's woman' "—and even with Gowan's open invitation to deceit and to self-deception.

> *Narcissa my dear*
> *This has no heading. I wish it could have no date. But if my heart were as blank as this page, this would not be necessary at all. I will not see you again. I cannot write it, for I have gone through with an experience which I cannot face. I have but one rift in the darkness, that is that I have injured no one save myself by my folly, and that the extent of that folly you will never learn. I need not say that the hope that you never learn it is the sole reason why I will not see you again. Think as well of me as you can. I wish I had the right to say, if you learn of my folly think not the less of me.* G.

Such hypocrisy leads in Jefferson to a religion of the artificial, the superficial, and the false; the town's conventions are death-dealing in themselves, its characteristic moral tidiness is only a sham. But not until his bitter remark on spring at the end of his visit is Horace able to see the depth of the quiet terror evil produces in his own native community.

Thus juxtaposed, these dramatized environments—at first discrete —supply us with a sense of unified corruptibility, of decay from within. At the Old Frenchman place, natural corn is fermented into a commercial product for the underworld of Memphis; the Memphis whorehouse trade, as in the case of Fonzo and Virgil, is drawn from Jefferson; but Jefferson also sends customers out to Goodwin's house. So the point of the triptych is in the correlation of its three panels. The Goodwin family is formally constituted on the models of family life in Jefferson, and Ruby fears that Lee will be tempted instead to the ways of Memphis; while even at Memphis Miss Reba, Miss Myrtle, and Miss Lorraine ape the social customs and unknowingly parody the social conversation of Jefferson. Since the Goodwins depend on customers from Memphis and Jefferson, their lawlessness is more disguised yet analogous to the lawlessness in the other two societies. Miss Reba's pretense of marriage is no more and no less real than Ruby's; their very names seem almost interchangeable. Red's funeral is a mockery not of its own means and ends but of the formal occasion of Jefferson which it parodies, just as Fonzo and Virgil, from Jefferson, parody Temple Drake in Memphis. Thus the decay that is so visible at the Old Frenchman place will also have its analogies in Memphis—and in Jefferson. Horace can tell his stories of the shrimp he gets for Belle and the grape arbor where Little Belle makes love regardless of where he finds himself.

These mirroring environments are doubling on a larger and more meaningful scale. This is most apparent in the ways in which people can pass back and forth among the geographies—people like Senator Clarence Snopes, Popeye, and Temple. Even Horace, who feels initial discomfort at the Old Frenchman place and in Memphis, is able to tell his autobiography at one and, hastening away from the other, analogize Temple with his own stepdaughter and thus incorporate her into his own life. But of all the characters, Temple is the one who ties this universe of decay and evil together best: everywhere she goes, she awakens in men the same reaction, the latent desire and violence that characterize them. She herself makes little distinction; she can call on her father the judge at the Old Frenchman place, she can think of Popeye as a kind of "daddy" in Memphis (since he provides for her and is her basic authority figure and sex figure, both other self and mirror), and she can meet Judge Drake in Jefferson. She can exchange Gowan for Tommy, for Popeye, for Red. The moral equivalencies here are bitter ones: the college coquette can also become the gun moll and whore. Little wonder, then, that Horace loses in championing goodness and truth in this cohesively evil world; little wonder that Temple, confronted by the illegality of the Old Frenchman place, the corruption of Memphis, and a court trial in Jefferson, is finally unable to distinguish among them and so, without hesitation, perhaps without self-knowledge, is able to perjure herself and convict Lee Goodwin. Possibly too, fittingly, Temple's perjury confirms Narcissa's view of Lee and Ruby and so secures her hypocrisy, annealing and strengthening the behavior of Jefferson society.

All three "sanctuaries" are indistinguishable in this modern, amoral world; all three are correlated finally in the violent murder in which activity in each ends: the shooting of Tommy, the slaughter of Red, the lynching of Lee. Each death replicates the others. Thus the trial which becomes the sole focus of Horace's narrative consciousness is not merely a trial to exonerate Lee Goodwin and himself, to exonerate the system of law and justice in Jefferson generally; in *Sanctuary*, mankind itself is put on trial.

Within this wide range of implication and statement, Temple Drake is the core character of *Sanctuary* as Addie Bundren is of *As I Lay Dying*. Her rape, like Addie's death, is the chief event of the novel and the focal image to which even the trial attends; clustered about the rape, several multiple perspectives converge which we as readers must reconcile.

The violence and significance of the rape are prefigured in Ruby's persistent warnings to Temple concerning her provocative innocence, for Ruby sees in the girl, despite their difference in social class, a fundamental secret self. When Temple continually ignores her, Ruby shares her own life story, a narrative about Frank which could be mistaken (and has been) for an incident in Temple's own life.

> "My brother said he would kill Frank. He didn't say he would give me a whipping if he caught me with him; he said he would kill the goddam son of a bitch in his yellow buggy and my father cursed my brother and said he could run his family a while longer and he drove me into the house and locked me in and went down to the bridge to wait for Frank. But I wasn't a coward. I climbed down the gutter and headed Frank off and told him. I begged him to go away, but he said we'd both go. When we got back in the buggy I knew it had been the last time. I knew it, and I begged him again to go away, but he said he'd drive me home to get my suitcase and we'd tell father. He wasn't a coward either. My father was sitting on the porch. He said 'Get out of that buggy' and I got out and I begged Frank to go on, but he got out too and we came up the path and father reached around inside the door and got the shotgun. I got in front of Frank and father said 'Do you want it too?' and I tried to stay in front but Frank shoved me behind him and held me and father shot him and said 'Get down there and sup your dirt, you whore.'"

But Ruby's instinct to protect and love others is, in the larger structure of the novel, a bitter comment on Temple; the point is that they could never be more than *mistaken* doubles.

Ruby is identified by love, Temple by its forceful perversion in the initial rape which leads to her habitual displays of fornication for Popeye, her persistent nymphomania. We are supplied with the account of Temple's rape five times, resembling structurally the several attempts to account for Caddy's loss in *The Sound and the Fury* and Bayard's attempt to reconcile himself to his twin brother's death in *Flags in the Dust*. The first account is by an omniscient narrator, but he stops short of the act itself; we are told Temple sees Popeye figured in a rat staring at her, and we are provided with details concerning Tommy's death, but Temple's violation is about to occur as the passage halts: " 'Something is happening to me!' " As usual, Temple confuses sex and death. Her corncrib here becomes a coffin, the corn shucks only sterile husks. Popeye holds only a stick, analogous to Judge Drake's cane in the closing scene of the novel. This epiphany, with Temple looking at Popeye in paralysis, closes the Old Frenchman place section of the novel.

The second version of Temple's rape is given us by Ruby at the midpoint of the novel; she views the rape as a singular and needless misfortune, a privileged carelessness she condemns from her world of toil.

> "Nobody wanted her out there. Lee has told them and told them they must not bring women out there, and I told her before it got dark they were not her kind of people and to get away from there. . . .
>
> But why must it have been me, us? What had I ever done to her, to her kind?"

Ruby's perspective is paired with Horace's; he makes light of it, unawares.

> "But that girl," Horace said. "She was all right. When you were coming back to the house the next morning after the baby's bottle, you saw her and knew she was all right. . . . You know she was all right."

The fourth view is Temple's recollection, which Horace hears from her at Miss Reba's in Memphis.

> Temple told him of the night she had spent in the ruined house, from the time she entered the room and tried to wedge the door with the chair, until the woman came to the bed and led her out.

> That was the only part of the whole experience which appeared to have left any impression on her at all: the night which she had spent in comparative inviolation.

She tells not of the rape but of her own fantasizing: that she is a boy, an old man, a corpse. At the conclusion of her narrative, she describes the rape in a way that reveals no particularity: the sensations have been elevated, generalized, assimilated. The final view, that of Eustace Graham, is not given to us directly, but it is the one which Jefferson hears and acts on; not until then can our constitutive consciousness account for the unusual recalcitrance in Temple or her excessive bleeding. What is common to all five accounts is the involvement of Temple; what is at stake is the willingness and degree of her complicity. The clues for this are not given us directly—they rarely are in Faulkner's narrative poetics as they rarely are in James and Conrad—but through Temple's natural attraction for Popeye on an unconscious level and her unnatural (but relatively easy) partnership with him.

We do not know if Temple's provocative actions at the Old Frenchman place were meant for Popeye initially or for Lee or the others; Temple does not know herself. Her actions appear indiscriminate and naive; she seems to bring to her new landscape the same gestures she has been accustomed to using at Ole Miss—gestures of flight, impulsiveness, vulnerability, invitation, confusion. When she retreats to her bed of cornhusks (and later to a corncrib) she robes and disrobes mindlessly, shedding any moral sense, any moral responsibility. Such innocence and arbitrariness are provocative to several men at the Old Frenchman place save the curious and protective Tommy; but she arouses to action only the impotent and syphilitic Popeye, one whose body is as deformed as her moral sense. Their affinity, once discovered, is deep and mutual. Popeye's face with its "queer, bloodless color" and his eyes which "looked like rubber knobs" are analogous to Temple's "bold painted mouth and soft chin, her eyes blankly right and left looking, cool, predatory, and discreet." Popeye is drawn to Temple as he was earlier drawn to Horace, and she invites him at the end by taunting him. Their departure together from the Old Frenchman place seems natural to Ruby, who sees it, and to Temple who, in looking in the car mirror, sees both Popeye and herself. At the filling station where they stop for fuel, Temple leaves the car to hide from college friends who might recognize her in Dumfries, and so invite her back to Ole Miss, but she does not think of leaving Popeye; when he finds that she is not waiting for him in the car, he has no trouble finding her waiting for him behind a "greasy barrel half full of scraps of metal and rubber," an object made of material that resembles Popeye himself. From this point on, these two corrupt, sullen, masochistic persons are always together until Temple tries to escape to Red, Popeye's sexual surrogate.

Their pairing underlines their relationship: both are selfish, both use others with abandon. Both act compulsively, randomly, amorally. Although they pretend to an interest in material things, they have none in fact; what they seek is limited to sensual gratification. They live only for the present. So joined are they, in fact, that one of Temple's orgasms is sufficient to satisfy both of them. For some time it does not seem to bother Temple that Popeye is not a fully active sexual partner, that he whinnies his animal pleasure at mere foreplay or in observing a surrogate, nor does it disturb him. Our constitutive consciousness therefore has no difficulty in correlating Temple as a "papier-mâché Easter [toy] filled with candy" to Popeye likened to a "wax doll" or mask pulled on a string: both seem subhuman. Nor does it surprise us when, at the end of the novel, both part by going off to their parents.

The central imaging of Temple, then, is with Popeye, and at the point of abnormal rape or sexual encounter. Such a central metaphor—Temple's rape writ large, writ endlessly—shows the sterility and meaninglessness in their selfish and corrupt existences; it seems at first ironic that the gruesome analogue to Temple's burning passion for intercourse is Lee's fiery death, itself meaningless, itself an uncontrollable passion stemming from the moral impotence of Jefferson. In the novel, this is a chief point. Lee's death, like Temple's fornication, is only the outer sign of a latent violence, only the most open admission of the corruptibility and evil in men. Popeye's essential impotence before Temple's needs is directly analogous to Horace's impotence before Lee's needs, another significant way in which Popeye and Horace are twinned. But, as Temple reveals a profound affinity with Popeye, so she suggests to Horace his own most dangerous and unrecognized self: it is in *that* that Horace sees his greatest fear as he returns on the train from Memphis and in *that* which, once realized in Jefferson in Temple's perjury, causes him to collapse altogether, to cry uselessly in Narcissa's car, and to declare a savage but useless indictment on spring. Within the larger context of a triptych of landscapes that suggests all mankind (as the ever widening circle does in *The Sound and the Fury* and the journey does in *As I Lay Dying*), the metaphor of trial in *Sanctuary* at

last pulls together Horace, Popeye, and Temple, making of this insinu-
ated congruence a severe condemnation of man's grotesque propensity
for evil.

Still this does not account for the entire novel. Although we can see
why Horace and Popeye were so drawn to each other at the Old
Frenchman place, why the opening scene is in fact an anticipation of
the larger novel, we still do not know why Popeye has come to the
Goodwin homestead. It is not his element; he feels awkward and uncomfortable, he is not welcome, and his anxiety is seen when he shoots
at Tommy's dog and later shoots Tommy. Goodwin runs the place well
enough, and he can drive sufficient whiskey into Memphis. Why, then,
is Popeye there? It is to answer this final question that, in revising
Sanctuary for publication, Faulkner added Popeye's biography as a
penultimate episode.

Popeye comes to the Old Frenchman place because he *needs* to come.
Born syphilitic, a backward child, grandson of an arsonist, mentally
retarded, Popeye, for all his eventual power and wealth, has never
known family love. His childhood is a case book study of the aggressive and vengeful child who seeks affection and attention: in killing
the lovebirds and in cutting up the half-grown kitten he not only seeks
a kind of punishment for his own misbegotten self but lashes out in a
general and blind hatred against what nature comes under his control.
Pain and harm become for him sources of joy and solace, like Temple's
cries of pain and ecstacy at orgasm. His regressive journeys home each
year are another form of self-punishment, but also frantic and empty
attempts at new beginnings. At the Old Frenchman place, Popeye
seeks a family, and it is the family environment that Ruby maintains.
In a sense, Popeye's unnatural rape of Temple is a sick attempt to
begin his own family relationship; more importantly, it is, in its open
admission of impotence, Popeye's greatest act of self-punishment. It is
this desire to hurt himself and thus guarantee his own worthlessness
that, finally, binds him to Horace and Temple. Unfortunately for Popeye, however, he can only rape Temple at the expense of Tommy's life,
and this in turn convicts Lee, robbing Popeye of the one home he has
found. With the Old Frenchman place gone, and with Temple returned
to her father, Popeye has no place left but his mother's—and his own
greatest payment, his execution. The fate which gave him such an ugly
heritage now arrests him for a crime he did not commit. Popeye is at
last confronted with nothing but the terror of such truth: justice mocks

itself, even outside the underworld. In attempting to regularize and organize crime in Memphis, Popeye sought to order his existence, a life disrupted first by his grandmother and now, more recently, by Temple. His concern with his appearance in his last moments—" 'Fix my hair, Jack,' he said"—is the last sign he gives us, a final gesture of futility which attempts to impart dignity to his undignified life. For he sees what our constitutive consciousness establishes, that in this world the innocent are persecuted and the guilty are set free.

Popeye's biography—as well as his execution—is comprehensible and necessary; in the larger sense of the novel, his term in jail recalls the black murderer in Jefferson who said, as if for both of them—" 'Aint no place fer you in heavum! Say, Aint no place fer you in hell! Say, Aint no place fer you in jail!' "—just as his trial echoes and parodies the trial of Lee Goodwin. We find the parallel established with pointed efficiency: in both instances, we learn, the "jury was out eight minutes."

This attempt to respond to futility with a significant gesture, which is Popeye's last act, is essentially a mockery which has its final correlation with Temple and Judge Drake in the Luxembourg Gardens of Paris. Whether they can find sanctuary in the world of this novel—either a secret or a sacred place, a place secure or a place hallowed—they too must make their response to the world of Jefferson and Jackson, Mississippi. They do so in the height of civilization; amidst a man-trimmed park, watching children play with toy boats at a man-made basin, listening to a brass band, they sit silently, the judge holding his stick as the sign of wealth and male potency in their society, Temple yawning between glances at herself in the mirror. They have displaced the natural spring of the Old Frenchman place with a more civilized milieu and with consequent boredom. Everything has happened to them—Temple has been an accessory after the fact in two murders and has committed prostitution and perjury; Judge Drake, although he does not know of all this travesty of justice, chooses his ignorance—and nothing has happened to them. She has come to resemble Narcissa Benbow more than ever, and Judge Drake still holds the bench, a position to which Horace Benbow may still aspire. Their quiet stroll and their seat in the gardens, all quite decorous and proper, unites them with conventional Yoknapatawpha and prepares them for a return to Jefferson; meanwhile, their presence does nothing to disturb the placid and routine activity of this, or their, world. They are, finally, citizens of a corroded, corrupted mankind, as they always were: in an evil world, *that* (fittingly) is their sanctuary.

"Absalom, Absalom!"

Absalom, Absalom! (like *Flags in the Dust*) is bounded by the sense of mortality: it opens and closes in rooms stifled with a sense of the past and of death. At the beginning of the novel, a letter summons Quentin Compson to Miss Rosa Coldfield's home, where

> From a little after two oclock until almost sundown of the long still hot weary dead September afternoon they sat in what Miss Coldfield still called the office because her father had called it that—a dim hot airless room with the blinds all closed and fastened. . . . in the gloom of the shuttered hallway whose air was even hotter than outside, as if there were prisoned in it like in a tomb all the suspiration of slow heat-laden time which had recurred during the forty-five years,

and five months later, when Quentin has a letter from Mr. Compson about Miss Rosa's death, he sits in his Harvard dormitory with Shrevlin McCannon "in this tomblike room in Massachusetts in 1910," "in the now tomblike air." Both environments resemble what Shreve calls the Coldfield home—an " 'overpopulated mausoleum.' " Quentin, already preparing to go to Harvard when we first meet him, listens patiently to Miss Rosa as if he were a stranger not only to her but to the South, as if he were listening to a strange story that must be corrected constantly by one who knows the tale.

> *his name was Sutpen—(Colonel Sutpen)—Colonel Sutpen. Who came out of nowhere and without warning upon the land with a band of strange niggers and built a plantation—(Tore violently a plantation, Miss Rosa Coldfield says)—tore violently. And married her sister Ellen and begot a son and a daughter which—(Without gentleness begot, Miss Rosa Coldfield says) —without gentleness. Which should have been the jewels of his pride and the shield and comfort of his old age, only—(Only they destroyed him or something or he destroyed them or something. And died)—and died. Without regret, Miss Rosa Coldfield says—(Save by her) Yes, save by her. (And by Quentin Compson) Yes. And by Quentin Compson.*

If we were not told that this was Quentin talking with himself at the outset, we should think it was Shreve corrected by Quentin at the end: the novel is, despite its anxious searchings, curiously moribund, static, itself a relentlessly voiced portrait of death.

Juxtaposed, the two environments—Miss Rosa's office, Quentin's room at Harvard—are made analogous. The dust motes in Miss Rosa's house are replaced by snow in Cambridge, the oppressive heat by the progressive cold as the novel slows to a chilled, tortured halt, a stalemate of emotional self-knowledge. This reversal is but the other side of the same coin. In the beginning, Miss Rosa sits in her office beside "the dead old dried paint" like "a crucified child," a corpse. There, figuratively dead, she is literally dead in the final scene: even the worm in her grave is frozen and still, Mr. Compson writes to his son. Listening at first to this woman swathed "in the eternal black," Quentin himself becomes ghostlike,

> his very body was an empty hall echoing with sonorous defeated names; he was not a being, an entity, he was a commonwealth. He was a barracks filled with stubborn back-looking ghosts still recovering, even forty-three years afterward, from the fever which had cured the disease,

prefiguring his contemporary Jim Bond, "wraith-like and insubstantial," in the last scenes of the novel. The "biding and dreamy and victorious dust" that is Sutpen's life, Miss Rosa's beliefs, even Quentin's spiritual biography, all seem spent, irrevocably past. Words repeatedly strike the resonant strings of remembering; "*You cannot know yet whether what you see is what you are looking at,*" Quentin admits to himself, "*or what you are believing.*"

Absalom, Absalom! is presented in three tableaux—Rosa and Quentin at the Coldfield house; Mr. Compson and Quentin on the Compson front porch; Quentin and Shreve in the dormitory. The book is composed of voices, and of their reflections on life rather than life itself, which, always beginning as dialogues, are transformed correlatively into monologues and then into self-rationalizing soliloquies. Events are approached from different perspectives, analyzed, reinterpreted, and so stilled. People only sit and talk: the narrators are trapped within themselves as much as in the past, all radiating from Sutpen, who seems also to be curiously trapped within his own "design." Narrative within narrative, circle within circle, *Absalom, Absalom!* is, finally, a novel of self-incarcerations.

Tell about the South. What's it like there. What do they do there. Why do they live there. Why do they live at all.

Shreve's request of Quentin is the novel's impersonal *incipit*; and the opening chapters with Miss Rosa and Mr. Compson become the first portions of Quentin's reply, as if Shreve's questions occurred before Miss Rosa's story and later, retold, timeless. For Quentin, telling about the South is synonymous with telling the biography of Thomas Sutpen. It is true of Miss Rosa and Mr. Compson as well—Sutpen's life in *Absalom, Absalom!* is the generating image, as Caddy is in *The Sound and the Fury* and as Addie's death and Temple's rape are in *As I Lay Dying* and in *Sanctuary*. Here, narrators trace Sutpen's significance as if they were tracing their own features, seeing him as a version of themselves and seeing in his life those patterns of human consciousness which mirror their own. Their stories are compulsive, obsessive, and the path through their reconstructions to Sutpen is circuitous: Quentin tells Shreve what he has heard from Miss Rosa and his father, but Miss Rosa has depersonalized Sutpen, schematized him, and Mr. Compson knows only what he has heard from his own father and what he conjectures with Quentin over the tombstones of the Sutpens set out by Judith and by Miss Rosa herself and in the relative isolation of his own front gallery. Behind these perceptual screens, we can locate Sutpen only once up close, for any extended period. It is the time he and Grandfather Compson are chasing the French architect like an escaped slave and Sutpen has time—perhaps the only time, except for the Carolina interview at the novel's close—for speaking of his own past, for defining himself.

> "they had gone far enough for that night, and the niggers had made camp and cooked supper and they (he and Grandfather) drank some of the whiskey and ate and then sat before the fire drinking some more of the whiskey and he telling it all over and still it was not absolutely clear—the how and the why he was there and what he was—since he was not talking about himself. He was telling a story."

So *even Sutpen* was *telling a story!*

The act of narration is a reiterative point of *Absalom, Absalom!*: personal history, like regional definition, is a story. Human consciousness operates the same way for both. Because empirical experience is, sooner or later, cradled in the mind's constructs, history, fiction, biography, and autobiography all take the shape of narrative. Yet so claiming,

Absalom, Absalom! redeems and reemphasizes the power and poetry of such human shapes for truth. Even while it admits the inadequacy of language and the fundamental mysteries in events, *Absalom, Absalom!* confirms the potency of words: the teacher's words and those in the schoolbook send Sutpen to the West Indies; Shreve's question forces Quentin to a full self-confrontation; even the graves for which Judith hoards her money have inscriptions which are a tribute meant to withstand the erosion of time. This, then, is Sutpen's most valuable legacy, for his own story has set the example, supplying the South with both the subject matter and the form for understanding the past.

Miss Rosa is most excited in telling her story; it redeems her, brings her temporarily back to life. She recognizes, deep within her, that *"there is no such thing as memory: the brain recalls just what the muscles grope for: no more, no less: and its resultant sum is usually incorrect and false and worthy only of the name of dream,"* so she has decided to go out to Sutpen's Hundred, to risk the significance of her own life by confirming or denying what she has willed herself to believe as the truth. She wants to keep the affair " 'in the family,' " Mr. Compson tells his son, " 'the skeleton (if it be a skeleton) still in the closet,' " yet she also sees herself mirrored in Sutpen, and so she would like her story in turn preserved—" 'maybe you will enter the literary profession as so many Southern gentlemen and gentlewomen too are doing now and maybe some day you will remember this and write about it' "—much as she has tried to memorialize the Confederate dead in her own poetry.

At first Miss Rosa strikes Quentin (and us) as remote and foolish, a caricature of Southern ladyhood in antebellum times who by sheer force of will has lived beyond her days. Her summary view of Sutpen seems shrill and distorted.

> Out of quiet thunderclap he would abrupt (man-horse-demon) upon a scene peaceful and decorous as a schoolprize water color, faint sulphur-reek still in hair clothes and beard, with grouped behind him his band of wild niggers like beasts half tamed to walk upright like men, in attitudes wild and reposed, and manacled among them the French architect with his air grim, haggard, and tatter-ran. Immobile, bearded and hand palm-lifted the horseman sat; behind him the wild blacks and the captive architect huddled quietly, carrying in bloodless paradox the shovels and picks and axes of peaceful conquest. Then in the long unamaze Quentin seemed to watch them overrun sud-

denly the hundred square miles of tranquil and astonished earth and drag house and formal gardens violently out of the soundless Nothing and clap them down like cards upon a table beneath the up-palm immobile and pontific, creating the Sutpen's Hundred, the *Be Sutpen's Hundred* like the oldentime *Be Light.*

Yet beneath the heightened language (as transmitted, apparently, through Quentin's understanding) there is an enormous admiration, a kind of awe for the strange man who like God created the South, who supplied Ellen with the opportunity to be "chatelaine to the largest, wife to the wealthiest, mother of the most fortunate." In her relentless attraction to Sutpen, Rosa Coldfield sees the possibility even for people such as herself to gain access to all that was great in the South, to build and preserve its best heritage. The more we come to know Miss Rosa, the more we find (with Quentin) that she knows things and that the things she knows have point. The implications of her dream approximate a news story in the Vicksburg *Sun* for April 9, 1860:

A large plantation and negroes are the *Ultima Thule* of every Southern gentleman's ambition. For this the lawyer pores over his dusty tomes, the merchant measures his tape, the doctor rolls his pills, the editor drives his quill and the mechanic his plane—all, all who dare aspire at all, look to this as the goal of their ambition. The mind is used, from childhood, to contemplate it, and the first efforts are all lost if the objects in life should be changed. The mind is thus trained from infancy to think of and prepare for the attainment of this end.

For Miss Rosa, Sutpen was one of the foremost builders of the Old South.

The stern charges which Miss Rosa levels against Sutpen borrow their language of authority and self-assurance from Calvinism, giving to Miss Rosa a temperament very much like Sutpen's own—cold, logical, commanding. Her severity would seem a response to Sutpen's proposal to her to provide him a son as prior grounds for marriage. Yet Mr. Compson tells Quentin that the language and attitude also belonged to her father, a small shopkeeper and steward of the Jefferson Methodist Church who ran his life as he did his business. When his wife died in giving birth to Rosa, Goodhue Coldfield gives over the girl's upbringing to her equally cold and equally selfish aunt. Mr.

Compson tells us that although Mr. Coldfield was an abolitionist, he freed his own two slaves only after "putting them on a weekly wage which he held back in full against the discharge of their current market value." Goodhue Coldfield also arranges Ellen's marriage to Sutpen as a business deal, supplying respectability and a necessary wife in return for a good match and a partnership in selling his goods. He even places a claim on his own church for the wedding.

> "Mr. Coldfield apparently intended to use the church into which he had invested a certain amount of sacrifice and doubtless self-denial and certainly actual labor and money for the sake of what might be called a demand balance of spiritual solvency, exactly as he would have used a cotton gin in which he considered himself to have incurred either interest or responsibility, for the ginning of any cotton which he or any member of his family, by blood or by marriage, had raised—that, and no more."

His visits to Sutpen's Hundred with Rosa are made on a regular basis, taking their economics into account: "they would get into the buggy and depart, Mr Coldfield first docking the two negroes for the noon meal which they would not have to prepare and (so the town believed) charging them for the crude one of left-overs which they would have to eat." Mr. Coldfield is as repressive with Rosa as he is with his servants.

> On certain days of the week she would go down town with a basket and shop at certain stores which Mr Coldfield had already designated, with no coin nor sum of money changing lip or hand, and that later in the day Mr Coldfield would trace her course by the debits scratched on paper or on walls and counters, and pay them.

Rosa is neither trusted nor respected; she lives a desolate childhood. Her only activity we know is theft: she steals scraps of cloth from her father's store (since she is never allowed money to spend) in order to make clothes for Ellen and her children. For Rosa's home is rigorously supervised by Mr. Coldfield, whose singular temperament has acknowledged that Calvinism and materialism are mutually reinforcing, two sides of the same logical coin. They blend in his self-righteous abolitionism, for he sees the War between the States as a foregone defeat and a needless business waste. Mr. Compson adds that Mr. Coldfield retreats into his house—"He spent the day, the neighbors said, behind one of the slightly opened blinds like a picquet on post, armed not with a musket but with the big family Bible"—and finds that his self-righteous isolation provokes the same anger and hatred that Sutpen's does. His manner comes to resemble Sutpen's even more, although they are on different sides of the war.

> Then one morning he learned that his store had been broken into and looted, doubtless by a company of strange troops bivouacked on the edge of town and doubtless abetted, if only vocally, by his own fellow citizens. That night he mounted to the attic with his hammer and his handful of nails and nailed the door behind him and threw the hammer out the window. He was not a coward. He was a man of uncompromising moral strength.

Mr. Coldfield's self-incarceration recalls Rosa's imprisoned childhood. Eventually his alienating temperament is assumed by Ellen, and Rosa is left without family, without friends. After her father's suicide, she sees life for the first time as *only* a patched dress, a filched vegetable.

With these juxtapositions, the source of Rosa's hatred of Sutpen and her accusations against him are clear to us: she sees his resemblance to her father, whose blindness to her was not only repressive but robbed her as well of self-respect and even of self-pity. As Goodhue Coldfield took the romance out of her family life, so Sutpen took it out of the dream of Southern aristocracy. But Rosa has a *double* narrative consciousness in *Absalom, Absalom!* and this only reflects her first story, when she judges Sutpen as a demon in an overview of her life. In her second narrative, Rosa is herself a participant, and here she generates all the natural warmth and romanticism which the adult world has repressed within her; she portrays Sutpen as a man rather than a demon. Rosa's sympathy for all outsiders is now revealed as real, instant, and profound. When Wash fetches her to Sutpen's Hundred, when she is welcomed in a home because she is needed there and is recognized as family, she is able to sympathize at once with Judith's loss.

> *The four years while I believed she waited as I waited, while the stable world we had been taught to know dissolved in fire and smoke until peace and security were gone, and pride and hope, and there was left only maimed honor's veterans, and love. Yes, there should, there must, be love and faith: these*

left with us by fathers, husbands, sweethearts, brothers, who carried the pride and the hope of peace in honor's vanguard as they did the flags; there must be these, else what do men fight for? what else worth dying for?

Rosa loves Charles Bon only hearing of him and seeing his picture, and she tries to sense him, too: "*I remember how as we carried him down the stairs and out to the waiting wagon I tried to take the full weight of the coffin to prove to myself that he was really in it.*" Working Sutpen's Hundred for the remainder of the war, Rosa gives herself to a revival of the Southern dream that she has secretly shared with Sutpen (but not her father) all along. She has difficulty treating Clytie as anything but a servant (as Sutpen treats her), and when young she could not imagine her sleeping with Judith; "*Even as a child, I would not even play with the same objects.*" Now her ability to understand the dispossessed causes her to understand Clytie, if not to embrace her; and Sutpen's return confirms her best hopes, for he wishes to rebuild his antebellum way of life. It is this Sutpen stands for, not (as Goodhue Coldfield had) his own self-gain. He tells his fellow Southerners "*that if every man in the South would do as he himself was doing, would see to the restoration of his own land, the general land and South would save itself.*" She asks no more, but when in addition he notices her, she finds her "*okra bed finished without remembering the completing of it.*" We know that both Rosa and Sutpen were ignored as children, were shut out by others. Perhaps Rosa senses this: she imposes on Sutpen's design her own dream, that the eminence, respectability, and security of Sutpen's Hundred are grounded on the bedrock of honor and decency, of a Methodist if not a Calvinist morality, and when Sutpen proposes to her not with a Southern cavalier's formal courtesy but in Goodhue Coldfield's terms—those of a businessman rather than a gentleman—she denies him in order to save the dream. Nor does she forsake the dream in her moral terms. Impoverished once more, living off baskets of food left anonymously on her doorstep, she still erects a tombstone for Judith (who dies while nursing the black son of her half-brother) that reads "*Pause, Mortal; Remember Vanity and Folly and Beware,*" and she now urges Quentin to take her to Sutpen's Hundred because of " 'Something living in it. Hidden in it' ": her courage, like Sutpen's, is total, and she will risk all to realize and accomplish her dreams for Sutpen's Hundred *and* fulfill her responsibility to her kin. She knows that any purpose to her forty-three years of self-imprisonment will now be judged, but she can face this total exposure because she, like Sutpen, would still work for the dream.

When we examine Rosa's position in its fullest context, when *we* reconstruct the past, we find that it is the Calvinistic morality which can alone tie together Rosa's mixed feelings about Sutpen, about what he stood for—and what he did. He was both her one chance to join the aristocracy and partake of the dream and her secret sharer, the outcast who made good. United in one man, these ideas are transformed by her consciousness into the single idea of Sutpen as temptation, for he is outwardly attractive and life-giving, inwardly immoral and death-dealing—it is for this reason that she labels him a devil or demon and his creation (he created Sutpen's Hundred "like the olden-time *Be Light*") only a parody of Paradise. Moreover, this convenient and orthodox explanation admits Rosa's *own* complicity, confesses to her own self-condemnation and her own self-punishment. In being attracted, she sinned herself, as Sutpen did. They both fell. Thus the town jingle—" *'Rosie Coldfield, lose him, weep him; caught a man but couldn't keep him.'* "—is sardonically apt. She does both love and hate Sutpen—an impossible, self-defeating proposition—as she loves and hates the South and loves and hates herself, and the paradoxical judgments and emotions have paralyzed her, in her chair and house, for forty-three years. Now, as the novel opens, it is precisely this anguishing compound of love and hate that draws her to Quentin: for she senses too that *they* are doubles more than either of them at first suspects.

"There is a might-have-been which is more true than truth," Rosa tells Quentin; *"there is that might-have-been which is the single rock we cling to above the maelstrom of unbearable reality."* This is the core-formulation of the novel, and Shreve rephrases it: " 'there are some things that just have to be whether they are or not, have to be a damn sight more than some other things that maybe are and it dont matter a damn whether they are or not.' " *Absalom, Absalom!* is about this need for narrative (mythic, historical, personal, fictive): we find acknowledged the facility of language to evade truth as well as confront it. Despite major lacunae in the information—concerning how Sutpen got his money, what he did in the West Indies, why his son shot another boy, perhaps another son—and the distorting elements of designed stories—elements of error, delusion, and imagination—the need of an integrated consciousness continually rearranges and re-

absorbs the facts and implications of Sutpen's life so as to make sense of it by reflecting (and so confirming) the storyteller. Rosa Coldfield's intentions and efforts are refracted in all the characters in the novel. *Absalom, Absalom!* is a book about self-projections far more than it is a novel about a "real" Thomas Sutpen.

Of the chief narrators during the autumn and winter of 1909/10, Mr. Compson provides the neatest story because he is more detached than any of the others. Drawing on his classical education, he accepts at face value Sutpen's own stated purpose as his father, Grandfather Compson, repeated it to him.

> " 'You see, I had a design in my mind. Whether it was a good or a bad design is beside the point; the question is, Where did I make the mistake in it, what did I do or misdo in it, whom or what injure by it to the extent which this would indicate. I had a design. To accomplish it I should require money, a house, a plantation, slaves, a family—incidentally of course, a wife. I set out to acquire these, asking no favor of any man. I even risked my life at one time, as I told you.' "

Thus teased into thought, Mr. Compson sets out to locate the cause of Sutpen's ultimate defeat, the "mistake": he finds it in Sutpen's background. " 'He was underbred. It showed like this always, your grandfather said, in all his formal contacts with people.' " Not surprisingly for us, Mr. Compson thinks Sutpen fails because he lacks the one thing which the Compsons still have. Mr. Compson pursues this single notion relentlessly; every act of Sutpen's is that of the low-bred man forcing his way on the world. "He now had a plantation; inside of two years he had dragged house and gardens out of virgin swamp, and plowed and planted his land with seed cotton which General Compson loaned him." Mr. Compson calls him a brigand, for there is no other way for Mr. Compson to explain (or to image) the way in which Sutpen manages to furnish his house and to set himself up as respectable aristocracy except by stealing an opportunity to simulate good breeding. When Sutpen returns with household goods from unknown quarters, Mr. Compson tells Quentin,

> "he was in a sense a public enemy. Perhaps this was because of what he brought back with him this time: the material he brought back this time, as compared to the simple wagonload of wild niggers which he had brought back before. But I dont think so. That is, I think it was a little more involved than the

sheer value of his chandeliers and mahogany and rugs. I think that the affront was born of the town's realization that he was getting it involved with himself; that whatever the felony which produced the mahogany and crystal, he was forcing the town to compound it. Heretofore, until that Sunday when he came to church, if he had misused or injured anybody, it was only old Ikkemotubbe, from whom he got his land—a matter between his conscience and Uncle Sam and God. But now his position had changed, because when, about three months after he departed, four wagons left Jefferson to go to the River and meet him, it was known that Mr Coldfield was the man who hired and dispatched them. They were big wagons, drawn by oxen, and when they returned the town looked at them and knew, no matter what they might have contained, that Mr Coldfield could not have mortgaged everything that he owned for enough to fill them; doubtless this time there were more men than women even who pictured him during this absence with a handkerchief over his face and the two pistol barrels glinting beneath the candelabra of a steamboat's saloon, even if no worse: if not something performed in the lurking dark of a muddy landing and with a knife from behind."

Because Sutpen is so successful at building for himself the Southern plantation that the Compsons do not have, Mr. Compson conveniently forgets (as we learn elsewhere) that the Compsons settled Jefferson in much the same way—that all the white settlers did. Sutpen's actions are as offensive to the Compsons, then, as to anyone, yet Sutpen's activity is modeled *on* such settlers as the Compsons. Sutpen reaffirms the values of the Compsons as much as he mocks them. So Mr. Compson responds with the same admiration for the form and hatred for the fact as Rosa does. In this they mirror each other.

But in his detachment Mr. Compson is not so much concerned about what might be at Sutpen's Hundred in 1909 as what caused the murder of Charles Bon in 1865. It is the puzzle and the abstraction that attract him most. His answer, surprisingly, is as inconsistent as Miss Rosa's might be. He argues that Bon, himself white, had had a black mistress and son, " 'the eighth part negro mistress and the sixteenth part negro son.' " That is, he forgets Sutpen's affront to the Compsons and assigns to him and to Bon all the characteristics of the traditional Southern cavalier. Even with this legerdemain, " 'It's just incredible. It just does not explain,' " for even then the Sutpen line as it extends through Henry is not tainted. He goes on to explain his dilemma.

> "They are there, yet something is missing; . . . you bring them together in the proportions called for, but nothing happens; you re-read, tedious and intent, poring, making sure that you have forgotten nothing, made no miscalculation; you bring them together again and again nothing happens: just the words, the symbols, the shapes themselves, shadowy inscrutable and serene, against that turgid background of a horrible and bloody mischancing of human affairs."

No, the taint must involve both Sutpen and his son because of their offensive character, their bad breeding. Mr. Compson finds his solution in Bon as the source of Sutpen's and Henry's corruption, a corruption no doubt fostered by Sutpen's arrogance and error. Relaxed now, he summarizes his Thomas Sutpen for Quentin.

> "He trusted no man nor woman, who had no man's nor woman's love, since Ellen was incapable of love and Judith was too much like him and he must have seen at a glance that Bon, even though the daughter might still be saved from him, had already corrupted the son. He had been too successful, you see; his was that solitude of contempt and distrust which success brings to him who gained it because he was strong instead of merely lucky."

This theory should help Quentin, for it coalesces almost perfectly with the view of Miss Rosa. Although Mr. Compson is too abstract, too cerebral to account for Sutpen's passion, he finds Sutpen as offensive to the Southern way of life, and to the Southern dream, as Miss Rosa did. He, too, comes to feel that Sutpen is mocking Southern aristocracy by achieving it so quickly, and that his achievement thus mocks them all. Mr. Compson uses his narrative to the same end Rosa does: our constitutive consciousness can see that each is at great pains to reveal Sutpen's weakness but at equal pains to hide his own. That is, by now, clear to us—and it is clear, too, to Quentin and Shreve at Harvard.

The unholy marriage of love and hate for the South coupled with the unbearable need to be involved—these are what Quentin and Shreve understand from Miss Rosa and Mr. Compson as the significance of Thomas Sutpen. Yet you cannot become disentangled. Mr. Compson conveys that. So too does Judith, upon hearing from Bon during the war.

> " 'Because you make so little impression, you see. You get born and you try this and you dont know why only you keep on trying it and you are born at the same time with a lot of other people, all mixed up with them, like trying to, having to, move your arms and legs with strings only the same strings are hitched to all the other arms and legs and the others all trying and they dont know why either except that the strings are all in one another's way like five or six people all trying to make a rug on the same loom only each one wants to weave his own pattern into the rug; and it cant matter, you know that, or the Ones that set up the loom would have arranged things a little better, and yet it must matter because you keep on trying or having to keep on trying and then all of a sudden it's all over and all you have left is a block of stone with scratches on it.' "

The intellectual and emotional conflicts in all these congruent consciousnesses seem irresolvable: Shreve voices our frustrations as well as his own. " 'What is it?' " Shreve says, exasperated,

> "something you live and breathe in like air? a kind of vacuum filled with wraithlike and indomitable anger and pride and glory at and in happenings that occurred and ceased fifty years ago? a kind of entailed birthright father and son and father and son of never forgiving General Sherman, so that forevermore as long as your children's children produce children you wont be anything but a descendant of a long line of colonels killed in Pickett's charge at Manassas?"
>
> "Gettysburg," Quentin said. "You cant understand it. You would have to be born there."

Like Miss Rosa and his father, Quentin withdraws into himself, pampers his isolation, while Shreve's question persists. *"Tell about the South. What's it like there."* What Miss Rosa and Mr. Compson have revealed has left too much unrevealed. " 'It just does not explain.' "

Rather than expose his father *or himself* any further, Quentin submits as *his own* version *Sutpen's* autobiographical story, as he told it to General Compson. It is the story of an innocent boy from the mountains of western Virginia, poor, parochial, isolated, in a land of

Scots culture that was essentially rural and egalitarian. It is the perfect picture of Jacksonian democracy.

> "Because where he lived the land belonged to anybody and everybody and so the man who would go to the trouble and work to fence off a piece of it and say 'This is mine' was crazy; and as for objects, nobody had any more of them than you did because everybody had just what he was strong enough or energetic enough to take and keep, and only that crazy man would go to the trouble to take or even want more than he could eat or swap for powder and whiskey."

But the family moves to Cavalier country, to the Jeffersonian democracy of Tidewater Virginia, where the culture is hierarchical, aristocratic, and static. People are not communal but separated by class, clan, and race. Young Sutpen is so bewildered that for the first time he takes to spying (as Miss Rosa was forced to do to learn about her world):

> "he told how he would creep up among the tangled shrubbery of the lawn and lie hidden and watch the man) in a barrel stave hammock between two trees, with his shoes off, and a nigger who wore every day better clothes than he or his father and sisters had ever owned and ever expected to, who did nothing else but fan him and bring him drinks."

Yet Thomas does not understand his own inferior position until his father gives him a message for the white man—a chance to see the inside of his house at last!—and the large black servant will not speak with him at the front door. Thus, Sutpen explains, what started him on the way to Sutpen's Hundred, to an embodiment of Southern life as a great planter, was

> "innocence. All of a sudden he discovered, not what he wanted to do but what he just had to do, had to do it whether he wanted to or not, because if he did not do it he knew that he could never live with himself for the rest of his life, never live with what all the men and women that had died to make him had left inside of him for him to pass on,"

his self-respect. Perhaps because Quentin is talking to a Canadian, a Northerner, geography becomes for him metaphoric in the retelling: from the mountains to the valley of darkness, Sutpen begins anew in a discrete land, an island: he learns at school that " 'there was a place called the West Indies to which poor men went in ships and became rich.' " This was for Sutpen " 'a spot of earth which might have been created and set aside by Heaven itself, Grandfather said,' "

> "a little island set in a smiling and fury-lurked and incredible indigo sea, which was the halfway point between what we call the jungle and what we call civilization, halfway between the dark inscrutable continent from which the black blood, the black bones and flesh and thinking and remembering and hopes and desires, was ravished by violence, and the cold known land to which it was doomed, the civilized land and people which had expelled some of its own blood and thinking and desires that had become too crass to be faced and borne longer, and set it homeless and desperate on the lonely ocean."

Earth and Heaven both, this middle ground, the island of Haiti, provides for Sutpen not only the hierarchical society he wishes to emulate and conquer but also the possibility of free admission and accession to the top; he does not see, apparently, that the blackness of the island also suggests loneliness, isolation, hatred, evil, and doom—that it is, literally, a Conradian *heart* of darkness. In Haiti Sutpen does achieve position, power, and wealth; he becomes a slave owner, heir to a large plantation, a husband and a father; in manipulating his plan, he learns to manipulate events and other people. The design fails because Sutpen is betrayed by others, not by himself.

> " 'I did not demand; I accepted them at their own valuation while insisting on my own part upon explaining fully about myself and my progenitors: yet they deliberately withheld from me the one fact which I have reason to know they were aware would have caused me to decline the entire matter, otherwise they would not have withheld it from me—a fact which I did not learn myself until after my son was born. And even then I did not act hastily. . . . I merely explained how this new fact rendered it impossible that this woman and child be incorporated in my design, and following which, as I told you, I made no attempt to keep not only that which I might consider myself to have earned at the risk of my life but which had been given to me by signed testimonials, but on the contrary I declined and resigned all right and claim to this in order that I might repair whatever injustice I might be considered to have done by so providing for the two persons whom I might be considered to

have deprived of anything I might later possess: and this was agreed to, mind; agreed to between the two parties.' "

The Haitian experience thus gives Sutpen his model for Sutpen's Hundred: history and fiction fuse, and both help to found the large plantation outside Jefferson, Tidewater Virginia reborn and realized in northern Mississippi. It is an incredible, indomitable act, vision matched with will, which makes of Sutpen as fine a Confederate hero as General Compson and one whose dreams could not be destroyed by mere defeat in battle with the Yankees. Perhaps the finest thing about Sutpen, in the end, is that he had the courage and fortitude to begin again: at nearly sixty years of age, he restores the dream, as Miss Rosa has it, to himself and his family and even to his retainer Wash Jones, who

> believed he could restore by sheer indomitable willing the Sutpen's Hundred which he remembered and had lost, labored with no hope of pay or reward who must have seen long before the demon did (or would admit it) that the task was hopeless— blind Jones who apparently saw still in that furious lecherous wreck the old fine figure of the man who once galloped on the black thoroughbred about that domain two boundaries of which the eye could not see from any point.

This is Quentin's story, drawn directly from Sutpen and extended beyond the range of Sutpen's modesty, of Sutpen's own admission to Grandfather. Thomas Sutpen's need for self-respect, Quentin implies, as well as his love, hatred, and bewilderment over what had happened to him, all reinforce Miss Rosa and his father, yet charge their incomplete, secondhand narrative consciousness with an extraordinary vision matched only by his extraordinary effort and endurance. It is a moving tribute to Sutpen by way of his autobiography and an abiding testimonial to the dignity and achievement of a beleaguered South. Quentin has found himself, too, in the grandness of Sutpen.

But this will not, of course, do any more for Quentin than it will do for us. The novel follows a patterned scheme of progressive fictionalizations as the narrators are in turn removed more and more from the acts of history they attempt to understand. Still Quentin's love-hate, although he is the third generation, remains obsessive. "*Am I going to have to have to hear it all again he thought I am going to have to hear it all over again I am already hearing it all over again I am listen-*

ing to it all over again." He must, for Quentin has shied away from Sutpen's story as the mirror of his own secret selving more than any of the others; he has been the most emotionless, detached, and as untrue to Sutpen's story, therefore, as to himself. Shreve senses this, as we do, in the very control of Quentin's narrative, in his anxiety to have no interruptions, in his fits of silence when narrative breaks toward dialogue. Quentin's story, moreover, like those of the others, " 'just does not explain,' " for it does not handle Henry's murder of Charles satisfactorily. Bon's marriage to Judith would in no way affect the Sutpens' male line of descent through Henry, although Sutpen confesses to General Compson that he would consider this tainted marriage a mockery of his plans. Our constitutive consciousness tells us (as it must have told Shreve) that as with Miss Rosa (who omitted the facts of Sutpen's insolent proposal) and Mr. Compson (who omitted his own lack of achievement), Quentin has omitted from his story what is most relevant to himself. Shreve sets out to help us learn what that is.

Mr. Compson told Quentin that Henry could enjoy an ideal incest with his sister Judith.

> "In fact, perhaps this is the pure and perfect incest: the brother realizing that the sister's virginity must be destroyed in order to have existed at all, taking that virginity in the person of the brother-in-law, the man whom he would be if he could become, metamorphose into, the lover, the husband; by whom he would be despoiled, choose for despoiler, if he could become, metamorphose into the sister, the mistress the bride."

The reasoning is dense, but it shows a potential relationship between Quentin and Henry that goes very deep, suggesting that Quentin's relationship is not, finally, so much with the father as with the son. The narrative consciousnesses in *Absalom, Absalom!* have circled, skewed, enfolded upon themselves, but always at the point where Sutpen comes too close as secret self, always where the narrative becomes too personal. Shreve decides to awaken Quentin's *emotional* commitment to the story, and thus to complete it. " 'No,' " says Shreve, interrupting his friend, " 'you wait. Let me play a while now.' " Shreve distances Quentin by repeating his salient points with enough wit and sarcasm to seem detached and disinterested himself, playing a safely opposing self to his roommate; then he begins his own fantastic story about Bon's mother and a family lawyer, spinning Charles back into the center of the story and Sutpen out to its periphery. In its way, this is the most dazzling and spellbinding story of them all, this adolescent romance with its wide arc toward Charles and Henry, for we can see Shreve's motivation behind it at every point. When Henry at last enters as a character *in a story* and, so formulated, removed from life, Shreve brings Quentin into the telling of it too:

> not two of them there and then either but four of them riding the two horses through the iron darkness, and that not mattering either: what faces and what names they called themselves and were called by so long as the blood coursed—the blood, the immortal brief recent intransient blood which could hold honor above slothy unregret and love above fat and easy shame.

Their minds marry; " 'And now,' Shreve said, 'we're going to talk about love.' " And "it did not matter to either of them which one did the talking, since it was not the talking alone which did it, performed and accomplished the overpassing." As narrative turns at last into drama, story back into life, Quentin pairs himself openly with Henry and Shreve assumes Charles's role; minor discrepancies are reconciled in the re*do*ing; all stories leap ahead to accommodate the new fact, and they rush on to the final fatal confrontation between Henry and Charles before the gates at Sutpen's Hundred.

So far, the restudying of Sutpen's story has led to a progressive disengagement. Shreve understands this and so this last time through the tale on *his* loom, he will have them both—the four of them—weave *everything*. We know now why Quentin cannot bear to have Shreve call Rosa "Aunt Rosa": Shreve is not permitted to claim a Southern heritage and cannot rob Quentin of his vitally close relationship with her nephew Henry, which through his natural projection, has fashioned Miss Rosa as *his* aunt, not Shreve/Charles's. But Shreve understands this, too, and repeats "Aunt Rosa," forces Quentin to realize his deep psychological involvement in the Sutpen story. This means not only the possibility of incest but the possibility of miscegenation too: to leave out these terms of selfish pride and extreme possession that embody hate as much as love would be to surrender to defeat, to have the new story approximate the half-true versions that Miss Rosa, Mr. Compson, and Quentin have told incompletely and hence imperfectly. Shreve hints of Mr. Compson's notion of incest, and then returns to Sutpen's own hint about his failure in Haiti: " ' "they deliberately withheld from me the one fact which I have reason to know they were aware would have caused me to decline the entire

matter . . . a fact which I did not learn until after my son was born." ' "
Shreve's reminder becomes choric, insistent, like a hammer: " 'And as
for a little matter like a spot of negro blood' "; " 'just "a little spot
of negro blood" ' ";

> four of them who sat in that drawing room of baroque and
> fusty magnificence which Shreve had invented and which was
> probably true enough, while the Haiti-born daughter of the
> French sugar planter and the woman whom Sutpen's first
> father-in-law had told him was a Spaniard (the slight dowdy
> woman with untidy gray-streaked raven hair coarse as a horse's
> tail, with parchment-colored skin and implacable pouched black
> eyes which alone showed no age because they showed no for-
> getting, whom Shreve and Quentin had likewise invented and
> which was likewise probably true enough) told them nothing
> because she did not need to;

and finally, at the very moment the two, the reenacted Henry and
Charles, break to leave for Sutpen's Hundred, Shreve imagines Sutpen
saying "—*He must not marry her, Henry. His mother's father told
me that her mother had been a Spanish woman. I believed him; it was
not until after he was born that I found out that his mother was part
negro.*" They arrive at Sutpen's Hundred, all four as two, breathless.
Shreve plays the role of Charles. "*I'm the nigger that's going to sleep
with your sister. Unless you stop me, Henry.*" And Henry/Quentin
stops Charles/Shreve. For there it is, at last, " 'there was no gentle
spreading glow but a flash, a glare' ": the moment of epiphany is the
moment of exposure for both Quentin and Henry. "*So it's the miscegenation, not the incest, which you cant bear. Henry doesn't
answer.*" Henry doesn't answer: in loving their South, the Sutpens
hate each other; they could not admit their own brotherhood when a
drop of black blood might have entered one of them. Their devotion
to the South meant their inhumanity as a family. And still, today,
Quentin is as full of hate and as inhuman. "The consciousness of the
past," Marx said, "weighs like a nightmare on the brain of the living."

> —*So it's the miscegenation, not the incest, which you cant bear.
> Henry doesn't answer.*

" 'Come on,' Shreve said," as Shreve now, " 'Let's get out of this re-
frigerator and go to bed.' "

There are at least two levels of consciousness in each narrative of *Absalom, Absalom!* At the explicit level, they are increasingly dependable reconstructions not of Thomas Sutpen but of the narrator who is using Thomas Sutpen to talk about himself; at a more subterranean and more authentic level, the narrators reveal their innermost secrets —what they fear and despise most in themselves that motivates their compulsive stories. Like Proust's *La recherche*, this novel comes to us as much in layers as in segments. We have been told (as Shreve has) that Quentin learned some critical information on his visit to Sutpen's Hundred and that that knowledge changed Mr. Compson's whole interpretation of Sutpen. But Quentin has been unable to confront that knowledge again until Shreve forces it upon him. We learn what that knowledge was—as much as we will ever learn of it, for it is all Quentin now knows—in the closing pages. We learn that it is Henry Sutpen who has come home, who is incarcerated in *his* own attic, yellowed and dying, and, three weeks later when Rosa comes for him, the cause of the final demolition of Sutpen's Hundred. The conversation they have, Quentin and Henry, the doubles across generations of the South, is peculiarly abbreviated and truncated.

> *And you are—?*
> *Henry Sutpen.*
> *And you have been here—?*
> *Four years.*
> *And you came home—?*
> *To die. Yes.*
> *To die?*
> *Yes. To die.*
> *And you have been here—?*
> *Four years.*
> *And you are—?*
> *Henry Sutpen.*

Ask the questions forward; backward, the questions ask. The astonishing thing is the circularity of the final interview: whole, self-contained, this is a rote catechism with foregone questions and foregone answers. Together Henry and Quentin merge, their roles interchangeable, coming back on themselves, their ends in their beginnings. They are in miniature what the Sutpen dynasty has become in large, for Sutpen's abrupt dismissal as a boy comes back on itself in his own dismissal of Charles, of Wash, and of Henry in the deed he required of him—and also in his dismissal of Eulalia, of Miss Rosa, of General Compson, of the very town of Jefferson itself after the war. His provocation of his own death, moreover—for it is, ironically, by his scythe in the hands of Wash Jones, who was not admitted to the front or back door of Sutpen's great house despite his loyalty and companionship—images not only Goodhue Coldfield's suicide in his attic but the spiritual suicide of all the rest. Now Quentin has tried to break that self-defeating circle by forcing the Compsons back into the lives of the Sutpens, and his own present back into their past. He looks on Henry as a Dostoyevskian other self and sees "the wasted yellow face with closed, almost transparent eyelids on the pillow, the wasted hands crossed on the breast as if he were already a corpse." So Quentin, the ghost from the barracks of the past becomes another corpse, another "crucified child," at one with Miss Rosa at last because both have forsaken the present, their lives as well as their values caught, fixed in history. They are both imaged at the end in the decaying shell of the house they visit together, but they are also imaged in Miss Rosa's house, to which they shall now return.

> It too was somehow smaller than its actual size— it was of two storys—unpainted and a little shabby, yet with an air, a quality of grim endurance as though like her it had been created to fit into and complement a world in all ways a little smaller than the one in which it found itself.

The end of the novel, too, is there in its beginning.

Quentin has a tender poignancy when, in his narration, he describes the idiot James Bond. His hatred of miscegenation, doubtless because it also involves incest, is reserved for Clytie, whom he pushes roughly to one side on his way to discover Henry. Shreve's final sardonic therapy is to fuse Clytie with Jim by fabricating an irrational parody of Jim Bonds inheriting the Western Hemisphere that calls forth from Quentin a cry of love and hate for the South echoing Miss Rosa's attitude—"*I dont. I dont! I dont hate it! I dont hate it!*"—a loud but resonant echo of " '*Rosie Coldfield, lose him, weep him; caught a man but couldn't keep him.*' " "*Maybe nothing ever happens once and is finished*": the song the town sings about Rosa is applicable to all of them. Everyone who tells a story in this novel loves Sutpen because he finds himself in Sutpen, and loses Sutpen because the interpretation is only a self-projection, is at the last but a flattering and usable fiction. "*Maybe happens is never once but like ripples maybe on water after the pebble sinks,*" Quentin tells us, *the ripples moving on, spreading, the pool attached by a narrow umbilical water-cord to the next pool which the first pool feeds, has fed, did feed, let this second pool contain a different temperature of water, a different molecularity of having seen, felt, remembered, reflect in a different tone the infinite unchanging sky, it doesn't matter: that pebble's watery echo whose fall it did not even see moves across its surface too at the original ripple-space, to the old ineradicable rhythm* thinking Yes, we are both Father. Or maybe Father and I are both Shreve [= shrive, confessor?], *maybe it took Father and me both to make Shreve or Shreve and me both to make Father or maybe Thomas Sutpen to make all of us.*

Absalom, Absalom! is bounded by the moribund, but the novel itself defeats its own atmosphere of death. At the beginning, Rosa Coldfield asks Quentin to

"write this and submit it to the magazines. Perhaps you will even remember kindly then the old woman who made you spend a whole afternoon sitting indoors and listening while she talked about people and events you were fortunate enough to escape yourself when you wanted to be out among young friends of your own age."

In *Absalom, Absalom!* our constitutive consciousness shows us how Quentin Compson fashions that story.

"Go Down, Moses"

As a novel, *Go Down, Moses* radiates from the emblematic core scene in the commissary, the long fourth section of the chapter titled "The Bear." Here Ike McCaslin and McCaslin Edmonds, second cousins on the sprawling plantation of Lucius Quintus Carothers Mc-Caslin, confront each other with their radically differing philosophies: it is a cruicial and telling moment. Potential doubles, they have come to the store at the heart of their forebears' land where for generations the McCaslins have kept their account books, sign and seal of their ownership, and where they have sold

that slow trickle of molasses and meal and meat, of shoes and straw hats and overalls, of plowlines and collars and heel-bolts and buckheads and clevises, which returned each fall as cotton—the two threads frail as truth and impalpable as equators yet cable-strong to bind for life them who made the cotton to the land their sweat fell on.

It is here, at the meeting ground of the labor of blacks and the supervision and sales of whites, that Ike and Cass choose to reexamine themselves. About them lies their most negotiable property; above them are stacked the McCaslin records—their identity and their legacy. For Cass these are ledgers of accounts receivable, but to Ike they are the family diary ever since, at the age of sixteen, he studied them late one night to determine why on *"Cristmas Day 1832"* the nigger Eunice *"Drownd herself."* These books direct them both, Ike implies, but he makes them the secular counterpart of more sacred Scriptures.

> 'There are some things He said in the Book, and some things reported of Him that He did not say. And I know what you will say now: That if truth is one thing to me and another thing to you, how will we choose which is truth?'

How, indeed? It is this single question that the novel persistently, urgently asks.

The debate in the commissary contains little real argument, for the perspectives of Ike and Cass are too dissimilar to permit much common ground for discussion. For Ike, life is visionary and sacramental; it is the view of life taught him as a youngster, when he was called Isaac, by Sam Fathers during their November hunts for Old Ben, "the yearly pageant-rite of the old bear's furious immortality." It is in this "ancient and unremitting contest" that he has discovered and cherished "the best game of all, the best of all breathing and forever the best of all listening," in keeping "yearly rendezvous with the bear which they did not even intend to kill." The hunt has taught Ike both hardihood and humility; it has made him skilled and self-sufficient at the same time that it has purified him. He has learned to see the significations of the natural world, feel its rhythms, locate himself knowingly in the interstices of woods and swampland without compass or gun, companion or guide. Much more than that, the woods have given him a sense of the mysterious and the wonderful, like the first time he saw Old Ben's tracks. He was only eleven then, and it was not even an autumn hunt but two summer weeks at the camp for fishing and for shooting squirrels, turkey, raccoons, and wildcats. Instead of joining the others Isaac had searched for Old Ben, for he wanted to know more of him. But he did not see Old Ben until he became lost, and then he saw,

> as he sat down on the log the crooked print, the warped inden-
> tation in the wet ground which while he looked at it continued
> to fill with water until it was level full and the water began to
> overflow and the sides of the print began to dissolve away. Even
> as he looked up he saw the next one, and, moving, the one
> beyond it; moving, not hurrying, running, but merely keeping
> pace with them as they appeared,

and following the tracks, he found Old Ben at last,

> he saw the bear. It did not emerge, appear: it was just there,
> immobile, fixed in the green and windless noon's hot dappling,
> not as big as he had dreamed it but as big as he had expected,
> bigger, dimensionless against the dappled obscurity, looking at
> him. Then it moved. It crossed the glade without haste, walking
> for an instant into the sun's full glare and out of it, and stopped
> again and looked back at him across one shoulder. Then it was
> gone. It didn't walk into the woods. It faded, sank back into the
> wilderness without motion as he had watched a fish, a huge old
> bass, sink back into the dark depths of its pool and vanish
> without even any movement of its fins.

For young Isaac's analogizing consciousness this has become a reitera-
tion of the claw marks he had seen scarring a log during his first
November hunt; his second year he had returned to the same log but
found that "It was almost completely crumbled now, healing with
unbelievable speed, a passionate and almost visible relinquishment,
back into the earth from which the tree had grown." Both were moments of fluid timelessness, of communion which awarded to Isaac "an
eagerness, passive; an abjectness, a sense of his own fragility and
impotence against the timeless woods."

Both visions prepared Isaac for his baptism in blood when he killed
his first deer. The buck was, for Isaac, almost precisely analogous to
Old Ben.

> At first there was nothing. . . . Then the buck was there. He
> did not come into sight; he was just there, looking not like a
> ghost but as if all of light were condensed in him and he were
> the source of it, not only moving in it but disseminating it, al-
> ready running, seen first as you always see the deer, in the split

second after he has already seen you, already slanting away in
that first soaring bound, the antlers even in that dim light looking like a small rocking-chair balanced on his head.

"Now," Sam Fathers said, "shoot quick, and slow."

The experience is recounted in "The Old People"; there Isaac and Sam
are alone too when the greatest buck of them all appears.

The boy saw the buck. It was coming down the ridge, as if it
were walking out of the very sound of the horn which related
its death. It was not running, it was walking, tremendous, unhurried, slanting and tilting its head to pass the antlers through
the undergrowth, and the boy standing with Sam beside him
now instead of behind him as Sam always stood. . . .

Then it saw them. And still it did not begin to run. It just
stopped for an instant, taller than any man, looking at them;
then its muscles suppled, gathered. It did not even alter its
course, not fleeing, not even running, just moving with that
winged and effortless ease with which deer move, passing
within twenty feet of them, its head high and the eye not proud
and not haughty but just full and wild and unafraid, and Sam
standing beside the boy now, his right arm raised at full length,
palm-outward, speaking in that tongue which the boy had
learned from listening to him and Joe Baker. . . .

"Oleh, Chief," Sam said. "Grandfather."

The visions are correlative: each animal has appeared, paused, and
departed, encapsulating in miniature the cyclic, renewing forces of
nature which Isaac first witnesses in the decomposition of the log, and
they have been granted to him when he has surrendered himself to the
greater power of the woods, of life generally. Isaac senses himself mirrored in nature as he finds his double in his mentor Sam Fathers, "son
of a negro slave and a Chickasaw chief," a man of white, black, and red
blood who best embodies for the boy the " 'communal anonymity of
brotherhood.' " In pledging his allegiance to the woods and to Sam,
Isaac learns the lessons of pride and humility, learns a way of life that
is classless, ownerless, and timeless. For Isaac the woods offer him a
sense of peace and of grace and a life that is, essentially, religious.

But Cass tells Isaac that Sam is " 'his own battleground' " because of
his mixed blood, " 'the scene of his own vanquishment and the mausoleum of his defeat.' " For Cass does not understand time as cyclic and
renewing; for him it is linear and progressive. He is most at home in

the commissary—it is where we often see him in *Go Down, Moses*—as Isaac was most comfortable in the woods; Cass's loyalty is to an efficient economic society. He has transformed the humanistic paternalism of the McCaslin plantation under Uncle Buck and Uncle Buddy into something mirroring his own sense of economic management. In his developing consciousness during the commissary scene, Ike can recognize how Cass has forsaken the precious qualities of the woods for the quantitative values of a place like Memphis, a city where Isaac and Boon on an errand from the hunting camp had once found "the high buildings and the hard pavements, the fine carriages and the horse cars and the men in starched collars and neckties made their [Boon's and Isaac's] boots and khaki look a little rougher and a little muddier and made Boon's beard look worse and more unshaven and his face look more and more like he should never have brought it out of the woods at all." To Ike's consciousness Cass does not resemble Sam or Boon but Major de Spain, who, like Cass, once hunted with them but had no special feeling for the holiness of the woods. Ike remembers when, at sixteen, he sought permission from de Spain to return to the woods and found him "sitting at the desk with a paper in his hand," wearing "sober fine broadcloth and an immaculate glazed shirt" instead of "boots and muddy corduroy." Returning then to the woods, part of which de Spain had sold off to lumbering interests, Isaac had

> looked about in shocked and grieved amazement even though he had had forewarning and had believed himself prepared: a new planing-mill already half completed which would cover two or three acres and what looked like miles and miles of stacked steel rails red with the light bright rust of newness and of piled crossties sharp with creosote, and wire corrals and feeding-troughs for two hundred mules at least.

Ike argues that such development is unnatural, for it destroys the miraculous heritage that he associates with nature, with the past, with family—and with God.

Cass and Ike meet, their separate attitudes join, in the commissary, "the square, galleried, wooden building squatting like a portent above the fields whose laborers it still held in thrall '65 or no," "the solar-plexus of the repudiated and relinquished." Ike has come to surrender his title to the McCaslin land, and he chooses Cass's special vocabulary to make it clear that Cass is to be the new heir: Ike wishes to give up any ownership because possession of land was what caused God to dispossess man from Eden.

'Because He told in the Book how He created the earth, made it
and looked at it and said it was all right, and then He made man.
He made the earth first and peopled it with dumb creatures, and
then He created man to be His overseer on the earth and to hold
suzerainty over the earth and the animals on it in His name,
not to hold for himself and his descendants inviolable title
forever. . . .'

About this Ike is unusually forceful: " 'Dispossessed. Not impotent:
He didn't condone; not blind, because He watched it. And let me say it.
Dispossessed of Eden.' " He hammers on the word especially dear to
Cass. " 'Dispossessed of Canaan, and those who dispossessed him dis-
possessed him dispossessed.' " Then Ike turns his argument to the
secular and the personal.

'He saw the land already accursed even as Ikkemotubbe and
Ikkemotubbe's father old Issetibbeha and old Issetibbeha's
fathers too held it, already tainted even before any white man
owned it by what Grandfather and his kind, his fathers, had
brought into the new land.'

Later, challenged by the historic fact of the War between the States,
Ike incorporates that into his theory, too, as God's punishment on the
South for exploiting land and men. Ike sees greed and rapacity as the
historical nature of socialized and economic man, and he swings in a
wide arc that may surprise us, an arc to

'the New England mechanics who didn't even own land and
measured all things by the weight of water and the cost of turning wheels and the narrow fringe of traders and ship-owners
still looking backward across the Atlantic and attached to the
continent only by their counting-houses'

until we remember that he is attacking Cass who, with him, stands surrounded by just such small tools and yard goods as the stuff to sell to
the blacks on the plantation. Ike's analogy, though implicit, strikes
home and Cass interrupts to divert him.

But Ike will not be distracted now. He has exchanged the word *dispossessed* for the more general and biblical *cursed:*

'Cursed:' and again McCaslin merely lifted one hand, not even
speaking and not even toward the ledgers: so that, as the stere-
opticon condenses into one instantaneous field the myriad
minutia of its scope, so did that slight and rapid gesture estab-

lish in the small cramped and cluttered twilit room not only the
ledgers but the whole plantation in its mazed and intricate entirety—the land, the fields and what they represented in terms
of cotton ginned and sold, the men and women whom they fed
and clothed and even paid a little cash money at Christmas-time
in return for the labor which planted and raised and picked and
ginned the cotton, the machinery and mules and gear with
which they raised it and their cost and upkeep and replacement
—that whole edifice intricate and complex and founded upon
injustice and erected by ruthless rapacity and carried on even
yet with at times downright savagery not only to the human beings but the valuable animals too, yet solvent and efficient and,
more than that: not only still intact but enlarged, increased;
brought still intact by McCaslin, himself little more than a child
then, through and out of the debacle and chaos of twenty years
ago where hardly one in ten survived, and enlarged and increased and would continue so, solvent and efficient and intact
and still increasing so long as McCaslin and his McCaslin suc-
cessors lasted.

This is a tormented and bitter indictment, and Ike's consciousness,
exhausted, juxtaposes to it a comic equivalent in the story of his legacy
from Uncle Hubert Beauchamp, a silver cup filled with gold coins and
wrapped and sealed in burlap that Ike is to open on reaching legal
majority. In Uncle Hubert's increasing secrecy about the cup and in its
suddenly metamorphosed shape, we are warned of what is to come.
When Ike does open the burlap all he finds is a shiny, new tin coffee-
pot stuffed with worthless I.O.U.'s for the gold coins—and an additional one for the silver cup. The story is an analogous indictment, for
it parodies Cass's interest in legacy, commerce, and investment and
comments on his sense of property and responsibility. But Uncle Hubert's exploitation of his own nephew is not without its darker side.
When Hubert stayed on at Warwick after Sophonsiba's marriage to
Uncle Buck, he took up a black mistress, luring her with Sibbey's
dresses. The younger Isaac's first view of the woman is oblique:

(And he remembered this, he had seen it: an instant, a flash, his
mother's soprano 'Even my dress! Even my dress!' loud and
outraged in the barren unswept hall; a face young and female
and even lighter in color than Tomey's Terrel's for an instant in
a closing door; a swirl, a glimpse of the silk gown and the flick
and glint of an ear-ring: an apparition rapid and tawdry and

illicit yet somehow even to the child, the infant still almost, breathless and exciting and evocative,

perhaps because her second appearance is so memorable and haunting:

in the empty lane solitary young-looking and forlorn yet withal still exciting and evocative and wearing still the silken banner captured inside the very citadel of respectability, and unforgettable.)

We know, now, at least part of the reason for Ike's anger and anxiety with Cass, because Uncle Hubert's exploitation and Cass's are concurrent in Ike's consciousness: he confronts them both *in the same year*, at the age of twenty-one. Like Cass, Uncle Hubert limns the McCaslin exploitation of property and person: he too is corruptible, cursed.

But Ike has deeper cause to be grieved with Cass. Two instances are supplied to our constitutive consciousness. During the argument in the commissary, between Ike's defense of the virtues of blacks and his theory of the curse on the white McCaslins, he recalls a time the two of them met five years earlier. Isaac had just sacrificed a close shot at Old Ben because he had instead rushed in to save the fyce dog from the bear. At first Cass is indignant.

'And you didn't shoot,' McCaslin said. 'How close were you?'
'I don't know,' he said. 'There was a big wood tick just inside his off hind leg. I saw that. But I didn't have the gun then.'
'But you didn't shoot when you had the gun,' McCaslin said. 'Why?'

Again Cass's sense of possession has violated Ike's sense of the sacred. But this time Cass had tried to counsel Isaac as well as understand him. He did so by taking down a volume of Keats.

'Listen,' he said. He read the five stanzas aloud and closed the book on his finger and looked up. 'All right,' he said. 'Listen,' and read again, but only one stanza this time and closed the book and laid it on the table. 'She cannot fade, though thou hast not thy bliss,' McCaslin said: 'Forever wilt thou love, and she be fair.'
'He's talking about a girl,' [Isaac] said.
'He had to talk about something,' McCaslin said. Then he said, 'He was talking about truth. Truth is one. It doesn't

change. It covers all things which touch the heart—honor and pride and pity and justice and courage and love. Do you see now?' He didn't know. Somehow it had seemed simpler than that, simpler than somebody talking in a book about a young man and a girl he would never need to grieve over because he could never approach any nearer and would never have to get any further away.

Then, at sixteen, the values Cass proposed did not disturb Isaac; only the example did. Why should Cass displace life for books, for art? Why should one live with abstraction and metaphor in a world of nature, where bears and deer roamed and stalked among trees and brush? Now, at twenty-one, Ike has further reason to doubt Cass's application of Keats. For he has witnessed a moment when life *did* become art, when the natural motions and the ongoing rhythms of nature *were* halted, stilled. It was at the death of Old Ben. "It fell just once. For an instant they almost resembled a piece of statuary: the clinging dog, the bear, the man stride its back, working and probing the buried blade." The scene resembles a frieze on the sort of Grecian urn that Keats was describing. What first disturbed the younger Isaac is now clear to the older Ike: in such frozen moments art betokens death; it resembles the life trapped in all the books like the accounts books in the commissary. It robs humanity of the right to breathe and makes men only symbols and statistics.

Ike may also be correlating another story from Cass, this time of Ike's father and mother before they were married, the tale called "Was" which was "not something he had participated in or even remembered except from the hearing, the listening, come to him through and from his cousin McCaslin born in 1850 and sixteen years his senior." It is a story of a hunt which Cass went on with Ike's father, Uncle Buck—"It was a good race." As Cass tells it, Uncle Buck, stopping only long enough to put on a necktie, went with Cass (then eight) on a ritual chase of Tomey's Turl, who had run off to the Beauchamps' to see his girl Tennie. It is a tale both romantic and comic, for it juxtaposes Miss Sophonsiba's pretensions at romance—her name itself a comic misspelling of Sophonisba, the legendary and beautiful woman beloved of Masinissa—and Uncle Buck's and Tomey's own little game. The difficulty is that when Uncle Buck passed the gateposts, "just two posts and a nigger boy about [Cass's] size sitting on one of them, blowing a fox-horn," he was in " 'bear-country,' " where the hunter was made the hunted. For Miss Sophonsiba and Uncle

Hubert tricked him into climbing into bed with her and so betrothing himself and only a poker game got him out of it, a game with preposterously high stakes,

> "If I win, you take Sibbey without dowry and the two niggers, and I dont owe 'Filus anything,"

or incredibly low stakes,

> "If I dont call you, 'Filus wont owe me nothing and I wont owe 'Filus nothing,"

or what they finally settled on, the future of Tomey's Turl and Tennie. But Tomey's Turl played a part, too, because (unknown to Hubert until the end, when he passes) Tomey's Turl dealt the cards.

This is Cass's version, but it is not the only version. For it does not matter how Tomey's Turl deals the cards, since in his society it is the white man who plays them. The real substance of the story, beneath its patois of tall tale and folk legend, is the analogy of blacks with animals. Tomey's Turl's attempt to see his girl is made the occasion for a ritual hunt by Uncle Buck much as the ritual escape of his caged pet fox is, and he and Hubert bring to the chase all the joys characteristic of a traditional fox hunt.

> So he never did know just when and where they jumped Tomey's Turl, whether he flushed out of one of the cabins or not. Uncle Buck was away out in front on Black John and they hadn't even cast the dogs yet when Uncle Buck roared, "Gone away! I godfrey, he broke cover then!" and Black John's feet clapped four times like pistol shots while he was gathering to go out, then he and Uncle Buck vanished over the hill like they had run at the blank edge of the world itself. Mr Hubert was roaring too: "Gone away! Cast them!" and they all piled over the crest of the hill just in time to see Tomey's Turl away out across the flat, almost to the woods, and the dogs streaking down the hill and out onto the flat.

What is worse, Uncle Buck does not acknowledge that Tomey's Turl is *his own half-brother,* for he is also the son—as well as the grandson— of Lucius McCaslin: Uncle Buck is chasing an enslaved part of his own blood! The decaying house of Warwick and the decadent behavior of Miss Sophonsiba and Uncle Hubert thus also correlate to (as well as help conceal) the white tendency to corruptibility, to what Ike now terms the McCaslin curse.

Juxtaposing these incidents, we can see why Ike is so insistent during the argument in the commissary to counter Cass's pragmatic economics with his own personalized humanism. At sixteen, Isaac found the sacrifice of Eunice as disturbing as the sacrifice of Old Ben—which *happened concurrently* and which brackets it in his memory—and far less natural.

> *June 21th 1833 Drownd herself. . . .*
> *23 Jun 1833 Who in hell ever heard of a niger drownding*
> *him self. . . .*
> *Aug 13th 1833 Drownd herself. . . .*

Why did Uncle Buddy think she had drowned herself? finding, beginning to find on the next succeeding page what he knew he would find, only this was still not it because he already knew this:

> *Tomasina called Tomy Daughter of Thucydus @ Eunice Born*
> *1810 dide in Child bed June 1833 and Burd. Yr stars fell*

nor the next:

> *Turl Son of Thucydus @ Eunice Tomy born Jun 1833 yr stars*
> *fell Fathers will*

and nothing more, no tedious recording filling this page of wages day by day and food and clothing charged against them, no entry of his death and burial because he had outlived his white half-brothers and the books which McCaslin kept did not include obituaries.

At sixteen, Isaac learned the official story of Tomey's Turl in the ledgers, and its variance with Cass's story called "Was," since Buck and Buddy recorded no hint of their treatment of him nor any sign that their father had sired him on his own black slave daughter. All Isaac could learn from the ledgers at age sixteen was that Lucius attempted to salve his conscience by willing one thousand dollars—to be paid *after* his death—to the three children of Tomey's Turl: James, Fonsiba, and Lucas. Buck and Buddy had in turn passed that legacy on to Isaac to pay; declining to pay it themselves they merely tripled the amount of the debt, their legacy, like their treatment of slaves (who could sneak out at night if they snuck back before morning) and like their treatment of Tomey's Turl, essentially a ritual and a game. No previous generation of McCaslins was willing to recognize or acknowledge its own black kin.

> *So I reckon that was cheaper than saying My son to a nigger* he thought. *Even if My son wasn't but just two words. But there*

must have been love he thought. *Some sort of love. Even what he would have called love: not just an afternoon's or a night's spittoon.*

Still, Isaac can find no sign that Lucius loved Eunice, only that he used her. Now in the argument in the commissary all of Ike's frustrations and bewilderment, rage and guilt return: Cass's attitude is like Lucius's, like Buck's and Buddy's.

Where Ike imports the experience of the woods to the ledgers, see-ing in them *human* nature and *human* growth, Cass finds only facts, records, and audits. So Ike makes his argument about the McCaslin curse and his personal relinquishment of the family inheritance turn on Eunice and Tomey's Turl and on the children of Tomey's Turl and Tennie and the necessary payments designated to their own heirs whose humanity has been strengthened from being partly black:

> if he couldn't speak even to McCaslin, even to explain his repu-diation, that which to him too, even in the act of escaping (and maybe this was the reality and the truth of his need to escape) was heresy: so that even in escaping he was taking with him more of that evil and unregenerate old man who could summon, because she was his property, a human being because she was old enough and female, to his widower's house and get a child on her and then dismiss her because she was of an inferior race, and then bequeath a thousand dollars to the infant because he would be dead then and wouldn't have to pay it, than even he had feared. 'Yes. He didn't want to. He had to. Because they will endure. They are better than we are. Stronger than we are. Their vices are vices aped from white men or that white men and bondage have taught them: improvidence and intemperance and evasion—not laziness: evasion: of what white man had set them to, not for their aggrandisement or even comfort but his own—' and [Cass]
> 'All right. Go on: Promiscuity. Violence. Instability and lack of control. Inability to distinguish between mine and thine—' and he [Ike]
> 'How distinguish, when for two hundred years mine did not even exist for them?' and McCaslin
> 'All right. Go on. And their virtues—' and he
> 'Yes. Their own. Endurance–' and McCaslin
> 'So have mules:' and he

'—and pity and tolerance and forbearance and fidelity and love of children—' and McCaslin
'So have dogs.'

And there it is: "himself and his cousin amid the old smells of cheese and salt meat and kerosene and harness" stand irreconcilably opposed. The two antagonistic views of life—as sacramental and given by grace, as progressive and earned by sweat and cleverness—bring them to a stalemate. There seems to Ike no communication, no family left. Ironically, his recourse is to surrender *any sense* of sacrament and grace, to relinquish his sole patrilineal rights to the economically minded Cass and to absolve himself of any responsibility. But in doing so, he displays an ignorance of his own: he rejects Sam's lesson of accepting responsibility; he renders Sam's death meaningless.

But it comes as no surprise to us, because the argument in the commissary was prefigured in chapter 2, "The Fire and the Hearth." There it was Lucas and Molly Beauchamp who argued for human dignity and self-respect. The night of Roth Edmonds's birth Lucas risks his life to fetch a doctor while his wife Molly goes to Zack's house to wet-nurse the child. But Molly stays six months, and Lucas, the son of Tomey's Turl, is certain that, as Lucius McCaslin did to his grandmother, so Edmonds is now doing to his wife. He demands that Molly return home, but that is not enough; he may still have been compromised, and he challenges Zack to a duel although he will die either way, since a black cannot kill a white man and go free. Honor demands that Lucas wait until dawn ("He was waiting for daylight. He could not have said why"), but then he confronts Zack with his razor.

"Put that razor down and I will talk to you," Edmonds said.
"You knowed I wasn't afraid, because you knowed I was a McCaslin too and a man-made one. And you never thought that, because I am a McCaslin too, I wouldn't. You never even thought that, because I am a nigger too, I wouldn't dare. No. You thought that because I am a nigger I wouldn't even mind."

They fight instead with Zack's pistol, across a bed which signifies their own blood relationship and the importance to Lucas of conjugal love.

Then Lucas was beside the bed. He didn't remember moving at all. He was kneeling, their hands gripped, facing across the bed and the pistol the man whom he had known from infancy, with whom he had lived until they were both grown almost as brothers lived. They had fished and hunted together, they had learned to swim in the same water, they had eaten at the same table in the white boy's kitchen and in the cabin of the negro's mother; they had slept under the same blanket before a fire in the woods [anticipating Henry and Roth].

"For the last time," Lucas said. "I tell you—" Then he cried, and not to the white man and the white man knew it; he saw the whites of the negro's eyes rush suddenly with red like the eyes of a bayed animal—a bear, a fox: "I tell you! Dont ask too much of me!"

Lucas resembles Tomey's Turl before Uncle Buck, but this is a much more serious game of life and death. He grabs the pistol but it misfires, and Lucas surrenders, since it seems to be a fated draw. He returns to farming his own small portion of the McCaslin land. But the quarrel remains unresolved in Lucas's mind because he does not know if he was treated as a slave and he does not know how to know. " 'How to God,' he said, 'can a black man ask a white man to please not lay down with his black wife? And even if he could ask it, how to God can the white man promise he wont?' " The threat of the possessed, the exploited, still hangs over them all.

The confrontation of Zack and Lucas adumbrates the commissary argument over the exploitation of men; the analogous envelope story, more expansive and comic, of Lucas and Molly in "The Fire and the Hearth" adumbrates the argument over the exploitation of land. For years Lucas Beauchamp has profited from his commercial enterprise in moonshine whiskey. He has grown greedy and ambitious; one night, when hiding his still from Roth Edmonds (who now runs the McCaslin plantation), he finds a gold piece in an old Indian mound and decides to rent a gold divining machine to see if there is more buried treasure. His own dream of getting rich soon overcomes him; he exchanges Ike's terms for Cass's in their later argument in the commissary: he "held the divining machine before him as if it were some object symbolical and sanctified for a ceremony, a ritual." His wife opposes him, for she (like the later Isaac) finds the land sacred and Lucas's greed sacrilegious. She appeals to him to stop his ruination of the land, digging it up at night hoping to find more gold coins, and when her position does not prevail, she goes to Roth requesting a divorce from Lucas. In explaining her beliefs to Roth, she shares Ike's later sentiments.

"He's sick in the mind now. Bad sick. He dont even get up to go to church on Sunday no more. He's bad sick, marster. He's doing a thing the Lord aint meant for folks to do. . . .

"Because God say, 'What's rendered to My earth, it belong to Me unto I resurrect it. And let him or her touch it, and beware.' And I'm afraid. I got to go. I got to be free of him."

In the course of his search for gold, Lucas has also corrupted George Wilkins and, more importantly, his daughter Nat, whose exploitation of her father for a dowry of some substance echoes Lucas's exploitation of Molly and others. Not until Molly steals the machine from Lucas and faints from overexertion trying to hide it from him does Lucas recognize the dimensions of his ambition, the impropriety of it. He wins Molly back by giving up the machine. The terms in which he surrenders the instrument show that he has come to see Molly's view of life as sacred. " 'Get rid of it,' " he tells Roth when he takes it up to the commissary.

"I dont want to never see it again. Man has got three score and ten years on this earth, the Book says. He can want a heap in that time and a heap of what he can want is due to come to him, if he just starts in soon enough. I done waited too late to start. That money's there. Them two white men that slipped in here that night three years ago and dug up twenty-two thousand dollars and got clean away with it before anybody saw them. I know. I saw the hole where they filled it up again, and the churn it was buried in. But I am near to the end of my three score and ten, and I reckon to find that money aint for me."

Lucas returns to his responsibility of plowing his own natural crops instead of defiling the sacred Indian mound and the land around it. But that act in the past has ironic ramifications for us: in giving up that economic gain which Ike later claims also motivates Cass, he *also returns to the land*, an implicit criticism of Ike's later too-easy relinquishment of the McCaslin plantation. To our constitutive consciousness Lucas like Tomey's Turl (and later like Rider) provides an ignored other self for Ike McCaslin.

The year he was sixteen, Isaac had a prescience it would be their last hunt.

It was like the last act on a set stage. It was the beginning of the end of something, he didn't know what except that he would not grieve. He would be humble and proud that he had been found worthy to be a part of it too or even just to see it too.

When Old Ben and Lion are killed and buried and Sam falls sick, Isaac asks to stay with Sam and Boon. Cass objects, since Isaac has missed too much schooling, but General Compson intervenes in their quarrel.

"And you shut up, Cass," he said, though McCaslin had not spoken. "You've got one foot straddled into a farm and the other foot straddled into a bank; you aint even got a good hand-hold where this boy was already an old man long before you damned Sartorises and Edmondses invented farms and banks to keep yourselves from having to find out what this boy was born knowing and fearing too maybe but without being afraid."

Isaac is given permission to stay four more days with Sam, his mentor and his secret self. But as soon as the hunting party departs, Sam asks Boon to kill him as he killed Old Ben, making their lives actually conterminous, and Boon does: it is a moment of deep pain and anguish for both Boon and Isaac, and it is blotted from Ike's otherwise active consciousness. But it is the way of the woods, of the cycles and rhythms of nature, for Sam and Old Ben were coequal. Cass guesses the truth on Sunday when he returns for Isaac, but intimations are not enough for Cass. He must overpower his inferiors and so *possess* the truth from them. His treatment of Boon is brutal and likely implies his treatment of blacks on the McCaslin plantation.

"Did you kill him, Boon?" he said. Then Boon moved. He turned, he moved like he was still drunk and then for a moment blind too, one hand out as he blundered toward the big tree and seemed to stop walking before he reached the tree so that he plunged, fell toward it, flinging up both hands and catching himself against the tree and turning until his back was against it, backing with the tree's trunk his wild spent scoriated face and the tremendous heave and collapse of his chest, McCaslin following, facing him again, never once having moved his eyes from Boon's eyes. "Did you kill him, Boon?"

"No!" Boon said, "No!"

"Tell the truth," McCaslin said. "I would have done it if he had asked me to." Then the boy [Isaac] moved. He was between them, facing McCaslin; the water felt as if it had burst and sprung not from his eyes alone but from his whole face, like sweat.

"Leave him alone!" he cried. "Goddamn it! Leave him alone!"

That was Isaac's first quarrel with Cass. But it was also his first lesson from Boon; Isaac learned then that he must recognize his own kinship with Sam as Boon had recognized his. He tries to make good the unpaid McCaslin legacy to the three children of Tomey's Turl: two years later, he trails James to Tennessee but is unable to find him. Then, while Lucas claims his own one thousand dollars from Cass, Isaac leaves like "one of the Magi travelling incognito" to seek out Fonsiba near Midnight, Arkansas. When he finds her, she is in distressing poverty, in "a single log edifice with a clay chimney which seemed in process of being flattened by the rain to a nameless and valueless rubble of dissolution in that roadless and even pathless waste of unfenced fallow and wilderness jungle." Fonsiba is named after Isaac's own mother, but she will have nothing to do with him, nor will her husband, who dismisses Isaac's attempt to lift the white McCaslin curse by claiming that the blacks have already done so, insisting " 'this country will be the new Canaan,' " oblivious of his own condition. Isaac is understandably anxious. " 'Fonsiba,' he said. 'Fonsiba. Are you all right?' 'I'm free,' she said."

Remembering Boon's love of that " 'communal anonymity of brotherhood' " and Fonsiba's poverty brought on by McCaslin blindness and ignorance and waste, Ike faces Cass in the commissary and repeats her words (ironically not understanding himself any more than Fonsiba had): " 'I am free.' " He too would seek like Fonsiba and her husband a " 'new Canaan.' " But how? He no longer has Sam to emulate, the children of Tomey's Turl—his own black kin—scorn him, and his attempt to teach Cass and so reconcile himself in some way to the McCaslin plantation he rejects outright. Ike decides to relinquish everything in emulation of Christ—no longer able to emulate Sam or Cass, he chooses the ultimate sacrificed man. He will become sanctified like the sacramental woods where he was educated. He will imitate Christ

> not in mere static and hopeful emulation of the Nazarene as the young gambler buys a spotted shirt because the old gambler won in one yesterday, but (without the arrogance of false humility and without the false humbleness of pride, who intended to earn his bread, didn't especially want to earn it but had to earn it and for more than just bread) because if the

Nazarene had found carpentering good for the life and ends He had assumed and elected to serve, it would be all right too for Isaac McCaslin even though Isaac McCaslin's ends, although simple enough in their apparent motivation, were and would be always incomprehensible to him, and his life, invincible enough in its needs, if he could have helped himself, not being the Nazarene, he would not have chosen it: and paid it back.

It is an astonishing and foolish, impossible decision made clear because, even at the first, it was one which was not easy to make: "if he could have helped himself, not being the Nazarene, he would not have chosen it." If the form Ike's narrative consciousness takes at this juncture is familiar to us—to emulate someone whose life embodies the values he cherishes most—the example is no less unsettling. The dialectic suddenly opened here between his reasoned (if passionate) argument with Cass and the extreme form his senseless relinquishment takes replicates the sharp disjunction in his own narrative consciousness between the first three sections of "The Bear," set in the woods, and the fourth section, set in the commissary. The final cause for the force and anxiety of Ike's argument with Cass in the commissary and the final reason for his decision to emulate the Nazarene—both extreme responses for the events we know at this point and for the weakened Ike we have come to fathom—are provided to our constitutive consciousness in the one event Ike does *not* tell Cass: his final climactic visit to the holy woods, which we are given in section 5 of "The Bear." With this, all is made clear.

In the unfolding consciousness of Ike as we are given it, this last visit is withheld from us until the end, for it is the most painful for Ike to remember. He had prescience of this experience, too. The summer following the deaths of Old Ben and Sam Fathers, when it came time for the customary hunt for small game, "there was no mention of it," and when November arrived "no one spoke of using Major de Spain's house"; instead, they went an additional forty miles into land Isaac had never seen before. The spring following, when he was eighteen, "they heard (not from Major de Spain) that he had sold the timber-rights" of the big woods "to a Memphis lumber company." In his businesslike way, Major de Spain has also relocated Boon, having him appointed town marshal at Hoke's where he can do least harm. It is a moment of sharp and bitter revelation for Isaac that this other mentor, the man who killed Old Ben and Sam and then grieved for what he had had to do, has been accommodated in a way alien to his nature and then forgotten. Such shared anguish cannot be so easily dismissed. So Isaac returns to Boon.

Isaac knows that Boon shares his sacramental vision of nature. Along part of his journey, the boy is confronted with the lumber train, but the noisy machine is still dwarfed for him by the past when he remembers how a "harmless" train then had disturbed a bear that did not know what it was. Even the present train is for Ike only "a small dingy harmless snake vanishing into weeds." At Hoke's he is met by Ash, for Boon is down at the Gum Tree where they once hunted squirrels together. This further journey does not bother Isaac, either, for, as "the solitude closed about him, green with summer," he can only recall *the day, the morning when he killed the buck and Sam marked his face with its hot blood.*" His vision is both external and internal, as cleansing as ever.

Although he is shocked by the "alien" concrete markers of the lumber company, he is reassured by the sight of the burial grounds of Lion and Sam, annealed by the still mysterious powers of nature:

> –the tree, the other axel-grease tin nailed to the trunk, but weathered, rusted, alien too yet healed already into the wilderness' concordant generality, raising no tuneless note, and empty, long since empty of the food and tobacco he had put into it that day.

This is "no abode of the dead because there was no death" in the woods, only transformations of life. But when he sees a snake he thinks of his own mortality. He welcomes the snake into the natural " 'communal anonymity of brotherhood' ": " 'Chief,' " he says to it, " 'Grandfather,' " as Sam had once addressed the mystical buck, but he omits "Oleh"; his faith in nature—this year when he visits his black kin—is already slipping. He can recognize but not greet, acknowledge but not accept.

In the commissary scene with Cass, Ike had forgotten the renewing power this return to the woods supplied him because this final holy moment was qualified by the snake and then destroyed by Boon. There was no warning that the woods could not accommodate Boon when Isaac heard the squirrels running about the branches of the Gum Tree; forty or fifty appeared to him, full of life, making the whole memorable tree "one green maelstrom of mad leaves." But

> Then he saw Boon, sitting, his back against the trunk [as when he killed Sam], his head bent, hammering furiously at some-

thing on his lap. What he hammered with was the barrel of his dismembered gun, what he hammered at was the breech of it. The rest of the gun lay scattered about him in a half-dozen pieces which he bent over the piece on his lap his scarlet and streaming walnut face, hammering the disjointed barrel against the gun-breech with the frantic abandon of a madman. He didn't even look up to see who it was. Still hammering, he merely shouted back at the boy in a hoarse strangled voice:

"Get out of here! Dont touch them! Dont touch a one of them! They're mine!"

To Isaac's analogizing consciousness Boon has returned to the position of overwhelming grief he assumed when Cass tried to force from him the admission that he had killed Sam. But now he is no longer Boon— he would *possess* squirrels as, later, Cass shows Ike *he* might. Isaac has found his new double—the successor to Sam and the man on whom he had planned to rely—in the woods of his present and has discovered that he is a madman. The last sacred communion the woods gives to Isaac is his epiphany of total despair in the ruination of Boon. And for our constitutive consciousness, it is also—here in *his* implied rejection of Sam's woods—the beginning of the ruination of Ike McCaslin.

The destruction of Boon, which personifies for Isaac the destruction of the woods, sends him later that same year to Midnight, Arkansas, if we reconstruct the chronology of Isaac's life—*that* is what sends him back to the McCaslin legacy, to black kin and to the plantation commissary: the last puzzling moment of Ike's consciousness in "The Bear" falls into a pattern for us at the end. But Fonsiba's abrupt dismissal of him only echoes Boon's and Cass's. It is on the basis of these powerful rejections that Ike chooses the life of the Nazarene, not in emulation finally but in signification. His own name seems to indicate this role of sacrifice and redemption, but from the outset he confesses the very futility of his action. He tells Cass in the commissary,

"If He could see Father and Uncle Buddy in Grandfather He must have seen me too.—an Isaac born into a later life than Abraham's and repudiating immolation: fatherless and therefore safe declining the altar because maybe this time the exasperated Hand might not supply the kid."

But he does not doubt himself sufficiently as the biblical Isaac and Jesus did—in electing to become a carpenter, Ike adopts the form of

Christ's life while simultaneously rejecting its substance in his career as a rabbi or teacher (like Sam). Ike does not realize that Christ *suffered for* mankind throughout his life rather than sacrificing his inheritance, suffered by entering *into* the alien society to save it rather than by leaving it in self-righteousness and self-pity, felt love and compassion rather than shame and guilt.

Ike's wife tries to teach him these lessons, tries to persuade Ike to a useful life of farming. Whether she sees that as a carpenter he will, ironically, foolishly, necessarily use lumber that comes from his own ruined woods we are not told; but she does sense the healing powers of plowing the land as Molly did with Lucas. Ike's wife fears his childhood withdrawal into the woods has matured into a fixed, analogous pattern of withdrawal even in the town. When Ike, challenged, assigns to her the motives and values of Cass, she responds the way Molly responded to Lucas: she advances the argument of human love. But Ike's argument with Cass has undone him. Even his wife's naked body shocks more than it attracts him. She cannot even give him the son—the McCaslin kin—he has wanted to recognize. Still misunderstanding,

> he thought she was crying now at first, into the tossed and wadded pillow, the voice coming from somewhere between the pillow and the cachinnation: 'And that's all. That's all from me. If this dont get you that son you talk about, it wont be mine:' lying on her side, her back to the empty rented room, laughing and laughing

What we can see—but what Ike fails to see—is that his argument with his wife is correlative to his earlier argument in the commissary except that now he has taken Cass's position; and that, moreover, his wife's despair, laughing from an abysmal grief, is the precise analogue to Boon's. Her self-destructive course echoes Boon's mutilation of his own gun and each reveals an unbearable desperation to realize a dream while acknowledging final defeat.

But we can anticipate Ike's failure because *Go Down, Moses* has, with Lucas and Rider, already shown us, outside the range of Ike's consciousness, dilemmas similar to his own. Lucas learned to live with his frustrations with Zack and to retain his love and faith in Molly. Rider's story in chapter 3, "Pantaloon in Black," is a miniature biographical consciousness which is in every way inverse to Ike's and so instructive to our understanding of Ike's more detailed (and more self-pitying) narrative. Like Ike (and even more like Tomey's Turl and

Lucas), Rider can see the deeply rooted bigotry of the white culture around him. Not only the sawmill and the law, but even the illegal still and dice game are run by whites who all refer to him as "nigger": their racial accusations ring repeatedly and analogously in his head (and in ours). But he rises above this by ignoring it, by marrying Mannie and building a new life around her. In apposition to Ike's "little new jerry-built bungalow" in Jefferson, Rider's successful life with Mannie is mirrored in their rented *home:* "in just six months he had refloored the porch and rebuilt and roofed the kitchen, doing the work himself on Saturday afternoon and Sunday with his wife helping him." When his wife suddenly dies from no known cause, he buries her himself with the same devotion and anguish that characterize the burial of Lion and Sam. He is offered help at the burial, but as with Boon, the unbearable job cannot be shared.

> Another member of his sawmill gang touched his arm and said, "Lemme have hit, Rider." He didn't even falter. He released one hand in midstroke and flung it backward, striking the other across the chest, jolting him back a step, and restored the hand to the moving shovel, flinging the dirt with that effortless fury so that the mound seemed to be rising on its own volition, not built up from above but thrusting visibly upward out of the earth itself, until at last the grave, save for its rawness, resembled any other marked off without order about the barren plot by shards of pottery and broken bottles and old brick and other objects insignificant to sight [like the axle-grease tins] but actually of a profound meaning and fatal to touch, which no white man could have read.

Although he is warned not to return to his home because Mannie's ghost will be walking there, he returns to meet her: it is as if he *wills* her back. His vision is like young Isaac's visions of the buck and Old Ben. Nor is Rider afraid; it is for him a splendid vision of reunion, adumbrating Isaac's first moments in the woods when he returns to visit Boon. When Mannie leaves again—appearing, pausing, and disappearing like the buck and the bear before Isaac—Rider devotes his life not only to grieving for her but to finding ways to rejoin her. He lifts logs too heavy even for him; he tries drink; he finally attacks a white man who has repeatedly cheated blacks at dice. He will not accommodate himself to this life—he will not therefore pray with his aunt and uncle—for his world cannot adjust to his own deeper sense of morality and justice; in his world, white men—the moonshiner, the diceman, the sheriff—always carry weapons to be used against him, his kin, and his race. So, in his growing awareness of his own alienation, of the futility of his and Mannie's plans to compromise with the white world where they find themselves, he makes his final act of provocation a testimonial to the corruption that abounds in it. By exposing the dishonesty of the crapshooter, he witnesses to the indignity of blacks and provides a memorial to Mannie on his way to finding her in another life. The degradation of his lynching, he knows, will reflect more on the Birdsongs—and on the white culture generally —than on him, on the blacks. But he does not live long enough to know that even the deputy's wife, like the diceman, cheats: "she had attended a club rook-party that afternoon and had won the first, the fifty-cent, prize until another member had insisted on a recount of the scores and the ultimate throwing out of one entire game." This, too, underlines the significance of Rider's choice. His death, like Eunice's, is a willed suicide of the body upon the surrender of the spirit. Both become, in *Go Down, Moses*, corrective analogies to Ike's behavior, lessons for the living he refuses to re-cognize—but more too than that: they also serve as sharp reminders of the dimension and the urgency of their needs.

Despite these significations, the good intentions of the best of the whites in *Go Down, Moses* are not sufficient to save them. In chapter 6, "Delta Autumn," the slow reduction of Ike's world is confirmed. The old hunt for bear is now restricted to deer, the woods are replaced by scrub country at the farthest reaches of the delta, and " 'the communal anonymity of brotherhood' " is succeeded by a general cynicism realized particularly in Roth's selfish presumption of a black mistress. His mistress is the great-granddaughter of Tomey's Turl: Roth's act reawakens for us once more the characters and forces of "Was." The woman knows this: " 'You're Uncle Isaac,' she said." Ike has one last chance to recognize his kin, but he does not fulfill that pledge as he might have once wished to do: he assumes Cass's role again (and his own, with Fonsiba) by handing her an envelope of cash that Roth has left for her. She properly scorns it: " 'That's just money,' she said." It is another sign of corruption for her—land, money, and material goods substituted for human affection and relationships. She even accuses Ike of the error of his relinquishment of property. " 'You spoiled him. You, and Uncle Lucas and Aunt Mollie. But mostly you,' " she says; " 'When you gave to his grandfather that land which didn't belong to him, not even half of it by will or even law.' " Ike was

correct in acknowledging that land corrupts when man thinks he
possesses it, but in passing over his inheritance he has only corrupted
his own white kin.

When the woman tries to share her life with him, she tells him that

> "I got a job, teaching school here in Aluschaskuna, because my
> aunt was a widow, with a big family, taking in washing to
> sup—"
> "Took in what?" he said. "Took in washing?" He sprang,
> still seated even, flinging himself backward onto one arm, awry-
> haired, glaring. . . . "You're a nigger!"
> "Yes," she said.

Ike learns her race by the menial job of her aunt; there is no " 'communal anonymity of brotherhood' " here as there once had been with
Sam, who was also part white, part black. But they are kin and, forced
to respond to her, Ike gives the woman his most generous legacy now,
General Compson's old hunting horn, "covered with the unbroken
skin from a buck's shank and bound with silver." She takes it, knowing that once again an object (even a symbolic one) is made to substitute for human concern. The horn thus mocks Ike, for it means
nothing to her and will be useless to her boy in Chicago, even if it
remarks on the happier times of the past and of the sacred woods
that did not know race; now, ironically for our constitutive consciousness, the horn for Ike is *cheaper than saying My* [niece] *to a nigger*."
Ike's advice to her, too, only mocks his earlier argument to Cass in
the commissary. " 'Go back North. Marry: a man in your own race.
That's the only salvation for you—for a while yet, maybe a long while
yet. We will have to wait. Marry a black man.' " His response is as
heartless as his reply to his wife: the scenes are deliberately analogous.
Ike, like Roth, leaves the woman as Lucius once abandoned Eunice. Like
them, Ike is not generative but sterile even in his kindness, "a widower
now and uncle to half a county and father to no one." His unbending
will in opposition to ownership is matched, inversely, by an unbending will regarding the separation of races. The woman's reply could
be his wife's, had she not been overcome with a grief akin to Boon's.
Departing, the woman

> blazed silently down at him. Then that was gone too. She stood
> in the gleaming and still dripping slicker, looking quietly down
> at him from under the sodden hat.

> "Old man," she said, "have you lived so long and forgotten so much that you dont remember anything you ever knew or felt or even heard about love?"

Unwittingly, Ike has become—as he once feared—a sacrifice God would ultimately reject. He realizes, at the end, his own complicity. "No wonder the ruined woods I used to know dont cry for retribution! he thought: The people who have destroyed it will accomplish its revenge." His secret self—once Sam, then Boon, then Christ—is now only Roth. When Legate returns and tells Ike that Roth has shot a deer, Ike answers for both Roth and himself. " 'It was a doe,' he said."

Chapter 7, "Go Down, Moses," is in deliberate parallel with "Delta Autumn." This time it is a black McCaslin, Samuel Worsham Beauchamp, who embodies the material values of Cass in the commissary argument (and who is, but more permanently, an analogue to the Lucas digging for gold in "The Fire and the Hearth"). Butch Beauchamp parodies Cass's values in his clothes,

> He wore one of those sports costumes called ensembles in the men's shop advertisements, shirt and trousers matching and cut from the same fawn-colored flannel, and they had cost too much and were draped too much, with too many pleats,

an outgrowth of his criminal activity in robbing Rouncewell's store in Jefferson and in working a numbers racket in Chicago. For Butch is finally not meant to be an analogy with Cass, but an extension of his position in the debate of "The Bear." Butch's true double, for our constitutive consciousness, is Roth, for they share the same attitude of easy dismissal of their wrong. He stands, moreover, for Roth's bastard son, the other mulatto boy condemned to Chicago.

Just as the Roth of "Delta Autumn" is analogous to Butch, so the Ike of "Delta Autumn" is analogous to Gavin Stevens. Gavin, too, has good intentions to help bury Butch in the style his grandmother Mollie wants, and he even collects money for the effort from the community Butch once robbed.

> During the remainder of that hot and now windless afternoon, while officials from the city hall, and justices of the peace and bailiffs come fifteen and twenty miles from the ends of the county, mounted the stairs to the empty office and called his name and cooled their heels a while and then went away and

returned and sat again, fuming, Stevens passed from store to store and office to office about the square—merchant and clerk, proprietor and employee, doctor dentist lawyer and barber—with his set and rapid speech: "It's to bring a dead nigger home. It's for Miss Worsham. Never mind about a paper to sign: just give me a dollar. Or a half a dollar then. Or a quarter then."

Gavin adds significantly more than that himself, as he insists the local newspaper editor do, but this generosity is correlative for us with Ike's gift of the hunting horn: it is more significant in form than in substance. As Ike cannot understand the woman's feelings of love in "Delta Autumn," so Gavin cannot fully appreciate Mollie's grief in "Go Down, Moses." He feels uncomfortable when he goes to see her, stumbles in his conversation, and leaves quickly; he does not attend the burial of Butch, but only the ceremonial ride from the railroad station to the town center and around the town square; the "unctuous, . . . almost bishoplike purr" of the hired hearse tells us that for white Jefferson this is merely a matter of ritual, of propriety. Gavin can no more appreciate the burial of Butch Beauchamp than Cass could the death and burial of Sam Fathers.

But " 'It's all right,' " Miss Worsham tells Gavin. " 'It's our grief.' " The white Miss Worsham joins the blacks Mollie and Hamp in mourning the Beauchamps' final loss, as Boon grieved for Sam and as Rider grieved for Mannie. The significant difference is that, for the first time, *both* white and black share their grief before a single fire in the hearth, and they suffer not only for themselves—as Ike and Roth selfishly do—but for the whole future of both races. In the context of the novel, this is at best a modest sign. For the direction of the book demonstrates that as that land in which we find a vision of life as sacramental decreases, so then the stature of the people also diminishes: the novel moves outward from its center in "The Bear." At both its edges, in the frustration of Tomey's Turl's attempts to marry Tennie and in the downward curve of Butch Beauchamp's self-respect (confirmed by his admission to the census taker), we have undeniable parables of all the McCaslins, white and black, caught in their cells of race and belief as even Sam Fathers was caught in the " 'cage' " of his body. Tomey's Turl as a fox, Lucas as a bear or a fox, Roth's woman as a doe, Butch as "the slain wolf" are all made correlative: things have grown subtler, but they have not essentially changed. The burden of *Go Down, Moses* is that the unproductive stalemate between Ike and

Cass in the commissary radiates outward to analogous ends in the fruitless search for a redeemer: "Was" forever translated into "Is."

Conclusion

"When fiction arouses very deep terror," Simon O. Lesser tells us, "it may also seek to enclose the terror in a kind of frame." Confronting the grim realities of race, human exploitation, and death, *Go Down, Moses* is distanced from us at first glance by the unfolding narrative consciousness of Isaac McCaslin, which is itself bracketed within more remote if analogous narrative episodes. In Ike's reference to the hunt and to biblical prototype as assimilative and accommodating narrative containers which might make sense of his life and so realize his most cherished values, he reminds us of Quentin Compson in *Absalom, Absalom!* and his search for a usable narrative form. Yet on closer inquiry we find that both *Go Down, Moses* and *Absalom, Absalom!* share another, quite separate mediating and temporizing frame, for both are essentially circular, their ends in their beginnings, as so much of Faulkner is: the past living in its impact on the present, the present significant largely as a verification of the past. Formed from the same narrative poetics, *Go Down, Moses* and *Absalom, Absalom!* are of a piece with each other and with Faulkner's other work.

Absalom, Absalom! and *Go Down, Moses*, furthermore, not only mirror each other structurally and technically, but in theme one responds to the other: where Quentin Compson raises the problem of miscegenation and its implications—an emblem of the problems of human love and endurance generally—Ike McCaslin seeks, however mistakenly, to answer it. And in turn, both works chart the fall of Thomas Sutpen and of the McCaslins as analogous to the fall of the Sartorises and the Compsons—and even to the fall of the Snopeses if we take as our chief examples Flem, Linda, and Mink and the desire of each of them for a fundamental self-respect. Faulkner's canon amazes us because it is as integrated as any one of his novels. He knew that too: "As regards any specific book, I'm trying primarily to tell a story, in the most effective way I can think of, the most moving, the most exhaustive," Faulkner wrote Malcolm Cowley in early November 1944. "But I think even that is incidental to what I am trying to do, taking my output (the course of it) as a whole. I am telling the same story over and over, which is myself and the world." In this, he agrees with Proust. "Style has nothing to do with embellishment, as some people think; it's not even a matter of technique," Proust said in an interview with Elie-Joseph Bois in 1913—Proust's only statement of what he was about. "Like the color sense in some painters, it's a quality of vision, the revelation of the particular universe that each of us sees and that no one sees. The pleasure an artist offers us is to convey another universe to us." Style is a matter of vision, not of technique.

Yet even such unity can pose its own problems. Art must continually erupt into reality since forms themselves risk becoming moribund, like the total allegiance to form we find in Horace, Aunt Jenny, Miss Rosa, and Ike. This is the rationale for Faulkner's more radically open form, based in a Cartesian doubt, dependent on evolving perspective, focused on the changing consciousness, and emphasizing the unresolved lights and shadows of experience. Faulkner's novels, even when they begin in chronological sequence like *Flags in the Dust*, *As I Lay Dying*, and *Go Down, Moses*, soon shed this principle of presentation for an interest in analogies, juxtapositions, inner progression, and inner parody. We have not been especially cognizant of this, although Faulkner always has been: the awkward scene of Harry Mitchell with his diamond stickpin pressing himself on Little Belle at her recital in the early portions of *Flags in the Dust* prepares us for the correlative scene at the close of the novel where Harry has given the diamond to a whore whom he likewise presses his hand against. She is as poor a substitute for Little Belle as Harry himself is as Young Bayard's secret self, but this final scene of Harry makes little sense in *Sartoris* because Faulkner's agent Ben Wasson had deleted the earlier analogue. Faulkner knew better, and in the later years of his life he repeatedly asked that *Flags in the Dust* be published.

Reality for Faulkner thus finally relies on such resemblance and contiguity as the deeper and more accurate *perceptual* reality; wherever Faulkner seems to press toward metaphysics, that metaphysics is epistemological. This at once complicates matters. But "in a complete and successful work there are hidden masses of implications," writes the Swiss architect Le Corbusier, "a veritable world which reveals itself to those whom it may concern, which means: to those who deserve it." Faulkner guarantees a deeper involvement from his readers because he places us (as his disciple Robbe-Grillet does) at the observational center of his fiction. From here radiates the multiplicity of meanings. Faulkner knew that, too.

> Q. Mr. Faulkner, in *Absalom, Absalom!* does any one of the people who talks about Sutpen have the right view, or is it more or less a case of thirteen ways of looking at a blackbird with none of them right?
>
> A. That's it exactly. I think that no one individual can look at truth. It blinds you. You look at it and you see one phase of it. Someone else looks at it and sees a slightly awry phase of it. But taken all together, the truth is in what they saw though nobody saw the truth intact. So these are true as far as Miss Rosa and as Quentin saw it. Quentin's father saw what he believed was truth, that was all he saw. But the old man was himself a little too big for people no greater in stature than Quentin and Miss Rosa and Mr. Compson to see all at once. It would have taken perhaps a wiser or more tolerant or more sensitive or more thoughtful person to see him as he was. It was, as you say, thirteen ways of looking at a blackbird. But the truth, I would like to think, comes out, that when the reader has read all these thirteen different ways of looking at the blackbird, the reader has his own fourteenth image of that blackbird which I would like to think is the truth.

Martin Price has put it another way: "The novel gives us . . . the complex awareness of seeing the tough opacity of the actual and at the same time seeing it as a radiant construction of meaning."

The beauty of Faulkner's narrative poetics is that it so manages our perceptual reading that it rewards us with the constitutive consciousness for which it strives. Significantly, Faulkner's poetics is an outgrowth of the work of his predecessors, most notably Flaubert and Balzac, Conrad and Joyce, whom he so much admired. Percy Lubbock summarizes the effect in *The Craft of Fiction:* "The well-made book is the book in which the subject and the form coincide and are indistinguishable—the book in which the matter is all used up in the form, in which the form expresses all the matter." The reader is the focal point of the fiction, where all the stories become congruent and coalesce; the author disappears. We may recall Flaubert's well-known letter to Mlle. Leroyer de Chantepie: "An artist must be in his work like God in creation, invisible and all-powerful; he should be everywhere felt, but nowhere seen," and we find it, echoing and resonant, in Faulkner's letter to Cowley: "It is my ambition to be, as a private individual, abolished and voided from history, leaving it markless, no refuse save the printed books; I wish I had had enough sense to see ahead thirty years ago and, like some of the Elizabethans, not signed them." He very nearly achieved his aim; the significant signature he leaves us is not that on the title page but that in the perceptual shapes of the novels themselves.

Conclusion

We are discussing the Art of Fiction; questions of art are questions (in the widest sense) of execution.—HENRY JAMES

The artist, whether or not he wishes it, discovers with the passage of time that he has come to pursue a single path, a single objective, from which he cannot deviate.—FAULKNER

Literature, in any case, would always, and systematically, consist in talking about *something else*. There would be a world that was present, and a real world; the first would be the only visible one, the second the only important one. The novelist would be supposed to act as a mediator: by his fake description of visible—but completely unreal—things, he would evoke the 'real' which was hiding behind them.—ALAIN ROBBE-GRILLET

UNTIL VERY RECENTLY, we have not done especially well by Faulkner. "There has been," Albert J. Guerard complains in his recent *The Triumph of the Novel*, "a general failure to talk about Faulkner's innovations and audacities." The first stages in the discovery and re-covery of an unusually difficult writer are always a searching out of his life and times, the exhumation of his papers and his compositional changes; what astonishes is still the widespread neglect of the man as a writer: the adolescent who found as much joy in reading *Les Chouans* of Balzac as in his own escapades with his brothers; the young effete drawn to Symbolist poetry and eager for any encouragement from his friend Phil Stone; the young man who was attracted, if only for a short period, to the Bohemian life in New Orleans and who sought out Sherwood Anderson's friendship each afternoon on the benches in Jackson Square; and the young novelist who hastened to Europe with letters of introduction to Pound, Eliot, and Joyce. Faulkner's interest in the current movements of Impressionism and Vorticism suggests his eagerness to learn narrowed early onto matters of technique, his growing appreciation of style as vision even then dismissing the transparencies of Anderson's bland prose for what lurked beneath. "It had the appearance of fumbling," Faulkner later commented on Anderson's fiction, "but actually it wasn't: it was seeking, hunting." The description might also serve to guide us past facile first impressions of *Soldiers' Pay* and *Mosquitoes*. It suggests too Faulkner's chief concern with narrative strategy. "The apparent narrative perversity of Faulkner's tales can be seen as justified, not to say inevitable, if one understands its hidden significance," Claude-Edmonde Magny contends; "he cannot help but immediately obscure whatever he touches, for his narrative method is in essence *enveloping* and implicative rather than developmental and discursive." From the very outset Faulkner's poetry draws most substantially on the Symbolists and his fiction most substantially on Impressionism. He seems to have concentrated on human perception and conception as his contemporary Virginia Woolf did; thinking perhaps of Flaubert—"*A luminous center, toward which the entirety of things converge*" was his goal— she writes that for them, for the Impressionists, "Life is not a series of gig lamps symmetrically arranged; but a luminous halo, a semitransparent envelope surrounding us from the beginning of consciousness to the end. Is it not the task of the novelist to convey this varying, this unknown and uncircumscribed spirit, whatever aberration or complexity it may display, with as little mixture of the alien and external as possible?" For Faulkner and his peers, the answer was obvious.

European critics and writers have best discerned Faulkner's European roots for a narrative poetics while we in America have been distracted by Southern regionalism, folktale, and myth. "Convoluted sentences and a cumulative syntactical pattern create the effect of thought flow," the British critic Richard Gray tells us; "it is almost impossible to separate the meaning of the story from its medium of communication, the various narrative and linguistic frames within which it is set." For dismissing Faulkner's predominant concern with style as vision and looking at his fiction as simple story-telling, his plots are unattractive and absurd. We would not, in the normal presentation of things, much enjoy the story of a family of failures like the Compsons, composed of a thirty-three-year-old, self-centered idiot, a mean and petty thief, a promiscuous teen-ager, a bed-ridden hypochondriac, and a slow, routine-ridden mammy where the climax is the teen-ager's theft from the thief alongside a black Easter service— surely we would not find it *as story* the splendidly powerful and deeply moving novel Faulkner gives us (dependent in some measure on the achronological meditations, years previously, of an incipient suicide). The coincidences of the foreigner Shreve and the incest-haunted Quentin finding their doubles in what are seen as Sutpen's only two sons, and of Rosa choosing to take Quentin with her on a visit to the dying Henry just before he meets Shreve are, in synopsis, incredible, as are the sudden meetings of the wanderer Joe Christmas, the abolitionist Joanna Burden, the defrocked Hightower, and the fanatic Percy Grimm. Other stories remain simply unappealing in the abstract: trailing a stinking corpse to a misbegotten burial by the largely inept and untutored family; following a twin brother's attempt to make a life for himself when his family and town surround him with a pressing model of how to die heroically or glamourously; examining a wasteland of cadavers simulating life by flying planes around pylons; or sympathizing with a naive medical intern who runs off with a married woman hoping to make their impossibly restricted world that of an ideal romance, even when he must fabricate sensational "true" confessions and she must make twisted paper figures to keep them alive on tinned food. Such precis are monstrous parodies of Faulkner's work as Sartre knew in connection with *The Sound and the Fury* (but as reviewers seemed willfully to practice in attacking *Sanctuary*) and as Malcolm Cowley knew, some years later in 1935, when he reviewed *Plyon* for the *New Republic*.

> Faulkner has found a fashion of his own, . . . forcing the real plot into the background and revealing it only in scattered dialogues. The direct action of his novel is confined to five days during the New Orleans carnival. The principal character, instead of being Roger or Jack or Laverne, is the drunken and sentimental reporter. Many of the episodes are seen through his half-glazed eyes, and are thereby refracted and distorted; the story proceeds in what military historians call "the fog of war." For the rest, the general construction is that of a play rather than of the usual novel. The story moves in two directions as in a tragedy by Racine—that is, toward a future catastrophe and also toward a fuller understanding of the past.

Although Cowley could not have known it then, Faulkner was already at work on the early drafts of *Requiem for a Nun* in which the traditional form of the novel broke explicitly into the form of drama, for generic distinctions held little interest for him. Form, even then, was a matter of vision, and vision was not a matter of genre but of the unavoidable consciousness of his narrative point of view and the necessary responses of his readers, in their constitutive consciousnesses.

From the very outset of his career as a novelist, then, Faulkner discerned the basis of modernist art and what would remain, even now, the basis of twentieth-century culture and thought. Even as I compose these concluding remarks, the newest and most contested (if also a necessarily reductive) book locally is *The Origin of Consciousness in the Breakdown of the Bicameral Mind* in which Julian Jaynes asserts as his premise that the problem of consciousness "has been at the very center of the thinking of the twentieth century," while two scientists in another intellectually popular book, *Origins*, argue that "the most dramatic structural advances through evolution" are in the cerebral cortex, "the crown of biological success" because it allows perceptions to integrate into concepts, the final flowering of being human which is, for them, "to be self-aware." Leakey and Lewin describe in a biological context Joyce's sense of epiphany, Quentin's sense of the flash and the glare, a moment of insight we have seen central to all of Faulkner's longer fictions and one which we can also trace back, as Hugh Kenner does, to Faulkner's early interest in the European Symbolists.

A definition of the Symbolists' art is in Mallarmé's *Divagations*: "We renounce that erroneous aesthetic (even though it has been responsible for certain masterpieces) which would have the poet fill the delicate pages of his book with the actual and palpable wood of trees, rather than the forest's shuddering or the silent scattering of thunder through the foliage." Mallarmé proposes what Kenner calls the "effort . . . toward simultaneity, the successive words dissociations of a chord"; the consequences saturate Faulkner's early poetry in *The Marble Faun* and recur persistently in his later collection, *A Green Bough*. Such a poetics is likewise apparent in Faulkner's 1920 play *Marionettes* where Joseph Blotner discovers "imagery Pound employed in his translations of Chinese poems." But the interest in the effect of the image rather than the image itself is most evident, and most successful, in Faulkner's novels; it is seen, for example, in the use of the church in *Soldiers' Pay*, the pipe in *Mosquitoes*, and the slipper in *The Sound and the Fury*, for these are objects charged with special meanings for the characters, for Joe *and* the Reverend Mahon, for Josh *and* Pat Robyn, for Benjy *and* Caddy. Once we realize this, we also re-cognize their usefulness and force, for our constitutive consciousness finds the images splinter into several meanings since the characters, agreeing on the images, interpret them differently, supply us with an inherent multiple perspective. Thus the church symbolizes a misguided faith for Joe but a refuge for Donald's father; the pipe is a work of art for Josh but a sign of masculinity, redolent of sex, for Pat; the slipper allows Benjy to place Caddy in the household, before the fire, but it may symbolize another slipper, that worn at a dance (as it does with Temple in *Sanctuary*, written just before *The Sound and the Fury*, although published afterward) for Caddy. The fragmentation of the Vieux Carré Faulkner knew—through the consciousness of a wealthy Jew, a priest, young lovers, a sailor, a cobbler, a longshoreman, a cop, a beggar, an artist, and a tourist in his neglected journalistic apprenticeship—constitutes his first extended series of publications, his *New Orleans Sketches*. In these he calls on our constitutive consciousness openly and persistently, as he does in his initial draft of Benjy as the idiot brother of a petty thief in "The Kingdom of God"—

> The face of the sitting man was vague and dull and loose-lipped, and his eyes were clear and blue as cornflowers, and utterly vacant of thought; he sat a shapeless, dirty lump, life without mind, an organism without intellect. Yet always in his slobbering, vacuous face were his two eyes of a heartshaking blue, and gripped tightly in one fist was a narcissus

—where we are given a bitter indictment of the petty greed and jealousy which characterize the others in the story, and their world of New Orleans generally. These few illustrations suggest we still have some distance to go in studying Faulkner's early poems and journalism as they display his growing concern with style as vision and with vision as style.

Wherever we turn in the apprentice work, Faulkner is experimenting with a literary Impressionism too, in his exploration of narrative consciousness. The unpublished Elmer papers, which he fussed with most of the way to Italy and again in France in 1925, show bolder shifts in time and freer association in thought development, drawing on the ideas of Freud and the strategies of Joyce as well as other Impressionists and Post-Impressionists, as Thomas L. McHaney has argued. The attempts to abstract that trip with the young artist William Spratling by transposing their experiences into fictional dialogues of Don-and-I in such early stories as the published "Mistral" and the unpublished "Snow" and "Evangeline" were, even then, the seeds of the dialogic reconstruction fundamental to *Absalom, Absalom!*, just as "The Big Shot," another Don-and-I story of that period about Dal Martin's great design initiated by a rebuff at the docr of a rich man's house when Dal was still a boy, is the seed of the story (and of the House) of Sutpen. Estella Schoenberg has recently shown us how this need to work out ideas in dialogue, first in life, then in the debates of his fiction, later in the Hollywood method of having writers talk their way to screenplays, is preparatory for Faulkner's final dialogue, that between the author and *reader* which relies on his acknowledgment of our constitutive consciousness. It is undeniably suggestive, then, that when Faulkner came late in life to arrange his *Collected Stories* he placed last the one most reliant on our constitutive consciousness to lend drama and significance to its concluding interior monologue.

> He lay still beneath the tarred paper, in a silence filled with fairy patterings. Again his body slanted and slanted downward through opaline corridors groined with ribs of dying sunlight upward dissolving dimly, and came to rest at last in the windless gardens of the sea. About him the swaying caverns and the grottoes, and his body lay on the rippled floor, tumbling peacefully to the wavering echoes of the tides.
>
> *I want to perform something bold and tragical and austere* he repeated, shaping the soundless words in the pattering silence *me on a buckskin pony with eyes like blue electricity and a mane like tangled fire, galloping up the hill and right off into the high heaven of the world.* Still galloping, the horse soars outward; still galloping, it thunders up the long blue hill of heaven, its tossing mane in golden swirls like fire.

The "opaline corridors," the "ribs of dying sunlight," the "windless gardens of the sea" like the wild pony ride charge the narrative and structural consciousness of "Carcassonne" with the techniques of Symbolism and Impressionism that, distant tributes to Balzac and Flaubert, determine Faulkner's poetics for the novel.

It is not so much that Faulkner refused to tell a straight story from the first; it is that his understanding of poetics permitted no other way but through the partialities and distortions of a concerned narrator. "A Rose for Emily," for instance, easily a subject for an omniscient perspective, must for Faulkner be filtered through the narrative consciousness of a townsperson, just as "That Evening Sun" had to be witnessed to by the young Quentin Compson. Even the hunting stories about Faulkner's own experiences in the counties of the delta country, the legendary riverbed of the Old Man in the counties neighboring

Lafayette, had to be seen through young Quentin's and Isaac's consciousnesses.

For this is the first cause of Faulkner's power as an artist. *Dark House* is a case in point; excitedly, he put it ahead of *The Peasants* (his early draft of *The Hamlet*) and his first work on *Requiem for a Nun* in early 1934, as he describes enthusiastically to his publisher Harrison Smith. *Dark House*, he writes Smith,

> is the more or less violent breakup of a household or family from 1860 to about 1910. It is not as heavy as it sounds. The story is an anecdote which occurred during and right after the civil war; the climax is another anecdote which happened about 1910 and which explains the story. Roughly, the theme is a man who outraged the land, and the land then turned and destroyed the man's family. Quentin Compson, of the Sound & Fury, tells it, or ties it together; he is the protagonist so that it is not complete apocrypha. I use him because it is just before he is to commit suicide because of his sister, and I use his bitterness which he has projected on the South in the form of hatred of it and its people to get more out of the story itself than a historical novel would be. To keep the hoop skirts and plug hats out, you might say. I believe I can promise it for fall.

This letter exposes the poetics: the structural consciousness juxtaposes two "anecdotes," while the story of "a man who outraged the land" is not told impersonally or even by that man himself but by Quentin Compson, a boy far removed in time; and what is more, the novel will be about *Quentin; he* "is the protagonist." Yet *Dark House* still had far to go then—development must be by the loopings backward and forward in time, the *retour en arrière* that John Porter Houston traces back to Balzac and the free indirect discourse he finds in Flaubert as well as the splintered vision Poulet traces to Proust; the narrative consciousness must be fractured into narrative debates and hypotheses; issues of incest and miscegenation must displace the theme of outrage on the land (relegated to *Go Down, Moses*); and Quentin must find his double in Henry as well as his subject in Thomas, must learn to love as well as to hate the South—before *Dark House* will emerge as the *Absalom, Absalom!* we know. Only when all of this congeals with the flash and glare that explodes simultaneously, imagistically, conceptually, for Quentin and Shreve and for our constitutive consciousness, will the novel take its permanent form and assert its greatest climactic power.

In the juxtapositions of Sutpen and Quentin and, later, of Quentin and Shreve and (for us) in the doubling of Quentin and Rosa, Faulkner also builds by planes of narrative his literary analogy to Cézanne (as Richard P. Adams and Linda Welshimer Wagner have noted). These discrete planes of perspective are better joined than those of *The Sound and the Fury* and of *As I Lay Dying*, supplying a composite that may substantially change our impressions, as the radical imaging of opposites for our constitutive consciousness to comprehend and align changes the meaning of *Go Down, Moses* for Guerard.

> The radical shift of mode at the end of Part Three [of Chapter 5, "The Bear"], from clear dramatic narrative . . . to deep obfuscation and involuted legal reasoning, makes startling demands on the reader. The complex and often sardonic windings of family history take us far from the deaths of Sam Fathers and the bear. But the very difficulty of this long section makes the hunting story, both as we return to it in Part Five, and as we reread the whole, a darker, more meditative experience.

We constitute and re-constitute what we read and re-read; Faulkner's narrative poetics—at once combining vagabond life and sedentary memory—is also distinctive in this: it is primarily a poetics designed for subsequent readings, when the *whole* is known and the *components* can be actively recombined. Given the conflicting ingredients of events, the provisionary nature of his narrative consciousnesses, and our own recombinations of what is conveyed, it is amazing that Faulkner's fiction, as R. W. Flint has it, "deserves to be called thoroughly composed, *durchcomponiert*, as the Germans say of music"; this, too is a legacy of the Symbolists and Impressionists. But it is not surprising— seeing Faulkner as artist caught up in the needs and strategies of art, a writer's writer—to find that some of his most astute critics (early and late) are themselves novelists: Robert Penn Warren, Conrad Aiken, Warren Beck, and Albert J. Guerard; Jean-Paul Sartre, Albert Camus, and Alain Robbe-Grillet.

Faulkner's narrative poetics of the constitutive consciousness not only illuminates Faulkner's unique employment of Symbolist and Impressionist techniques; it also helps to explain how, in the last twenty years of his life, he was to falter and even to fail so badly. We can perhaps best see this decline in the trilogy *Snopes*. The first volume (to be later named *The Hamlet*) was begun at the time of *Flags in the*

Dust, when Faulkner was most aware of the other novelists of consciousness; in it discrete stories of love and economic advancement are sustained, as we have already seen, by the connective ideas of self-respect and possessiveness which our constitutive consciousness learns to assign to the separate episodes so as to integrate them. For Faulkner, however, they are also glued into place by the narrative consciousness of V. K. Ratliff, a consciousness that takes on some surprising colorations.

> [Flem] entered the store, carrying the pail, and Ratliff and his companions sat and squatted about the gallery all that day and watched not only the village proper but all the countryside within walking distance come up singly and in pairs and in groups, men women and children, to make trivial purchases and look at the new clerk and go away. They came not belligerently but completely wary, almost decorous, like half-wild cattle following word of the advent of a strange beast upon their range, to buy flour and patent medicine and plow lines and tobacco and look at the man whose name a week ago they had never heard, yet with whom in the future they would have to deal for the necessities of living, and then depart as quietly as they had come. About nine oclock Jody Varner rode up on his roan saddle horse and entered the store. They could hear the bass murmur of his voice inside, though for all the answer he got he might have been talking to himself. He came out at noon and mounted and rode away, though the clerk did not follow him. But they had known anyway what the tin pail would contain, and they begin to disperse noonward too, looking into the store as they passed the door, seeing nothing. If the clerk was eating his lunch, he had hidden to do it. Ratliff was back on the gallery before one oclock, since he had had to walk only a hundred yards for his dinner. But the others were not long after him, and for the rest of that day they sat and squatted, talking quietly now and then about nothing at all, while the rest of the people within walking distance came and bought in nickles and dimes and went away.

The perspective belongs to Ratliff only nominally; we are *really* at a second remove, the remove of the hamlet itself. The wry humor that often makes events in Frenchman's Bend bearable (and sometimes amusing, sometimes wildly funny) is Ratliff's, but this is not the same as the obsessive Snopes-watching which captures so many in the

Bend. Our constitutive consciousness, that is, has *already* been partly constituted *by Faulkner himself;* and our involvement—our *participation,* to recall Irving Howe's sense of *Light in August*—has been seriously diminished. We become spectators, *audiences* at the telling of tall tales and at the escapades of all the people of Frenchman's Bend—the Armstids and Littlejohns and Bookwrights as well as the Snopeses. By doing too much, Faulkner lets us do too little.

Despite this, *The Hamlet* does not fail entirely as a novel because there is still a great need for our constitutive consciousness. We must join the wild hyperbole of Pat Stamper's air-pumped horse and the savage humor of the horse auction with the idyllic romance of Ike Snopes, on which Faulkner lavishes considerable sympathy, and Labove's painful frustrations, which contain autobiographical sentiments. We must see these varied fragments integrated into a single hamlet and constituents, therefore, of a single communal perspective indicated most often (but far from always) by Ratliff. This loosening of vision and power is easily seen if we compare *The Hamlet* with its contemporary novel of discrete episodes, *Go Down, Moses*—episodes conveyed through the component narratives of Lucas and Rider, Cass, Ike, and Gavin. Conversely, the sprawling anthology and events in *The Hamlet* signals a flaw in Faulkner's latter-day poetics: he came to see no differentiation between his earlier use of a provisional, partly blinded narrative consciousness and the narrative and structural consciousness of the detached, omniscient *raconteur* of folk tales. For Faulkner, they seem to share the same interest in vocal rhythms and colloquial language, the same need for signification over verisimilitude, and a similar unity in perspective rather than in plot or in character. Failing to realize that the *raconteur* is nevertheless only a pale imitation of the involved narrator, Faulkner seeks at times in *The Hamlet* to rely on a participant narrator, at other times on a detached storyteller, while at still other times he confuses the two. The result is uneven, a work we cannot integrate either: the episodes narrated directly by Mink or indirectly by Jack Houston and Labove have considerably more depth and force than the tall tale of Pat Stamper or—what is worse—the missed opportunity with Ike's toy cow.

The effect of such a slackened, confused, and uninspired poetics grew to be crippling. In his later years, Faulkner came to rely on imitating his earlier techniques. He *constructs* narrative perspectives from the outside rather than *realizing* them from within, as with the three narrators of *The Town*—there all three narratives are mannered, predictable, ineffective. Rather than the *"radical* novelty" which Polanyi and Prosch relate to the *"poetic* imagination," characterized by a condensation of thought and feeling and an insulation of perspective that enables our constitutive consciousness to respond more freely and creatively, the narratives of Charles Mallison, Gavin Stevens, and Ratliff in *The Town* become more than self-aware—they become self-conscious, and hence unintended parodies. Here, for example, is Gavin:

> The poets are wrong of course. According to them I should even have known the note was on the way, let alone who it was from. As it was, I didnt even know who it was from after I read it. But then, poets are almost always wrong about facts. That's because they are not really interested in facts: only in truth: which is why the truth they speak is so true that even those who hate poets by simple natural instinct are exalted and terrified by it.
>
> No: that's wrong. It's because you dont dare to hope, you are afraid to hope. Not afraid of the extent of hope of which you are capable, but that you—the frail web of bone and flesh snaring that fragile temeritous boundless aspirant sleepless with dream and hope—cannot match it; as Ratliff would say, Knowing always you wont never be man enough to do the harm and damage you would do if you were just man enough.—and, he might add, or maybe I do it for him, thank God for it. Ay, thank God for it or thank anything else for it that will give you any peace after it's too late; peace in which to coddle that frail web and its unsleeping ensnared anguish both on your knee and whisper to it: There, there, it's all right; I know you are brave.

The bemused stockpiling of such adjectives as *fragile temeritous boundless* and the serpentine patterning of *poets, truth, hope, frailty, God,* and *peace* fold in on themselves, go nowhere; and the note we start with is clouded, lost. Rather than develop ideas, Gavin merely plays with them. His narrative is neither engaged with the activity of life nor with examining its significance, but only with his personal inward bemusement over the capacity of his own meditations and phraseology. Charles's youth naivete—his ripening wisdom under the pressures of Snopes-watching—is meant to act as counterpoint, as the tall convict was a brilliantly inspired counterpart to Harry Wilbourne. But in *The Town*, Charles's narration comes more and more to imitate the older Gavin.

> So she couldn't tell me because she could not. And Uncle Gavin couldn't tell me because he wasn't able to, he couldn't have

stopped talking in time. That is, that's what I thought then. I mean, that's what I thought then was the reason why they—Mother—didn't tell me: that the reason was just my innocence and not Uncle Gavin's too and she had to guard both, since maybe she was my mother but she was Uncle Gavin's twin and if a boy or a girl really is his father's and her mother's father-in-law or mother-in-law, which would make the girl her brother's mother no matter how much younger she was, then a girl with just one brother and him a twin at that, would maybe be his wife and mother too.

Where in a successful novel like *Absalom, Absalom!* every synapse of the brain and each ounce of nervous energy is fixated on the learning more while frightened by the truth such learning might reveal, the concentration nearly unbearable and the tension unrelieved, in *The Town* the narrative consciousness and consequently both the structural and constitutive consciousness must be, laboriously, *manufactured*. Gavin and Charles are not driven to stop the Snopeses, nor do they find their own fate desperately involved. Gavin is too easily seduced by a teen-ager as a safe surrogate for her more desirable (and more driven) mother while Charles is too freely able to see the threat posed by Flem as a threat to his uncle rather than to himself. The contagious narcissicism even reaches Ratliff. He too comes to imitate Gavin.

It was like a contest, like Lawyer had stuck a stick of dynamite in his hind pocket and lit a long fuse to it and was interested now would or wouldn't somebody step in in time and tromple the fire out. Or a race, like would he finally get Linda out of Jefferson and at least get his-self shut forever of the whole tribe of Snopes first, or would he jest blow up his-self beforehand first and take ever body and ever thing in the neighborhood along with him.

No, not a contest. Not a contest with Flem Snopes anyway because it takes two to make a contest and Flem Snopes wasn't the other one. He was a umpire, if he was anything in it. No, he wasn't even a umpire. It was like he was running a little mild game against his-self, for his own amusement, like solitaire.

"It is as if Faulkner, once so fertile and free in his technical innovations, were now their prisoner," Irving Howe writes, "driven to go through the motions of virtuosity and to complicate the point of view from which his story is told, regardless of inner need or plausibility. *The*

Town and *The Mansion* both enjoy a textbook sophistication in technical matters which is quite superior to that of *The Hamlet*; and it does them little good." Unlike his earlier novels which broke away from the narrative experiments of others to fashion their own new forms, forced to audacity under the pressures of their searching, driven narrative consciousness, *Snopes* is content to pattern itself after technical strategies used before and so, now, fixed as mere method. *Snopes* does not create, it duplicates. The failure of *Snopes* is a failure of the poetic imagination.

Faulkner's enriched realizations of the interior being—his selving by way of the narrative and structural consciousness—is in direct proportion to the power and success of his novels. He knew this; "I had just written my guts into *The Sound and the Fury*," he recalls in his introduction to the Modern Library edition of *Sanctuary*, because the true artist, in the white heat of creating, is overcome with committed energies; writing a novel, Faulkner once said, is like trying to nail together a henhouse in a hurricane. This excitement could be for him, as it can be for us in the major novels, nearly palpable. "I have just written such a beautiful thing that I am about to bust," he wrote his mother in 1925 upon completing the first draft of what would be the conclusion of *Sanctuary*.

> 2000 words about the Luxembourg gardens and death. It has a thin thread of plot, about a young woman, and it is poetry though written in prose form. I have worked on it for two whole days and every word is perfect. I havent slept hardly for two nights, thinking about it, comparing words, accepting and rejecting them, then changing again. But now it is perfect—a jewel. I am going to put it away for a week, then show it to someone for an opinion. So tomorrow I will wake up feeling rotten, I expect. Reaction. But its worth it, to have done a thing like this.

The eagerness and labor in starting out and the worry and anguish in the years of his major fiction—the death of his brother and his own baby girl, the responsibility for three families, the burden of Rowan Oak and the hatred of Hollywood—all forced him into a powerful and organic fiction. "I cant send you Light in August because none of it is typed yet," he wrote Ben Wasson in January 1932. "It is going too well to break the thread and cast back, unless absolutely necessary." The result was equally stimulating: "I have just finished reading the galley of LIGHT IN AUGUST. I dont see anything wrong with it. I want it to stand as it is."

By contrast, his later works of self-imitation were difficult and disappointing. There was the false start in *The Town* when he began with Gowan Stevens rather than Charles Mallison. Straining for the sort of analogy he had used in *Absalom, Absalom!* he also altered and damaged the story of Wallstreet Panic Snopes by introducing a relationship with Miss Vaiden Wyott that would reflect as parody on Gavin's relationship with Linda. Unsure even of direction and theme, he wrote new passages that expose his own fumbling for clarification. He tries to make an apparently muddled theme explicit by adding,

> He didn't always listen to all Ratliff would be saying at those times, so that afterward he couldn't even say just how it was or when that Ratliff put it into his mind and he even got interested in it like a game, a contest or even a battle, a war, that Snopeses had to be watched constantly like an invasion of snakes or wildcats and that Uncle Gavin and Ratliff were doing it or trying to because nobody else in Jefferson seemed to recognise the danger;

and, only six pages later, he adds once more

> that idea of Snopeses covering Jefferson like an influx of snakes or varmints from the woods and he and Uncle Gavin were the only ones to recognise the danger and the threat.

Faulkner wrote Saxe Commins, who had succeeded Wasson, in late 1955 or early 1956 about *The Town*, "Have not taken fire in the old way yet, so it goes slow, but unless I am burned out, I will heat up soon and go right on with it," and, a month later to Jean Stein, "I still feel, as I did last year, that perhaps I have written myself out and all that remains now is the empty craftsmanship—no fire, force, passion anymore in the words and sentences." He even misjudged *The Town*, so frayed and misdirected were his efforts. "Just finishing the book," he tells her on August 22, 1956. "It breaks my heart, I wrote one scene and almost cried. I thought it was just a funny book but I was wrong." The surprise at the effect of Eula's death superseding the raid on Jefferson by the little Texan Snopeses has curiosity in it but no joy and little pride of accomplishment; three days later, he wired Commins an identical message: "FINISH BOOK TODAY. WILL BREAK THE HEART. THOUGHT IT WAS JUST FUNNY BUT WAS WRONG. BILL."

Yet except for the miraculous moment when he realized Mink Snopes —when he re-cognized him for the opening brilliant passages of *The*

Mansion—Faulkner went on simulating the older poetics he had once carved out of necessity, out of the technical precedents of the Symbolists and the Impressionists, of the novelists of consciousness and of his own requirements of the moment. *Intruder in the Dust* attempts a re-run of *The Unvanquished* with the boy's consciousness growing once more into a man's regional awareness, realizing this time not so much the need for the New Law as for programmatic compromise. But Bayard's sudden realization, caught in Ringo's irrelevant invitation to a second ambush and Drusilla's outmoded challenge to duel, is relegated in *Intruder in the Dust* to a long speech by Gavin, explicit and self-contented: another failure of the imagination. *Requiem for a Nun* uses earlier scraps of Yoknapatawpha history for a summing up of retrospective vibrancy, constituted of both sociological fact and fantastic legend, but the desire to parallel this with Temple's fallen state strains the use of analogue in a way that comparing Temple with Popeye and Horace had not. Even Nancy becomes an attenuated Dilsey. Worst of all—and bitterly disappointing—is *A Fable*, for Faulkner worked longest on this and it contains still some of his most profound and subtle discussions of guilt and innocence. But the form here too is masturbatory; Faulkner's own remembrance of things past incorporates into an allegory as its own compelling situations those motifs from his earlier writing which maintained their residual force for him but have less or no point here. The mounting crowd and its sense of doom recalls the Jordan passage in *The Unvanquished*. The division commander's attempt to resign at the chateau is reminiscent of the last days of Joe Christmas. The sentry's insurance racket and his pleasures in the petty operations of it recall Jason Compson. Levine's need to find a new opportunity for heroism replays *Flags in the Dust*. The multiple perspectives on Gragnon remind us of *Absalom, Absalom!*, while the Quartermaster General's attempt to resign his post and relinquish all responsibility recalls Ike McCaslin. Ignoring the death of the pilot and the use of carnival masks for religious celebration echoes *Pylon*, as the final account of the corpse eventually returned to the farm of Marya and Marthe, where it is thought to belong, uses motifs in *As I Lay Dying*. Everywhere we turn in *A Fable*, we see ghosts of the past, an entirely *open* poetics of self-imitation.

Conversely, "What constitutes the novelist's strength," Faulkner's disciple Robbe-Grillet writes, "is precisely that he *invents*, that he invents quite freely, *without a model*. The remarkable thing about modern fiction is that it asserts this characteristic quite deliberately, to such a degree that invention and imagination become, at the limit, the very subject of the book." For Faulkner's narrative poetics at its most successful, the invention and imagination of the novelist insists on a parallel imaginative creativity by the reader, who must note the discrepancies between his own awareness and that of a narrative consciousness and his or her preconscious or unconscious drives, while at the moment of highest pitch, the narrative and constitutive consciousness face identical problems. *"You cannot know yet whether what you see is what you are looking at or what you are believing,"* Faulkner writes in *Absalom, Absalom!,* but the observation is equally appropriate for characters in *The Sound and the Fury, As I Lay Dying, Sanctuary, Light in August,* and *Go Down, Moses,* and for us when we read these novels.

But our constitutive consciousnesses are never precisely the same when they quicken in response—yours and mine—and one of Faulkner's novels is never re-constituted by us in precisely the same way at any re-reading. Doesn't Faulkner's narrative poetics rest, then, on a kind of willful solipsism? Doesn't the uncertainty of the result undermine the whole dynamic of his narrative art? It would, if the study of epistemology did not teach us, as it taught Faulkner, that our ways of thinking, while diverse, are also similar. If there are thirteen—or fourteen—ways of looking at a blackbird, to all fourteen there is an ineradicable blackbirdness. Even so new a writer as Julian Jaynes and so fresh and inventive a view as that of the origin of consciousness occurring in the "breakdown" of the "bicameral mind" stresses those ingrained patterns of consciousness we have seen in Faulkner all along: spatialization by the use of geography as metaphor; excerption in which emblem passages and images stand as synecdoches for the whole; analogies and doubling as self-projections and means of "narratization"; and assimilation as "conciliations." In something so thoroughly autonomous as our imagination, as our re-creation and re-cognition of a character in narrative, the integrating powers of the cerebral cortex and the ingrained habits of our methods of reading lead us to widely predictable responses. We may not agree that Horace Benbow's crimes of omission make him as culpable as the openly and actively criminal Popeye, but we will—none of us—fail to see that Faulkner means to suggest certain similarities between the two apparently dissimilar men that cause them to attract each other, for two hours, over the natural spring at the Old Frenchman place. There may be thirteen ways of looking at blackbirds, but Faulkner felt reasonably assured of the reader's own, fourteenth view toward which he claimed to strive. In his sense of our active imagination in league with the author's as, in Whitehead's terms, "the triumph of consciousness," Faulkner pursued, in the major years from *Flags in the Dust* to *Go Down, Moses*, an autonomous art to match the autonomy of our—of his and my and your—imagination. "To me," Faulkner writes, "the book is its own prologue epilogue introduction preface argument and all."

A final confirmation of Faulkner's narrative poetics rests in our current study of language (and of the arts of language) as metaphor. "Metaphor is not a mere extra trick of language, as it is so often slighted in the old schoolbooks on composition," Julian Jaynes reminds us; "it is the very constitutive ground of language." As illustration, he supplies customary metaphors of the body—"The *head* of an army, table, page, bed, ship, household, or nail, or of steam or water; the *face* of a clock, cliff, card, or crystal"—and even the metaphoric properties once forming our most abstract verbs—*to be* derived from the Sanskrit *bhu*, " 'to grow, or make grow' " and *is* from the Sanskrit *asmi*, " 'to breathe.' " Faulkner's contribution is perhaps even more decisive: he insists that *human consciousness is a similar, parallel act of metaphorization*. We are conscious of something only as it *stands for* something else working symbolically, or as we abstract it, metaphorically. The final cause of Faulkner's narrative power is thus to awaken all our resources of metaphor-making—our language, our consciousness, and our imagination. He requires of his audaciously experimental fiction that we make it, as we make our world, make sense. This is what we saw Byron Bunch do at the outset of his essay: he made sense of Joe Christmas by also making sense of himself and of his world, the world of the professional and the world of the saw-mill worker.

Likewise on a broader scale in the constitutive planes of this essay—the close analysis of a passage in *Light in August*, the abstract discussions of perception and conception, the examination of Faulkner's predecessors and his own techniques, a review of Faulkner's finest achievements and of his sources, growth, and failures—we too have assembled and assimilated levels of metaphoric language, in our consciousness and our imagination, in order to understand the production and process of his fiction. Such a "desire for meaning is perhaps the defining characteristic of the life of the mind," Jonathan Culler writes. He is speaking particularly of Flaubert, but his conclusion is drawn from the art of modernism and the latest studies in philosophy, psychology, and linguistics, the studies of mind and of language. "Readers," he goes on, "are not to be easily thwarted in their attempts to make things signify." Faulkner was aware of this; he knew the nature and need of the readers'—of our—constitutive consciousnesses; and he also knew the task this set for him. Man's tragedy, Faulkner told Loïc Bouvard, " 'is the impossibility—or at least the tremendous difficulty —of communication. But man keeps on trying endlessly to express himself and to make contact with other human beings.' " So Faulkner kept trying, too, the power of his own imagination released through his narrative poetics because of the determined consciousness of his characters to understand themselves and their worlds—you and me and our world, metaphorically—and to sustain them further through projected, imagined ideals. There is always, for Faulkner's best realized characters, *"that might-have-been which is the single rock we cling to above the maelstrom of unbearable reality."* At its most successful, Faulkner's narrative poetics of style as vision enriches us with a miraculously vital, magnificently haunting beauty even when it reveals, to our metaphor-making imaginations, our constitutive consciousnesses, its blood strange to each other blood and strange to our own, and shows us too how terribly doing goes along the earth.

End Matter

Acknowledgments

Few writers of literary criticism are fortunate enough to recall the beginning of a long study stretching over many years—but I am one of the lucky ones. It came during the spring of my freshman year at Syracuse University when, as an anonymous student in one of a hundred sections of freshman English, my instructor Alfred Marks assigned me Faulkner to read over the spring holiday. I took the long bus ride home carrying two books—*Intruder in the Dust* and *Absalom, Absalom!*—and I can still vividly remember the absorbing, even electrifying experience of reading Faulkner for the first time, from cover to cover, cramped in one corner of our family's old gray mohair sofa: lunch came and went, and dinner; dusk came and night, but I never left the books nor that couch. I had avidly read and written much fiction by that time, but I had never been so consumed by fiction nor, afterward, so thoroughly exhausted by it; and this has not happened to me since. Now, after more years than I care to count publicly or privately, I have tried to explain that experience.

In the reckoning I have been fortunate in many ways, too. If no American writer approaching Faulkner's stature has yet succeeded him, we have enjoyed a period unusually rich in theory and critical analysis; and this essay shows my indebtedness to the work of Ernst Cassirer and Rudolf Arnheim, of Jean Piaget and Michael Polanyi, of Sartre, Merleau-Ponty, Sapir, Levi-Strauss, and R. D. Laing. In literary theory, I have learned from Wayne Booth and Wolfgang Iser, Frank Kermode and Roger Shattuck, Georges Poulet and Jonathan Culler; and I have had my occasional quarrels as well as insights from Alain Robbe-Grillet and Roland Barthes. Nor, once begun, has my study of Faulkner ever slackened. As an undergraduate I learned much from Leonard Brown and David Owen; as a graduate student, I continued to learn from frequent discussions with Arno Bader, Robert Haugh, David H. Stewart, Lynn Z. Bloom, and Francis L. Utley. I have found books on Faulkner by Warren Beck, André Bleikasten, Cleanth Brooks, Panthea Reid Broughton, Walter J. Slatoff, and Jean Weisgerber and essays by Robert Penn Warren particularly instructive. And a number of students of Faulkner have encouraged or criticized my work: Olga W. Vickery, R. W. B. Lewis, Ursula Brumm, and Irving Howe early, and later Joseph Blotner, Lewis P. Simpson, Ilse Dusoir Lind, Dorothy Tuck, and James W. Webb (during my stay in Oxford and Lafayette County, Mississippi); Richard P. Adams, after his voluntary reading of the first draft of *Faulkner's Narrative Poetics* (then masquerading under another title), went off to Paris to check my remarks on the Luxembourg Gardens in connection with the close of *Sanctuary* and then wrote me his corrections, wryly noting that no one had travelled so far to amend an early draft of someone else's book. My most stimulating months in preparing the present essay were spent in Charlottesville, where the estate of Jill Faulkner Summers, Linton Massey, and the staff of the Alderman Library of the University of Virginia allowed me to study the Elmer papers and to examine and collate Faulkner's various corrected manuscripts, typescripts, and galleys; there too the penetrating questions and explorations with Michel Gresset, Francois Pitavy, and Charles Dean helped me to focus my own thoughts. Several years later, the Humanities Research Center at the University of Texas also gave me access to their Faulkner manuscripts and galleys. A number of my former students at the University of Michigan, Yale University, Clark University, and the University of Massachusetts, Amherst, also pointed to new possibilities; I remember with special gratitude remarks and papers by Joyce Spencer, Edwin M. Barney, George Shumacher, John M. Lannon, and Harrison Gregg.

Most of the criticism of Faulkner until recent times has been concerned, as it had to be, with explaining story lines and genealogies, with tracing the biographical, historical, and regional backgrounds of so difficult a writer, and determining his ideas and use of religion and race. We have recently begun to see Faulkner in the broader contexts of artistic, philosophical, and psychological movements that generally characterize modernist writing such as his. My thanks are due those who agreed to read and criticize earlier drafts of *Faulkner's Narrative Poetics*— Claude Simpson, Lewis P. Simpson, Robert Richardson, Jonathan F. S. Post, and Leone Stein; and to my colleagues at Massachusetts who likewise are students of modernism—David Porter and Paul Mariani and especially Sarah N. Lawall, Priscilla Gibson Hicks and Kirby Farrell—who helped me to see what I really wanted to say.

An early version of *Faulkner's Narrative Poetics* was delivered as a series of public lectures for the English Faculty at Oxford University during Hilary term 1977 and I am grateful to the faculty and their chairman, Professor John Carey, for that trial run. While at Oxford, John Bayley, Christopher Butler, Roger Sale, and Lazar Ziff read my remarks on Faulkner and offered valuable suggestions for revision, as did Brian McHale and Robert Garnett. This essay has also benefitted substantially from the remarks of still-anonymous University Press readers; from the skillful editing of Barbara Palmer, Pam Campbell, and Carol Schoen; and from the distinctive design and sympathetic production of Mary Mendell. For the several efforts of these colleagues—stern and monitory, patient and supportive, inquisitive and dubious—I remain in their debt.

I have repeated here certain phrases and paragraphs from a few of my earlier publications—"Faulkner and the Possibilities for Heroism" in *The Southern Review*, N.S. 6:4, 1110–25; "Faulkner's Fourteenth Image," *Paintbrush* 2, 36–43; and "Faulkner and Flaubert," *Journal of Modern Literature*, 6:2, 222–47—and I am grateful to their editors, Lewis P. Simpson, B. M. Bennani, and Maurice Beebe, for permission to reprint them here. Permission rights have also been granted by Random House, Inc. for quoting those portions of Faulkner's novels which seem to me most helpful in studying and illustrating the dynamics of his narrative art.

A.F.K.

Sources

Regarding Faulkner's fiction, references are to the first editions of *Soldiers' Pay* and *Mosquitoes* (Horace Liveright) and to the present standard Modern Library and Vintage editions of the remaining works published by Random House, Inc.

v   *Requiem for a Nun*, pp. 220, 225.

xi   Hellström: "Presentation Address," *Nobel Prize Library* (New York, 1971), p. 5.

xii   Hellström: p. 5. Sartre: "On *The Sound and the Fury*: Time in the Work of Faulkner," *Literary and Philosophical Essays*, trans. Annette Michelson (London, 1955), p. 79; q. *Faulkner: A Collection of Critical Essays*, ed. Robert Penn Warren (Englewood Cliffs, N. J., 1966), p. 87.

xiii–xiv Seyppel: *William Faulkner* (New York, 1971), p. 101.

1   Frye: *Anatomy of Criticism: Four Essays* (Princeton, 1957), p. 271. Lukacs: *The Theory of the Novel*, trans. Anna Bostock (Cambridge, Mass., 1971), p. 38. Faulkner: *The Sound and the Fury*, p. 145.

2   *Flags in the Dust*: p. 10.

6   Ford: *Joseph Conrad: A Personal Remembrance* (Boston, 1924), pp. 129–30. "Lo": *A Fable*, p. 70.

7   "momentary avatars": "Interview with Jean Stein vanden Heuvel" in *Lion in the Garden: Interviews with William Faulkner 1926–1962*, ed. James B. Meriwether and Michael Millgate (New York, 1968), p. 255.

8   Ward L. Miner: *The World of William Faulkner* (New York, 1952), chap. 2. Old Reel-Foot: John B. Cullen, *Old Times in the Faulkner Country* in collaboration with Floyd C. Watkins (Chapel Hill, N. C., 1961), p. 27. W. C. Falkner: Joseph Blotner, *Faulkner: A Biography* (New York, 1974), pp. 9–53. Popeye: cf. Blotner, pp. 607–8. Page: *Faulkner's Women: Characterization and Meaning* (DeLand, Fla., 1972), p. 5. Howe: *William Faulkner: A Critical Study*, 3rd ed. rev. and exp. (Chicago, 1975), p. 212.

11   " 'telling a story' ": *Absalom, Absalom!*, p. 247.

15   Arnheim: *Visual Thinking* (Berkeley, 1969), p. 226. Cocteau q. Bonamy Dobrée, *Modern Prose Style* (Oxford, 1966), pp. 220–21. Garzilli: *Circles without Center: Paths to the Discovery and Creation of Self in Modern Literature* (Cambridge, Mass., 1972), p. vii. Faulkner: *Absalom, Absalom!*, p. 247.

16   *Light in August*: pp. 27–28. *Hard Times*: Book I, chap. 2, ed. George Ford and Sylvère Monod (New York, 1966), p. 6.

17   Arnheim: p. 13. Williams: "Paterson," *The Dial* LXXXVII:2 (February 1927), pp. 91–93. This is likely the version Faulkner knew; the line is thematic and choric—see ll. 5, 22, 25, 85.

18   Ribot: Théodule Armand Ribot q. Arnheim, p. 115. Arnheim: p. 19.

20   Langer: *Philosophical Sketches* (Baltimore, 1962), pp. 71–73.

21   Georges Braque q. Arnheim, p. 239.

22   Shahn: *The Shape of Content* (New York: Vintage ed., 1960), p. 55.

23   Sergei Eisenstein: *Film Form: Essays in Film Theory*, trans. Jay Leyda (Cleveland, 1957), p. 236.

24   Sartre: *Imagination*, trans. Forrest Williams (Ann Arbor, Mich., 1972), p. 146.

24–25   *Light in August*: pp. 28–29.

28   *Light in August*: p. 111.

31   Polanyi: *The Tacit Dimension* (Garden City, N. Y., 1967), p. 4.

32–33   Joyce: *Stephen Hero*, ed. Theodore Spencer, rev. John J. Slocum and Herbert Cahoon (London, 1956), p. 216.

33   Joyce: *Stephen Hero*, p. 218. *Portrait of the Artist as a Young Man* (New York, 1956), p. 212.

33–34   Faulkner: *Faulkner in the University*, ed. Frederick L. Gwynn and Joseph L. Blotner (Charlottesville, Va., 1959), p. 96.

37   Cassirer: *An Essay on Man* (New Haven, Conn., 1962), p. 143. Liddell: *Robert Liddell on the Novel* (Chicago, 1969), p. 203. Faulkner: *The Hamlet*, p. 21. Edel: *The Modern Psychological Novel* (New York, 1964), p. 201.

38   "hill-cradled": *The Hamlet*, p. 3. Henry James: "The Art of Fiction," rep. *Theory of Fiction: Henry James*, ed. James E. Miller, Jr. (Lincoln, Neb., 1972), p. 35. Bergson q. Edel, p. 29. Ralph A. Ciancio: "Faulkner's Existentialist Affinities," in *Studies in Faulkner*, "Carnegie Institute of Technology Series in English 6" (Pittsburgh, 1961), p. 75.

39   W. J. Harvey: *Character and the Novel* (Ithaca, N. Y., 1965), p. 71.

39–40   "twisted little apples": Sherwood Anderson, *Winesburg, Ohio* (New York, 1960), p. 36.

40   "little pyramids of truth"; *Winesburg, Ohio*, p. 35. "ghosts": *Winesburg, Ohio*, p. 240. *Absalom, Absalom!*: p. 12.

41   Simone de Beauvoir: *The Prime of Life*, trans. Peter Green (London, 1962), pp. 149–50. She is talking particularly of *As I Lay Dying* and *Sanctuary*. Blotner: *William Faulkner's Library: A Catalogue* (Charlottesville, Va., 1964), p. 3.

41–42   "deliberately choosing": unpublished introduction first published in *The Southern Review*, N. S. 8:4 (1972), 709.

42   James: "The Art of Fiction," rep. Miller, p. 33; p. 36; p. 35; p. 35; p. 35. Weinstein: *Henry James and the Requirements of the Imagination* (Cambridge, Mass., 1971), p. 9.

43 "The central object": *The Awkward Age* in *The Bodley Head Henry James* (London, 1967), II, 26–27. Stone's purchase: Blotner, *William Faulkner's Library*, p. 125. Lubbock: *The Craft of Fiction* (New York, 1957), pp. 234–35. Conrad: "Henry James, An Appreciation," *Notes on Life and Letters* (London, 1924), pp. 18–19. Hardy: *The Appropriate Form: An Essay on the Novel* (Evanston, Ill., 1971), p. 48.

44 Flaubert to Sand: *Selected Letters*, trans. and ed. Francis Steegmuller (New York, 1957), p. 248. The letter was sent after December 20, 1875 from Paris. Flaubert to Mlle. Leroyer de Chantepie: (June 2, 1872) q. Benjamin F. Bart, *Flaubert* (Syracuse, N. Y., 1967), p. 573.

45 *"Everything should sound simultaneously"*: *Correspondence* in *Oeuvres Complètes* (Paris, 1947), III, 75; q. Joseph Frank, *The Widening Gyre: Crisis and Mastery in Modern Literature* (Bloomington, Ind., 1968), p. 15. Frank: *Widening Gyre*, p. 15.

46 James: "The Lesson of Balzac," *Two Lectures* (Boston, 1905), pp. 75, 97.

47 "scaling off": Balzac, *Père Goriot*, trans. Jane Minot Sedgwick (New York, 1963), p. 4. "handsomely set in pearls": Balzac, *Eugénie Grandet*, trans. Ellen Marriage (New York, 1961), p. 163. "saddest prison cell': *Père Goriot*, p. 151.

49 *Moby-Dick*: Ed. Charles Feidelson, Jr. (Indianapolis, 1964), p. 48; p. 486; p. 65.

50 *Moby-Dick*: p. 22; p. 362; p. 724.

51 *Moby-Dick*: p. 36; p. 26. " 'It just does not explain' ": *Absalom, Absalom!*, p. 100. Grigoriev: cited by Edward Hallett Carr, *Dostoevsky 1821–1881* (London, 1962), p. 148. Underground Man: *Notes from Underground* in *Three Short Novels of Dostoevsky*, trans. Constance Garnett rev. and ed. Avraham Yarmolinsky (Garden City, N. Y., 1960), p. 209. Ivan tells Alyosha: *The Brothers Karamazov*, trans. Constance Garnett (New York, 1950), p. 278.

52 " 'Man is broad' ": *Brothers Karamazov*, p. 127. " 'the greatest and most important social type' ": Dostoevsky q. Carr, p. 34. " 'nothing but hosannah' ": *Brothers Karamazov*, p. 780.

53 " 'Who doesn't desire' ": *Brothers Karamazov*, p. 834. Vivas: *Creation and Discovery* (New York, 1955), p. 69. " 'There is no place' ": Faulkner, *The Wild Palms*, p. 136. "To snatch": Conrad, "Preface" to *The Nigger of the "Narcissus"* (Baltimore, 1963), p. 13; p. 13.

54 "Confronted": "Preface" to *The Nigger*, p. 11. "très cher maître": Conrad q. Edward Engelberg, *The Unknown Distance: From Consciousness to Conscience* (Cambridge, Mass., 1972), p. 172. Gurko: *Joseph Conrad: Giant in Exile* (New York, 1962), p. 113. Conrad to Curle: Letter of July 14, 1923, in *Joseph Conrad: Life and Letters*, ed. G. Jean-Aubry (Garden City, N. Y., 1927), II, 317. "brooding": *Heart of Darkness*, ed. Robert Kimbrough (New York, 1963), p. 3. "whited sepulchre": *Heart of Darkness*, p. 9.

55   " 'The wastes' ": *Heart of Darkness,* p. 69. " 'You can't understand' ": *Heart of Darkness,* p. 50. " 'had kicked himself loose' ": *Heart of Darkness,* p. 67. " 'These were issues' ": *Lord Jim,* ed. Morton Dauwen Zabel (Boston, 1958), p. 68. " 'one of us' ": *Lord Jim,* p. 58.

56   " 'follow the dream' ": *Lord Jim,* p. 154. " 'only on sufferance' ": *Lord Jim,* pp. 27–28. Conrad to Clark: *Life and Letters,* II, 205. " 'The horror!' ": *Heart of Darkness,* p. 71. Shreve: *Absalom, Absalom!,* p. 174.

57   "falling faintly": Joyce, "The Dead," *Dubliners* (New York, 1958), p. 224. "smugging": *A Portrait of the Artist as a Young Man,* p. 43.

58   "skull": *Portrait of the Artist,* p. 193. "Beauty expressed": *Portrait of the Artist,* p. 206. Stanzel: Franz Stanzel, *Narrative Situations in the Novel,* trans. James P. Pusack (Bloomington, Ind., 1971), p. 125.

59   Iser: "Indeterminacy and the Reader's Response in Prose Fiction," in *Aspects of Narrative,* ed. J. Hillis Miller (New York, 1971), p. 38. Levin: *James Joyce: A Critical Introduction,* rev. and aug. (New York, 1960), p. 129. "Real adventures": *Dubliners,* p. 21. "There was no doubt": *Dubliners,* p. 73.

60   Rabkin: *Narrative Suspense: "When Slim Turned Sideways . . ."* (Ann Arbor, Mich., 1973), chap. 1. Grossvogel: David I. Grossvogel, *Limits of the Novel: Evolutions of a Form from Chaucer to Robbe-Grillet* (Ithaca, N. Y., 1968), p. 268. the father of them all: cited Blotner, *Faulkner: A Biography,* p. 1230. Shattuck: *Marcel Proust* (New York, 1974), p. 76.

61   "a building which occupied": Proust, *Swann's Way,* trans. C. K. Scott Moncrieff (New York, 1956), p. 75. "trauvaux d'architecte": Proust q. Lewis Galantière, "Introduction" to *Swann's Way,* p. vii. Fowlie: *A Reading of Proust* (Garden City, N. Y., 1964), p. 52.

62   Faulkner to Bouvard: *Lion in the Garden,* p. 72.

63   Beckett: *Proust* (New York, 1957), p. 68. Fowlie: *A Reading of Proust,* p. 256. Bergson: Henri Bergson, trans. T. E. Hulme (New York, 1912), pp. 16, 17; also q. Richard P. Adams, "The Apprenticeship of William Faulkner," *Tulane Studies in English XII* (1962), p. 154.

64   Beckett, pp. 54–55. "we hear endlessly": *Swann's Way,* p. 108. "When I saw": *Swann's Way,* p. 104. Shattuck: p. 105.

65   "Man is the being": Proust q. Shattuck, p. 98. Bersani: Leo Bersani, *Marcel Proust: The Fictions of Life and of Art* (New York, 1965), p. 187. Poulet: Georges Poulet, *Studies in Human Time,* trans. Elliott Coleman (Baltimore, 1956), p. 313. Old Testament: *Lion in the Garden,* pp. 250–51. *Martin Chuzzlewit: Lion in the Garden,* p. 251.

66   Cervantes: *Lion in the Garden,* p. 251. "old verities and truths of the heart": Faulkner, "Upon Receiving the Nobel Prize for Literature," in *Essays, Speeches and Public Letters,* ed. James B. Meriwether (New York, 1965), p. 120.

67   Aswell: "The Puzzling Design of *Absalom, Absalom!,*" *Kenyon Review* XXX:1 (1968), p. 67.

71 Schorer: "Technique as Discovery," in *The World We Imagine: Selected Essays* (New York, 1968), p. 3. Valéry: q. Wayne Booth, *The Rhetoric of Fiction* (Chicago, 1961), p. 376. Faulkner: Unpublished "Introduction" to *The Sound and the Fury*, *The Southern Review*, N.S., VIII:4 (1972), p. 709. Coindreau: Maurice Edgar Coindreau, *The Time of William Faulkner: A French View of Modern American Fiction*, trans. George McMillan Reeves (Columbia, S.C., 1971), p. 36. He is speaking specifically of *Light in August*.

72 Szanto: George H. Szanto, *Narrative Consciousness: Structure and Perception in the Fiction of Kafka, Beckett, and Robbe-Grillet* (Austin, Tex., 1972), p. 17. He is speaking particularly of Kafka. Faulkner to Cowley: Letter from Hollywood, August 16, 1945; rep. in *The Faulkner-Cowley File: Letters and Memories, 1944–1962* (New York, 1966), pp. 25–26; *Selected Letters of William Faulkner*, ed. Joseph Blotner (New York, 1977), p. 197.

73 *Light in August*: p. 111. *The Reivers*: p. 3.

74 Gass: (New York, 1970), p. 71.

77–78 *A Fable*: p. 437.

78 "dressing a showcase window": *Faulkner in the University*, p. 45. Stevick: *The Chapter in Fiction: Theories of Narrative Division* (Syracuse, N. Y., 1970), p. 18.

79 "one of the emergency ships": *The Wild Palms*, p. 314.

80 "counterpoint": *Faulkner in the University*, p. 8. "Listen, stranger": *Requiem for a Nun*, p. 225.

81 "nigger dope-fiend whore": *Requiem for a Nun*, p. 104.

81–82 Stevenson: "On Some Technical Elements of Style in Literature," *The Contemporary Review* (April, 1885), rep. *Works* (New York, 1898), 22; rep. Philip Stevick, *The Theory of the Novel* (New York, 1967), pp. 187–88.

82 *Pylon*: p. 7.

83 *The Sound and the Fury*: p. 387. *Absalom, Absalom!*: p. 11.

84 *The Unvanquished*: p. 175.

86 *The Unvanquished*: p. 292. James: "The Art of Fiction," rep. Miller, p. 35. Lesser: *Fiction and the Unconscious* (New York, 1957), p. 171.

86–87 Crane: "The Concept of Plot and the Plot of *Tom Jones*" in *Critics and Criticism*, abr. ed. (Chicago, 1957), p. 67.

87 Robb: *William Faulkner: An Estimate of His Contribution to the Modern American Novel* (Pittsburgh, 1957), p. 15. "believe": *Requiem for a Nun*, p. 234.

88 Morris: *The Territory Ahead* (New York, 1963), p. 177. Stephen Dedalus: Joyce, *Portrait of the Artist*, p. 215. Kazin: *The Inmost Leaf* (New York, 1959), p. 271.

90 Lesser: p. 166. Bosanquet: Bernard Bosanquet, *Three Lectures on Aesthetic* (London, 1915), p. 70. *As I Lay Dying*: p. 11; p. 115.

91   *As I Lay Dying*: p. 169; p. 169; p. 169; p. 170; p. 170; p. 226. Gombrich: E. H Gombrich, "Meditations on a Hobby Horse of the Roots of Artistic Form," in *Aesthetics Today*, ed. Morris Philipson (Cleveland, 1961), p. 120.

92   Dostoyevsky: q. Lesser, p. 149. "just a log cabin": *Go Down, Moses*, p. 277. "mended and faded": *Light in August*, p. 342. Swiggart: Peter Swiggart, *The Art of Faulkner's Novels* (Austin, Tex., 1962), p. 22. "A woman stood": *Sanctuary*, p. 8.

93   "flowered china": *Sanctuary*, p. 144. Frye: p. 81.

94   Ovid: *Metamorphoses*, III, 466–67.

95   *Ulysses*: (New York, 1934), p. 210. Temple Drake: *Sanctuary*, p. 29. Ike: *Go Down, Moses*, p. 330.

96   Rogers: *A Psychoanalytic Study of the Double in Literature* (Detroit, 1970), pp. 109–10.

97   Lubbock: p. 7.

98   Coindreau: p. 62. He is speaking of *The Wild Palms* in particular.

99   *Pylon*: p. 90; p. 45.

101–02 Pitavy: *Faulkner's 'Light in August,'* trans. Gillian E. Cook (Bloomington, Ind., 1973), pp. 69–70.

102   Burke: *A Grammar of Motives* (Cleveland, 1962), p. 504.

102–03 Ortega: José Ortega y Gasset, *The Dehumanization of Art* (Garden City, N. Y., 1956), pp. 13–14, 16.

104   "Plurisignificant" and "multidimensional": Heinz Werner and Bernard Kaplan, *Symbol Formation* (New York, 1963), pp. 213 ff.; cf. Jean O. Love, *Worlds in Consciousness: Mythopoetic Thought in the Novels of Virginia Woolf* (Berkeley, 1970), p. 28.

108   *Mosquitoes*: p. 54.

109   "a geographical place": *Intruder in the Dust*, p. 152. " 'It's not finished' ": *The Wild Palms*, p. 59.

110   "on fire": *Sanctuary*, cf. p. 233. " 'have the marble' ": *Absalom, Absalom!*, p. 127.

111   Shattuck: *The Banquet Years*, rev. ed. (New York, 1968), p. 332.

112   "Red Leaves": *Collected Stories*, p. 313; p. 334.

113   *Light in August*: p. 111.

115   *Light in August*: p. 462.

117   *Light in August*: p. 111. Brooks: *William Faulkner: The Yoknapatawpha Country* (New Haven, Conn., 1963), chap. 4, esp. p. 53 ff.

118   *Mosquitoes*: p. 210. Conrad: "Preface" to *The Nigger of the "Narcissus,"* p. 12. *Light in August*: p. 191; p. 380.

118–19 Beck: *Man in Motion: Faulkner's Trilogy* (Madison, Wisc., 1961), p. 160.

119   Stendhal: *Henri Brûlard* q. Stephen Gilman, "Meditations on a Stendhalian Metaphor," in *Interpretation: Theory and Practice*, ed. Charles S. Singleton (Baltimore, 1969), p. 155.

121   Shahn: *The Shape of Content*, pp. 80–81. Woolf: *The Voyage Out* q.

Edel, pp. 127–28. Bayer: "The Essence of Rhythm," in *Reflections on Art*, ed. Susanne K. Langer (New York, 1961), p. 194. Faulkner: *Lion in the Garden*, p. 253. *The Town*: pp. 315–16.

122   *The Town*: p. 316; p. 315; p. 315. "postage stamp": *Lion in the Garden*, p. 255.

123   *The Town*: pp. 317–18. *Flags in the Dust*: p. 11; p. 49; p. 95; p. 93; p. 60.

124   *Flags in the Dust*: p. 5; p. 41; p. 14; p. 15.

124–25   *Flags in the Dust*: pp. 140–41.

126   *Flags in the Dust*: p. 126; p. 6; p. 133; pp. 134–35.

127   *Flags in the Dust*: p. 282.

127–28   *Flags in the Dust*: p. 370.

128   *Flags in the Dust*: p. 81; p. 81; p. 291; p. 228; p.229; p. 237.

129   *Flags in the Dust*: pp. 239–40; p. 314.

130   *Flags in the Dust*: p. 315; p. 323; p. 320.

131   *Flags in the Dust*: p. 320; p. 217.

132   *Flags in the Dust*: p. 223; p. 404; p. 205; p. 215.

133   *Flags in the Dust*: p. 300; p. 305; p. 285.

134   *Flags in the Dust*: p. 356.

135   *Flags in the Dust*: p. 357; pp. 360–61; p. 377; p. 373; p. 381; p. 374.

136   *Flags in the Dust*: p. 75; p. 412; pp. 413–14.

137   *Flags in the Dust*: p. 415; p. 416.

138   *Flags in the Dust*: p. 388; p. 428.

139   *Flags in the Dust*: p. 426; p. 177; p. 433.

140   *The Sound and the Fury*: p. 23.

141   *The Sound and the Fury*: p. 30; p. 48.

142   *The Sound and the Fury*: pp. 57–58.

143   *The Sound and the Fury*: p. 100; p. 185; p. 100.

144   *The Sound and the Fury*: pp. 93–95.

145–46   *The Sound and the Fury*: pp. 143–44.

146   *The Sound and the Fury*: p. 144; p. 145; p. 145; pp. 111–12.

147   *The Sound and the Fury*: p. 131; p. 112; p. 113; p. 114; p. 152; p. 213.

148   *The Sound and the Fury*: p. 185; p. 137; p. 172; p. 98; p. 98; p. 98; p. 96.

148–49   *The Sound and the Fury*: pp. 219–20.

151   *The Sound and the Fury*: p. 290; p. 243; p. 196; p. 324.

152   *The Sound and the Fury*: p. 299; p. 237; p. 228; p. 320.

153   *The Sound and the Fury*: p. 306.

153–54   *The Sound and the Fury*: pp. 328–29.

154   *The Sound and the Fury*: p. 223.

154–55   *The Sound and the Fury*: pp. 330–31.

155   *The Sound and the Fury*: p. 342; p. 338; p. 334.

156   *The Sound and the Fury*: p. 34; p. 345; p. 352; p. 372; p. 363; p. 352.

156–57   *The Sound and the Fury*: p. 364.

157   *The Sound and the Fury*: pp. 364–65; p. 362; pp. 365–66; p. 367.

157–58   *The Sound and the Fury*: pp. 367–68.

158   *The Sound and the Fury*: p. 371; p. 371; p. 370; p. 382.

159   *The Sound and the Fury*: p. 388.

160   *The Sound and the Fury*: p. 393; p. 401.

160–61 *The Sound and the Fury*: p. 404.

161–62 *As I Lay Dying*: pp. 3–4.

163   *As I Lay Dying*: p. 165; pp. 196–97.

163–64 *As I Lay Dying*: pp. 10–11.

164   *As I Lay Dying*: pp. 11–12; pp. 12–13.

165   *As I Lay Dying*: p. 76; p. 76.

166   *Mosquitoes*: p. 210. *As I Lay Dying*: p. 95; p. 198.

168   *As I Lay Dying*: p. 227; p. 99; p. 243; p. 163; p. 164.

169   *As I Lay Dying*: pp. 161–62; p. 161.

169–70 *As I Lay Dying*: pp. 166–67.

170   *As I Lay Dying*: p. 171.

171   Laing: *The Divided Self: An Existential Study in Sanity and Madness* (Baltimore, 1965), pp. 145–46. *As I Lay Dying*: p. 8; p. 8.

172   *As I Lay Dying*: pp. 42–43.

173   *As I Lay Dying*: pp. 34–35.

174   *As I Lay Dying*: p. 249; p. 74; p. 82.

175   *As I Lay Dying*: pp. 77–78; p. 224.

177–78 *Sanctuary*: pp. 3–5.

179   *Sanctuary*: p. 271; p. 178.

180   *Sanctuary*: p. 17; p. 15; p. 127; p. 273; p. 214.

181   *Sanctuary*: pp. 215–16.

182–83 *Sanctuary*: pp. 114–15.

183–84 *Sanctuary*: pp. 7–8.

184   *Sanctuary*: pp. 18–19; p. 5; pp. 137–38.

184–85 *Sanctuary*: pp. 150–51.

185   *Sanctuary*: pp. 143–44; p. 155.

185–86 *Sanctuary*: p. 110.

186   *Sanctuary*: p. 107; p. 113; p. 126.

188   *Sanctuary*: pp. 55–56; cf. Olga W. Vickery, *The Novels of William Faulkner* (Baton Rouge, La., 1959), p. 106.

189   *Sanctuary*: p. 99; p. 157; p. 160.

189–90 *Sanctuary*: p. 208.

190   *Sanctuary*: p. 4; p. 5; p. 29.

191   *Sanctuary*: p. 136; p. 67; p. 5.

193   *Sanctuary*: p. 308; p. 111; p. 284 and p. 304.

194   *Absalom, Absalom!*: pp. 7–11; p. 336; p. 299; p. 176; p. 9.

195   *Absalom, Absalom!*: p. 7; p. 8; p. 7; p. 12; p. 375; p. 8; p. 314; p. 263.

196   *Absalom, Absalom!*: p. 174; p. 247.

197   *Absalom, Absalom!*: p. 143; p. 13; pp. 9–10.

197–98 *Absalom, Absalom!*: pp. 8–9.

198   *Absalom, Absalom!*: p. 69. *Vicksburg Sun*: q. Miner, pp. 35–36.

199   *Absalom, Absalom!*: p. 84; pp. 49–50; p. 66; p. 77.

199–200 *Absalom, Absalom!*: p. 82.

200   *Absalom, Absalom!*: p. 82.

200–201 *Absalom, Absalom!*: p. 150.

201   *Absalom, Absalom!*: p. 151; p. 140; p. 161; p. 163; p. 211; p. 172.

202   *Absalom, Absalom!*: p. 9; p. 168; p. 143; pp. 149–50; p. 322.

203   *Absalom, Absalom!*: pp. 263–64; p. 46; p. 40.

203–04 *Absalom, Absalom!*: pp. 43–44.

204   *Absalom, Absalom!*: p. 100.

204–05 *Absalom, Absalom!*: p. 100.

205   *Absalom, Absalom!*: p. 101; p. 103.

206   *Absalom, Absalom!*: p. 127; p. 361; p. 174; p. 100.

207   *Absalom, Absalom!*: p. 221; pp. 227–28; p. 220.

207–08 *Absalom, Absalom!*: p. 242.

208   *Absalom, Absalom!*: p. 250; pp. 250–51.

208–09 *Absalom, Absalom!*: p. 264.

209   *Absalom, Absalom!*: p. 184.

209–10 *Absalom, Absalom!*: p. 277.

210   *Absalom, Absalom!*: p. 100; p. 96; p. 280.

211   *Absalom, Absalom!*: p. 295; p. 316; p. 316; p. 176.

211–12 *Absalom, Absalom!*: p. 264.

212   *Absalom, Absalom!*: p. 308; p. 308; p. 335; pp. 354–55; p. 358; p. 313;
         p. 356. Marx: Karl Marx, "The Eighteenth Brumaire of Louis Bonaparte"
         in *The Marx-Engels Reader*, ed. Robert C. Tucker (New York, 1972), p.
         437. *Absalom, Absalom!*: p. 356; p. 359.

213   *Absalom, Absalom!*: p. 373. ·

214   *Absalom, Absalom!*: p. 373; p. 8; p. 10; p. 378; p. 168; p. 261.

215   *Absalom, Absalom!*: pp. 261–62.

214–15 *Absalom, Absalom!*: p. 10.

215–16 *Go Down, Moses*: pp. 293–94.

216   *Go Down, Moses*: p. 267; p. 260; p. 194; p. 192; p. 192; p. 194.

217   *Go Down, Moses*: pp. 208–9; p. 209; p. 205; p. 200.

217–18 *Go Down, Moses*: p. 163.

218   *Go Down, Moses*: pp. 183–84; p. 206; p. 257; p. 168; p. 168.

219   *Go Down, Moses*: p. 231; p. 317; p. 317; p. 317; p. 318; p. 255; p. 255.

220   *Go Down, Moses*: p. 257; p. 258; pp. 258–59; p. 287.

220–21 *Go Down, Moses*: p. 298.

221–22 *Go Down, Moses*: pp. 302-3.

222   *Go Down, Moses*: p. 303; p. 296.

222–23 *Go Down, Moses*: pp. 296–97.

223   *Go Down, Moses*: p. 241; p. 4; p. 5; p. 9; p. 22.

224   *Go Down, Moses*: p. 28; p. 28; p. 14

225   *Go Down, Moses*: pp. 267–69.

225–26 *Go Down, Moses*: pp. 269–70.

226–27 *Go Down, Moses*: pp. 294–95.

227   *Go Down, Moses*: p. 255; p. 52; p. 53.

227–28 *Go Down, Moses*: p. 55.

228   *Go Down, Moses*: p. 59; p. 87.
229   *Go Down, Moses*: pp. 101-2; p. 131.
230   *Go Down, Moses*: p. 226; p. 250.
230–31 *Go Down, Moses*: pp. 253–54.
231   *Go Down, Moses*: p. 277; p. 277; p. 279; p. 280; p. 257; p. 299; p. 279.
231–32 *Go Down, Moses*: pp. 309–10.
232   *Go Down, Moses*: p. 316; p. 316; p. 316.
233   *Go Down, Moses*: p. 319; p. 318; p. 323; p. 323; p. 327; p. 328; p. 328; p. 257; p. 330; p. 184; p. 331.
233–34 *Go Down, Moses*: p. 331.
234   *Go Down, Moses*: p. 283.
235   *Go Down, Moses*: p. 315.
236   *Go Down, Moses*: pp. 147 and 152; p. 281; p. 137; p. 135.
237   *Go Down, Moses*: pp. 154–55; p. 257; p. 358; p. 358; p. 360; p. 360.
238   *Go Down, Moses*: pp. 360–61; p. 257; p. 363; p. 269; p. 363; p. 3.
238–39 *Go Down, Moses*: p. 363.
239   *Go Down, Moses*: p. 364; p. 365; p. 369.
239–40 *Go Down, Moses*: pp. 378–79.
240   *Go Down, Moses*: p. 382; p. 381; p. 168; p. 382.
241   Lesser: p. 185.
241–42 Faulkner to Cowley: Written early November 1944; rep. *Faulkner-Cowley File*, p. 14; rep. *Selected Letters*, p. 185.
242   Proust to Bois: q. Shattuck, *Marcel Proust*, p. 172. Le Corbusier: q. Reuben Arthur Brower, *The Fields of Light: An Experiment in Critical Reading* (New York, 1962), p. xi.
243   Faulkner interview: *Faulkner in the University*, pp. 273–74. Price: "The Irrelevant Detail and the Emergence of Form," in *Aspects of Narrative*, ed. Miller, p. 82. Lubbock: p. 40. Flaubert: Written from Paris March 18, 1857; rep. *Selected Letters*, p. 194.
244   Faulkner to Cowley: Written February 11, 1949; rep. *Faulkner-Cowley File*, p. 126; rep. *Selected Letters*, p. 285.
245   James: "The Art of Fiction," rep. Miller, p. 42. Faulkner: "Speech of Acceptance for the Andres Bello Award" (Caracas, 1961); Faulkner delivered the speech in Spanish. His text and an English translation are rep. in *A Faulkner Miscellany*, ed. James B. Meriwether (Jackson, Miss., 1974), pp. 164–66. Robbe-Grillet: *Towards a New Novel*, trans. Barbara Wright (London, 1965), p. 179; also q. Arnold L. Weinstein, *Vision and Response in Modern Fiction* (Ithaca, N. Y., 1974), p. 26. Guerard (New York, 1976), p. 204. Faulkner on Anderson: "A Note on Sherwood Anderson," *Essays*, pp. 3–4.
246   Magny: *The Age of the American Novel*, trans. Eleanor Hochman (New York, 1972), pp. 179, 181. Flaubert: *L'Education sentimentale* q. Georges Poulet, *The Metamorphoses of the Circle*, trans. Carley Dawson and Elliott Coleman (Baltimore, 1966), p. 265. Woolf: "Modern Fiction," *The Common Reader* (First Series) (New York, 1925), pp. 212–13. Gray: *The*

Literature of Memory: Modern Writers of the American South (Baltimore, 1977), pp. 246, 243.

247 Cowley: "Faulkner: Voodoo Dance," *New Republic*, April 10, 1935; rep. Cowley, *Think Back on Us . . . : A Contemporary Chronicle of the 1930s*, ed. Henry Dan Piper (Carbondale, Ill., 1967), p. 269.

248 Jaynes: (Boston, 1976), p. 4. two scientists: Richard E. Leakey and Roger Lewin, *Origins* (New York, 1977), pp. 192, 189. Kenner: *A Homemade World: The American Modernist Writers* (New York, 1975), chap. VII. Mallarmé: Stephane Mallarmé, "Crisis in Poetry," in *Mallarmé: Selected Prose Poems, Essays, and Letters*, trans. Bradford Cook (Baltimore, 1956), p. 40. Kenner: p. 197. Blotner: *Faulkner: A Biography*, "Notes," I, 51. Cf. Noel Polk, "William Faulkner's *Marionettes*," *Faulkner Miscellany*, pp. 3–36.

249 "The Kingdom of God": *New Orleans Sketches* (New York, 1961), p. 113. McHaney: "The Elmer Papers: Faulkner's Comic Portraits of the Artist," *Faulkner Miscellany*, pp. 37–69.

250 Schoenberg: *Old Tales and Talking: Quentin Compson in William Faulkner's 'Absalom, Absalom!' and Related Works* (Jackson, Miss., 1977), p. 147; and esp. chap. IV. *Collected Stories*: "Carcassonne," p. 899.

251 Faulkner to Smith: Probably written February 1934; rep. *Selected Letters*, pp. 78–79. Houston: *Fictional Technique in France: 1802–1927; An Introduction* (Baton Rouge, 1972), pp. 40–41; p. 64. Poulet: *Proustian Space*, trans. Elliott Coleman (Baltimore, 1977), pp. 37–38.

252 Adams: "Apprenticeship," pp. 128–29. Wagner: *Hemingway and Faulkner: inventors/masters* (Metuchen, N. J., 1975), p. 136. Guerard: p. 207. Flint: "Faulkner as Elegist," *Hudson Review* VII:2 (1954), p. 257.

253 "[Flem] entered the store": *The Hamlet*, p. 52.

254 Howe: p. 212.

254–55 Polanyi and Prosch: Michael Polanyi and Harry Prosch, *Meaning* (Chicago, 1975), p. 87.

255 *The Town*: p. 88.

255–56 *The Town*: p. 305.

256 *The Town*: p. 347.

256–57 Howe: p. 286.

257 "I had just written my guts": *Essays*, pp. 176–77. Henhouse: q. Kenner, p. 204. Faulkner to his mother: Postmarked September 6, 1925; rep. *Selected Letters*, p. 17. Faulkner to Wasson: Received January 26; rep. *Selected Letters*, p. 59.

257–58 Faulkner to Wasson: Probably late September 1932; rep. *Selected Letters*, p. 66.

258 *The Town*: p. 106; p. 112. Faulkner to Commins: rep. *Selected Letters*, p. 390. Faulkner to Stein: January 13, 1956; rep. *Selected Letters*, p. 391. Faulkner to Stein: rep. *Selected Letters*, p. 402. Faulkner to Commins: rep. *Selected Letters*, p. 403.

259–60 Robbe-Grillet: Alain Robbe-Grillet, "On Several Obsolete Notions," in

For a New Novel: Essays on Fiction, trans. Richard Howard (New York, 1965), p. 32; italics added.

260   *Absalom, Absalom!*: p. 314. Jaynes: pp. 59–65.

261   Whitehead: Alfred North Whitehead cited in Edward S. Casey, *Imagining: A Phenomenological Study* (Bloomington, Ind., 1976), p. 233. Faulkner: Letter to Robert N. Linscott in late May 1946; rep. *Selected Letters*, pp. 236–37. Faulkner is speaking specifically of *The Sound and the Fury* and *As I Lay Dying*. Jaynes: p. 48; p. 49; p. 51.

261–62 Culler: *Flaubert: The Uses of Uncertainty* (London, 1974), p. 91.

262   Faulkner to Bouvard: *Lion in the Garden*, pp. 70–71. *"that might-have-been"*: *Absalom, Absalom!*, pp. 149–50.

Index

Italics denote major discussion(s). Except for writing by Faulkner, works are indexed by author. Faulkner's works and characters have separate listings.